The Amorous Umbrella

MARVIN KAYE

DOUBLEDAY & COMPANY, INC.

GARDEN CITY, NEW YORK

1981

All of the characters in this book
are fictitious, and any resemblance
to actual persons, living or dead,
is purely coincidental.

Library of Congress Cataloging in Publication Data

Kaye, Marvin.
The amorous umbrella.

I. Title.
PS3561.A886A8   813'.54
AACR2
ISBN: 0-385-15509-3
Library of Congress Catalog Card Number 79-8561

First Edition

This one is for my delightful in-laws,
NANCY AND WAYNE PORT
and their children
AMY AND LOUIS—
may they always be happy under the umbrella
of their love for one another.

Acknowledgments

An hosanna and a couple of hallelujahs for those fine fellows, onlie begetters and mavens of impeccable taste, Moshe Feder and Lou Stathis, for early brandishing the "umbrella." My seals and shibboleths art thine to command, sires!

A pair of farandoles and a tarantella for Jim Frenkel, who set the measure for the professor to tread beneath the Dell banner, and three gigues for Dan Steffan's amusing illustrations in that edition.

Two art songs, a watercolor and a schottische for faithful reader Ross Clements' gadfly request for more Boris, granted herein.

A Grand Waltz is set aside on my dance card for that fresh insight into the psychology of fairy princesses and soap opera villains granted me by Ms. Louise Shaffer, a fey friend from the parallel world of "Ryan's Hope."

Lastly, but not in the least leastly, at least half a dozen tons of brotherly love and a low mass for Pat LoBrutto, who proves it's still possible for an editor to be a member of the family.

Exegesis

Publishers of sequential volumes (such as this) are wont to proclaim that readers need not peruse the precedent tomes to understand and (hopefully) enjoy the latest installment. It is a claim that generally is as valid as walking in during the shower murder of *Psycho*, then staying in the theatre long enough to catch up on the part of the film that was missed.

Despite this caveat, it *is* possible to embark on the amatory pursuits of Professor James Phillimore without reference to his virgin voyages in *The Incredible Umbrella*. The data requisite to comprehending the present narrative is included in the Prolegomenon, but those already acquainted with the professor and his bumbershoot may skip directly to the first part.

However, repeat students will be held responsible for all material included in this text.

— Marvin Kaye
Manhattan, 1979–80

Prolegomenon

J. Adrian Fillmore (Gad, what a name!) recently taught English literature, American drama, and Shakespeare at Parker College in central
Pennsylvania. He was a dour, thirtyish professor, his chief frustrations
being his own name, a profound disparity of opinion with his department superior and thesis advisor, and an inability to relate to the opposite sex in a manner to which he wanted to become accustomed.

One fateful day, the teacher purchased a strange object in a curio
shop, "a long, heavy pole that ended in a large flounce of some silky
material emblazoned with orange-and-yellow stripes on which various
cabalistic symbols seemed to dance in pastel figurations. It was clearly
an umbrella, but its size was rather impractical: too large for everyday
use, too small for beach-basking. . . ."

He soon learned it was really a dimensional-transfer engine. It
whisked Fillmore away from his mundane academic life to a succession
of "literary" worlds peopled by such colorful figures as Count Dracula,
Mr. Pickwick, Sherlock Holmes and the assembled *dramatis personae*
of nearly all the Gilbert and Sullivan operettas.

Oddly, none of the denizens of these strange worlds ever heard of
the authors with whom Phillimore naturally associated them . . . and
yet their customs hewed closely to the styles and conventions of the
writers the professor knew so well—e.g., without any awareness of
Gilbert or Sullivan as aesthetic influences, the G&S world's people
often broke into song that either matched or closely parodied melodies
and lyrics of existing Savoyard choruses and arias. There was an unseen universal accompaniment—"Holy Tone" according to one inhabit-
ant—and all thought Fillmore odd for *refusing* to sing.

Eventually, Fillmore learned the rationale of the umbrella's opera-
tion: it took the user to the place determined in his mind. Since Fillmore taught literature, it was inevitable he'd be deposited on alternate
worlds that, in the infinity of possibilities that comprise the cosmos,

happened to resemble recognizable patterns of human literary endeavor.

Sherlock Holmes himself stressed the professor's error: "Those worlds do not exist because they were written about on your original earth. Instead, the fiction with which you are familiar must consist of notions and conceptions telepathically borrowed across the barriers of the dimensions. Your artists may unwittingly tap the logical premises of parallel worlds. . . ."

In effect, J. Adrian Fillmore (Gad!) could employ the parasol to visit virtually any place he'd ever read about. But there was a trap. His mind, professionally and professorially attuned to literary structure, found it hard to force the umbrella to transport him *out* of a world where danger lowered . . . for he had a pedantic subconscious compulsion to "finish sequences." His adventures tended to follow the shape of the plots he'd read in those literary analogues of the places he visited.

Even worse, his pre-umbrella life was reclusive and emotionally deprived. The infinitely alluring worlds of his imagination, even when dangerous, held the possibility of "subsuming" him into the base logic of that planet. He learned there was a fine line between calculated participation and total acceptance of a parallel earth's underlying tenets; the latter could permanently immure him in that world, and the umbrella would not function.

Only greater self-knowledge and repeated use of the umbrella might enable Fillmore to master the device and successfully steer past the shoals of interdimensional exploration. Yet the first thing he did in his altered life-plan was to attempt to negate certain aspects of his spiritual upbringing; this Gyntian aversion from Self was characterized by the professor's changing his name to an older spelling, so that he *clept* himself James Phillimore.

His new persona did not alter his root personality, however, and soon he became enmeshed in yet new interdimensional dangers partially brought about by his inescapable pedantry.

During his latter flights, Phillimore met and befriended the Frankenstein monster, whom he appropriately named Boris. The monster—grateful to be rescued from the bleak fate awaiting him in Shelley's novel—proved a loyal and useful companion. As eventual repayment for the creature's assistance, the professor flew Boris to the Gilbert and Sullivan world where, in typical Gilbertian fashion, the comely are often shallow and selfish, while the ugly generally are honest, moral, mellow, and ultimately well-rewarded.

Having bestowed Boris Frankenstein (the monster insisted on adopting his father's surname) in G&S-land, James Phillimore resolved to seek new adventures on other as-yet-unvisited planets.

He did so, but the tale has yet to be told. The history of *The Amorous Umbrella* commences with the return of the professor to G&S-land after exploits in other parts.

Part I

Once upon a time, an adoring bevy of immortal women danced about an enchanted glade feeding sweetmeats to a large, ungainly gentleman named Boris. As they busied themselves in this adulatory pursuit, the gorgeous troupe of fairies, for so they were, caroled forth sweetly . . .

> Tripping hither, tripping thither,
> Nobody knows why or whither;
> We must dance and we must sing
> Round about our fairy ring!

The Frankenstein monster, for that was the identity of the man they fussed over, neither marked nor minded their lyric. All in all, he preferred their ministrations to foraging for food amongst the less-than-friendly Germanic peoples of his homeland; yet the discerning eye might note the merest trace of surfeited appetite in the monster's mien, an attitude not wholly traceable to the fairies' Arcadian fare.

On the fairies' part, there was still enormous Baroque fascination with Boris' uncompromisingly frightful aspect, and they loved him for it, one and all.

All four-and-twenty.

Not far from the glade an oddly-encumbered personage suddenly appeared. It was James Phillimore, late professor of Parker College. He was a trifle weary, but not with the exhausting adventures he'd recently concluded; rather, his spirit bent under the burden of ennui.

"Probably just lonely," he told himself, turning his steps toward the fairy forest where his old friend, Boris Frankenstein, made his home. In the distance, he thought he saw the creature lolling languidly in the middle of a circle of the sisters of Iolanthe, the fay for whom W. S. Gilbert named one of his most popular operettas.

As he drew near, he heard the pattering chorus and grumbled to himself, *Don't they ever sing anything else?*

The damsels skipped delicately about the rustic landscape, which was graced in the distance by a gentle river spanned by a rude wooden bridge. Their mincing dance eternally revolved about the reclining giant whose shriveled skin, lustrous black hair and lips of the same tone immediately proclaimed his identity to the approaching professor.

"Boris!" he called. "How are you?"

The monster looked up, recognized Phillimore and leaped happily to his feet. He ran forward and hugged the other in an embrace that nearly broke the teacher's ribs.

"Kindly modify your rapture!" he gasped. The monster released him immediately, grabbed a nosegay from the nearest naiad and proffered it to the scholar, who promptly sneezed and pushed it away. "Hay fever," he groaned, wiping his eyes and nose.

Boris beamed benignly before his benefactor.

"O peerless friend! O Mighty Phillimore, it hath been all too long sith I beheld thee in these parts. What marvels hath since passed? I perceive thou'rt not the same staid sorcerer that last I looked on!" (The monster attributed the powers of the umbrella to necromancy on the professor's part, a notion that Phillimore encouraged on the grounds that it was sound business to keep a seven-foot giant a bit in awe of one, even if the emotion *was* founded on sham. *Wizard-of-Oz ploy No. 1*, he thought.)

The scholar settled himself on the ground and leaned against a tree-trunk. "I suppose, Boris, that I *have* changed a little since the last time we saw one another."

"You hath said it!" saith the monster.

Phillimore's customary dull academic garb was nowhere in evidence. Instead, he wore scarlet pantaloons cinched about the waist by a green silk sash. Save for a buttonless leather vest, his hirsute chest was bare. A multicolored bandanna circled his brow. His sole remaining accoutrements were an unwieldy curved snickersnee thrust into the sash and, of course, his transdimensional parasol (whose garish hues seemed less startling at that moment, viewed as they were against the professor's new raiment).

Boris joined him on the ground. They breathed the perfumed air and Iolanthe's fey sisters flitted from one to the other, fitting nuts in their mouths, pouring drafts of nectar, offering them ambrosia in abundance, as well as pignuts, gossamer pastries and moonlight melon.

Phillimore longed for a cheesesteak loaded with onions, peppers and hot sauce, and a flagon of Foster's to wash it down.

Boris eventually asked what his friend had been doing since last he saw him.

"Ah," Phillimore sighed, filled with *acedia,* "I've been wandering the worlds and sailing up and down on them."

"From thine numerous scars, I surmise thou hadst a devil of a time."

The other nodded. "Had quite a job just staying afloat." He shrugged. "I've always loved the sea and ships and thought if I had the time to pursue a nautical career, rather than an academic one, I'd be happy." He shook his head. "Oh, boy, was I wrong!"

Boris waved away a shellful of sugared raisins and airily told Leila and Fleta to flit off. Then he begged the professor to narrate the particulars of his recent adventures. "Perhaps," he reasoned, "I might detect some vital missing element which, once discovered, might enable thee to conquer thy present apathy."

Phillimore shrugged again. "Don't see what, but all right. First of all, though, do you think you could order me something a little less colorful to wear?"

Boris said a word to Iolanthe; the peri waved her wand and magically altered Phillimore's clothing to his customary gray vested suit and ascot.

The professor thanked the fairy, acknowledged Boris' courtesy, and began to tell his story.

It took several hours. By the time he finished, the forest was bathed in moonlight and the weary fairies sat curled upon the sward, heads daintily cradled on their forearms like ballerinas miming sleeping swans.

Nodding sagely, Boris yawned, stretched his joints and rose, all seven feet of him. A grin widened his big lips. "O Puissant Professor," said he (unaware how Phillimore detested this particular encomium, possibly because Boris' pronunciation was shaky), "at last I can repay some doit of that boundless kindness thou hast still shown me!"

"You can?" Phillimore asked, puzzled, as he creakily got to his feet, bracing his weight against the umbrella-shaft. "How?"

In reply, the monster flung his arms wide apart. Phillimore flinched, afraid that Boris meant to subject him to another painfully untrammeled display of affection. But the creature merely turned and indicated with outstretched hands their rustic surroundings.

"Observe," he grunted, "the many wonders of this magical forest. Yet we have but to consider the travails of our past lives to realize that the evanescent glories of this wood are as dust without the solace of companionship."

"True," Phillimore agreed, "I *have* been too much a loner. Maybe I should have asked you along on my nautical adventures, except—"

"But nay!" Boris interrupted, amused that, for once, he was more knowing than his illustrious mentor. "Thou hast mistaken mine meaning, Noble Friend! To me, 'tis apparent that thou lackest, not friendship, but rather, distaff affiliation."

Conceding the delicate distinction, the professor pensively twisted his lips. "True, true," he murmured, "I've always been unhappy about my shyness with women."

"Then you need ask no more, Mighty Benefactor!" Boris patronizingly patted his friend's head. "But take thee another glance about this glade, Master. . . ."

The professor regarded the voluptuous sleeping damsels with new interest. In typical Gilbertian fashion, each maiden—though a mythical sprite who mainly dined on low-cal dewdrops and polyunsaturated starlight—yet boasted the alluring proportions of a West End music hall chorine.

Phillimore carefully mulled over Boris' offer, but at last, thanking him for the generous impulse that prompted him to make it, nevertheless demurred. "I must admit, Boris, I *am* tempted . . . these immortal waifs *are* knockouts. But after all, you are virtually their husband—their sultan, anyway, so to speak. I can't intrude upon your sylvan existence, I'd be nothing more than an interloper."

"O say not so!" the creature wailed wearily. " 'Tis true I am possessed of preternatural stamina, but there *are* limits, even for a monster! I am but one, and they are four-and-twenty, not counting the Fairy Queen who, at present, mercifully is on a buying trip at the J. W. Wells supply house, London!"

Sinking onto the grass, Boris turned his watery eyes full upon the professor and beseeched him to reconsider.

"O Mighty Phillimore," he wheedled as he rested his great head on sandwiched hands, preparatory to sleep, "taketh my waifs . . . *please!*"

But joy incessant palls the sense, and after a few idyllically inactive weeks in Gilbertian Arcady, the professor began to feel a bit like Harold Shea stuck in Xanadu. The mild-climed glade, the caroling sprites, the insubstantial fare surfeited his jaded palate.

But the deciding circumstance was that the airy fairies treated Phillimore with the utmost respect, and that was the only treat he enjoyed of them. He wondered whether they avoided him because his own mind (which always dictated the tenor of his adventures in spite of his conscious wishes) perceived Gilbertian morals in the Victorian stage tradition in which the operettas were rooted. Or maybe it was just a simple function of the world's topsy-turvy nature: to reward the unhandsome Boris and not the much handsomer (so the professor thought!) James Phillimore.

Whatever the reason, he was an honored guest, nothing more. And it didn't suit him one bit. In a kind of proud desperation, he told himself he didn't really fancy any of them, anyway. *All looks, no brains!* But a mocking inner voice contradicted, made him turn the matter over in his mind more than his ego wished.

The truth is, he admitted, *women never pay me much attention. I'm always thirteenth at table, Cyrano in the gloom of Roxane's garden, Sganarelle outside the bedroom-door, Lazarus at the feast.* It's easy to insist on brains, but in his heart, Phillimore knew physical comeliness *was* important to him. The fair that toil not, that are the product of lavish nature, not their own industry, were so agonizingly out of reach that they naturally fascinated the professor mightily.

Beyond that, though he was essentially a soured romantic, deep within he considered the Quest for the Eternal Feminine perversely appealing. He longed for Goethe's *das ewig-weibliche* with as little comprehension of the term as Peer Gynt, but still Phillimore craved Her nearly as much as he longed for a mint edition of *Dark Carnival.*

He told Boris, "I'm going, that's for sure, and it has to be another world than this. The Gilbertian scheme inescapably matches physical comeliness with shallowness of character."

Boris didn't understand most of what he said, but dutifully inquired where Phillimore planned to go.

"I don't know, Boris. Some world where I can find a woman that embodies all I desire in a mate."

The monster paused to quaff some mead. "The possibilities are endless," he murmured in his cup.

"You're telling me?" Butting his back against a bole, Phillimore tapped his forefinger against his forehead. "It's all in here, Boris! Every desirable woman I've ever read about . . . Shakespeare's Cleopatra, Grimm's princesses, Trollope's high society coquettes . . . Glencora and Guinevere and Galadriel and Queen Mab (as if I didn't have enough of woodland sprites!). Don Juan might envy me, Casanova turn green with jealousy!"

"Yes, yes," said Boris, "but where will you try first?"

The professor shrugged. "I think I'll just trust to luck. Whatever is in my subconscious is what I'll go with. I'll think of The Perfect Mate and press the umbrella-catch!"

The great creature rolled his watery eyes. "It sounds rather risky to me, O Professorial Phillimore!" He glanced about the glade. "Cannot aught here stay you? The Fairy Queen, you know, has just returned from London. She has ample charms."

"*Quite* ample," Phillimore murmured. "No, thanks. I may crave, indeed, a fairy princess, but these ladies are a bit too ground-treading. Every time they trip about the glade, I swear they hike up their garters."

"But they don't wear any," the monster innocently confided.

Which information only further confirmed the professor in the opinion that he didn't belong in G&S-land.

Next morning, after a brief farewell and a promise to come back and introduce Boris to his future betrothed, Phillimore betook himself to another part of the forest, where he attuned his mind to tender thoughts and delicate emotions. Then he pressed the catch of the umbrella.

It opened. A mighty wind plucked him off the ground.

Flying beyond the tinted heartwall of the pulsing universe, night screaming in his ears, the scholar did his best to concentrate solely on visions of distaff loveliness, wonder and delight. . . .

Without warning, the umbrella snapped shut. Phillimore dropped heavily, sprawling on a patch of grass pale in the cloaking shadow of tall, twisted trees.

clump clump clump

A sinister music filled the air, an ominous melody he recognized from *Pictures at an Exhibition.*

clump clump clump

The ground shook with the pounding tread of approaching feet. Gigantic feet . . .

What's wrong? He rolled over, sat up, stared into the dark forest . . . and gawked at a monstrous *thing* drawing steadily nearer.

Clump Clump Clump

Phillimore scrambled to his feet, horrified. He stood in a thick, wild-looking wood in which unfriendly animal eyes peeped out all about, watching him. The brush was so tangled and tall that it choked out most of the afternoon sunlight. Somewhere nearby, angry bees droned. A hoarse raven croaked from the direction of the coming catastrophe.

CLUMP CLUMP CLUMP

No use using the umbrella, it won't work till it's cooled off! He tried to move his feet, attempted to run away from the *thing* that was now hardly twenty yards distant, but his legs were transfixed by a powerful spell of staymagic.

CLUMP CLUMP CLUMP

The nightmare hurrying toward him was a great thatched hut girded round with a fence of grinning skulls. Instead of resting on the earth, the frightful little house grew out of two mighty *living* fowl-legs that resembled the clawed feet of a giant turkey or rooster.

It was these bird-feet that produced the clumping sound as they carried the bizarre hut straight towards him.

It's going to trample me to death!

But suddenly the fowl-legs halted, scant inches away from him. Out of one of the hut's windows suddenly was thrust the face of a woman with shriveled skin, baleful eyes, a big pimple-ornamented nose, few teeth, many warts, and filthy gray hair combed in an untidy sweep secured by a coil of chicken-wire. She wore a frayed gray fragment of fichu around her gnarly shoulders.

Phillimore roundly cursed the umbrella. *This is what it gives me when I specify womanly beauty?*

As if in answer to his mental grumble, the crone cackled and addressed him in a raspy voice.

"Yoohoo, sonnyevitch! Have I got a girl for you!"

Phillimore sat in a comfortable, if slightly mildewy armchair in the old woman's parlor and tried to get a word in edgewise.

It wasn't easy. She rattled on, fussing over the professor as if he were the Prodigal Hen come home to roost. Below and beneath the floorboards, the hut's fowl-feet stomped through the woods, making the tiny house pitch and tremble. But compared with the last voyage he'd taken, he was scarcely troubled by the motion.

The professor knew enough about Russian folklore to identify the witch. Her name was Baba Yaga, and she was a Slavic variant of the British bogeyman or the American foolkiller; she existed chiefly to frighten wilful children into better behaviour. There was another detail connected with her, too, but he couldn't recall it. The thing that convinced him of her identity was the famous hut on fowl's legs itself. An essential part of the Baba Yaga legend, the strange dwelling, circled by victims' grinning skulls, constantly stalked the woods, seeking bad youngsters for the witch to capture and devour.

But I hardly fit the classification, he mused wryly. *Then why am I here?*

"Nu, sonnyevitch, put down your umbrella, it ain't raining inside! Take off your shoes, get comfortable! Maybe you're cold? I'll get you a nice *glayzala tay.* . . ." As she spoke, she patted and prodded him fondly with bony fingers. But a sly light glinted from her one green eye.

And yet, even though he distrusted her, Phillimore rather liked the old woman: she reminded him vaguely of someone dear, he couldn't remember exactly who.

As she pottered about getting the tea ready, he scanned the surroundings with interest. It was a small single-chamber hut, with two chairs, a kitchen table and a cot comprising the principal furniture. A large iron cauldron hung over a stone fireplace, next to which was curled a chubby gray cat with yellow eyes. The animal regarded the newcomer with sour amusement.

Baba Yaga stirred the cauldron once or twice, then ladled out an amber mixture which Phillimore presumed must be the tea. As he watched her tender ministrations, he suddenly realized who she reminded him of.

Can't do enough for me, wants to fix me up with a woman. Won't let me get a word in edgewise!

Wistfully, he thought about his late foster mother.

"You know, you're different from what I would have expected," Phillimore remarked.

"How could you expect?"

"Well, you're Baba Yaga, right?"

For some reason, the witch clapped both her hands over her mouth. She waited a moment before uncovering so she could speak. "How would you know my name?" she asked somewhat nervously, but nothing happened and she exhaled with apparent relief.

What's wrong with her? Something to do with . . . But Phillimore couldn't bring it to mind.

"I said, how do you know who I am?"

"Sometimes," he said, "I'm a bit fey. Anyway, I've heard stories about Baba Yaga. All about how you eat up wicked children."

"Ho-boy!" she snorted, with a disgusted sweep of her hand. "I knew I never should have accepted that retainer!"

"I don't understand."

"Whole bunch local peasants commission me to keep the brats in line. I ride around the forest scaring the crap out of the little darlingskis."

"Then you don't actually eat them?"

Again she startled Phillimore by clapping both her hands over her mouth. Then, finger by finger, she pried them away and replied circumlocutiously, "I'm not saying I eat kids, I'm not saying I don't, son-nyevitch—all I'm saying is there's a lot of PR connected with this kid-scaring sideline I've got, and if you want to believe one way or the other, how can I say the opposite?" But she slapped one hand against her cheek and rocked her head and moaned, half to herself, "Oy vey! The things a old lady's gotta put up with!" She gave him an affronted squinty glare and waggled a thin finger at him. "I'm not saying what I do or don't do, mine little guestnik, but this I'll say: eating kids is *feh!* Take my word for it or don't!"

With that, she dismissed the subject and poured the tea into a somewhat chipped crystal tumbler. She handed it to Phillimore. He raised it to his lips, feeling the warmth of the brew through the glass. But before taking a sip, he stopped and stared at the fat feline in the corner.

Its mouth turned down in disgusted disapproval and it slowly and emphatically shook its shaggy head.

Baba Yaga caught the movement from the side of her eye. She swiveled around angrily and shouted at the cat.

"Don't be a buttinski, Rimski! Go catch mice!"

"Hmph," the cat sniffed disparagingly, "if *you* don't eat kiddies, Babaleh, then *I* don't eat mice." He yawned, then licked his paws in lordly fashion.

The witch made an indignant appeal to the professor.

"I *ask* you, where today is it possible to find good help?"

Phillimore's eyes goggled from his head. "But the cat talked!"

"Such a miracle?" she sneered. "It would be more amazing, son-nyevitch, if only he knew when to shut up!"

Rimski shrugged. "So, all right, I'm bothering you. So I'll go out."

And the cat vanished.

The teacher recovered his wits with difficulty. His trembling hands spilled some tea as he set down the tumbler. A drop or two splashed on the floor and killed a pair of amorous cockroaches.

"You're nervous, dollink?" Baba Yaga inquired solicitously. "Sip a little *tay*, it'll put you to sleep."

"I'll *bet* it will."

"Maybe you think I'm from poisoning guests? *Feh!* In such business is no profit, take my word from it!"

"You're telling me this is just a sleeping potion?"

"Would *I* give you something that wouldn't be good for you?" Baba Yaga asked, carefully countering his question with a question.

Some detail of the Baba Yaga legend kept niggling at Phillimore's mind. A little more concentration and he'd have it. *Something to do with questions . . .*

"All I wanted is to make my little guesteleh nice and comfy, so I figured you'd be happy if you could *gaien shlafen* for a while and—"

"And then," interrupted Rimski's bored voice from midair, "she'd zap you with a geas."

"Hoo-boy, am I gonna give it to you, cat!" she shrilled, leaping to her feet. "If I ever catch you, I'll turn you into a tax collector!"

The awful threat didn't faze the invisible Rimski. "In that case," he meowed, "I'll make sure you don't catch me."

Turning back to Phillimore, the old biddy flashed him a sycophantically ingratiating smile, but he was on his feet, umbrella in hand, ready to push the catch and escape. His thumb joggled against the button as the hut on fowl legs clumped over some particularly rocky terrain below.

"So that's what you're up to," the professor accused. "Magic spells so I'd have to do whatever you will me to perform!"

"We-e-ell," she wheedled, "I *was* going to ask you a little favor, but I have to be careful, see? Anytime—"

"Why fool around with magic when you could just ask?"

"NO QUESTIONS!" she yelled, startling Phillimore. "DON'T ASK ME QUESTIONS!"

"Look," he snapped, "I've had about enough of this mystification. Why don't you tell me what you want?"

Baba Yaga's face went white. A fearful curse escaped her lips and she began stumping around the room and venting her temper on the scant furnishings. She kicked over a rush-broom, pounded the table and smashed a sugar bowl, whirled three times on her left toe and spat in the teakettle.

Wonder how often she does that? He was doubly glad he didn't drink any.

"OOOHHH!" Baba Yaga howled, wringing her wrinkled hands, "now you've *done* it!"

"Done *what?*"

His second question provoked an even louder yowl. She bashed her head against the fireplace in frustration, then, in a paroxysm of rage, ripped a bag of dried bear-snouts out of an herb-box and scattered them wildly about the room. "STOP WITH THE QUESTIONS!" she screamed, then suddenly threw herself into a cane-bottom chair and began to sob.

Feeling sorry for her without knowing why, he patted her shoulder and asked what was wrong. But that made her shriek again and knock his hand away.

"Now it's three *unavoidable* questions! Idiot! SHUT UP!" She tore her hair in rage and despair. "A year a question! Now I'll lose three years because you can't stop with the *dumke* questions . . . and *that's* what's wrong, Shlubya!"

No sooner were the words out of her mouth than she began shaking so violently that she flopped off her chair and banged her pimply proboscis on the unplaned planks of the rustic flooring. As she flailed about, Phillimore remembered the missing piece of the Baba Yaga myth.

After quite some time, she quieted and feebly crept back to her seat. The furrows in her forehead were etched deeper than before, and the sparkle in her single blue eye had perceptibly dimmed.

"Nu," she wheezed, "ain't you gonna wish me happy birthday?"

He did.

"That," the witch gasped, "is what happens when I have to answer a question. I age twelve months in a minute . . . and *that's* what you've done, shmendrick!"

As soon as she said it, she was seized by another convulsion, exactly like the first. It tossed her about for precisely sixty seconds and so enfeebled her that, when it was over, Phillimore had to help her hobble over to the bug-infested pallet by the far wall of the hut.

"A picnic it ain't," she complained. "Whenever I get a visitor, sooner or later some question pops out that I can't avoid answering and then *wham-bam!*" She exhaled shakily. *"Gevalt,* I ain't as young as I used to be!"

He nodded. "Then I assume that's why you were going to knock me out and fix a quest-spell on me. That way I'd go do your bidding without asking questions."

"Is that"—she glared suspiciously—*"another* question?"

"No, it's an assumption."

"Good," she murmured, plopping her head on her pillow, "assume all you want, sonnyevitch."

She lay still for quite a while. Finally, the professor suggested it was about time she explained what she wanted him to do.

"Not now," she demurred, "that would answer your third question and I ain't up yet to another four seasons. Let me rest a while. Instead, you should tell me about yourself. Like how come a big *boytchik* like yourself walks in the forest with an umbrella but no galoshes?"

To pass the time, he spoke about his adventures in various worlds and told Baba Yaga all he knew of his umbrella's peculiar properties. She looked so feeble lying there he could see no harm in being totally honest.

It was a serious tactical error.

The hut stood motionless in the middle of a moonlit clearing. Every so often, one or the other of its bird-feet lifted to scratch an itch on the opposite leg. Trotting around the side of the shack, Baba Yaga stuck two shriveled fingers in the corners of her mouth and vented an ear-splitting whistle.

"That," she cackled, "will fetch Walter, right enough. Wait, son-nyevitch, he'll be here in a couple minutes."

Out of deference to her penchant for instant chronology, Phillimore refrained from asking who or what Walter might be. *Just hope it's nothing too gruesome.*

The professor was ready to start out on the witch's quest, or at least to make a great show of doing so for her sake. He was tired of her company and especially of the sour chicken-fat odor of her hut. But his main reason for wanting to get away from her (and any spells she might have the power to cast should he seem recalcitrant to her wishes) was that he intended to escape her world entirely. *The umbrella can do better than Russian fairy-tales!* Other than Baba Yaga, he knew practically nothing of Slavic myth; the only reason her tale was vaguely familiar to the professor was because of his lifelong interest in fantasy-horror literature.

Earlier, after Baba Yaga somewhat recovered from two years of on-the-spot aging, she offered him supper and a blanket for the night. Fearing the first (though perhaps not so much as the second), Phillimore politely declined. To spare her feelings (on the grounds that it was poor policy to wound a witch's vanity), he expressed a keen desire to set out right away on her errand.

"How come suddenly you got *shpilkes?*" she wondered, squinting at him suspiciously. "I ain't even said yet what my favor is."

"I'm in a generous mood. I can't refuse you anything."

"You just did." She sighed. "However, health comes foremost, and I can't wait too much longer to drink the magic elixir. Another year or two could kill me!"

He began to ask what she meant by a magic elixir, but hardly were his lips open than she angrily gestured for silence. "Clamp a lid on it, blabbermouth! I'm *telling*, I'm *telling!*"

"Sorry, I forgot. But it's hard to restrain curiosity."

"Oh, is it?" she asked sweetly. "Would it help if I turned you into a tarantula?"

"That's all right," he gulped, "very kind of you, but I think I can manage from now on."

"Go-oo-ood, sonnyevitch, go-oo-ood," Baba Yaga crooned, "now give a listen—there ain't no way I can stop myself from growing a year older when I answer questions, that's in my original contract. However, my agent managed a kind of escape clause so's I can backtrack and get young again. I have to whomp up a drink made outta falernum, pig-sweat, slivovitz and black sunflower, put in a blender and run ten seconds at Mix—*yah, yah, I see you dying to ask, I got blenders, I'm a witch, ain't I?*—and serve stirred, not shaken, on the rocks. After I swig it down, I drop couple hundred years maybe, and believe me, is *that* a *machaiya!*"

"I suppose," said Phillimore, "it's impossible to home-grow these black sunflowers."

"Was *that* a question?" she yelped, reaching for a book with the ominous title, *Wells' Magic and Spells: Blessings, Curses, Ever-Filled Purses, Prophecies, Witches, Knells.*

"A supposition, only a supposition!"

"It better be, buster!" she snarled, replacing the tome. "Now *the* black sunflower grows on a certain enchanted island. One at a time, see? It gets picked and then another grows a long, long time later." She paused fearfully, but evidently Phillimore's last remark was credited as a mere supposition, so nothing happened to the witch. Heartened by her escape, she continued with greater enthusiasm.

"Okay, sonnyevitch, now pay attention 'cause soon is coming the part you're gonna like! On this enchanted island lives the prettiest, sweetest, purest, most innocent young lady you'd ever want to meet! A real *zoftich maidele*, and *stacked* like you wouldn't believe! Over there is a magazine, pick it up and flip, you'll see!"

Phillimore plucked a tattered copy of *Necromantic Age* out of a small pile of tidily-arranged soot. It was evidently a trade magazine for sorcerers, warlocks, witches and other magical practitioners. The issue evidently had been bent back many times to a certain story, for when he picked it up, it fell open to a colorful spread of photos and text that told about an unusual spell of staymagic holding a young woman (simply identified as the Beautiful Child) on an unnamed verdant isle, latitude and longitude unknown. He noted with vague disquiet that certain passages of the article's text had been blacked over so they were totally illegible. And at the bottom right of the right-hand page he saw a picture had been torn out of the periodical. *No point asking her about it, she'll get mad and won't tell me, anyway.*

"Nu, sonnyevitch," she grinned, "some knockers, hah? If Mama Yaga was just telling, you wouldn't be believing, but there you are, the magazine is showing, so now get ready to go fetch me that black sunflower and when you bring it back, the broad should come, too, and I'll fix it up permanent between the two of you! Now excuse me for one minute, I just answered your remaining question and— *HOO*—BOYYYYYYYYYYYYYYYYYYYYYYYYY!!!"

While she quivered and quaked, Phillimore tried to decide what was niggling away at the back of his brain that made him so uneasy about the enchanted island. The thought would not come, *but it doesn't really matter, anyhow, because I'm not going in the first place.*

At least, having seen the picture of the damsel on the isle, he had to admit the umbrella *had* been trying to do its job right, after all.

The witch, having gotten back her breath, told the professor she had a friend named Walter who'd be of immense help on his journey. Before he could protest that he preferred traveling alone, Phillimore suddenly was hurtled across the room where he landed head-downwards in a barrelful of rancid pickle-brine. This circumstance was the direct result of the crone's abruptly ordering her hut to come to a screeching halt.

Phillimore extricated himself with considerable spluttering from the gherkin-juice. Before he could recover his wits, Baba Yaga whirled him merrily around by both hands in a grotesque peasant dance, then yanked him outside the door, down the steps and into the summery gloom of the deep woods.

She whistled a second time. From somewhere in the midst of the trees, not too far away, came a cross bass voice.

"I'm coming as fast I can, you old bone-sack! Contain your urine! I'm not a bagpipe!"

Recognizing the Shakespearean allusion, Phillimore strained his eyes to see the speaker, but the moonlight did not illuminate the depth of the forest. He did not have to wait long, though. Soon, to his ears there came the muted *clipclop* of hooves. Out of the night suddenly cantered the most remarkable creature the professor had seen in quite some time.

It was a lean, sinewy stallion with mournful red eyes and a dour expression that twisted its large muzzle sideways, giving it the appearance of one about to spit in disgust. The most unusual thing about the riderless creature was its coat; it glowed bright pink in the rays of the waxing moon.

"Walter," said the witch, "I want you should meet a friend of mine."

"Pfui," Walter rumbled in his raspy, deep voice, "any friend of yours is bound to be a real *zhlub*." He regarded Phillimore darkly. "What're you gawking at, shorty?"

"You're pink!"

Curling his lip contemptuously, Walter complimented the professor on his perspicacity. "If pink is good enough for elephants, then how come you object to the way I look?"

"I don't object," the man soothed the animal. "I just never saw such a hue on a horse before."

"Damn right I'm hoarse," Walter growled and lapsed into contemplative silence.

"Walter here will be your noble charger," Baba Yaga informed the professor. "He can read road-maps good, and on his back, you'll make better time, too."

Walter snorted at the last notion, but said nothing.

"But I don't need to ride," Phillimore reasoned, "I can fly wherever I want to go with my umbrella." He started towards the hut. "I'll be just a minute, I left it inside."

He didn't notice the witch make a certain hand-signal behind his back, but he immediately observed that as soon as he approached the hut, its two clawed legs began to hobble towards the forest.

Phillimore stopped. The hut stopped. He sprinted forward three steps. It trotted backwards the same distance. He sidled sideways. It edged laterally, but in the opposite direction.

Disgusted, he turned to the witch. "Ask your skittish house to stand still!"

Smiling a broad, unpleasant grin, she apologized for the hut's recalcitrance. "What can an old lady do with a *dumke* chicken without a head? I'll be lucky to get back in it myself!"

"But I have to get my umbrella!"

"Not with Walter handy." She bowed and ducked her head in conciliatory fashion. "Nu, you shouldn't worry, sonnyevitch, Mama Yaga will take good care of your umbrella *till you come back with the black sunflower.*"

Phillimore got the point. He sighed, defeated. "It won't work for *you,* you know. It's imprinted with my brain-set and won't operate for anyone else."

She looked positively scandalized. "Are you accusing that *I* would touch your crummy umbrella? Since when have I given you cause to make such nasty thinkings?"

"Two questions," the teacher snapped. "Why don't you answer them yourself!?" He turned away, thoroughly disgruntled with his own stupidity, with the witch's duplicity, with Boris' original suggestion that he seek The Perfect Mate and finally, as always, with the unpredictable caprices of the umbrella itself. "Come on, Walter," he glumly grumbled, "let's go."

"Okay," the stallion snorted, "but if you climb up on me, I'll dump you in a cesspool!"

Oh, boy, Phillimore mused silently, *some quest this is going to be!* With a resigned shrug, he followed Walter out of the clearing.

Immediately, the hut pranced over to Baba Yaga, paused while its mistress entered, then resumed its customary sylvan perambulations.

Man and beast trudged along a broad path that cut, with few twists, through the forest. The foliage was thick, too tangled to permit much light to penetrate, yet here and there a pallid patch shone with surprising distinctness in the irregular illumination of the wistful moon.

Walter knew the trail well, but Phillimore often stumbled over unexpected stumps and stones. The horse did his best to endure it patiently, but when the other tripped and landed rather heavily against his flank, Walter neighed nastily, "Pick up your feet, klutz!"

"Sorry. I lost my footing."

"*Do* tell!" the animal grumped in his gravelly bass. "If I'd known how clumsy you are, I would've borrowed Baba's firebird so you could see where you put your feet."

"I'll attempt to be more careful," Phillimore said rather stiffly.

Walter disdainfully shook his mane. "Thanks for trying, shorty, but you'll probably break your neck long before you reach the island." Beneath his breath, the horse mumbled, "Which'll probably be more pleasant, anyhow."

Phillimore caught it. *Uh-oh.* A too-familiar chill tickled an arpeggio along the length of his backbone, an unwelcome sensation frequently experienced on umbrella-jaunts. "Suddenly," he addressed the horse, "I have a feeling this errand isn't quite as easy as Baba described it."

Lustily clearing his hoarse throat, Walter tried to change the subject. "You commented on my scratchy voice before. Wanna know how I got this way?"

"Not particularly."

"Cigar-smoking."

"You smoke cigars?!"

"Naw, a toad I once knew, when I used to hang around the swamp, was always puffing away. Said he was a congersman."

"The word is *congressman*," Phillimore punctiliously emended, but with little real interest. "And would you like a ladder to get down off this story?"

"It's true," said the horse. "And that's the way *he* pronounced the word. Anyway, he was always blowing cheap smoke in my face. Y'see, sometimes I used to let 'im ride on my neck, and I think that's when I developed this chronic hoarseness. I must've been allergic to his stinking stogies."

"Serves you right for not taking care of the frog on your throat," the professor replied. "Now stop avoiding my question. You won't discourage me about this quest . . . I *have* to get back my umbrella! But at least you might prepare me for what I'm going to run into on that rotten island."

"How should *I* know? I never set hoof there."

"You haven't?"

"Nope. I only take you as far as the final boat. I'll hang around on the shore for a few days and if you don't come back, I'll tell Baba you screwed up, too."

"*Too?*"

"You bet your borscht-belt. Whaddaya think, you're the first sap she's suckered on this gig? In the old days, there was nothing to it, I'd escort her errand-boys or -girls back and forth, but ever since the island got magicked, it's been strictly a one-way trip for them." He licked his great lips with a light-pink tongue. "Sorry, but you wanted the truth."

"Thanks," Phillimore glumly replied. "Now I know the worst."

"That all depends," said Walter, "on how you feel about Hessians."

"*What?*" Phillimore shook his head, thinking he'd heard incorrectly. "Did you say *Hessians?*"

"You repeat like a radish," the horse replied dourly. "Actually, it's just one Hessian, but he's behind us. You'd better get a move on."

Phillimore looked around to see what Walter was talking about. There on the trail several yards further back but slowly approaching was a coal-black charger on which was mounted a tall, dark-caped figure with a vaguely military air about him. The professor thought he spied the glint of dress-uniform brass buttons and braid, but he couldn't be positive, it was too dark.

"Who *is* he, Walter? Why's he following us?"

"Not us, buster, just you. He occasionally shows up on this road around this time of night. He'll disappear once he reaches the bridge a little way ahead."

The mention of the bridge caused an unpleasant thought to pop into Phillimore's mind. Glancing back again, he studied the rider more closely. The Hessian plodded along at an easy gait, but though his horse paced unhurriedly, still it steadily diminished the distance between mounted horseman and horse and man on foot. Suddenly the soldier cantered into a sickly pool of moonlight and in that instant Phillimore got his first clear glimpse of his pursuer.

Just as he'd feared, the gigantic, cloak-muffled man had no head above the stiff, high circle of his collar. But on his saddle-pommel he balanced a grisly object that the professor did not care to inspect too carefully.

Walter confided, "He's got an incurable hankering for other people's craniums. I don't know if he's looking for his own head, or just one that fits."

"He has a head already," Phillimore whispered weakly.

"Yeah, but as soon as he gets a new one, he'll throw the old model away."

The professor swallowed with difficulty. "Uh, how far ahead *is* that bridge?"

"From here? Maybe eight hundred meters."

"That far?" Calculating quickly, he groaned, "That's almost half-a-mile!"

The horse nodded. "Better shake a leg, shorty."

"Uh . . . I don't suppose you'd change your mind about letting me ride on you, just for a little while?"

The pink steed snorted, refusing to dignify the question with any further reply.

"I didn't think so," Phillimore sighed, then, taking a deep breath, started off at a sprint. He called over his shoulder to Walter, "See you at the bridge!"

"If you make it," the horse observed darkly.

As soon as the professor began to run, the ghostly horseman lightly touched spurs to his charger and his midnight stallion quickened its pace.

While Phillimore scrambled and stumbled along the path, he wondered what the hell the Headless Horseman was doing in Russia. *Sleepy Hollow is in upstate New York! Maybe—*

But there wasn't time to calmly contemplate the implication. He jogged on as fast as he could safely manage without tripping over roots, rocks or other impedimenta.

He shot a brief glance backwards. The spectral horse trotted along silently, little by little closing the gap. *Perhaps he's a sportsman,* Phillimore thought, noticing that the Hessian had not yet urged his steed to its swiftest gait.

Beneath the professor's speeding feet, the dry leaves crackled, the only sound in the deep woods.

Or is it?

Maybe it was the strangeness of the surroundings, or the ghastly nature of his pursuer, but Phillimore began to imagine he heard the soft subtle sound of something running alongside him on the forest trail. He couldn't be sure; it was only a faint rustle, yet it seemed slightly out of phase with his own hurrying footsteps.

"Dammit!" he gasped. "IS there something running beside me?" He muttered sourly, "My luck, it's The Damned Thing!"

"I *beg* your pardon!" said an affronted voice practically beneath his feet. It so startled the professor that he broke stride, stubbed his toe, yelped and sprawled flat on his face.

"Hmph," a voice he'd heard before sniffed. "Better get up before the dummy grabs you."

Shoving himself quickly to his knees, Phillimore stared fearfully back down the path. The horseman was now only some fifty feet distant. As he watched, he saw him draw a long saber that glinted dangerously in a vagrant shaft of lunar light.

"Get *up*, goofball!" the voice urged. "Follow me!"

"Are you kidding?" the professor protested, rising. "I can't even *see* you."

"Oh, yeah, I forgot . . . sorry!" With that, Baba Yaga's large gray cat, Rimski, instantly materialized. "Now stay close behind." He padded across the road and ducked through a gap between two distressingly conspicuous maple trees.

However, inasmuch as (a) the Headless Horseman was by now a scant thirty feet away and (b) it was Rimski who stopped the professor from swigging the witch's hypnotic and (c) he could see no other hope for escape, anyway, Phillimore decided to trust the feline. He ran between the maples and hurried over to the place where the cat's eyes glinted in the gloom.

"Let him ride past," the cat whispered. "He will."

Phillimore was skeptical, but he did his best to hold his breath, which wasn't easy, since he'd been running. Still, he forced himself to avoid twitching a single muscle. Soon, to his astonishment, the phantom reached the place where he'd left the road, but neither slackened pace nor even glanced in the direction of the unmistakable lofty maples.

"How'd you know he wouldn't—" Phillimore began, but the cat hissed for silence.

"He's dumb, but not deaf," Rimski whispered.

They waited a good two or three minutes before the cat spoke again. "That'll take care of him for the night. Pretty soon he'll be at the bridge."

"How'd you know he'd do that?"

"He's as dim-witted as a rhino. By the time he got to the spot, he forgot you even existed. No brains at all."

"You mean because he doesn't have a head?"

"I mean because he's a Hessian." The cat stretched and yawned. "I hope you don't mind that I've been following you and Walter all this time."

"I'm glad you did!" said Phillimore. "Would you mind, though, if I asked you a few questions?"

"Not at all," Rimski meowed importantly.

"First off, how'd you learn to disappear like that?"

"Pretty flashy, huh?" The cat was obviously proud of his talent.

"Did Baba Yaga bestow the power on you?"

"Hmph!" Rimski grunted. "From that old biddy I don't get *bupkis!* Naah, I picked up the trick a couple years back from an English cat I met on vacation."

"An *English* cat?" Phillimore smiled. "Was he, by any chance, from Cheshire?"

"As a matter of fact, he was. You know him?"

"No, but I've heard of him. He vanishes and just leaves his smile behind, right?"

"Yeah," Rimski drawled disapprovingly, "he pulls that sometimes. Cheap trick, if you ask me."

Sour grapes, perhaps? Phillimore tried wheedling the cat. "I've always wondered about it, though. I mean, how *can* one see a grin without also seeing at least part of the cat behind it?"

"Wonder away, professor, you'll never catch me doing it."

"Why not?"

"Around here," Rimski said scornfully, "what's there to smile about? *Next question?*"

Sitting down to rest, Phillimore asked the cat how it had been possible for the Headless Horseman to see him in the first place. "Does he use the eyes of the head he carries?"

"I doubt that," the cat said, after mulling it over for a moment. "Allowing for the possible piecemeal survival of the victim's spirit, and assuming that same *geist*, so to speak, chooses to hang around its separated head, still it's very unlikely it would allow its appropriated orbs to do service to the predator who stole the head in the first place. No, no," the cat meowed mellowly, "I would postulate that the horseman sees with astral optics."

"You appear to be something of a philosopher," the professor remarked, impressed.

"Thanks for noticing," said Rimski, gratefully rubbing himself against the man's legs. "That's what I once was."

"I don't follow."

"You see before you the transmogrification of a fledgling philosopher. But though my thoughts pursue their arcane windings as before, I cannot write them down since Baba klopped me with a spell."

"You mean she changed you into a cat?"

"Precisely. Which is how I can speculate with authority on the behaviour of victims of the supernormal."

"What did you do to provoke her?"

"It's what I *didn't* do," the cat purred.

"Namely?"

"I wouldn't go fetch her a sunflower."

"If that's so," Phillimore asked, "why are you here with me? Change your mind?"

"Hardly. It's just that it's safer than hanging around the hut. Baba threatened she'd change me back into a tax collector."

"*Back* into? I thought you said you were a philosopher!"

"Avocationally. Who can make with the Venns and zens and earn a living?"

"Well," Phillimore mused, "in the world I originally came from, there was sometimes a lot of money to be made playing guru or pragmatic philosopher. There was even a foreign businessman who made a fortune by persuading teenagers to attain inner peace by relinquishing all their personal property to him."

The cat chortled. "And I thought *this* place is loony!"

"I'm still confused, though, Rimski. If you used to be a tax collector until Baba Yaga turned you into a cat, then why would you run away now that she wants to remove the spell?"

"Because," the animal sighed, "*she* knows and *I* know that, compared with collecting taxes, it's not *so* bad being a cat."

"Why do you emphasize *so?*"

Rimski shrugged. "Catting has its drawbacks, like any other line."

"Such as?"

"The worst part," he replied, grimacing, "is trying to acquire a taste for mice."

Despite the unappetizing lead-in, Phillimore realized that he hadn't eaten in several hours. He mentioned it to the cat.

"Okay, I know a house where you can mooch some dinner," Rimski said. "It's a little out of the way, but eventually we'll get back to the bridge. Are you game?"

"Yes."

"Then follow me." The cat started over a nearby knoll. It led to a narrow path that paralleled the road, but with frequent detours and roundabouts. The professor did his best to keep Rimski in view, but it was dark and he often lost sight of him. However, the considerate feline soon sensed the other's confusion and made sure to turn around every so often so Phillimore could catch the yellow glimmer of his eyes.

They wove a twisted circuit for perhaps a quarter of an hour. Then, spying a tiny cottage a little way off nestling snugly in a dim dingle, Phillimore hailed the cat.

Rimski loped over to him. "Better not stick around here," he warned. "This is a very popular neck of the woods for all sorts of mischief."

"But that house over there . . . I thought that might be where you were taking me."

"Normally I would," the cat said, "but tonight, it's bad timing. The place we want is right next to the road, three rises from now."

"What do you mean by bad timing?"

The cat flicked his tail in the direction of the cottage. "The owner's kind of grumpy, he just got burgled this morning. It's not a good time to ask him for charity."

"Burgled?" The professor repeated the word, surprised; somehow he always associated that crime with city dwellers on the idyllically distorted assumption that the country is the last outpost of a more innocent civilization.

"It's no big deal," the cat explained with a yawn. "While the family was out, some snotty kid busted in, broke some furniture, ate up their kid's food, then, to top it off, clumps all over the bedspreads with muddy boots yet. Now I *ask* you—what's happening to good old respect for private property?" He paused for an answer but Phillimore, to Rimski's surprise and annoyance, just stood there, eyes wide and mouth half-agape. "Professor," he mewed with some pique, "haven't you been listening to me at all?"

"What? Oh, *yes!* Yes, I have—I'm sorry! It's just that while you were talking, an idea I've been chasing around in my head for almost an hour finally surfaced. Your tale made it happen."

"It *did?*" Rimski stared suspiciously at his nether member.

"Listen, were you still in the room when I told the witch about my umbrella?"

"Yes. Invisible and listening."

"Did you believe what I said?" Phillimore asked.

"Once you've tasted Baba's cooking, anything is possible," he replied with a shudder.

"All right, Rimski. Now since you're a philosopher, I doubt that you'll have any difficulty countenancing the preternatural implications of what I'm about to explain—"

But before the professor could utter another word, the cat emitted a hair-raising shriek.

Phillimore shrugged, somewhat nonplussed. "Well, of course, if metaphysics upsets you, I wouldn't think—"

"*Noodnick!*" the cat snapped, leaping up. "Somebody just stepped on my tail!"

Jumping to his feet, the professor looked around, but all he could see was the night-shadowed forest . . . then, without preamble or permission requested, countless dainty hands suddenly reached out of the darkness and seized him.

Drums rumbled. Trumpets blared. A brilliant burst of light sprang up all around, dazzling the professor's eyes and totally confusing him. The woods rang with merry laughter, sparkling but heartless.

The music rollicked and swelled. Phillimore was swirled about so swiftly that he was powerless to resist. Coronets shined and flashing diadems twinkled past while he was delicately compelled to quickstep all about the green. In the midst of the melee, he thought he caught the hilarious roar and spoor of a wild good-humored beast cavorting nearby, but could not possibly stop to study the source.

When the tempo accelerated, something quite remarkable happened. Perhaps it was the kinesthetic consequence of his exertions and exploits of the past few hours, but suddenly the professor no longer required the press of soft, insistent fingers to speed him along; Terpsichore possessed him and he gave himself over to the fury of the dance.

Whirling and leaping, Phillimore spun in madcap pirouettes that decidedly outdervished the surrounding stately mincing that his captors affected. As for those other dancers, they paused, two at a time, to mark the unexpected prodigy until, at length, only one reveler remained beside the professor to tread the measure. Sensing one another's proximity, the pair logically veered into each other's arms—and Phillimore found himself swaying cheek to jowl with a great sharp-toothed grinning lion.

And yet the frantic music carried him beyond logic; clutching the beast's golden mane and accepting its proffered upheld paw, off he stepped with redoubled vigor, dipping, dodging and delving a two-step up and down the sward. Now here, now there, the odd carousers swung with the spirit of the mirthful melody and all the world was a meld of verdant scenery whose hues bled one into another while merry watching eyes glinted and laughter mocked a counterpoint unminded by man and beast as the two, panting and sweating, scampered the precipice of a *prestissimo tutti* that blurred them to a wash of tawny tweed.

But then, too soon it seemed, the hidden consort of tympani and brass trembled on the brink of the penultimate tonic, quavered a last reluctant *ritard* before plunging, dead, into the gleeful final ejaculation of the crashing dominant chord that concluded the dithyrambic dance.

Tottering for an instant on the tips of his toes, the breathless professor toppled in temporary collapse beside the crumpled lion on the turf.

"Bravo!" shouted a single enthusiastic voice. The rest of the assemblage mingled polite condescending comments with a smattering of indifferent applause, then lost interest in the winded professor and his tired feline companion.

At length, Phillimore sat up groggily and surveyed his surroundings. He was surprised to find he sat just within the mouth of an immense cavern, the nature of which he'd never seen before, although he was a moderately enthusiastic amateur spelunker. Though above his head there loomed a great overhang of rock that served as the outer lip of the subterranean landscape, the ground resembled no cave he'd ever known. Instead of stone, he rested on a rolling short-cropped lea dotted with leafy orchards bearing gold and silver fruit. Nearby, a castle sported pastel pennants above the meadow; from it had proceeded the martial din and blare of the kettles and horns. A river running beside the grassy lawn spilled from the cave into the exterior wood where deep night still held sway.

Looking out into the forest, Phillimore saw an old bridge that spanned the stream. He presumed it was the one mentioned by Walter the hoarse, but there was no pale-scarlet stallion standing there waiting for the professor.

Rats! the professor grumbled to himself, glancing about in vain for his philosophic friend, Rimski, *the cat vanished, and now I'm also damn well minus pink Walter!*

Musing on Rimski reminded Phillimore that he still shared a potentially imprudent proximity with another kind of cat. He began to rise, but the lion, emitting a deep bass purr, put a paw on his shoulder and effectively restrained the professor from getting up.

"All right, all right," Phillimore nervously soothed the beast, "don't worry, I'm not going anywhere!"

The lion's cold, wet nose nuzzled him. It was not a delicious tactile sensation, but the professor did his best to tolerate it. He had no desire to hurt the lion's feelings. *Wouldn't want it to be mutual.*

Just then, a man approached, the same who shouted so enthusiastically in favor of their recent choreographic display. Though Phillimore guessed him to be in his middle years, his boyish smile made him appear younger. He was of medium height with curly dark abundant hair and wore nothing but a gray toga draped loosely about his spare body and flung carelessly over one arm. His feet were bare.

Patting the big beast's head, the newcomer reassured the professor that the lion would not injure him. "He's usually harmless."

"*Usually?*"

"He doesn't hurt those he likes . . . and he seems to have taken quite a fancy to you." He lowered his voice. "That may prove beneficial, considering the circumstances. . . ."

"What do you mean?" the professor asked, alarmed. "*What* circumstances?" He sprang smartly to his feet, a feat accomplishable by virtue of the fact that the lion was temporarily transferring his affection to the second man.

"I am alluding to our hosts," said the man in the toga, indicating the other dancers, who, between sets, milled about tables laden with provender, pastries and pale punch. "They have rather a peculiar attitude toward strangers."

"Their attitude is certainly peremptory," Phillimore sourly stated, eying the company distastefully.

The group was composed of a dozen dazzling damsels dressed in pastel tutus, flesh-colored tights and slippers studded with gems, as well as a like number of sleek-haired young men in burnished military garb replete with gold braid and brass buttons. Both sexes sported jeweled circlets on their brows, indicative of their noble caste.

Hmph! Phillimore sniffed silently. *Looks like a stranded touring ballet troupe and a second-string male chorus from* The Student Prince *about to team up and perform* The Black Crook *to earn fare home!*

While Phillimore watched the fairy princes and princesses, they in turn cast covert glances in his direction. He sensed their sly disapproval.

Far from friendly.

"While you remain here," said the lion's confidant, "I don't think you're in any immediate danger."

"Well," the professor replied, "at the moment I have no intention of going anywhere till I satisfy my appetite. Or does their hostility extend to denying me access to their table?"

"Oh, they'll let you eat. Will you join me?"

"With pleasure. By the way, my name's Phillimore. Professor James Phillimore."

"Delighted to meet you," said the man in the toga, taking Phillimore by the arm and steering him to the banquet. "You may call me Andy. Come along now, best stay close to me."

The lion arose, stretched and yawned so that his powerful teeth and claws were prominently displayed. Then he ambled after his cherished human companions.

They sat down on the sward, Phillimore balancing an exquisitely-fashioned china plate and a crystal goblet of punch. Andy contented himself with a single silver chalice of ruby-red wine, and the lion gobbled down a succession of raw steaks.

"He is rather a remarkable beast," the professor said. "Other than in certain forms of Oriental theatre, I've never before encountered a dancing lion."

Andy nodded proudly. "I taught him all the graces. Once, he roamed the wild like any predator. But then, after we met under singular circumstances, we became fast friends, and he decided to remain with me and adopt the ways of civilization. He's since grown especially fond of diversions such as feasts and masquerades and balls. As a matter of fact, he's become much sought-after as a desirable guest by many aspiring hostesses."

"I imagine he *would* provide a certain novelty at soirées."

"Indeed, yes!" Andy averred. "During *the season*, he's a regular party lion and, don't you know, he's *always* busy." He paused to quaff some wine.

Swallowing a morsel of mutton, Phillimore brought the conversation back to the topic of his personal predicament.

"You said I'd be running no risk if I remained here, but unfortunately, I must soon be going."

"They won't let you."

"Why not?"

"They're afraid you'll try to tell their father, the king, where they've been."

So that's it! Phillimore nodded vigorously. "I believe I know all about it! The princes are under an enchantment, right?"

Andy nodded. "The exact nature of the spell has long been forgotten, but according to rumor, the curse will wind down eventually, so long as these maidens keep them company for an indefinite number of nights."

"And while they do, they dance their shoes to ruins!"

"Correct. The cobblers clamor for payment constantly and the cash drain is driving the king to distraction. He's offered substantial rewards (including marriage to any one of the young women) to whoever reveals where they go each night." Andy tossed off the rest of the wine, wiped his lips and stared sorrowfully at Phillimore. "So, you see, they'll never permit you to escape to claim the reward."

"Except that's *not* what I intend!" the professor protested. "Anyway, what *can* they do, after all, to prevent me from leaving?"

"Around here," Andy said, "they consider cutting off one's head a remarkably effective deterrent."

Just as he spoke, the professor swallowed a sip of punch. The lion solicitously pounded his back till he stopped coughing.

"Are you, too, in danger?" Phillimore asked, wiping his eyes.

"Not at all. They know I'm already married."

"You are? Where's your wife?"

"She moved out when the lion moved in."

"I can understand that," the professor said, then, smiling at the lion, quickly added, "No offense intended."

"None has been taken." Andy laughed, clapping the professor upon the shoulder. "No, no, dear fellow, I was quite aware that my spouse *might* prefer some other vicinity to that in which this lovely beast dwells." He cuddled the animal's head affectionately. "*Good* boy, *goo-oo-ood* boy!"

"Do you think he'd stand them off if I decided to leave?" Phillimore asked, indicating the animal.

"Oh, undoubtedly he would, he's a loyal, loving lion. But the princes are trained hunters and there *are* arms in the castle. I doubt if you could get very far. Even a lordly beast is not impervious to musket and ball."

The professor nodded. "True. And I wouldn't want to risk any lives, anyway. But see here, I *am* under obligation to complete a quest for a crone who won't return my property till I do. I simply *must* get going!"

"Well, you might try taking it up with the eldest princess. She pretty much decides things around here."

"Which one is she?"

"The brunette with the baggy eyes."

"I didn't notice. Baggy eyes?"

"Certainly. What can she expect? She's turning thirty, but never gets any sleep (what with all this dancing) unless she naps in the day-time—and if she does, it's not enough. She's always cranky."

"*Is that so?*" a new voice exclaimed.

They whirled about. There, hovering a few steps away, was a tall dark-haired princess with thin, stern lips, a straight patrician nose and, in truth, rather baggy eyes.

Certainly the plainest of the lot, thought Phillimore.

"How dare you speak so of me, churl?" she sneered at Andy. "If you were not of such low birth as to render your effrontery of no great significance, I should see your curly head separated this instant from your shoulders!"

The lion curled the side of his mouth back from his great teeth and began to snarl.

"On the other hand," the princess said, "I am of generous nature, and see no real injury in remarks which, perhaps, have the seeds of truth in them, after all."

The lion sniffed disdainfully and closed his mouth and eyes. In *his* social set, such jumped-up nobility were hardly worth a yawn.

"You, sir," the princess addressed Phillimore, "claim to be bound upon a quest that has nothing to do with our nightly revels."

"That's true," said the professor, rising respectfully. "I have an errand to perform for the witch Baba Yaga."

"Never heard of her," the princess yawned, failing to cover her mouth as she did. "If this be true, then *why* did we discover you skulking about the woods near this enchanted spot? Was it not to learn our secret and discover it to the king, my father?"

"Not at all!" He vigorously shook his head. "I was taking a shortcut through the forest, that was all. I didn't even see you, and *wouldn't* have, if you hadn't kidnapped me!"

The princess frowned thoughtfully. "You may, of course, be telling the truth—in which case, it is unfortunate enough. But I'm afraid however it happened, we cannot now permit you to leave."

"But I have *no* interest in wedding a princess!"

One eyebrow raised and she pursed her lips. "And why," she demanded, "should you be different from any other commoner?"

Commoner! Phillimore's temper began to boil. "I'll have you know, first off, that I am the native of a country where royalty was ousted centuries before in favor of a republic!"

"Do you speak of Rome?" Andy asked eagerly.

"No. Not quite." The professor faced the princess with elaborate dignity and hauteur. "As for marrying one of your vile lot, it *is* true I came to this world to seek a female companion, but I should never elect to settle for spoiled brats who have so little regard for human life as to condemn to execution all who'd strive for your frivolous selves!"

"I *see*," she said icily. "And now, speaking of the latter subject, you will permit me to retire and arrange your own imminent demise."

Swiveling sharply on one slipper, she stormed off, snapping her fingers at the first prince whose eye she caught.

"Uh-oh," Andy murmured mournfully, *"now* you've done it!"

"Yes, I'm afraid so," Phillimore concurred. "However, here's my plan. . . ."

Phillimore, Andy and the lion sat down and waited by the side of the river, near a dock where twelve bright blue boats bounced on the billows. Andy said the princes rowed upstream each evening to pick up the twelve dancing princesses and paddle them to the vicinity of the subterranean castle.

"They *ought* to be paddled," Phillimore grumbled. "What a grim lot!"

Nearby, the sisters wrangled over the best way to terminate him. Some were in favor of drowning, some preferred simple strangulation, one foolishly suggested feeding Phillimore to the lion.

Eventually, however, Drusilla (the eldest) had her way, and traditional decapitation was agreed upon.

A company of musicians in the castle struck up a solemn march. Lackeys emerged carrying the appurtenances of a public beheading. One bore a plush cushion on which rested a gleaming sword. Another carried towels. A third's arms encircled a large, sinister wicker basket. In the rear, the professor noticed two servants dangling between them a big black net. *Probably to throw over the lion during the ceremony.*

He stood up as the procession halted a little ways off. The thumping and blaring of the music ceased. Drusilla stepped forward.

"Are you prepared to die, stranger?" she asked haughtily.

Exchanging a look with his two friends, Phillimore addressed the eldest princess in a tone as challengingly chilly as her own. "And do you mean to tell me," he sneered, "that yours is a country barbarous enough to send off a man with so little ceremony?"

Her brows contracted and her lips turned down. "It lacks an hour of dawn, stranger; we have no time for elaborate charades. What would you have? You've already partaken of your final meal!"

"In the civilized world, from which *I* hail," he replied with a touch of pride, "a condemned prisoner is always granted one last simple request."

She shrugged. "Time is scant. We must return to our father's castle. You'll get no special favors unless your demand is easily and speedily fulfillable."

"It is."

"Then *name* it!"

"I crave a chance of treading a final measure with this noble beast."

The lion grinned appreciatively.

Drusilla talked it over with her siblings. Though inclined to be suspicious, none of them could raise any tangible objection to the odd request, so they reluctantly agreed to permit the pair one last dance together.

"What tempo? A fast one?" Drusilla demanded.

"No, this time I should prefer a slow, measured rhythm—a ponderous quadrille, if the musicians can manage it."

"Executions are certainly becoming a bother," Drusilla sighed. "However, I'll see what they can do for you."

She strode up the hill and spoke to the conductor. He gave one knowing nod and, whispering to his players, signaled the downbeat.

They managed it nicely. As the band struck up a four-square strain, repetitive and compelling in its simple melody, the professor bowed to the lion. He stood on his hind legs. Phillimore put an arm about the beast's waist, and the animal propped a paw about his. They stood side by side.

"What kind of dance position is *that?*" one of the younger sisters wondered.

"It comes from Greece," Phillimore replied. "It's known as a chain dance."

"A *chain* dance?"

"Yes. That's because more than two at a time may take part. It's possible to form a veritable chain of dancers."

The youngest princess, a somewhat unsure little auburn-haired lass, clapped her hands enthusiastically. "Ooh, that sounds like fun!" She looked for approval to Drusilla, did not find it forthcoming, yet did not altogether subside.

The professor said the Grecian chain dance was one of the world's great communal cultural artifacts and was quite simple to learn. With that, he and the lion stepped off deliberately with their right feet, described a large circle with their left, took a few sideways crossovers that placed them in a position to step out rightwards again, circle to the left, step-step-step, outward and circle and step-step-step and . . .

Andy got into position beside the dancers, placed his hand on the lion's other hip and joined the chain.

Step-step-step, outward and circle and step-step-step.

The court musicians played the slow, stately, monotonous music, repeating again and again an air that never modulated nor changed, but sang itself into the time-tapping feet of the princes and princesses who watched.

Step and step and step and outward step and circle, step and step and step and as they passed near the youngest princess, Phillimore reached out one hand invitingly toward her waist and she pranced obediently into place and stepped and stepped and stepped and took one outward step and circled with one foot and then she curved her tiny hand about the waist of her admiring opposite youngest prince and together the five danced and danced and soon it was six and then seven who stepped and stepped and stepped and took that one deliberate outward step and circled and the company grew and grew until only the frowning eldest sister, Drusilla, momentarily refused to lilt with the impelling mind-deadening refrain, but at length even she— for she *was*, after all, one of the renowned twelve dancing princesses— even she encircled the end prince's waist and led off into that outer step that was almost a foot-stamp and completed with her left foot the circle that riveted the mind to the life-bestowing earth beneath fifty-four compulsive dancing feet, stepping and stepping and stepping, over and again, and over and yet again.

The mesmerizing *perpetuum mobile* communicated itself to the players of the music; enrapt, they repeated the principal subject of the piece, eyes closed, abstracted, on a plane whose pleasures are primarily known by musicians. As they tootled, keened and thumped out the swelling steady accents of the composition, the evening hours waned.

And now the central links of the chain—Phillimore, Andy and the lion—shifted their weights subtly and introduced an undulation into the great curve of dancers, a snaking ripple that billowed gently out to the furthermost ends of the line. The three repeated the maneuver a bit more forcefully, a trifle wider; again the caravan of flesh heaved to the motion.

Andy, the professor and the lion stepped wider and continued to ply the human ribbon with slowly increasing insistence. The rapt nobles coiled and contracted and dilated in fluctuating arcs that, by imperceptible degrees, carried them to the edge of the river. Their feet strutted upon the down-sloping bank and the drag and thrust of more than two dozen bodies aided the work of gravity as they footed it faster to avoid stumbling or losing the time.

Suddenly, the trio leaned into the cordon of flesh with all their weight and the professor nodded. With one mighty effort, they *snapped* the chain as hard as they could.

An unexpected melee: shouts and bewildered exclamations; twenty-four waking princesses and escorts, knotted together in a complicated tangle of intertwined limbs, falling and jostling and rolling in the same direction. . . .

"*Release!*"

When Phillimore shouted, he and his friends yanked their hands away from the crowd and gave mighty shoves to anyone they could reach, thus creating an effective riptide that added to the confusion. The furthest tottering royal representatives had begun to regain a little of their equilibrium but the professor's new tactic conquered whatever momentum they had started to reestablish.

With a mighty splash, half of the dazed and dizzy dancers plunged simultaneously into the river. The others either collapsed breathless by the shore or followed the bulk of the company into the water.

"*Now! Hurry!*" the professor yelled, but Andy and the lion were already speeding toward the dock and Phillimore matched them in a race to throw off as many mooring ropes as they could manage while the beached nobles were still too vertiginous to collect wits and combat them.

They managed to loose most of the punts before one of the princes groggily drew his sword and started uncertainly in their direction. Andy nudged the professor, who turned and saw the approaching adversary. With a confirmatory nod, Phillimore and his companions scrambled into one of the two remaining boats, cast off the rope and furiously started to paddle away from the dock into the middle of the river.

The lion roared delightedly as the men rowed with all their might. Andy nodded at the beast.

"Yes, yes, I totally agree."

"What did he say?" asked Phillimore.

"That it was the best damn party in years!" He chuckled. "That was quite a dance at the end. How did you know it would work so well?"

"I didn't for sure. It was a chance I had to take. The Greek chain dance was supposed to be a public ritual in which, say, the populace of an entire town might hypnotize themselves into dancing off a cliff rather than surrender to marauders." Phillimore craned his neck around. "Look and tell me whether we're being pursued, Andy; I can't see well enough."

Andy looked. Back on the dock, the prince who'd given token chase stood in doubt for a moment as to whether to jump in the one remaining boat or hurry down to the beach and help rescue some of his floundering kinfolk. At last, with a disgusted wave of his arm, he dismissed the professor and stumbled off to yank Drusilla out of the drink.

"Row on," said Andy merrily, matching Phillimore stroke for stroke. "We're in the clear."

Overhead, the sky paled with the approaching dawn. The punt rode the river out of the cave and into the forest, through which the great flood twisted.

"The bridge is one more bend downstream," said Andy. "Are you making for it?"

The professor shook his head. "I *was* supposed to meet Walter, my guide, there, but that was hours ago and by now, he's probably gone home, figuring I was killed on the road." He yawned. "I sure got myself stuck in one hell of a world."

"I beg your pardon?"

"Never mind, it's too complicated." He yawned again. "I'm exhausted. Just a few seconds ago, I saw a cottage over on the near shore, a little ways into the woods. I believe I'll beg a bed for a few hours before continuing my quest. Will you join me?"

"I'm afraid not," Andy replied, rowing toward the indicated riverbank. "We're on our way to town to a cotillion the lion promised to dance at."

"Do you want to use the punt?"

"No, it's not that far by foot. You keep to the river. It'll be faster for you and possibly safer than the woods."

At the bank, they stepped into the shallows and hauled the small boat onto dry land. The lion gave Phillimore a farewell hug and Andy shook hands with his new friend. Then the amiable Roman and his peculiar companion ambled down the trail and were soon lost to view. . . .

"It's *about time* you got rid of that monster!"

The professor yelped. Jerking his head in the direction from which the unexpected voice proceeded, he saw, sitting in a clump of weeds, the half-invisible philosopher cat.

"*Rimski!*"

"Nu," the cat yawned disdainfully, "you were expecting maybe Puss in Boots?"

"Some friend you are! Where've you *been* all night?"

"As close as I could safely come without getting trampled by those klutzes with ferryboats for feet! And as far away as I could stay from that overgrown alleycat's teeth!"

"You mean Andy's lion? He's harmless."

"To you, maybe." The feline padded out of the woods and deigned to rematerialize completely. "As for me, I didn't have any too sure an idea that he wouldn't've regarded me as an *hors d'oeuvre.*" Rimski rubbed appreciatively against Phillimore's legs. "Anyhow, it's good you got away safe. I'm glad to see you again."

"Likewise," said the professor, wondering whether it was proper manners to pet a former tax collector.

Rimski guided Phillimore underneath the trees to a small clearing lit by early morning sun. A neat small lawn with flagstones set in its midst beckoned the way to the tiny cottage the professor had seen from the river.

"Wait here," the cat suggested. "The men of the house will be leaving for work soon. Then you can ask for a place to lie down for a while, and when you wake, the girl will fix you a good meal before we start again. By the way, before you snooze, maybe you could sneak me a saucer cream? I couldn't get near the food in the cave."

"Why can't you ask for it yoursself?"

"I'll be invisible in the house."

"How come?"

"In these parts," Rimski whispered, crouching behind a berry bush, "it's *tsooris* traveling with a cat. You'll be suspected of being a warlock, and me, your familiar."

"Hmm." Phillimore mused. "And something else falls into place."

"What?"

"Is it possible that seven men live in there? Seven *small* men?"

The cat's eyes widened. "How'd you know that?"

"Bit of a fey quality, I fancy."

"Fey-shmay!" the animal scoffed. "To a philosopher you shouldn't talk *kasha!*"

"We-ell, if you *really* want to know—"

But the cat, shushing Phillimore, closed his eyes for a moment and cogitated. His small whiskery lips pushed in and out thoughtfully. At length, he inclined his head knowingly and opened his eyes. "Of *course* . . ."

"Of course?"

"Yes," he mewed, "I think I see. Given an umbrella that whisks you to other dimensions by attunement with your thoughts, it is logical to postulate that it might take you to places that correspond in some mysterious metaphysical fashion with your own mental expectations of your destinations."

"Well reasoned, Rimski," Phillimore said, impressed, "and generally correct. When I pushed the umbrella's release this time, I didn't have any clear definition of the best place to go, but I *was* thinking along the lines of what our world sometimes calls 'fairy tales.' However, I seem to have gotten more than I bargained for."

"Namely?"

The professor ticked them off on his fingers. "Baba Yaga, the Headless Horseman, Goldilocks, the Twelve Dancing Princesses, the Seven Dwarfs, Andy and his lion . . . and I suspect the island I am bound for is none other than one I know of in a story entitled *Beauty and the Beast!*"

"Sounds accurate, from what I've heard around Baba's place," the cat purred reflectively.

"In other words," said Phillimore, "I seem to have landed in a world of Faërie, one that may include any legend, folktale or invented myth in my head." He groaned. "The only thing I considered at the time was fairy-tale princesses; I forgot about the witches and monsters I might meet in such a place!"

"Yes," the cat agreed, "and you didn't do so hot in the princess department, either." He ambled over to the professor and nudged him gently with his head. "Look, doc, you're a nice fellow, but you shouldn't get all kinds of hopes up, *f'shtay?*"

"What do you mean?"

"You've got extra data in your head from your own preconceptions of this world, so maybe you'll actually get Baba her black sunflower. But don't trust witches! They all have this insatiable desire for objects of power. The day you get old Baba to let go your umbrella is going to be some special morning!"

"But it won't work for her. It's set on *my* mental frequency."

The cat eyed him gravely. "Even if you're dead?"

"You have a point, Rimski. But look, if she doesn't give it back, she won't get her sunflower."

"All the same, I'd be *very* careful, if I were you," the cat warned. "And another thing—you should be glad you got rid of that *zhlub* Walter. He—"

But just then, the door to the cottage swung wide.

"He what?" Phillimore demanded. "What about Walter?"

"Shh! Not now . . . here come the dwarfs!"

They waited silently while a baker's half-dozen of diminutive miners issued from the cot and trudged down the forest-path, pickaxes slung over their shoulders. Risking a peek, the professor saw the last of them stomping off. They all sang a hearty hiking song as they strode away.

"Funny," Rimski ruminated, "I never heard them sing before." He waved his tail in rhythm. "Catchy little thing. . . ."

But Phillimore did not hear him—or, for that matter, the song. He spied a blithe raven-haired maiden framed in the doorway, smiling and waving at her seven protectors. She was scarce twenty, simple and unspoiled. Though her shoulders had a regal pride to their set, she emanated gentleness and good humor. Her clear skin displayed no trace of time's encroachment, but about her parted rose-pink lips were a few laugh lines, exquisite parentheses to the dainty perfection of her small, perfectly-shaped mouth.

"Come on," Rimski said, "let's go before she closes the door. What's the *matter* with you?"

"I think," said the professor in a faint voice, "I just fell in love!"

The chubby gray cat made a derisive sound like a razzberry and disgustedly disappeared.

Sailing into the graceful harbor, Phillimore steered just north of windward, dipped his oar and impelled the punt toward the doming crest that was the nearest shore.

It was a beach of spun-sugar sand that rolled gently back and upward to a small hill but lightly downed with early spring grasses. The island itself put out two peninsular projections to either side of the bay, tame curvets of land that circled so far around the water they nearly enclosed the flood and made it a lagoon. But not quite; the waters opened to the sea and Phillimore, having negotiated the narrow gap, drove steadily onward till the punt scraped lightly on the rising floor of the bay. He got out and pulled the craft upon the beach, shipped the oar, then trotted off toward the neighboring hillside.

All was silent, all was calm. The perfumed breeze bore a hint of lush tropic vegetation, but mostly the air was thin and fresh as the world's primal morning. Somewhere overhead caroled a lark of paradise.

Phillimore's feet printed their trail in the pristine sand. At length he left the beach and trod lightly on the dewy ground out of which sparse blades of grass thrust up here and there. The hill was close now and he quickened his pace to reach it. As he did, he cast about for some trail cresting the rise, but could find none.

Then he saw, a little ways up from the level of the ground, a darkness in the hummock of earth. Approaching, he identified it as a cave, not very large, sunk into the hill. Memories of the lair of the purple troll, a dreadful creature in one of his earlier adventures, flooded into his mind; he tarried his pace, reluctant now to proceed further. . . .

But he had no choice. Without warning, the gentle clime darkened and the wind quickened to howling gale force. All, all was sham, and the seeming-pleasant harbor was an evil lure. Lightning flickered in the lowering sky, the lark changed to a bird of night, croaking dire instances of death. He tried to turn and make good his escape, but the bare earth suddenly sprouted noisome growths everywhere, stinking twines and vines that corded about his ankles and rooted him fast.

The ground tilted; the creepers released his legs and he slid, slowly at first, then with nightmare acceleration, directly toward the hill that now was a twisted, malevolent mountain. The cave's edges shivered and altered, and its perimeter was a jagged saw-toothed mouth that dilated to a wide cavern, then irised tight, a puckered channel of death. Phillimore flailed his arms to wrest free of the danger, but his efforts were useless. Doom hurtled closer; the world gaped and devoured him and he screamed as he felt the prickling of a million teeth and he woke on the floor in the middle of a rug whose harsh weave scratched him all over.

He sat up and blinked at the brightness of late afternoon sunlight. Memory returned: he was in the home of the seven dwarfs. The elfin maiden had treated him kindly, preparing him breakfast, putting him to rest in her own bedroom, where he'd suffered the nightmare and tumbled out of bed in the process. But as he thought of her, the terror fled and his heart fluttered with the flame of his infatuation.

Phillimore noticed a movement in the corner of the room. Turning, he saw the cat, Rimski, seated in front of a mirror, half-invisible. As he watched, the animal faded repeatedly in and out of sight.

"What *are* you doing?" the professor asked, getting to his feet.

Rimski abruptly zapped into focus. "Well, it's about time you woke!" he purred. "You've been asleep all day."

"I needed the rest," said the professor. "What were you doing just now?"

"Doing?" the cat echoed, somewhat embarrassed.

"Appearing, disappearing, coming back and vanishing again." Suddenly the man grinned. "*I* know what you were trying to accomplish!"

"What?" Rimski asked surlily.

"You were attempting to fade out of sight while leaving your grin behind!"

"Nonsense," the cat grumped, looking deeply wounded. "Why would I do anything so meretricious?"

But before Phillimore could reply, an anguished shriek froze them both.

The professor's face went white. "It's her! She's in trouble!"

"Brilliant deduction," the cat yowled, darting toward the door. "Stop jawing and *move!*"

Needing no second hint, Phillimore shot out of the bedroom and clomped toward the stairway that led down to the rustic ground-floor kitchen, nearly stepping on Rimski's tail as he did.

The kitchen was a large cheery place bedecked with flowers and lacy curtains. In the middle stood a great iron stove, at the side of which hung a big pot of heating water, suspended over an enormous hearth. Snow White had evidently just begun dinner preparations.

Thundering downstairs, Phillimore missed his footing and tumble-shot the landing. He skidded into the kitchen, Rimski right behind. Fortunately for the professor's seat, the kitchen floor was stone, unlike the thick-grain lumber in the rest of the house.

Snow White was at the far end of the room, near the vestibule to the outer door. Her dainty hands clutched at her throat and breast, and as they watched, dismayed, she sank into a swoon. Phillimore managed to hurl himself forward and catch her before her head hit the flagging.

Rimski sniffed nervously at her. "I think she's dead. Let's get out of here before the dwarfs return!"

"No!" Phillimore snapped. "Control yourself. It's something she ate. I can save her!" He lofted her in his arms, fumbled the constraints at her waist loose and quickly untied the ribbon circling her slender neck. Then, joggling the maiden into the proper first-aid attitude, he jounced her till a morsel of poisoned fruit dislodged itself and fell from her lips.

No sooner did it escape than her eyelids fluttered. "What happened?" she asked faintly as Phillimore eased her to a sitting position.

"What happened," the cat said, "is that my friend just saved your life." Rimski turned to the professor. "I presume you knew why she was choking in the usual manner?"

Fetching a napkin to clean away the expelled foodstuff, Snow White wondered what other way there was to choke. Rimski attempted to explain he was referring to the professor's "fey" faculties, but soon gave it up; she was unable to comprehend the subject.

However, Snow White fully understood Phillimore's heroism. Demurely stepping up to him, she said, "If thou wouldst treasure one such as I, but say so, and I am yours."

Pleased as he could be, the professor embraced the young woman and would have spoken his love in rapturous phrases, but for Rimski's insistence that she relate what fell thing felled her.

"A decrepit peddler woman," she said, "came to the door and gifted me with a fresh piece of fruit. I bit into it and the world spun about.

My throat closed in, my pulse pounded . . . and naught else do I recall till this gentleman restored me to life."

Rimski shook his head. "Peddler woman? Sounds uncomfortably like a typical trick of the witch-queen."

At the instant he said it, the door blew open.

"*Correct, cat!*" a horrible voice shrilled. Rimski disappeared.

The crone was whisker-lipped, with dry-straw hair and fierce yellow-amber eyes. Cloaked all in black, with a basket upon her arm, she was unmistakably the peddler-witch of Snow White's recent peril and Phillimore's hallowed memories.

The witch was not in a good mood.

"Swine prince of toads!" she hissed, pointing a bony finger at the professor. "How *dare* you interfere in the purposes of a queen?"

Phillimore shrugged offhandedly. "Probably because I'm a Democrat." He eyed the kettle in the corner speculatively. Meanwhile, Snow White, trembling like a frightened hind, snuggled against her protector.

"Mortal, you do not even display proper obeisance. I shall make you suffer!"

"Possibly," he replied, tenderly extricating himself from the girl's grasp, "but at the moment, I suspect I have you at a bit of a disadvantage." He took three rapid strides toward the hearth, grabbed a pair of pot-shields and hefted the full kettle from the flames. *Wonder whether Baum's remedy works on* all *witches?*

The horrible crone blanched when she saw the vessel of water. Skipping back as fast as possible, she waved an imperious hand at the front door, which gaped wide at her magical command. On the threshold she paused long enough to warn Phillimore in dire tones to stay out of her way—if he could.

"Just try!" she cackled. "But I'll get you. . . ." She glowered at Snow White. "You, too, my pretty!" The witch stared at an empty spot in the living-room. "And that goes for your little cat, too!"

The invisible Rimski meowed miserably.

A loud burst of thunder shook the cottage, though the day was bright and sunny. In the midst of the hurly-burly, the witch vanished, leaving behind a noxious yellow cloud of billowing sulphur.

"My hero!" Snow White cried, flinging herself into Phillimore's arms. Wheezing from the sorcerous pollution, he hugged her with avuncular affection, surprised that such unaccustomed feminine propinquity stirred so little libidinous personal response.

Must be the stress of the moment, he reasoned silently, gazing fondly down at her lovely visage.

"Let's get the hell out of here—*fast!*" the cat advised. "The first thing we should do is put distance between us and this cottage. Make her chase after us. Here we're easy game!"

"But you must not abandon me!" Snow White begged, clutching the professor's lapels.

"I meant all of us!" the animal yelped.

"But how can I leave my dear friends, the dwarfs, without even saying goodbye to them?"

"They'll be safer, I suspect," said Phillimore, "without our presence. Best leave them a note."

"Make it a short one!" Rimski pleaded.

"Yes, yes," the man reassured the animal, "we'd all better move our tails."

The idiom greatly puzzled the cat.

After she jotted a terse missive to her diminutive friends, Snow White packed a basket of food, threw a shawl over her slender shoulders, affixed the letter to the front door and shut it fast. Though she longed to hear the particulars of her new protector's history—and especially how he happened to travel with a sometimes-invisible cat—the maiden spared them her curiosity and hurried with Phillimore and Rimski to the water's edge.

"Using the punt," said Phillimore, "we can cover a great deal of distance yet before it grows dark."

But their escape plans were foiled. A great cleft in the small boat had somehow materialized since last he'd ridden in it. The gap was so wide, the punt was nearly shorn in two.

"How did this happen?" Phillimore mused.

"The witch must've done it," Rimski mewed. "You sure made one powerful enemy, *tovarich.*"

The professor shrugged hopelessly. "If I had my umbrella, I could save us all, but there's no chance of that now. Two witches to worry about . . . one I can't satisfy unless I complete her damned quest, while the other may get me while I try. If only I'd met Walter when I was supposed to!"

"As for him," said Rimski, "put Walter out of your mind. He doesn't deserve trust."

"Why not?"

"Baba Yaga has him under an enchantment. He's wholly devoted to doing her will. He's a mathologic animal."

Phillimore blinked. "I beg your pardon?"

"I said he's mathologic."

"Don't you mean mythologic?"

"Nope. Mathologic. You can't count on him."

Snow White, impatiently enduring the conversation, decided to get things back to more immediate practicalities. "What are we supposed to do now? How shall you save me, mighty champion?"

"Well," Phillimore drawled, shifting uncomfortably from one foot to the other, "I suppose we have no choice now but to hoof it."

Snow White opened her sparkling eyes wide. "In sooth, do you expect me to destroy my dainty feet hiking?"

Rimski interrupted. "Let's hide in the woods tonight. There's a ferry due six miles upstream, but it won't come till tomorrow morning. I know a fairy ring where we'll be safe this evening."

"Okay," answered the professor. "We'll catch up on some needed sleep."

"Hmmf," the cat sniffed, "you've been snoozing all day."

"And I'm sure I'll need a lot more rest before this adventure's done."

They started off for the enchanted clearing and reached it soon after dark. The professor bundled his jacket for Snow White to rest her head on.

The night passed without incident, but Phillimore didn't get much sleep, after all. Snow White kept him awake for hours asking him questions.

Rising early in the morning, the three companions made a hasty breakfast from Snow White's basket of goodies, then briskly proceeded along the water's edge to the spot where Rimski claimed the ferry would moor.

Arriving at a rude wooden dock, the cat and the man sat upon the blanched sand to await the vessel. Meanwhile, Snow White, trilling merrily like some bird of the morning, scouted the perimeter of the woods for berries.

The shingle sparkled in the morning light. Phillimore was pleased to see an absence of civilization's litter in the cool dawning vista. Scanning the opposite shore, he noted a cluster of cottages. Rimski explained they were close to the capital, and the tiny houses marked the edge of the suburbs.

No sound but the breeze's breath ruffled them. Snow White gamboled hide-and-seek around the boles and branches of the forest until Phillimore tired of following her blithe form dancing midst bush and bramble. The morning lulled him; all danger seemed remote, all travail transient; he wondered on the arbitrariness of Meaning. . . .

"Excuse me, is this where the ferry docks?"

The lilting voice at his elbow startled him, half-asleep as he was. He turned, surprised, having heard no footsteps—and there before him stood the most serenely beautiful blonde he'd ever been privileged to view. Tall she was, regal in bearing without any trace of hauteur; wide blue orbs twinkled mischievously in an oval heart-face whose creamy skin was draped and caressed by long gold tresses. The woman was clad in gossamer green and carried a sparkling emerald diadem in one hand. Upon her feet she wore an exquisitely-fashioned pair of pure crystal slippers.

"I said, is this where I catch the ferry?" The damsel spoke in a mellow, throaty tone that tingled Phillimore's spine.

"Yes, it is," he replied. "Will you sit and wait with us?"

"In a minute," she promised, striding off to inspect the horizon where the river kissed the sky. But she barely took two steps when she tottered. Uttering a startlingly earthly imprecation, she hobbled to the dock, leaned against a piling and yanked off one of her slippers. "Damn," she grumbled, massaging her foot, "these things are sure hell on the arches!"

"Women," Rimski observed, "will kill themselves in the name of Fashion."

"It's not *my* fault," she retorted. "Designers never consider how our feet feel when they come up with their torture devices." She held the shoe up to the light and squinted. "Of course, this *is* rather a fetching number." She inverted the slipper, dumped a quantity of sand out, then put it back on and repeated the business with the other.

"I presume," said the professor, "that you are none other than Cinderella?"

"And what if I am?" she demanded, glancing at him suspiciously. "Are you one of the prince's spies?"

"Hardly. I'm just curious. I associate glass slippers with Cinderella."

"Who doesn't?" the blonde sighed. "Ever since I crashed that lousy Grand Ball, glass slippers have been *the* thing. You can't buy a simple pair of sensible shlumpfing-around-in shoes anyplace!"

"So," Rimski purred, regarding her with mild interest, "you're the famous Princess?"

"Not any more, catnik! I've had it with that royal bum!" Her mouth described a disgusted moue. Wetting her lips, she looked out for the ferry but, failing to see it, left the dock and sat down by the professor's side.

Phillimore, shocked, asked, "Are you saying that you left the prince?"

"You bet your bird I did!"

He winced at her colorful argot, but realized he must make allowances for the fact that, after all, she *had* started as a chimney-sweep. It dismayed him, though, that one of his favorite childhood stories had somewhat not managed to end happily ever after. He expressed his feelings in so many words and urged Cinderella to confide in him.

"Don't call me Cinderella," she said, placing a hand on his. "Only my stepmother and her lousy daughters like to tack on the 'cinder' part. I'm *Ella*, but you can call me Ellie." With that, she smiled at Phillimore with that vague unspoken promise which is the natural province of only the most innocent or the most flirtatious of women.

The press of her hand on his caused Phillimore's pulse to beat in rapid syncopation that, paradoxically, lulled his critical faculties to sleep.

"Why *did* you leave the prince?" he asked, holding her dainty hand.

"He's not the man I married." She sighed. "Godmother knows, I should've seen the signs sooner, it was obvious enough. But I was too infatuated."

"Nu?" the cat impatiently prompted, but the professor gestured for him to be silent.

Ella leaned her head conspiratorially close. "It was the slipper business. I lost one of them at the Grand Ball."

"Yes, I've heard about that." Phillimore nodded. "In order to find you, the prince said he'd have the slipper tried on the feet of all the eligible maidens in the land and he sent out a messenger to—"

"Messenger, hell!" Ella interrupted. "He went himself!"

"I beg your pardon?"

"The prince *personally* tried the glass slipper on all the eligible women of the land. That should have clued me in!"

"To what?"

"He's got a foot fetish."

"ALL 'BOARD!"

The handsome young skipper called out lustily as the last of the arriving passengers disembarked. The ferry was a paddle-wheeler gaily bedecked with bunting, reminiscent of a Nineteenth Century Mississippi riverboat.

Phillimore, Ella, Rimski and Snow White were the only embarking passengers at the quay. Ella walked a bit ahead, hiking up her gossamer gown so it would not trail in the splashes or get caught on the splinters of the ramp. She deliberately held herself aloof, shoulders high and proud. The cause of her chilly attitude was Snow White's seemingly innocent query, upon being introduced to the ex-princess, as to "what mode of alchemy accomplished the striking paleness of yon cornsilk tresses?"

Rimski trotted after Ella. Phillimore brought up the rear, his arm firmly linked to Snow White's own and securely held there by her delicate little fist. As they stepped on the gang, he looked up and saw Ella at the top rearranging her skirts in such fashion as to reveal one immodest, fleeting glimpse of tapered thigh.

"Ah, sweet champion," Snow White sweetly suggested through

clenched teeth, "pay heed to thine own legs lest they unwittingly deposit thee in yon river. . . ."

To underscore her loving advice, she gently punctuated her caveat with an educational hip-nudge that instructionally introduced Phillimore's breadbasket to the handrail of the gangway.

Though his sole monosyllabic utterance hardly shed light on his views of Snow White's pedagogic pretensions, mentally he observed that her rustic lack of breeding *ought* to be taken into account. Also, he noted his ego *ought* to be flattered by what might be construed as jealousy on her part. Yet these silent considerations held little persuasive force compared with his need to negotiate the remaining segment of gangway in a posture reminiscent of a Groucho Marx sidle.

They all sat down together, Ella on a bench just opposite James Phillimore.

The lines were loosed, the ferry slipped into the current, and soon the captain left the pilothouse to greet his passengers.

The skipper was a sun-bronzed youth of perhaps twenty-two or -three. Sinewy and skinny, he was all angles; his ruggedly good-looking face included a lantern-jaw and enormous handlebar mustache, and when he grinned, he flashed a gold incisor. His eyes were steely blue that matched a uniform studded with brass buttons. On his head perched a visored cap. To the professor, he resembled the sort of riverboat pilot one reads about in Twain or Ferber, so Phillimore was not surprised to hear him speak in a recognizably southern U.S. drawl.

"Ah'm Cap'n Mike," he introduced himself. "Jes' make yourselves comf't'ble and tell me what we can do t' make yer ride *fun.*" He grinned; his tooth glinted. "And what's yer name, li'l lady?"

Snow White blushed, curtsied and told him. Ella complied with a similar request, but with no personal confusion and without getting up. The professor introduced Cap'n Mike to Rimski and gave his own name. As soon as he spoke, the seaman squinted curiously and asked whether he might hail from the "Yewnited States."

When Phillimore avowed that he did, the captain pounded him on the back so heartily that the professor dropped Snow White's basket.

"Ah'll be hawg-tied and double-damned! Yer the fust Yankee I set eyes on in a coon's age!" With that, he pumped Phillimore's hand so hard he might have been priming for oil. "That's the sperret, son! Put 'er there! What brings you all th' way over t' here?"

Phillimore started to explain, but Rimski pressed his lips together and gave a frowning shake of the head. He stemmed his tale in mid-tide.

"Got a secret, huh?" Mike asked with a sage nod. "'S okay, son! You won't find a closer ear for a fellow countryman, even if ye do be a Yankee!" He grinned again, but the professor demurred from closer discussion. The sailor shrugged. "It's yer hand, Jimmy-boy; if you wanna play close t' the vest, that's your privilege, but if yer running from trouble, feel free t' change yer mind."

With that, he bowed deeply to Snow White and invited her to accompany him to the wheelhouse where he would allow her to steer the ferry. She demurely dimpled and said she would join him presently.

Phillimore frowned.

"Rimski," the professor said, once Cap'n Mike was gone, "why did you shake your head before? What harm would there be in telling the captain our troubles?"

The feline preened as he spoke, pleased that the professor took his word as sterling. "He *may* be harmless, but . . . he's a bit nosy for my taste. And he volunteered his assistance a little too quickly, don't you think?"

Before Phillimore could reply, Snow White interrupted huffily. "How canst thou suspicion such an one? To scan his visage is to know his mind!"

Rimski grunted. "I'm sure your opinion counts, Snow-baby. But remember, the queen has spies everywhere!"

"Nonsense, cat! She could never suborn such a specimen! He hath sparkling blue eyes! How canst *not* trust him?"

The professor's own orbs sought the heavens in unspoken exasperation. Then he turned to Ella. "What was *your* opinion of the skipper?"

Brushing a wayward strand of blonde hair into place, Ella made a *who-knows?* gesture with one hand and smiled at Phillimore. "I believe he's too straightforward to worry about," she said. "Of course, if he *were* in the employ of our neighborly witch-queen, he might well affect that bluff, hearty manner. But we *must* take into account what this raven-haired maiden has brought in evidence."

Snow White was delighted to have her views apparently confirmed from a quarter where she least expected an ally. She smiled at Ella and asked, "Then you agree that our skipper is too divine to be in any way suspect?"

"Dear child," the other sweetly answered, "you completely mistake my meaning. I meant to call notice to the fact that he paid you a good deal of attention. Now if he's *that* undiscerning, how can anyone credit him with sufficient brains to be duplicitous?"

Snow White jumped to her feet, fury blazing scarlet in her cheeks. She glowered at Phillimore. "Dost thou sufferest this low person to address *me*—thine own beloved—*thus?*"

"Uh . . ." the professor stammered, "let's . . . let's not have a scene, ladies. . . ."

The angry girl began to frame a scathing reply, but then waved Phillimore away with one disgusted gesture and confronted the blonde, instead.

"I warn thee, strumpet, from now on thou'd best keep a civil tongue in thy head."

Ella rose slowly, pushing back her sleeves. "You better watch how you talk to an ex-princess, junior!"

"Ex-princess?" Snow White laughed. "*You?* Your origins proclaim you, plain enough! Ignoble scullery wench!"

"Now that's enough!" Phillimore begged. "Both of you, calm down!"

But his suggestion was not acknowledged. The disputants, incensed beyond words, threw themselves at one another, pinching, slapping, yanking hair, squealing and caterwauling sufficient to make the professor cringe and the cat wince.

"Let's step aside," Rimski suggested, scuttling out of the path of one of Ella's slippers, which scudded across the deck to smash to bits against a recumbent anchor. "The true philosopher finds it prudent to observe all such phenomena from an objective distance."

Phillimore joined him by a bulkhead, pausing only to dodge a wild roundhouse that went wide of Ella's midriff. "And what moral precepts are you able to derive from a study of the present phenomenon?"

"That I'd rather be a cat than married," Rimski replied fervently.

The brouhaha brought the captain on deck.

"What in tarnation is—?" He stopped, cognizant all of a sudden of the source of the ruckus.

"A minor difference of opinion," meowed the cat as Snow White tugged a quantity of hair from her opponent's skull and uttered a triumphant exclamation: "Dark roots! What did I tell you?"

Ella neatly rebutted her opponent's argumentation by butting her. The tactic did not daunt the younger woman, though; she smartly ad-

vanced the issue of balled fist against jutting chin. Ella switched tech-
niques at that stage and shredded Snow White's logic with a systematic
tattering of her outer garments.

Cap'n Mike joined Phillimore by the bulkhead.

"I suppose we should do something," the professor remarked.

"I dunno," said the sailor, obviously enjoying the pyrotechnics of
distaff debate.

"But oughtn't we try to part them?"

"Are you itchin' to step in between them hellcats?"

"Well," Phillimore sighed, "I guess they'll wear each other out eventually."

"Or kill themselves," Rimski yawned.

But the tussle ended sooner than any of the observers anticipated,
and in an unexpected manner.

The men were facing starboard, so did not immediately see the
reason for the sudden diplomatic détente. The women, during a brief
pause to catch breath, happened to glance out off the port rail.

Their combined screech set the cat's hair on end.

"What in hell's wrong?" Mike swore. By way of reply, the women
pointed to the river portside. The men and Rimski followed their trembling fingers and spied, at a distance of perhaps forty yards, a huge and
surprisingly unappealing serpent churning up the surface in a pellmell
rush towards the ship.

"Aww, grape-shot and gopher-guts!" the captain grumped. "It's
gonna be one o' them kind-a days!"

With that, he rushed into the wheel-house.

Rimski mewed miserably. "Either the skipper's a coward, or he set
this all up." He huddled against Phillimore's pants-leg.

The women hunkered down under one of the benches; in spite of
their recent enmity, they clasped one another tightly.

"Ah, dear champion," said Snow White to the professor, "wilt thou
protect me 'gainst yon fell beast?"

"D-ditto with n-n-nuts on top!" Ella stammered.

"Quit nagging," Phillimore replied. "Rimski, what *is* that thing?"

"Looks like Nessie."

"*Nessie?* From Scotland?!"

"The same."

"But what's he doing *here?*"

"I imagine," the cat answered, "that the witch-queen sent him."

The man gave a low whistle. "She *does* play rough."

As if to punctuate the sentiment, the creature uncoiled itself until its head was perhaps twenty feet above the surface of the water and roared like an iron foundry at rush-hour.

"*Chuttarachmaunos!*" Rimski wailed, blanching beneath his shaggy gray coat. "We're doomed!"

"Buck up," Phillimore said. "I'll reason with him."

The cat looked at him as if he'd gone mad.

Phillimore didn't feel especially courageous, but someone had to refuse to give in to panic. *Maybe I can stall for time?*

Actually, the monster wasn't quite as dreadful as the purple troll. Phillimore hoped that the serpent's vast bulk was not commensurate with a like quantity of intelligence.

As the water-worm hove into view some fifteen yards from the ship's rail, Phillimore held up one hand like a traffic cop and said in a stern voice, "HOLD IT, NESSIE! LET'S SEE YOUR LICENSE!"

The beast stopped short, raised its head another few feet above the surface and fixed Phillimore frostily with an immense yellow eye.

"Lee-cense?" Nessie growled in a deep fortissimo *burr*. "I ken nae lee-cense! Wha' dostha jabber about, mon?"

"I asked for your lee—for your *license!*" The professor employed his sternest *where-is-your-term-paper?* tone and snapped his fingers impatiently. "Come, come, produce your license at once, Nessie! If you don't have it, prepare to tread water all the way back to Scotland!"

The threat was so unexpected that Nessie actually retreated an inch, eyes wide at the cool air of authority projected by the insignificant mite. But then the serpent remembered he was on queen's business. Bringing more coils out of the water, he used the additional yardage to crane his head down level with the professor's.

"Lee-cense?" he repeated, fixing the man with a baleful glare. "I say I ken nae lee-cense! Lee-cense for *wha'?*"

Phillimore crossed his arms and insolently returned Nessie's glower. *Look for a bare spot!* he thought, remembering that dragons and serpents often have a single unprotected patch where they can be assailed. Not that Phillimore had any weapon handy. *Doesn't matter, anyhow,* he told himself, examining the body of the monster in vain for a place without a protective layer of scales. His neck was covered with scarlet wedges like overgrown armadillo-plate; his breast was similarly protected, though there the shingles were a dull amber in hue.

"*Lee-cense for wha'?*" Nessie demanded once more.

"Attack and despoilment!" Phillimore replied. "You can't wreck ferries out of season without the proper papers!"

"*Really?*" Nessie asked, nonplussed. "Truly, lad," he grumbled, lofting another fourteen feet of his gargantuan body from the river-bottom, "I dinna ken tha local customs!"

"Oh, ay," the professor nodded sagely, "ask anyone, you'll discover I'm telling the truth. . . ."

"And I'll jus' do tha' richt na, I weel," the monster replied, suddenly diving below the surface—but not before Phillimore glimpsed a tiny spot near the belly that was bereft of scaly protection.

As soon as Nessie disappeared, Cap'n Mike popped his head out of the wheelhouse and cursed roundly.

"Dawg-bone double-damn!" he shouted. "Ah had 'im in mah sights! Whyn'tchoo keep 'im talkin' another couple seconds?"

The professor shot a dirty look at the tar, but before he could frame an appropriate rejoinder, a perfect geyser of water boiled up from the river not five feet away from the port railing. Phillimore gestured toward the disturbance. "Well, as for that, skipper, I believe you're about to get a second chance."

The captain immediately ducked back into the wheelhouse.

Out of the water stormed a livid Nessie, the pale yellow glow of his enormous eyes now flecked with a dangerous shade of scarlet.

"Varlet!" he roared. "How dast-tha trifle wi' me? There's no sich thing as thy lee-cense!"

"Says who?"

"Says all th' denizens below! I consulted with a school o' eminent sturgeons, and nane e'er heerd a' sich a ridiculous thing!"

"Bosh!" Phillimore bluffed. "How can you take their word for it? What do *they* know about topside regulations? Are you trying to defy authority with this fishy tale?"

"Och, I've had weel enow!" the monster bellowed. "Tha queen hast commanded me t' wreck this vessel, an' wreck it I shall, lee-cense or no lee-cense! If there be aught i' the way o' a fine, the dame hersel' can richt weel assume th' debt!"

Further parlay was useless. Nessie rose as far out of the water as was serpently possible, emitting an ear-splitting screech in the process. Phillimore hurled himself beneath the bench where the ladies still quavered with fright.

"Maybe we'd do better overboard!" he yelled at them, but the monster's mighty bellow drowned him out.

Rearing back with his massive skull, Nessie gave the ferry a powerful ram that set the ship rocking sickeningly—though it managed not to founder. With a playful snort, the serpent butted the side of the vessel a second time, obviously toying with it before its final onslaught.

Phillimore clung desperately to the bench, which, fortunately, was solidly fastened to the deck planking. With one hand, he cushioned Rimski against his side. The cat nervously flexed his claws to the detriment of the professor's epidermis.

The two women's mouths were open, but it was impossible to hear them scream. The river crashed over all the passengers as the ferry rocked from port to starboard to port, righting itself only to yaw in a decidedly alarming fashion.

In the midst of the turmoil and artificial tempest, Phillimore cast one desperate glance aft. To his surprise, the captain, whom he'd written off as a hopeless craven, straddled the port rail with his long legs and aimed a rifle at the rampaging Nessie.

Not a chance, thought Phillimore, deciding that the very desperation of their plight must have lent Cap'n Mike the courage of a raging berserker. But with the pitching ship threatening to broach to any second, and with the lake monster vulnerable only in one minute patch, *and* with the target in violent motion, it was clear that the skipper hadn't the slimmest chance of—

CRACK!

When the boiling whirlpool swallowed up the dead fresh-water serpent and the captain maneuvered the ferry out of danger of being sucked down with the creature, and only when the deck-surface returned to a reasonable facsimile of an horizontal plane, Rimski agreed to stop burrowing his whiskers in the professor's belly.

"What happened?" the cat mewed, still terrified.

Phillimore petted him to reassure Rimski he was no longer in danger. (He still felt peculiar about lavishing affection on a onetime tax collector. Somehow, it seemed a trifle *gauche*).

"What happened," said Snow White with adulation in her every syllable, "is that yon brave seaman hath rid us of the dastardly demon!"

"Shucks," said Cap'n Mike, " 'twarn't nothin,' ma'am."

"Well," the blonde ex-princess Ella admitted, "it *was* a lucky shot. But the greatest bravery was shown, I ween, when this dear man"— Here she put her arm in Phillimore's "—when this dear man, I say, faced the creature and gave the skipper the opportunity of locating Nessie's one weak point, which, by happy fortune, he managed to penetrate with a single bullet."

"Fortune?" the captain fumed. "Chance? Gol' dang it, ma'am! Don't yew know crack marksmanship when y' sees it? *Luck* mah Aunt Nellie's aspadistra!"

Something at that moment clicked in Phillimore's memory. Pointing to the skipper, he blurted out in a positive voice: "Fink!"

The captain squinted supiciously. "Who y' callin' a fink?"

"Aren't you *Mike Fink?*"

The other displayed his gold tooth in a broad grin. "Y' mean y' heard o' me, chum?"

"I should say I have! The best sharpshooter on the Mississippi river! One of the greatest folk heroes of the American Midwest!"

Mike Fink turned scarlet to the tips of his hair. "Aw, shucks, y' shouldn't oughtta say them things."

"But they're true!"

"Waal, *shore* they are! But they still put th' flush on a man's face, right 'nough. . . ."

Now that the captain's identity was firmly affixed, Phillimore was able to assure Rimski that they couldn't hope for a better ally. The cat was still skeptical, but considering the accuracy of the skipper's shooting, decided to accept the new companion for the time being. As for Snow White, she literally clung to the tall man's sleeve. There was no doubt she'd totally switched allegiance to a new champion.

"Never mind," Ella whispered to Phillimore, "*you* don't need a schoolgirl! *You* deserve a maturer mate. . . ."

The professor shrugged. *Some gentlemen* do *prefer blondes, I suppose.*

They quickly described to Fink their plight in reference to the witch-queen and Phillimore also outlined his quest for Baba Yaga's black sunflower. When he was finished, the captain clapped him on the back.

"*Two* witches!" the stringy sailor exclaimed. "You are sure one Yank with more troubles than a possum in a kettle o' pot likker! Well, we just gonna hafta cancel th' ol' ferry run for a time an' see you-all get hold of that li'l ol' sunflower safely."

"Thanks," the professor said, heartily shaking his hand, "that'll be an enormous help, if you can pilot me to the enchanted island." He turned to Rimski. "Can you tell the captain how to get there?"

The cat shook his head. "No, and neither could Walter, if he were here."

"But Walter said he guided other searchers there."

"He did. But that wouldn't make any difference."

"Why not?"

"The island is enchanted, remember?" the cat explained. "It moves around."

"Oh, terrific!" Phillimore groaned. "How do we catch up with it?"

"By consulting a magic atlas."

"And where do we get one of them?"

"In a magic library, shmendrick!" Rimski yelped, his patience at an end.

Cap'n Mike broke in. "There's a castle just upstream that I hear tell has a bookroom like what y' need. I often shuttle visiting sorcerers over thataway."

"Sounds like the right kind of place," Phillimore nodded.

"Only one thing," the skipper said. "It ain't the safest place, I hear, t' fetch a visit on."

The professor sighed deeply.

"I'm delighted to hear that," he murmured. "I was so afraid life might begin to grow dull. . . ."

Brambles everywhere.

Brambles crackling underfoot, brambles choking progress along the faint footway. Brambles twined with brake and branch, brambles twisted around tree-trunks. Brambles tearing sleeves and catching trouser-legs. Brambles forbidding access to the ancient castle, brambles screening the way and brambles blocking it.

The only edge-tools the two men had were boat-hooks. The going, therefore, was tortuously slow. While the women waited with Rimski back on the docked ferry, James Phillimore and Mike Fink grimly hacked a passage through the barrier of thorns.

"How long have these damned things been sprouting?" the professor growled, taking a vicious sideswipe at one bristly bush.

"Accordin' t' local stories," Fink said, "these here sticklers've bin shootin' up well over a hunderd y'ar."

"I *thought* so, but let me make sure. . . . What, precisely, is the nature of the danger to those who enter the castle?"

"I heerd if y' stay too long, y'drop off t' sleep and don' wake up."

Just what I thought! Phillimore paused in his labors to wipe sweat from his forehead with the back of his hand. "All right, Mike, now listen to me—when we finally chop our way through these damnable weeds, you go straight to the castle library and search for the map that'll show us where the enchanted isle is."

"But how 'bout you?"

"Trust me. I have a plan to gain time for us. . . ."

The main reason Phillimore sought the tower, Phillimore told himself, was to save the two of them from falling into a magical slumber. Yet the task did not totally repel him, either. After all, what *had* he come to Faërie for in the first place?

He put all thoughts of Snow White and Ella temporarily out of his mind.

It was not easy to locate the legendary tower room. When the young princess called Sleeping Beauty first climbed up to that fatal hideaway, it was to a part of the castle unknown or forgotten by her royal family. (In the Disney film, the professor recalled, the garret-room was concealed by a secret entranceway. He wasn't sure which version his subconscious might conjure up in the world-set he was in.)

He had no recourse but to trust to luck. Up and up he went, traversing dusty, drafty corridors, poking his way through venerable cobwebs, timidly testing the treads on rotted wooden staircases, clambering like a goat up stone steps chewed and pocked by time's devouring teeth.

The air grew increasingly stuffy. He found it harder and harder to breathe.

Wonder how Fink's doing down in the library?

Phillimore stopped to catch his breath. He leaned against a tapestry-covered wall.

It was so quiet he could hear the pounding of his heart laboring for oxygen. Dim sunlight filtered through dust-caked casements. It was as close as an attic packed with curios.

Phillimore yawned.

In the library, Mike Fink cracked open a huge Atlas. Its title was *Necromantic Age: Cartographic Supplement, Annual Sites & Plots.*

He turned the great pages, one at a time. The book was so big it was a tiring effort just to turn the leaves. The repetitive action drained and lulled him; his glazed eyes found it difficult to focus properly.

A familiar contour roused him, a curve of river in one blue-dominated chart. Squinting, he moved close to the page and discerned the very waters on which they navigated . . . and here was the spot he'd tied up to less than two hours before. Beyond, the stream swept past town and harbor and out to sea. . . .

And there—perhaps twenty-five leagues from shore and concealed by a chain of coral islets—was a single green hummock of land. The legend beneath noted it as the approximate location that season of the enchanted domain of the Beast. Instructions for plotting its precise position were offered in a footnote whose letters were so tiny that Fink had to slit his eyes to read them.

Bit by bit, he deciphered the cabalistic formula. Then, flopping flat on the tabletop, scattering maps and books right and left, he fell fast asleep.

"What's keeping them?" Rimski mewed for the tenth time, anxiously pacing the deck.

"Mayhap they've fallen afoul of the witch again," Snow White worried, chewing her lip. "Perhaps it were good that we absent ourselves from the vicinity?"

"A splendid idea," Ella cheerily concurred. "Why don't you leave first?"

"Giving you a free hand with my champions? Never!"

"*Your* champions?" The blonde laughed. "They don't need a girl, there's a lady aboard!"

"True? *I* see her not. . . ."

"Please," Rimski begged, "don't quarrel. We've got enough *tsooris* without another free-for-all."

"Odd that you quote this maiden's going rate," Ella remarked with a toss of her golden locks. Snow White's cheeks flushed angrily, but before she could reply, the blonde walked to the exit ramp and declared her intention to go to the men's assistance. "Coming, Snowy?"

"I'll wait here, thank you," she replied frostily.

"Really?" Ella inquisitively cocked an eyebrow. "Aren't you concerned I'll steal away your champions?"

"Only common women traipse after men," Snow White declared airily, arranging the pleats of her peasant skirt.

"I suppose you'd be the one to know." Turning away from her, Ella bent down and affectionately patted the shaggy cat. "Better stay here and protect Snowy's putative honor."

"What's that supposed to mean?" hissed Snowy.

"A charitable fiction, child." Ella smiled blithely and stepped onto the gangway.

Somehow managing to rouse himself, the professor forced his heavy feet to work, one shuffling step at a time.

Don't fall asleep . . . don't fall asleep . . . asleep . . . fall asleep . . . sleep. . . .

He shook his head vigorously, alarmed at the way his thoughts conspired to lull him. He fell to cursing Baba Yaga for taking his umbrella, but the imprecation assumed the quality of ritual, repeating itself and repeating itself, so he tried to think of other things.

Hope Mike's found the map. Hope he's not asleep . . . asleep . . . asleep. . . .

Once more, Phillimore wrenched himself back from the abyss of unnatural slumber. He concentrated on his catly companion, Rimski, philosopher-feline, but soon monotonous mewed syllogisms reiterated propositions in his skull. . . .

Just then, he noticed a subtle sound, a drone. Save for his own footsteps, it was the first thing he'd heard since leaving Fink on the ground floor. The muted buzz woke him a little.

He blinked. Up ahead he spied a narrow, winding staircase that led yet higher to a shadowy eyrie at the very apex of the castle. *Must be it!* Step by sluggish step, he staggered up and up and up. Three-fourths somnolent, he negotiated the latter portion of the stairs on hands and knees. He pinched himself to stay awake. At last he crawled onto a small stone landing, thick with dust. His hands and knees were coated with grime.

There was a tall oaken door giving off the landing. He padded to it on all fours.

Got to rest a second. . . .

Phillimore leaned his head against the door. It swung inward, depositing him with a smart smack on the flagging. *OW!* The pain woke him up.

Scrabbling at the portal, he hauled himself to his feet and took a tottering step across the threshold.

Here the buzzing was louder. It was a lofty garret, oval-shaped and fashioned entirely from green stones. The close atmosphere which choked the whole castle evidently emanated from the attic he was in, for nowhere else was the thick air so concentrated, dense, and still. A new wave of ennui washed over him.

And then he saw Sleeping Beauty.

In a far curve of the cell, beneath a thin, dusty window, there stretched a long pallet. The only other objects in the room were a mirror hung on one wall and an antique spindle at the head of the bed. On the cot lay the princess.

Tall she was, well over six feet, a veritable Amazon. *Never liked rangy girls!* Her flaming scarlet tresses were complemented by a bright red mustache and chin-whiskers of the same startling hue.

Good Gad, Phillimore winced, *her hair's been growing all the time she's been asleep!* He closed his eyes.

The buzzing now was so loud it jangled every synapse he owned. The sound came from the dreaming princess—no less a phenomenon than her regal snores.

Gorblimey, the professor shuddered, *do I really have to kiss that?*

In spite of the sleeper's lumber-camp suspirations, he felt tired once more. The spell fought to subdue him. *Really no choice, I have to break the enchantment.*

He tottered to the foot of the bed and climbed onto the cot next to her. Eyelids drooping, brain whirling into night, he began to add his own snores to those of the princess. But as he flopped beside her, he managed to aim his lips accurately at hers.

Downstairs, Ella took a welcome breath and got up from the floor where she'd fallen. She continued her search, soon found the library door, peeked inside and saw Cap'n Mike stretching his arms and yawning with wide-open mouth.

"B'gosh," he muttered thickly, "that *were* a refreshin' forty winks!" He rubbed the sleep from his eyes and saw her. "Hey, gal, good news! I found Jim-boy's map!"

"Wonderful . . . but where is he?"

"Upstairs someplace."

"Come on, then—he may need our help." She took his hand and pulled him along. Now peering here, now there, they mounted steps, peeked into bedrooms and pantries. Nobles and slaveys alike sat up, trying to recollect the business of a life long laid aside. All were too disoriented to pay much note to the pair of strangers prying into every niche of the waking castle.

"Look," Ella suddenly exclaimed, pointing to a line of footprints in the deep dust of a remote hallway.

"He must've come this way, Ellie!"

They dashed along, following the trail.

It eventually led them to the narrow stone staircase. Climbing to the top, they heard sounds of a struggle within.

Ella burst through the door first. She saw a furious professor vainly trying to free himself from the ardent embrace of a giant red-haired maiden.

"Let me go, will you!"

"Nay, wee champion, nay!" the Amazon crooned. "Ye've roused me from a wicked fairy's spell, and now tha'll reap the reward of thine brave action!"

Mike Fink, observing her mustache and chin-whiskers, silently agreed such a rescue was, indeed, brave—if not downright foolhardy.

"What in hell is going on here?" Ella demanded, arms folded, foot

tapping impatiently. She squinted at the princess in decidedly unneigh-
borly fashion.

"This cute wee morsel," said the red-haired woman, "woke me from
a sorcerous sleep with the salute of his lips. I know my rights—who
rescueth me, marries me!"

"*Marry you?*" Phillimore spluttered. "If I could've woken up some
other way, I wouldn't even have kissed you!"

"Ah, well," Unsleeping Beauty philosophically observed, "ye'll grow
accustomed to me in time."

"I'll *never* grow accustomed to your face."

She frowned. "What's wrong with my face? I was always rated
comely."

"But have you looked at yourself recently?"

Hefting Phillimore under one arm, the princess tramped to the suspended looking-glass and studied her reflection. After a few seconds,
she grinned broadly and emitted a delighted giggle. "O wondrous rare!
And my stuffy father once boasteth that only a man can be thus
resplendently ornamented."

Marvelous, Phillimore groaned to himself, *an incipient libber*. He
stared at Fink and Ella and coldly asked whether they might stop
laughing long enough to help him get away from the redhead.

"Sure," Ella said, doing her best to straighten up. "Come, Captain,
let's take care of yon crimson pirate."

But the skipper was too busy holding his sides together to be of
much assistance. Undaunted, Ella strode smartly up to the princess
and, without pause or preamble, briskly belted her in the brisket.

Quoth the princess: "Oof!"

Releasing her hold on Phillimore, she staggered backward, clutching
her tummy. Her bent position presented a generous target to the waiting point of the potent spindle.

Quoth the princess: "Owoo!"

Plucking the offending object from her seat, the redhead glared at it,
exasperated, then sank down upon the couch.

Quoth the princess: "Here we go again. . . ."

And she recommenced to snore.

"Quick," said the professor, "we have to get out of the castle before
the spell puts us all to sleep!" He punctuated the comment with a great
yawn.

Fink grasped Phillimore's arm with one hand and Ella's with the other. They plunged out the chamber-door and tumbled downstairs, flailing end over end.

At the bottom, the professor wobbled to his knees, but immediately began to sway rhythmically, eyes closing.

"Help me stand him up," Ella said, extricating herself with difficulty from the tangle of intermingled limbs.

Somehow the trio managed to descend to the ground floor. But by then, the professor, who'd been in the higher reaches of the castle longer than the others, was deep asleep and could in no way be shaken out of it. Mike and Ella lugged him by the arms toward the front door, but it was still a long way off.

Ella's legs rubbered beneath her. "I . . . I don't think I . . . can . . . make . . . it. . . ."

"Lie down, then, honey-puss," the captain told her. He was strangely alert. "Naaw, Ellie-gal, let ol' Jim go, I c'n manage 'im th' rest o' th' way. Once we's outside, he'll wake up 'n' we c'n both hightail it back here 'n' carry you out."

Nodding gratefully, Ella slumped onto the cold floor and slept.

Fink, though not altogether unaffected by the enchantment, managed to keep his word and jostle Phillimore to the entrance portal and through it. The professor immediately woke. After a few grateful breaths of fresh air, he was sufficiently revitalized to reenter with the skipper and rescue the sleeping blonde.

At last, all three stood in the forest. Ella's fluttering eyelashes flickered at the sailor.

"Dear Captain Fink," she cooed, "how on earth *did* you manage to resist that sleep-spell so long?"

"Waal, Ellie, it were either that or g'wan back and *personally* smooch Ol' Daddy's Mustache!"

Phillimore heartily slapped Fink on the back. "Good work, Mike! You got the map, I see!"

"Yep, but shucks, I on'y did part o' th' job." He tipped his hat as he helped a frankly-admiring Ella to her feet.

If Phillimore noticed any look pass between them, he said nothing about it.

They began to walk toward the path the men hacked earlier through the forest. "At least," Phillimore remarked, "we've earned a brief respite from danger. . . ."

As if in ironic punctuation to the sentiment, an ominous growl rose from a spot not far off and to their left, screened from view by the thick tangle of brambles that networked the woods.

The men stared uneasily at one another.

"Probably just a wild animal," the professor suggested.

"NOT . . . WILD . . . ANIMAL!" a throaty growl objected.

Ella whimpered. "What *is* it?"

"Whatever it is, I tell ye what," Fink whispered. "You draw the critter round th'other side o' th' castle, then have it chase y' to th' ferry."

"And what will *you* be doing?" Phillimore demanded with some asperity.

"This!" said Fink, running like hell up the forest-path.

"Whenever it gets the least bit dicey," the professor grumbled, "that Fink manages to duck out."

Ella came to the skipper's defense. "That's not fair! When the serpent attacked, Mike only went to his cabin to get his rifle."

"Maybe," Phillimore grumpily conceded, "but *this* time—"

"THIS TIME YOU GET EAT!" the as-yet-unseen thing growled. It was much closer; they could hear it scuffling and stomping through the undergrowth.

Grabbing Ella's arm, Phillimore sprinted around the side of the castle, stopping at the corner to see what manner of danger stalked them.

A tremendous crash. Suddenly a great flailing bludgeon flashed into view, flattening a section of thorny interposing branches. From the woody ruins emerged a single-eyed ogre that looked something like a fourteen-foot-tall goat standing on its hind legs.

"Uh-oh," gulped Phillimore. "Wonder if the witch-queen sent him?"

"Who cares?" Ella yelped. "Let's move our butts!"

But the monster heard the professor's question. It grinned nastily. "NOT FREELANCE!" came the throaty reply.

So they led the beast a chase about the castle. It could not see well out of its one centrally-located eye, but the shag-legged thing had an excellent sense of smell. Though they ducked behind buttresses and dropped beneath eaves and hid within porticos, it but paused each time long enough to sniff once or twice before licking its protrusive canines in anticipatory pleasure and prancing in their precise direction.

"Come on," panted Phillimore, "that's enough eaves-dropping. Let's run!"

He had observed that the ogre was incapable of speed and therefore decided a protracted sprint was the best plan. It was true that the thing's gait was hampered by a peculiar dragging hunch of its haunches—but in partial compensation, it took large steps. Another factor militating against the wisdom of the professor's scheme was that both he and Ella were physically exhausted from their foray in the enchanted castle.

Still, now that the initial shock upon first seeing the monster had worn off, the two experienced a brief surge of adrenalin that carried them around to the castle-front.

"Hurry, Ella! To the forest!"

They dashed across the clearing to the narrow path hewn earlier by the two men. Stopping at its edge, Phillimore stooped and retrieved the two boathooks they'd employed. He passed one to Ella.

"Try to hit it in the eye!"

The ogre thumped menacingly into view.

"Wait till it's closer . . ." said the professor. "All right . . . *NOW!*"

They both threw the boathooks. One stuck in the beast's leg. The other, thrown by Phillimore, came close to its forehead, but the ogre managed to catch it in midair. In a leisurely fashion, it brought the iron point up to its mouth, bit off the entire hook and began to chew it methodically.

"AHH!" the creature belched. "IRON GOOD IN DIET!"

The sight appalled the professor and his companion. But worse was a sudden crash from a point some thirty yards off to their right.

A new voice—loud, deep and gravelly-textured—rang out in the woods. "SAVE ME ONE, MANNY!"

The ogre waved a claw in acknowledgment and yanked Ella's boathook from its leg. "APPETIZER WAITING, JACK!" it roared in reply.

"Oh, Good Lord!" Phillimore complained. "Now there's *two* of them!"

"USED TO BE THREE!" said Manny. "BUT DRAGON ATE BROTHER. WE AIN'T GOT NO MOE!"

Weariness was taking its toll of the two mortals, but they started through the woods, nevertheless, forcing their legs to carry them as fast as they were still capable.

The day was near its end. The trail between the trees was narrow and gloomy and brambles conspired to snag their garments. More than once, they tripped, bumping elbows or knees.

The diversion of the boathooks gained them a few precious minutes, but now the hunt was up again. The second ogre swung its club from side to side, wantonly smashing branches as it gave chase.

SMASH! SMASH! SMASH! The twin horrors drew inexorably nearer.

Phillimore and Ella broke through to the beach, but the ferry was another fifty feet along the shoreline.

"We *have* to make it!" Phillimore insisted, half-shoving, half-carrying Ella.

"I can't do it!"

SMASH! SMASH! Out of the forest emerged the ogres. Grinning evilly, they spread out to right and left. One of them cut off their passage to the ferry, the other circled round their flank.

"What can we do?" the blonde cried. "We're trapped!"

"Keep moving, Ella! Fake them out! Run zigzag!"

"I *can't!* My ankle hurts!" She sank to the sand.

"Get up!" he yelped, tugging at her sleeve. The material ripped.

SMASH! The second ogre swung its club against the bole of a cherry tree and broke it in half. Then it stamped further into the sand, nearing its prey.

On the other side, the first ogre marched steadily onward, slavering and chomping its teeth. It was close enough for them to smell its fetid breath.

"*Jim-boy!*"

Phillimore whirled, sudden hope flaring. He anxiously scanned the seascape but could not see the skipper.

"Over *here!*" Fink shouted, waving his arm. The professor spotted him at the edge of the forest, rifle in hand, standing ankle-deep in a small stream.

"Quick!" Phillimore yelled. "Plug 'em!"

"Not yet!"

"Huh? What do you *mean?*"

"I mean, *not yet*, mate! Make 'em chase y' a while."

"*What?*"

"Get 'em t' chase after y', Jimbo!"

Before Phillimore could protest the two ogres turned in his direction, grinning.

"HO-KAY BY US!" roared Manny.

"YOU BET!" Jack agreed.

And they both converged on the professor.

Phillimore dodged and twisted and scampered along the beach in a desperate effort to escape becoming an ogre's entrée.

Little by little, the great beasts closed in on him. All the while, Fink lounged patiently, feet in the water, rifle trailing negligently by his side.

"How long do I have to keep this up?" Phillimore croaked. "I've been dodging them for five minutes!"

"IT OKAY TO STOP," Manny said considerately.

"WE DON'T MIND!" Jack echoed.

"Just a little longer," Fink called. "Make 'em come t' you, then drop down on the sand!"

"Are you *crazy?*"

"*Just do like I say!*"

"YEAH! DO LIKE HE SAY!" Manny advised.

"SOUND LIKE GOOD PLAN TO ME!" Jack opined.

Now they were only a few feet away. Phillimore spun and tried to run to the water, but Manny interposed himself between the professor and the sea. Pivoting, Phillimore dodged the other ogre's reaching arm and attempted to run between its legs, but it closed them.

"That's *perfect!*" Fink shouted. "Now hit th' sand!"

Phillimore collapsed in a heap upon the beach, resigned to the inevitability of his destiny as a nutriment. Behind him, Manny rasped hot breath on his neck. In front, Jack hobbled up hungrily.

Mike Fink hefted his rifle and squeezed off a shot.

Crack!

Both monsters howled in rage and pain, clutching the remains of their eyes.

Manny emitted a bellow, crumpled to the sand, and died.

The other ogre blindly reached out one talon, raking the air in an attempt to rend Phillimore to bits. But then it, too, folded over, dead, and landed smack on top of the professor.

"*See?*" Ella exclaimed while Fink shoved the ogre off his friend. "Mike saved us both! Now aren't you ashamed you spoke so ill of him before?"

Rising painfully to his feet, Phillimore ignored her and demanded why Fink made him wait so long before shooting the ogres.

"Shucks, son," he replied, "I on'y had one bullet left: had t' wait till they got in a straight line so's I could hit 'em both."

With that, Phillimore rather abruptly stretched out again upon the beach.

Once they were all back on board, Fink instructed his crew to set off and sail as long as the moon shone bright. He hoped to make town by morning, stopping just long enough to replenish supplies—cartridges in particular.

Once he found a linament for the professor to massage on his stiff spots and after he'd prepared a cold pack for Ella's ankle, the ferryman sat down with his friends. Rimski happily snuggled on the professor's lap, glad Phillimore was safe.

"Is it true, Rimski," the professor asked, "that Puss in Boots once swallowed an ogre?"

"Hmpf. I wouldn't be surprised. That cat has one *big* mouth."

Ella, gritting her teeth against the ache in her *tarsus*, remarked upon Snow White's absence. The maiden was nowhere upon the boat.

"Well, after you left, Ella," said Rimski, ruffling his whiskers, "the whole *shmegeggle* of dwarfs showed up. They've been looking for Snowy ever since we all ran out of her cottage with the witch after us. Anyway, she thought maybe she better stick with her original protectors."

Ella nodded. "Naturally. After all, there's *seven* of them." She yawned. "Tedious topic. Is there any food aboard?"

Rimski said, "Oh, I forgot to mention: she left her picnic basket behind. Said there's an apple in it for Ella."

The blonde dug into the folds of the basket, found an empty thermos and a single pome with tooth-marks and a missing chunk.

"Don't eat that," Phillimore warned.

"I know better," said Ella, tossing the apple over the rail. Where it splashed, a sudden foam of bubbles gurgled in the moonlight.

"Poisonous little bitch," Ella cursed. "What *did* you ever see in her, Jim?"

Phillimore had no answer.

"Waal, never mind, thar's plenty o' grub in th' cabin."

Ella beamed. "And would *you* serve me sup?"

"Why, shorely, ma'am!" Fink rose, touching his cap in salute to the blonde.

The professor and the cat exchanged a knowing glance.

"*La donna è mobile*," Rimski mewed beneath his breath.

The night air was mild and there was a pleasant breeze. They decided they all would sleep beneath the stars on the top-deck. Fink provided bedrolls for the humans and a warm blanket for the animal. Phillimore worried the accommodations might offend Rimski, but the cat dismissed the notion with an off-tailed gesture.

"When I was a tax collector, believe you me, I *shlaffed* in a lot worse beds!" Abruptly vanishing, he padded invisibly to the blanket, snuggled down and reappeared a little at a time.

Long after Rimski and Ella fell asleep, Phillimore and Mike Fink sat and talked. The lanky riverman, looking rather uncomfortable, chewed thoughtfully at a tobacco-plug.

"Waal, I know why y' might uv bin ticked off when I hotfooted it back t' th' ferry, but mah rifle was the best bet, doncha see?"

"Perhaps. But why couldn't you take it along in the first place?"

"Aww, son, don't ask me that. . . ."

"But I *am* asking."

"I'd druther not tell ya. It's kind-a personal." Expectorating the tobacco-chaw, Fink shamefully lowered his head. "I'll say this much, Jimmy: if'n I had brought muh rifle 'long, it wouldn't of done *no* good, and that's a fact!"

Just then, an odd bit of data concerning the Mike Fink legend dislodged itself from Phillimore's memory. "Of course!" he exclaimed, snapping his fingers. "You're only a crack shot when you fire *across water!* We were too far inland. On land, you can't hit the side of a dead dragon!"

Swiveling so he faced the professor, Fink stared at him in amazement, not altogether friendly. "Now how the deuce," he demanded, "did y' know that? It's m' closest kep' secret."

Phillimore shrugged. "Bit of a fey quality, I fancy."

"Fey, my granny's nanny!"

So Phillimore explained about interworldly travel and the marvels of owning a thought-controlled dimensional transfer engine in the form of an umbrella.

"Man, *man,*" Fink murmured when the other was through. "An' I thought I heerd tall tales before!" Still, he was at a loss to find any better explanation.

Suddenly, the ferryman pulled a long face. "You ain't gonna go tell Ella about this, are y', Jim?"

Phillimore sighed. "No, I suppose not."

"Yer a real pal!"

Hmph, the professor thought sourly, but could find nothing specific to complain about in Fink's behaviour to the blonde, so he held his tongue.

"Funny how I cain't hit nothin' on land," Fink mused. "Mebbe it's 'cause I growed up on th' river and got used to a deck beneath mah feet."

"Hold on," Phillimore said, suddenly puzzled. "When you shot the ogres, you were on the beach."

"Yeah . . . but I had m' tootsies in a brook. Long as I got water near mah feet, I c'n hit the left earlobe of a moth at fifty yards! I gotta shoot across water to make it count."

Phillimore screwed up his face in deep concentration. "Pardon the pun, Mike, but you just triggered something."

"Like what?"

"A way for you to shoot well on land."

"*Real?* What *is* it?"

"I can't remember it yet. But give me time, I'll bring it to mind."

"We're both pretty tuckered," Fink said, patting Phillimore gently on the arm. "Let's turn in now and talk some more t'morrah. We gotta get up early if'n we wants t' see the magic isle by mid-afternoon."

Fink crawled into his bedroll and said good night, but Phillimore sat up a while longer, deep in thought.

He reflected sourly on his many troubles: on Baba Yaga's high-handed appropriation of his escape-route *y clept* umbrella (which Rimski believed was gone for good); on the crone's geas to locate her blasted youth-restoring black sunflower; on the unflagging malice of the queen-witch and her menacing minions—ogres and serpents *and who-knows-what's-coming-next?* Not to mention the miscellaneous perils of Hessians, horses and headsmen. . . .

So far, Phillimore grumbled, *this trip has* not *been a picnic!*

As for his original amatory reason in coming, it was not only un-fulfilled, but Phillimore now had grave doubts that he'd even come to the best of all possible worlds for his purposes. Most of the women he'd met were extremely unappealing, Snow White being a particularly in-sidious bit of poor judgment on his heart's part. How easily he might have succumbed to her superficial charms, how tardy *might* have been his disillusionment!

Even Ella was no prize, he told himself (not totally successfully). He had to admit she was refreshingly down-to-earth and, in her own feisty fashion, quite loyal. But still, the blonde was no intellectual giant *and, anyway, she's just as fickle as Snow White!* And that *was* what mattered, ultimately, wasn't it?

But on the other hand, what if Phillimore's ill luck in distaff quarters were really his own fault? *Do I expect too much? Do I invite women at first, but finally drive them off?*

It was an impenetrable maze. At first thought, he could think of nothing specific he'd done or said to justify the unexpected personal speculation. But at root, the professor knew he regarded life too often from a distance, weighing it and finding it not up to his personal standards. He admitted being guilty of a particularly unbending formality that might initially intrigue a woman, but ultimately bore her.

But the ego always expects to meet its equal, even though the privilege is rarely warranted! And what, then, were the perquisites of the Phillimorean Perfect Mate? The professor ticked off the necessities on the fingers of one hand:

1. *Beauty*—though he blushed to admit the shallow truth, the fact was, he couldn't imagine himself taken with any but the comely.

2. *Intellect*—he noted the difference between mere intelligence (*a kenning for homely common sense*) and the quality he craved: a recondite command of the secreted treasures of the mind, a rarified joy in the subtle play and tang of words in profuse gradations of subtlety.

3. *Good humor*—a sweet temper was a soothing commodity, much to be valued . . . but more important to Phillimore was the capacity to see every situation in its most ridiculous light and laugh at it despite any gods that might deem the matter sacrosanct. (Sad to relate, Phillimore, in his pre-umbrella days, was thought to be totally devoid of humor by his Parker College colleagues. But he stoutly maintained that his risibility was of so dry a character as to be perceptible solely by discerning sympathetic souls . . . an exclusive company that naturally *would* include his ardently-craved Hypothetical Heart-of-Hearts.)

To the professor, then, *das ewig-weibliche* must be invested with the above commodities, cunningly intermingled with a lusty interest in practicing (or rather, *rehearsing*) for the production of progeny.

But where, O where, is she to be found? his spirit apostrophized.

No place, buster! his mocking mind answered. *She doesn't exist— and even if she did, you wouldn't deserve her!*

He wondered why he was always prepared to believe the worst of himself. But even as he considered it, Phillimore lay down to sleep, resolving to give up his foolish search for *la belle dame sans pareil* and confine himself, instead, to recovering his umbrella. *Then I'll go home. Wherever that might be.*

By late afternoon, they reached the magic isle.

The morning was spent resupplying the ferry. Captain Fink pointed out the chart he'd studied indicated there was no fresh-water source on the island, so, since the professor had no idea how long it might take to discover the whereabouts of the sunflower, it was deemed wise to stock up on sweet water and jugs to carry it in. Fink himself took to carrying the thermos left behind by Snow White.

There was one other commodity that the skipper scoured the town for: silver bullets. It almost delayed them past sailing, but he insisted on waiting till a smith fashioned a few, "jest in case th' witch sends somethin' wuss at us!"

Despite the late departure, they reached their destination while the sun still shone on the face of the waters.

"Thar 'tis, Jimmy!" Mike Fink declared, pointing to the verdant mound lying low in the sea. "It's 'zackly where I figgered it. Wanna set out for't now? Or wait till mornin'?"

"I'd just as soon go immediately," Phillimore said.

"Okay, I'll stow gear in th' jollyboat an' we'll—"

"Hold on, Mike," the professor interrupted. "There's no 'we' this time. I'm going alone."

"Aww, now, don' start playin' hero, Jim-boy! 'Tain't safe t' go an'—"

Phillimore forestalled him with an upraised palm. "The last thing I feel is heroic! But this started out my quest, and it's likely to be dangerous on the island."

"All the more reason I better go with y'!"

"All the more reason I cannot permit my friends to come along! I've appreciated your protection, Mike, but the understanding was you'd help me reach the island, not come along with me. I don't think at this stage fancy shooting would be of much use . . . and besides, your marksmanship deteriorates dramatically on dry land."

Mike Fink argued with the professor, but the scholar proved adamant. At the last, he reluctantly agreed to permit Rimski to come along on the venture, but only if the cat promised to stay invisible, a stipulation to which Rimsky gladly agreed.

The professor's courage momentarily turned Ella's head. At the last instant, she tried to bull her way into the boat. Phillimore, shaking his head, gave her a friendly kiss on the cheek, a salute that was totally without passion. Then he turned away and clutched the oars.

Just before he faded from view, Rimski nuzzled his shaggy head against his friend's arm. The look on the cat's face was decidedly grim.

"You don't seem sanguine about the outcome of this foray," Phillimore remarked. "Are you sure you won't wait on the ferry?"

"Sure I'd like to, *zhlub!*" the unseen cat replied with unaccustomed severity. "But I got you out of trouble with Baba in the first place, so I better stick with you now her quest is near the end!"

"Thanks, Rimski." With that, the professor hastily turned his face toward the island where dwelt Beauty and the fabulous Beast.

It looked peaceful enough from far off.

Sailing into a graceful harbor, Phillimore rowed toward the doming crest that was the nearest shore.

He and the invisible cat stepped onto a beach of spun-sugar sand that rolled gently back and upward to a small hill lightly downed with early spring grasses.

On either side of the bay, the island extended peninsular projections, tame curvets of land that circled so far around the water they nearly cut off the sea and made the place a placid lagoon.

All was silent. The perfumed breeze bore a hint of lush tropic vegetation, but the air was mainly thin and fresh as the earliest dawn in Eden. Somewhere above, a lark trilled.

"I don't like this," Rimski grumbled, printing a line of feline footpads along the sand.

"Why?"

"Can't say, *tovarich* . . . but there's something infernal in it."

"Nonsense," Phillimore scoffed, "it's a veritable paradise." But he didn't believe it. Something disturbed him about the beach, he couldn't define what it was.

They trod lightly on the moist ground from which sparse grassblades stuck up. They were closer to the hill. The professor quickened his pace. Rimski hung back.

"There must be a trail to get over that rise," said Phillimore.
And then he saw the mansion.

A little way above the level of the ground, he noted a darkness in the hillock. As he peered into the cave's dimness, the professor discerned—glinting in a wayward shaft of late afternoon sun—the marble columns and ornamentations of a great hidden building, wide doors invitingly agape.

"I'm not going in there," Rimski whined.

"Of course not. Wait for me."

The feline did his best to dissuade Phillimore, but to no avail.

Although the entire place was below the surface of the earth, a resplendent glow softly lit it. All was gleaming pink and white: vaulting ceilings bedecked with rococo friezes; glimmering flooring cunningly worked with tiled designs swirling and shimmering; winking dimples of mother-of-pearl sparkling in the iridescent blush of coral walls; scintillating chandeliers that shed crystal drops of light.

Gently Phillimore stepped along, afraid lest one heavy footfall dispel the delicate magic and leave him lorn upon the lonely shingle. And so he passed the outer chambers, following the curving tiles that swept him toward the promised mysteries of the house's innermost recesses.

At the heart of the abode was a bedroom buffered with folds of satin and rich velvet. In the middle of the room, on an oval bed, reclined a smiling woman with skin so fair it seemed too soft to touch with aught harsher than a feather.

Young she was and so beautiful that, beside her, Snow White would have appeared an unweaned infant; Ella would but reflect femininity like a muddy pond feebly returning the glory of the dawning sun.

Her body was slim and perfectly proportioned. Her arms were graceful without being either too thin or fleshy, and they ended in long, artistic fingers that traced the blue gossamer of her gown and decorously draped it over a thigh sculpted, he was sure, by the Muse herself. Her sparkling eyes—merry with the irrepressible spirit of good humor—shone blue as her diaphanous chamber-wear; her long hair was so light in color as to be nearly white; its glorious sheen thrilled with silver highlights as she turned her bewitching smile full upon the professor.

Her graceful pink lips parted to reveal even white teeth, small and exquisitely shaped like the buds of new-picked early corn. Her eyes found his and held them in a long, searching look that was almost an embrace. And then, at last she spoke.

> "My Love," quoth she, "is of a birth as rare
> As 'tis for object strange and high . . ."

Emotion surged in Phillimore's breast. Fervently he replied, "My love is begotten by Despair—"

"Upon impossibility," she breathed in perfect unison with the professor.

Marvelous! thought Phillimore.

How long he rested with her he did not know. It might have been a moment or the better part of an hour, he could not keep track of the enchanted seconds that elapsed as they spoke of things little known and long forgotten. He found her as clever as she was wise, as brilliant as she was beautiful, and withal, possessed of a wit so nimble that he had much to do to scamper to comprehend its capering subtleties. All *he* knew, she knew . . . and more. Every transient mood and whim and dread he'd ever pondered laboriously upon in his solitude *she* danced lightly over, understanding all and dismissing the old terrors with conquering laughter.

At length, they held each other close and kissed, and James Phillimore found the shape and terms of love.

"So you must pluck *the* black sunflower in my keeper's garden," Beauty said sometime later.

"It's all I need to repossess my umbrella. Then I can take you away from all this."

"Yes," she sighed, "I *am* weary of this castaway life. The Beast is kindly to me, but I find his thought shackled and his manners coarse. I can never love him . . . certainly not now that I have sampled perfection."

The professor beamed and pressed his lips to her fingertips.

"And will you return for me when the flower is in your possession? Shall we flee together?"

"Yes!" he fervently replied.

"Then I will tell you where to find it." Uncertainty appeared briefly in her azure eyes. "You *will* return? You haven't simply used me to discover—"

"Hush," breathed the professor. "I love you!"

At that, she smiled and traced the contour of his cheek and chin with the nails of one hand. Where her fingers touched his skin, they left thin red lines.

Outside, he walked where she'd instructed, oblivious to all but the promptings of his heart. He thought he still heard Beauty calling his name, but so ensorcelled was he that Rimski had to repeat himself thrice before he could get the professor's attention.

"Oh, Rimski, it's only you. I thought—"

"*Only* me?" the cat grumbled. "You were expecting maybe the Bremen Town Musicians? I'd just about given you up! What took you so long?"

"Ah, Rimski, I just met the most magnificent lady in my entire life!"

"Is *that* what you've been doing? *Shmutzing* around when you're supposed to be looking for that *f'shimmelte* sunflower?!"

"You don't understand! I'm in love!"

The animal snorted in disgust. "Again?"

"No, for the *first* time."

"May I remind you," Rimski yawned, "of your great passion for Snow White, and your unarticulated, but woefully obvious hankering for Ella?"

"I didn't know better then. They were infatuations—this is the real thing!"

"Excuse me for being skeptical."

The professor tolerated his companion with the pity of the truly enlightened. "I don't blame you for not understanding, Rimski. A love like this comes along seldom."

"For which, much thanks," the cat replied. "When it comes to Great Romance, I'd rather have a gall bladder attack!"

"How would *you* know? You're only a cat."

"Let me remind you I was once a tax collector," Rimski huffed. "And I chased plenty of women in those days, even landed a few. I suffered lots of grand passions, and I even got married once. For all I know, I still am."

"Really? What happened? Did you leave her?"

"Just the opposite. She took up with that damned English cat you're so inordinately fond of! Love! Feh! At least gas stays with you all your life."

They entered the garden that covered the innermost acres of the isle. All was lushly planted, all was neatly arranged. The evening air was heavy with the perfume of the myriad blooms, and the last gleams of the westering sun shone along the stalks and cups and blossoms.

"You could search for years and never find that *f'shlugginah* flower!"

"Don't worry," Phillimore reassured him. "I've got inside information. It ought to be just on the other side of that dell to the left. . . ."

They stepped along, careful not to trample the flowers. Beauty had specifically warned the professor about that, but he would have avoided spoiling anything so lovingly tended, anyway.

Ducking around the low-hanging branches of a slanting willow, Phillimore saw the shallow bowl of a peaceful glade before him. The trees to one side thinned out and the full glory of the dying sun illuminated the spot. There, in the very center of a close-cropped circle of turf, grew a tall sunflower, ebony in shade.

Unique, Phillimore thought. But he approached the single flower; reluctantly he reached out a hand to grasp its slim stem. . . .

"Come now, sir," a thick voice grated near his ear. "You look too decent a sort to be a common poacher."

Stifling a yelp, Rimski (forgetting he was invisible) put distance between himself and the newcomer.

Phillimore turned, hand still extended toward the black sunflower. And there was the Beast.

Neatly attired in Edwardian frock coat with tweed vest, cravat and silk handkerchief tucked into the breast pocket, the Beast had tangled wild hair, a wet snout, great fangs and glowing green eyes, one of which was shielded by a monocle on a cord. His hairy paws emerged from spanking-white sleeves that were affixed by diamond cufflinks; a matching ring bedecked the appropriate talon of his left claw, which clutched an ebony walking stick with silver handle.

Looks like Edward Hyde!

"I say, old chap," growled the Beast, "you *weren't* actually attempting to divest me of my prize helianthus, were you?"

"It's needful," Phillimore replied.

"Best let me judge, sir. Come, sit you down in my arboreal retreat a few steps away, and explain all."

He led him across the clearing, through a screen of ferns and onto a flagged terrace where several chairs and a table were set with the appurtenances of teatime, or rather the remnants of that afternoon's repast.

"I do believe the pot is still warm enough," the Beast observed, gingerly testing its sides. "May I offer some tea to you, sir? Unfermented brew, decidedly delicious, transcendentally heady. . . ."

"By any chance, is it pinhead gunpowder?"

"The precise brew!"

"My favorite!"

"Egad!" exclaimed the Beast. "For a flowerly filcher, you have uncommonly civilized tastes! Sit you down! I've not had company on these shores for at least three years."

The professor chose a chair and reclined in it, relieved that the Beast was decidedly unlike the fairy tale original, or for that matter, the Cocteau version. His initial impression that the creature resembled cinematic depictions of Stevenson's Mr. Hyde was soon affirmed in the course of a delightful chat, during which Phillimore discovered that the Beast's sole recreation, other than tending the flowers, was to watch fictional entertainments on a dimensional receptor once sold him by an enterprising sorcerer named John Wellington Wells on one of his sales trips via umbrella.* Thus the resemblance to Hyde was deliberate.

"I may be doomed to wear this hirsute embodification," the Beast remarked between sips, "but don't you know, it is not one's appearance that counts, but rather the style with which one chooses to live out one's life. I may be stranded on this backwater, but at least I can conduct my few activities with dash and verve. I daresay no beast of land or air or sea can boast as much!"

"You are certainly urbane," the professor concurred. "But I had construed your existence here as pleasant to your apperceptions. After all, these flowers—"

"An engrossing hobby, right enough, and one I should miss, were I finally to leave this isle. But," he continued with a sigh, "I really appear fated to suffer the absence of any social nicety, so I make the best of my confinement. I cannot leave the isle in any shape but this unless the maiden who dwells here commits herself to loving me." A rueful smile flickered on his whiskery lips. "There's a small mercy, at least. I frighten her. Indeed, I make it a point to do so. There's little chance she shall grow fond enough to rescue me from the spell."

Phillimore blinked. "What are you saying? That you prefer remaining a beast? I don't follow."

* Phillimore's own umbrella was manufactured by Wells' firm. See *The Incredible Umbrella* (Doubleday, 1979).

"Oh, I should like to be a man, once more. But the curse is that she who speaks love to me shall not only loose the spell, but also will marry me."

The professor's head spun. There was some slip in the logic of the Beauty and the Beast tale as he knew it. *Well, it's happened before.* But if there were some variation, what might it be? A sudden thought struck him, and he delicately voiced it.

The Beast shook his mane disdainfully. "Not a bit of it, sirrah! I am fond enough of distaff company, but this Beauty creature now—she's so awfully dull, don't y' know? A regular empty-headed lass. One might bed such an one, but never would I wish to wed her!"

Phillimore was totally confused. Could they be thinking of the *same* woman? He questioned the Beast further, but there was no mistake. The magnificent lass he'd met in the subterranean palace, a damsel upon whom his entire heart and mind were irretrievably fixed, filled the Beast with boredom and contempt.

"She prates of naught but clothes, the shallow slip! I'd rather wed a bearded lady from the circus than be tied down to such a vacuous filly!"

Shaking his head positively, the Beast was unaware of how his declarations offended his guest. But before the professor could argue, the creature brought the topic of conversation back to the thwarted theft of the black sunflower.

Happy to change the subject, Phillimore discussed his plight in some detail. Fortunately, the Beast knew all about the Wellsian umbrella device, so some of the usual expressed incredulity and detailed explication demanded by other auditors was eclipsed. He outlined to the Beast his original purpose in flying to the world of Faërie and how it had been diverted from full-time consideration by Baba Yaga's enforced quest. (At mention of her name, the Beast displayed a panoply of pointed teeth. Phillimore, after all, was but the latest in a long line of mostly unsuccessful emissaries from the Russian witch. The monster did not supply details as to his predecessors' fates, and Phillimore did not press for it—though he did learn that he was one of the few to be stopped *before* picking the sunflower . . . a fortuity for which the Beast said he ought to be grateful.)

Quickly, the professor sketched in the latter events of his search. One portion of it vastly interested his host, and Phillimore had to repeat it.

At length, the Beast put down his empty cup and leaned back, contemplating. The sun had long since gone down and the only feature Phillimore could see was the twin glint of his host's baleful green eyes.

"I believe," said the Beast, after a long silence, "we have the rudiments of an arrangement that might benefit me mightily, as well as you . . . although there is one circumstance I cannot easily recommend to your thoughtful consideration. So, all in all, I suppose I *dare* not hope . . ."

"I pray you, try me!" Phillimore urged. "I might be thoroughly amenable to your plan."

"Well," the other said doubtfully, "you require from me a blossom that grows slowly and would take years to replace. Normally, I would never permit such a liberty. But I should consider sacrificing *any* of my blooms if it meant I might escape my fate!"

"And how have I created such a possibility?"

The Beast thoughtfully ruffled the hairs of his chin. "I should not object to remaining in my present form if I could but find a mate suitable to my aspect and station . . . and your narrative suggests one, indeed!"

"It does? Whom?"

"The maiden with the scarlet tresses."

"*Sleeping Beauty?!*"

"I believe that is what you called her."

"But she—" The professor stopped himself.

The Beast was not offended. "Precisely," he said. "Her appearance would match mine sufficiently to pair us in the public eye. I would not object to her red mustache or whiskers if she were in other ways gracious. As for me, I suspect she would automatically accept me, such is the stuff of spell-breaking."

"Then you propose to seek her out and kiss her?"

"Ay, sir, if I could but rid myself of *this* lass with whom I am inextricably conjoined. The curse has it that I must be her mate . . . unless some other claim her, in which case I continue as the creature you see before you."

"I'll be happy to take her off your hands," Phillimore assured the other. "I love her deeply!"

Rising, the Beast stared into the other's eyes with genuine concern. "Lad," he said huskily, "I would not ask you to do this unless you are willing. I was sure that could not be! Do not be hasty, you have not met her yet."

"Ah, but I have!"

"You *have?*"

"Yes! And I adore her!"

The Beast shook his head. "You are, I perceive, a man of considerable intelligence and somewhat rarified taste. How can you be content with this vapid mannequin?"

"Sir," said Phillimore stiffly, "you are speaking of the woman I love!"

"Well, well," sighed the Beast, "*de gustibus, chacun à son,* and all that. If you've a mind for her, my good man, then it's settled. No doubt dimensional travel has loosened your wits, but *I* shall hardly be the one to suffer from the circumstance. Pick my sunflower, do, and be good as your word."

"I shall, never fear!" Then, because it was too dark to see, he was led by the Beast to the stalk of the bloom. He reached out his hand . . .

"Stop!" the Beast begged. "Even though our pact is set, I cannot bear to witness the sad despoilment. Permit me to retire before you pluck the plant."

Phillimore waited till the Beast was gone from the glade. Then he drew the black sunflower from the ground and folded it tenderly within his inner jacket pocket.

"My quest is completed!" he said. "Now to claim Beauty for my own!"

The garden was too dark to find a path, but luckily for the professor, Rimski—now that the Beast was no longer in the dell—rejoined his comrade. The cat shimmered into view, and Phillimore recognized him by the sparkle of his feline orbs.

"Nu, it's turned out easier than I expected," the animal admitted. "You're still alive, and now we can get out of this place before something happens."

"If I recall, you can see in the dark, can't you, Rimski?"

"I'd be some kind of dopey cat if I couldn't, now wouldn't I?"

"Then take me back to the underground mansion."

"*What?*" the shaggy gray cat squawked. "Are you totally *meshugah?* Let's move off here while the getting's good!"

"Not until I fetch the woman I love!"

The cat uttered a rude sound.

"Spare me your antiromantic demonstrations. It's part of the pact I made to secure the sunflower from the Beast."

Rimski rolled his eyes skyward. "It *was* going too easily. . . ."

Gladstone bag in hand, the Beast rowed to the ferry, accompanied by Rimski to prevent Mike Fink from blowing the fearsome apparition out of the water. When all was explained, the cat returned with the skipper.

"What's up?" Fink asked the professor, hopping out of the jolly-boat.

"I'm going to fetch Beauty. As soon as I do, we all can go."

"Be glad t'come 'long, Jim-boy," Fink grinned.

"Never you mind! This lady is *very* special to me."

"Attaboy! Go get 'er!" He slapped Phillimore playfully on the back.

"Well, Rimski, do you want to come with me or wait here?"

"Feh," the cat uttered in disgust, "I don't like either choice. If this gal is so hotsy-totsy, why doesn't the Beast want her? He knows her far better than you. Don't—"

"I refuse to discuss it," the professor stated with great precision. "Coming or not?"

"Lead on," Rimski replied, "but 'this cannot come to good.' "

They quickened their pace. Phillimore saw the trail a little above ground level, a darkness in the deeper black of the hillside. Pallid moonlight limned their way.

"The trail moved," Rimski stated worriedly.

"What?"

The animal lowered his voice. "I'm saying there's something weird. The trail moved."

"Nonsense. You're just disoriented in the darkness. It's the night-shadows."

"It is not! We'd better get out of here, there's something wrong, I can *feel* it like I was ready to put my paw in a mouse trap."

"You're just trying to get me to leave Beauty behind. If you were a woman, I'd think you were jealous!"

"Don't give me such *kasha!*" Rimski growled in a sullen *sotto voce.* "Cats have well-developed sixth senses, and mine is tingling like a bolt of lightning!"

"All right, all *right!* So you wait here for me, like you did this afternoon."

"And let you walk into danger? I'll *plotz* first!"

The professor bent down and petted his friend's shaggy back. "Look, Rimski, you're upset. Maybe it's better you *do* wait. If you're wrong, no harm is done. But if you're right—and I'm not admitting you are— well, you could make a dash for the beach and fetch Mike."

The cat saw the sense of the plan. Reluctantly, he agreed to wait just below the trail for Phillimore's return.

The professor stepped upon the narrow footway. Truthfully, he *was* beginning to feel a trifle uneasy. *Bah! I'm just letting Rimski's warnings affect my nerves* . . . and yet, why did the moonlit scene seem so tantalizingly, forebodingly *familiar*?

But danger or no, he was fully determined to keep his promise to his own true love and return. The exquisite Beauty was the apotheosis of those desires which initially prompted him to undertake yet another umbrella-flight. Head high, heart bravely striving to be light, Phillimore purposefully tread the path to the underground palace.

Now the shadowy portal was near, the cave-mouth opening into the hill. Memories of the lair of the purple troll flooded his mind . . . and he briefly paused, suddenly reluctant, in spite of his romantic resolve, to proceed further. He looked over his shoulder and saw, a good way off, the shine of Rimski's eyes in the darkness. *Wish he was here to help me make my way in the gloom. I can't see a thing up ahead!*

But suddenly, the blackness was dispelled by a blinding burst of light from within the hill. Phillimore turned in amazement, but the glare instantly died and it was night once more. Yet in that instant of unnatural illumination, Rimski's vague fears washed over the professor a thousandfold, augmented by his own burgeoning terror. He turned to depart the sinister neighborhood.

But now he had no choice. His feet stuck fast in the footway that suddenly was stickily undulant. Somewhere, ominous organ music rolled and the clouds skimmed swiftly across the sky, blotting out the moon. The wind quickened to the force of a shrieking gale. Lightning flickered under and over hill and a bird of night shrilled above the *profundo* fluctuation of the swelling organ-tone. He felt creepers twist about his ankles, rooting him even faster in the roiling earth—and then the trail tilted and began to hustle him towards the cave in the hill.

Wrenching his head around, he yelled to Rimski to get help. He couldn't see the cat, but thought he heard the thin whine of his voice.

Whether Rimski was reassuring him that he was speeding for rein-forcements, or whether he was also caught in some deadly trap, Phillimore had no way of knowing.

And now the cave's edges altered and shivered as a glare of sickly yellow light pulsed from the malevolent mountain. Phillimore flailed his arms to wrest free, but icy laughter mocked him as he plunged within the portal and smashed with bone-jarring force upon the marble flooring of the mansion.

"Won't you wake, my pretty?"

He cracked open one eye. The voice sounded like Beauty, but there was a cold mirth in it that was thoroughly unfamiliar. Tilting his head, he saw her a little way off, arms outstretched to enfold him.

"Here I am, lover!" she laughed, white teeth gleaming like the fangs of a serpent. "Your dream awaits! Come, claim me, you precious—*meddler!*" Her voice rose to a hideous shriek. The lovely lineaments of her face and body melted and ran together like pustulant liquors.

"Who *are* you?" Phillimore gasped.

"'Tis Beauty!" she mocked. "Your precious Beauty!"

"Impossible!"

"Not at all, vain champion! The Beauty that dwelt on this isle is properly disposed of, but what care you for *her*? You never met her."

"Yes, I did!"

"No, 'twas *me* you encountered—the embodiment of every attribute your puerile mind conceives as the perfect match: someone as uselessly pedantic as yourself. 'Twas *me* you met, in the guise of the one thing you most desire, a womanly version of your own tedious self! You met *me* . . . ME!"

And as her thick laughter rumbled, the flesh of her face and form reshaped itself and there, towering before him, thinner and taller than the first time he saw her, was his dreaded enemy, the witch-queen.

Being a traditionalist, the witch whistled for her broomstick. It scudded obligingly between her legs. She swooped up her prey and shouted directions. The broom shot into the air so swiftly that the air was knocked out of the professor's lungs. By the time he regained his breath, they were soaring out of the underground castle into the night.

"Where are we going?" Phillimore demanded.

"It's *Walpurgisnacht*, my quixotic buffoon! I've arranged a little ceremony on your behalf." She uttered an unctuous chuckle and said no more. But she'd told him enough. He was pretty sure of their destination.

They flew over the isle. Clouds no longer obscured the moon and as Phillimore glanced desperately down, he could see, far below, the silhouette of Mike Fink waiting on the palely-glowing beach.

"HELP!" the captive howled. "UP HERE!"

Fink looked and saw the shadow of witch and broom and pedagogue etched against the moon.

"What'r y' doin' up *thar?*" he called.

"TRYING TO STAY ON!" Phillimore replied. "HELP ME! USE ONE OF THE BULLETS! SHE'S TAKING ME TO THE HARZ MOUNTAINS!"

"Cry out all you want," the witch mocked; "he can do nothing to aid you. Naught but a silver bullet or cold iron slayeth creatures of darkness."

"He *has* silver bullets!"

"In that case," the witch said, addressing her broom, "Fleet! Get *moving!*"

The broom accelerated, but Phillimore, looking down, knew the sorceress stood in no danger, anyway. There was nothing but air between the rifleman and the witch.

Maybe that's why he's hightailing it for the ferry?

Indeed, Mike Fink *was* speeding across the beach to the jolly-boat.

By the time he stepped into it, Rimski close behind, the witch-queen and the professor were lost in the shrouding depths of the night-sky.

Phillimore wondered how far from the island the Harz chain was situated on this particular world. (Because the witch had specified they were headed for *Walpurgisnacht* rites, he never doubted there *was* a Harz range somewhere.) After several minutes of soul-freezing flight in the upper atmosphere, he heard a weird familiar strain of music float up from the earth. The ghostly melody, though far-off, steadily grew louder. Phillimore recognized it now: *Night on Bald Mountain!* He wished he were a better geography student, he couldn't recall where that haunted peak was, *probably in Russia?* But since his subconscious linked it with the Harz region, maybe that fact would dictate proximity of the crags, not that he hoped for much from Mike Fink. *Even if he does know where to find me, he'll never get here in time, and anyway, how many silver bullets can one man fire? There's bound to be witches galore where we're going!*

There were.

There were also several dragons, fourteen warlocks, three wizards, nine generals, four hundred-and-eighteen statesmen, innumerable will-o'-the-wisps, three parvenu-witches, a like number of huckster-demons, Mephistopheles, Lilith (looking decidedly out of place but determined to see the dreary business through), five hundred-and-eleven members of the stagehands' union, and a single apoplectic proktophantasmist ranged along the niches and ascending trails of the mountain.

Somewhere in the middle of the witchly crowd, an incredibly ancient crone bobbed up and down, trying to catch Phillimore's eye. She shrilled out a greeting: "YOOHOO! SONNYEVITCH! DID YOU GET IT FOR BABALEH? I'M NOT GETTING NO YOUNGER, Y'KNOW!"

A wild surge of hope swelled up in Phillimore's breast! Baba Yaga was there! Perhaps he could arrange to trade off the black sunflower—still in his jacket pocket—for his umbrella! Once he had his marvelous bumbershoot back, he could instantly escape.

But the witch-queen had other plans for him. Her strong, long fingernails stabbed into his shoulder as she dragged him to the top of the mount, just below the swirling wings of the king-demon who beckoned spirits of evil from all points to join in the grisly revels below.

As for those unhallowed delights, Phillimore took a single look into the heart of the roiling throng and saw too much; afterwards, he kept his eyes closed or, if he had to study the path ahead, turned as much skyward as was commensurate without breaking his neck *en route*.

"This," snickered his witchly nemesis, "is a bit of poetic justice derived from the muddy depths of your own subconscious."

With a sweep of her gnarled hand, she indicated a colossal amphitheatre that took up one large sector of the mountain-top. Its edges shimmered hazily, and Phillimore suspected it was created solely by demonic magic. In form, it resembled a Roman gladiatorial arena, surmounted as it was by tier after tier of marble benches, on which squatted obscene spirits-in-the-making, jeering and braying and committing miscellaneous noxious social errors.

The detail that distinguished it from any depicted replica of the Circus Maximus in Phillimore's memory was the presence of two doors, side by side, at ground level on the far side of the amphitheatre.

"Once you set foot on the sand," said the witch, "there will be no turning back. A barrier will form. You must open either of the doors at the further end."

The professor groaned inwardly: *The Lady or the Tiger!*

"Since you sought this world for amorous companionship," quoth the mind-reading sorceress, "I shall permit you to seek it here. The lady whom you *thought* you adored awaits you. You have but to summon her out of her proper portal. But take heed—" (and here the witch smiled bloodthirstily) "—that you do not select the incorrect door, for behind it lurks a beast of savage ferocity."

Phillimore started to say something, but the witch gestured impatiently, and a sudden energy-field plucked him high, depositing him unceremoniously onto the sand of the arena.

The salamanders, swine and toad-things in the bleachers snortled and snuffled with glee at his discomfort, and in a special reserved box above the double doors, a fleshly journalist scribbled up an account of the event for the early evening edition of the *Bloksberg Post*.

Phillimore whirled and tried to escape, but as the witch said, he was hemmed in. An iridescent veil covering the open end of the arena flickered with a fluctuant radiance that spoke of enormous untapped powers. The professor did not try to defy the energy-membrane, he had a fair idea of what might happen if he did.

His mind raced, ticking off options. He'd flown too far. Even if

Mike Fink sped at top speed to assist him, he could not arrive in time. As for Baba Yaga, she obviously was outranked by the queen-witch and never could force her way through the energy barrier to rescue him. It occurred to Phillimore that *Walpurgisnacht* was a diabolic ceremony delimited by the approach of the sun. How long might he stall? But he doubted the witch's great wrath at his thwarting of the apple-death of Snow White would allow him to escape disaster merely by adopting a dilatory tactic.

No, there's no other option, he gloomily decided. *Might as well try the doors.*

Absurdly, selfishly, even as his reluctant feet stepped slowly in the direction of the paired portals, Phillimore wished Rimski was with him. The dour cat had shared so many of his tight spots, had indeed helped him out of at least one of them, that he yearned for his companionship at this moment of ultimate danger.

But he's not here, so . . . press on!

He pressed on.

The ghouls and hobgoblins and trolls in the stands yowled and grunted mocking, conflicting advice to him:

—*Open the left door*—

—*She's behind the right door!*

—*Open both and take your pick!*

—*Open either! Then climb up it*—

(This last was particularly malevolent. The surfaces of the doors were studded with sharp spikes.)

Shutting out the shrill cacophony as best he could, Phillimore stepped midway between both doors and attempted to recall the original Frank R. Stockton story, "The Lady or the Tiger?" In it, the enigma was not which door the prisoner opened, the professor told himself, but what came out. . . .

Got it! Stockton's prisoner was beloved of the king's daughter, but she'd lost him. With great difficulty, she found out the secret of her father's doors that fateful day. If one were opened by her lover, a fierce tiger would bound out and rend him to pieces. But behind the other portal waited the princess' most hated rival, a woman of the court to whom the prisoner would immediately be married if he chose *her* door. Either way, the princess lost him. Which was worse, to see him torn apart and go to another plane, there to await her when she herself died? Or watch him wed her detested rival and live, enjoying another's secret delights? The princess agonized over her decision for days, but

gave her lover an answer in an instant when he entered the arena and
sought her eyes with a question he *knew* she'd have the key to
. . . and (in Stockton's own words), "without the slightest hesitation,
she had moved her hand to the right."

The right!

That ironic phrase, "without the slightest hesitation," had always
hinted to the professor of the true answer to the riddle. That, plus the
fact that Stockton spent a mere half-dozen lines depicting the princess'
mental agonies at imagining her lover devoured by the tiger, while the
suffering she would feel if he selected the lady took a good score of
print-rows for the author to describe—in a telling paragraph that began
with the extremely suggestive omniscient third-person declaration, "*But
how much oftener* had she seen him at the other door!"

I'm sure of it! thought Phillimore. *The tiger was actually behind the
right-hand door indicated by the princess!*

And since the witch-queen freely admitted she'd derived the notion
of the amphitheatre with the two ominous portals from Phillimore's
own subconscious, it was extremely likely that the placement of the
lady and tiger would correspond with *his* own opinions of what Frank
Stockton originally intended, so if the tiger *was* behind the right-hand
door, as Phillimore hypothesized, the door he must open *has to be the*
left *one!*

Doesn't it?

He paused, hand grasping the left doorknob.

*But what if the witch is depending on me to follow my own theory?
She may have read that, too, when she peeked into my mind. . . .*

Phillimore removed his hand from the knob and stepped back.

Which? Which door would the witch expect me to choose? Perhaps
she guessed he'd avoid his natural inclination because he'd figure she
was depending on that, therefore she might hide the tiger behind the
door he wouldn't normally pick. But, on the other hand, knowing *that,*
he might revert to his original selection and, shrewdly judging his behaviour, the witch-queen then would . . .

Or would she?

Or wouldn't she?

Or . . . or . . . or . . .

At that moment, a broad-shouldered apparition stepped onto the
sands of the arena and approached the professor. Clad in vaguely
Arabian garments, he was of cheery disposition and carried, hilt in his

right hand, broad blade resting on his broad arm, an enormous cimeter, the upturned edge of which was keen and bright as any razor.

Phillimore shuddered. He had a pretty good idea who the smilingly threatening personage was.

"I," said the big man with a courteous grin, "am the Discourager of Hesitancy. My mistress, the queen, grown weary of your dallying, hath despatched me to persuade you to pursue your course more speedily." Lowering the blade from its cradle, the Discourager plucked a hair from his head and dropped it on the sword, neatly splitting the single strand. "You may choose between me and the doors."

Now the point is: which door did the professor pick? The question cannot be glibly answered, involving, as it does, such niceties of reasoning as might be expected to revolve within James Phillimore's pedagogic brain. His own course would have been to avoid the door indicated by Stockton's fictional princess, but the fact that the witch had looked into his thoughts turned the problem into one of Talmudic complexity.

Hardly could I, dear reader, presume myself the sole authority capable of solving this dilemma, so I leave the question with you: *which door did he choose? And why?*

And what emerged from within?

The tiger? The lady?

Or . . . *or* . . . ?

As the portal swung wide, the professor heard a deep growl emerge from within. In horror, he took a step back, but the point of the Discourager's cimeter prodded his posterior.

That was no lady! Phillimore groaned inwardly, *But that was his knife!*

And now, out of the open door, bounded the great beast that was intended to devour the professor. Stepping back a few paces, the witch's broad-shouldered lackey regarded the scene with a soapy grin, awaiting the impending bloodshed with keen professional interest.

The animal roared lustily. It sounded delighted.

Phillimore blinked, hardly able to believe his eyes. "Hey!" he exclaimed, glancing at the Discourager. "That's not a tiger!"

"So, sue us," the Stocktonian slayer yawned. "Her Majesty couldn't find one at short notice, not even by conjuration. This critter was ambling around the neighborhood, so we snatched the opportunity . . . *and* him. Don't worry! I'm sure he's hungry enough to take you to heart!"

In a fashion, the Discourager was correct, but not in the way he'd intended. The wild feline that pounced through the door was a tawny lion of immense girth and stature. When he recognized the professor, Andy's lion roared in bright delight, stood on his hind legs and hugged Phillimore with wonder and great affection.

The professor automatically grasped the animal's outstretched paw and they stepped off smartly, providing their own offkey accompaniment to the animated dance they did on the sands of the witch's arena. As they whirled dizzily about, the slimy creatures of evil attending as spectators howled in bafflement and disgust.

The Discourager of Hesitancy rubbed his eyes, unable to believe the merry spectacle taking place before them.

From someplace beyond the circumscribed perimeter of the amphitheatre, the witch-queen shrieked, lividly horrified at the profanation of fouldom with the professor's decidedly un-*Walpurgisnacht*ian display of genuine affection and terpsichorean pleasure.

Far above the witch, His Satanic Hostship smirked at her discomfiture—anything that reminded the damned of the quintessential joylessness of their Being was not without use. . . .

Below, James Phillimore whispered something to the lion. They separated, caroling and winding and waving celebratory limbs aloft. The Discourager tried to watch them both, could not, swiveled and turned to keep them each within view. He nervously fingered his sword, but was at a loss on whom to use it; his instructions had not covered the present contingency.

And now the professor minced and danced and dived this way, and now the lion crooned a throaty musical *purr* and trotted in concentric circles, irregular, yet always fixing the Discourager of Hesitancy as their center-point. The Discourager howled at them to stop, but his adjuration only succeeded in making them swirl about at a greatly accelerated tempo, the lion roaring in mocking melody, the professor confusing the Discourager with *prestissimo* renditions of Gilbert and Sullivan patter-songs.

"MAKE THEM STOP!" howled the witch from her lofty vantage-point. "KILL THEM BOTH!"

The Discourager heaved a sigh of relief. Now he had orders! Now he knew how to think! Taking a firm grasp on the hilt of the cimeter, he advanced toward Phillimore. But his legs were wobbly and his head swam from watching the dizzy dance so long and before he could reach his prey, the professor was gone and the lion was there, and the Discourager hefted his weapon, but had to swing to the left to follow the beast, and wasn't fast enough because now the lion was all the way on the other side, but here again was Phillimore, loping into view. With a frightful yell, the Discourager sliced the air in a wide swath, but the professor nimbly ducked and pranced *en point* to a position 180 degrees away, but up danced the lion, instead; again the witch's servant swept high his blade, preparing to part the animal's head from his shoulders. But suddenly the lion feinted, passing under his impotent sword-cut, and there the creature was! Inside his guard! Towering above him on hind-legs! No longer did the lion grin, but with a devastating roar of anger, he bared his great glistening fangs, bathing the Discourager with hot, fetid breath.

The Discourager screamed with fright and backed away—only to trip over James Phillimore, cunningly crouching behind him. Head over heels he tumbled, flopping to the sand with a mighty expulsion of breath. His cimeter flew from his grasp and stuck, some distance away, in the ground.

The professor hopped up, gave the lion a satisfied nod, and sped over to the sword. Grabbing it, he called an order to the friendly beast: "Run over to the other of the two doors! All fours! You'll have to save us both!"

Even as he shouted, the animal was on his way. Phillimore also ran to the closed portal, yanked it wide, shouted to the occupant of the chamber on its other side, "Come on! Hurry! I'll save you!"

Overhead, the trolls and gnomes and toad-things gibbered and grunted furiously, champing teeth and hurling enraged curses at their enemies below. Some of the fouler fiends scrambled over the engirdling parapets and dropped heavily onto the floor of the arena, snuffling as they came.

Beauty walked into the harsh light and blinked in confusion at the obscene things squirming their way in her direction. She smiled uncertainly at the professor, on whom she obviously had never set eyes in her life.

Understandable. I only met the witch disguised as Beauty, Phillimore told himself, noting briefly the transcendental loveliness of the woman who stood before him now. She outshone her sorcerous replica as the sun might shame a glowing stick of punk. But there was no time to admire her, the first of the infernal revengers was almost on them.

"Quick! Hop on the lion! I'll explain later."

"But 'tis not seemly!" she balked. "Such a position wouldst revealeth too generous a quantity of mine maidenly flesh!" Flushing demurely, she averted her eyes.

Oh, hell!

A slug-like cacodemon extended its sucker-arms toward them. Phillimore sliced at the tentacles, at the same time grabbing the squealing Beauty and unceremoniously dumping her onto the lion's back. "Someday you'll thank me for this!" the professor assured her as he leaped onto the beast's shoulders and grabbed a handful of mane.

Roaring so loud that the front rank of ghoulies halted one single precious second, the lion bunched mighty haunches and sprang over their startled semi-heads. Another bound and he cleared the first parapet and landed with his passengers in the bleachers.

He scampered along the first row, ducking over the massed monsters when he could, snapping with powerful jaws when he had no alternative, spitting out the repulsive goblin parts his sharp teeth could not help biting off every so often.

Scrambling to a higher row of the arena, the lion broke clear of the hellish pursuers and put distance between them. The fading growls and snorts and grunts and mutterings made Beauty break into uncontrollable sobs and even the professor shivered at the ghastly malevolence of the damned.

"Make for that arch!" Phillimore advised the lion, pointing to a gap between a pair of supportive columns through which he could see a portion of the night sky. Baleful forks of lightning split the dark.

The lion galloped through the space between the towering columns and skittered to a stop on the marble shelf beyond. Beauty shrieked. Phillimore paled.

Beyond the outer lip of the polished stone flooring was nothing but mocking night, alive with fiery forms and chaotic colors.

The professor dismounted and helped Beauty off the lion's back. They stood forlornly on the marble paving and stared out into nothingness. Behind them, the pursuit, still faint, grew steadily nearer, louder.

"Prithee tell me where we are," Beauty whimpered.

"On the edge of illusion," Phillimore grimly replied. "This bogus arena is fashioned out of magic on the very brink of Bald Mountain."

It was true. Stepping gingerly to the edge of the ledge, Phillimore saw below the steep slopes of the precipice and far, much further down, the floor of a broad, tree-covered plain enclosed by other lesser peaks. And then, a horrid sound made him look up.

Hovering in mid-air, grinning balefully, the witch-queen straddled her broomstick and laughed heartlessly at their plight.

"Soon, soon, my troublesome friend, I shall rollick with joy as my minions mince your bones!" She swooped whistling down on them. "But I shall have the pleasure, first, of plucking out your eyes, one by one!"

Her laughter rang shrill in the chill mountain air. Phillimore wondered how near it was to dawn, but no sooner had he thought it than the witch, landing upon the ledge, bared her teeth in malevolent mirth. She waggled a crooked finger at him.

"Don't delude yourself, there is fully an hour of darkness before us, during which I shall prolong my vengeful delights!" She suddenly whirled and stuck a gnarled forefinger in the direction of the lion, poised to spring. He paused, suddenly transfixed.

Beauty moaned and cowered in a corner.

Now the sound of the legions of hell was quite loud. The witch strode across the terrace and held up an admonishing hand.

"Later, my pets!" she laughed cruelly. "The initial bloodletting is mine!" With that, she advanced toward Phillimore.

He gave back a step and hefted the sword of the Discourager in a feeble effort at self-protection.

The witch chuckled as she gestured at the cimeter. It trembled and shimmered and turned into a nosegay of poison ivy. Phillimore flung it at her in disgust, but it vanished in mid-air before a single envenomed branch touched her shriveled skin.

And now she strode forward, unchecked, and the professor stood his ground, smartly planting his feet in the middle of the lofty ledge. *No point in running, there's no place to go! Maybe I can grapple with her, pitch her over the edge?*

But as soon as he thought it, he knew she'd caught the thought. The leering light of her baleful eyes told him he had no hope of surprising her.

And now her long-nailed claws reached forth and raked the air in front of the professor's bulging eyes.

Fitting justice, he chastised himself. *I've been blind enough in the pursuit of a mate!*

Reading the thought, the crone cackled. Then she caught Phillimore's head in a steely grasp and bent it upwards so the last thing he might see was her suddenly-transfigured visage; which she'd shaped once more to resemble his illusory beloved Beauty.

Phillimore flinched, as much from the irony as the proximity of the witch's talons. But now there was a spell upon his eyelids and he could not lower them to avoid the spectacle of the lewd travesty of his Immortal Beloved getting ready to tear out his organs of sight.

Her nails grazed his gaping eyelids.

Crack!

In an instant, Beauty's second visage melted into the startled glare of the witch's own face. No sound but a whistled intake of breath escaped her lips, but her nails, gone wide of their intended mark, suddenly ripped smartly along the professor's cheeks, tracing thin red lines.

And then, all around, the hosts of Hell howled in anger and dismay. The marble beneath Phillimore's feet tottered and started to crumble.

But in the same second, the staymagic seeped away, and his head was no longer fixed. Andy's lion roared and sprang to Phillimore's aid, tossing him onto his back. His paws skidded over the deteriorating marble, but the beast managed at length to similarly rescue the genuine Beauty, who stood in abject fright at a far corner of the swiftly-disappearing terrace.

The lion turned his head toward the twin columns from which they'd first emerged. The entranceway was clogged with spectres and sin-spawn, chittering and shaking amorphous menacing appendages in their direction.

Just then, a mighty shout resounded through the valley. So impossibly loud was it that Phillimore could not hear for many seconds after. With the sound the terrace totally surrendered, disintegrating in a massive terminal shiver, plunging the dead body of the witch-queen into the valley below.

At that very instant, the lion leaped over the heads of the demons (now too concerned with their own immediate salvation to pay further heed to the professor's squad). The lion aimed for the place between the columns, but the amphitheatre was breaking up. The beast landed in slippery grass, fouled with the effluents of the night's rites.

"What in Hell is happening?" Phillimore exclaimed. A mighty din resounded around and upon the mountain, bellows and shouts and the keen whine of bullets.

The cavalry got here in time!

It was still night, though the moon was down. Warlocks and crones and council-members swarmed shrieking over the mountainside. Leathery wings fluttered overhead, but most plunged earthward as silver bullets pierced their owners' vital organs.

Dashing down a narrow side-path, the lion entered a small dale through which slithered frightened elementals hurriedly heading back to the security of their native elements. Here Phillimore and Beauty dismounted and allowed the panting beast to catch its breath.

"What hath transpired?" the trembling woman asked.

"Not sure," the professor panted. "We seem to be rescued, but how, or by whom, I don't know. How *he* could have gotten here so fast, I have no idea!"

"He? Who?"

Phillimore held up one hand, restraining her questions. "Just a minute, I thought I heard—"

"*What?*"

"Shhh!"

Into the dim seclusion of the tiny valley rode a stranger, dressed all in black. Riding up to the professor, he touched the brim of his hat with solemn respect. A pearly six-shooter shone at his side.

"You Jim Phillimore?"

"I am."

Turning in his saddle, the stranger called over his shoulder. "I found him, Fink!"

The familiar voice of the skipper sounded a little ways off in the wood. "Who you calling a fink?"

Mike Fink trotted into the glade on horseback. Curled about his shoulders was a gray shaggy cat with yellow eyes that gleamed happily as they saw the unharmed professor.

"Rimski! Mike!" Phillimore shouted gleefully.

All but Beauty squatted on the grass. Rimski was still timid when it came to meeting the lion, but when he heard how the animal had repeatedly helped the professor, he warmed up considerably to him, though he still preferred to sit some distance away.

Beauty stood to one side, shyly darting glances at the three men, each in turn. Mike Fink grinned openly at her, but the stranger in black didn't seem to notice she was there; his eyes, brooding with too much knowledge, turned inward on the private griefs that the man carried with dignity and quiet grace.

When Phillimore brought his story up to the moment when the witch was about to tear out his eyes, Fink took over and explained how he'd "rounded up a posse to he'p out!"

"But how did you get here so fast?" Phillimore wondered. "And was that *you* who shot the witch?"

"Nope," Fink shook his head sheepishly, "not a lake or river in the hull dawgoned valley! M' pal here snapped off that shot, all th' way from th' bottom o' th' mountain."

The professor thanked the stranger and took the thermos-cap full of Tennessee whiskey that Fink passed to him. "That was mighty fancy shooting, sir."

"Nothing to be proud of," the stranger replied. It was not, coming from him, an admonishment, but rather the observation of one who'd shot too many wrongdoers in his day and found that, maybe, deep down, he really liked to kill.

They all sipped whiskey in silence.

"We stocked up, quick-like, on silver bullets," Fink resumed. "Lucky I bought some in town."

"Yes," the stranger added, "and it's a good thing that masked man agreed to come along, too. Never saw so much silver in my life outside a bank!"

"Where's Ella?" Phillimore asked abruptly.

"Back in the ferry," Mike said. "Didn't want her t' get hurt!"

"Who is Ella?" Beauty suddenly interrupted.

The captain shrugged. "Guess y' might describe her as th' lady I'm sorta sweet on."

"Oh," said Beauty, "I see," and turned her attention to the stranger in black. "And art thou perchance affianced?"

The stranger's brow knitted. "Only loved one woman, and I no way could have her." He rose swiftly to his feet. "You'll pardon me. There's work yet to be done." Without another word, he swung into his saddle and cantered off, headed up the path.

Mike Fink rose to his feet, too. "He's got a point, Jim-boy. There's a lot o' moppin' up t' be done yet." He sighed. "Wisht we was on th' water, so's I could assist."

"Well, there's not much that Rimski or I can do, either," Phillimore stated, "and I think Andy's lion here has worked hard enough for one night. But I *am* curious as to what's happening on the mountaintop."

"Okay," Fink agreed, "let's take a look." He rubbed his hands briskly and led them back in the direction of the peak.

They paused at the edge of the woods and watched the battle. The forces of darkness were taking a terrific beating. Everywhere Phillimore looked he saw silver swords and silver bullets destroying the fouler denizens of the world of Faërie.

The professor whistled. "Wow! Where'd you manage to enlist such a large army so fast?"

"Got a friend who spread th' word round real quick!"

"But there's hundreds of champions in the field!" the professor marveled.

"Yep!"

"Who could possibly gather them so swiftly?"

"Hold off with th' questions, Jimbo, I don' wanna miss th' best part!"

Before them, a great host of heroes rallied and flanked and charged and attacked. Phillimore recognized some of them instantly: Snow White's dwarfs, stout axes in hand, heartily hewed down demons, singing a catchy tune as they did. Elsewhere a company of archers clad in Lincoln-green fired silver-tipped arrows into the heart of the diabolic throng. A company of knights clashed mail against the armor of flame-breathing dragons, while, on another part of the mountain, a rather dim-witted lout in a Scotch kilt laid about him with a billy-club, cracking unhallowed skulls. He was aided by a large, ferocious monkey, whose teeth and long claws tore the hides of hobgoblins.

Pointing to the dolt and the ape, Phillimore asked who they might be.

"A strange pair," Rimski observed. "Doomed to live their lives over and over again condemned to the shapes you see. Once both were evil, but evidence of nobler hearts persuaded the gods to commute their fates, and now they live forever and battle the forces of chaos."

"What's their names?"

"Oh, the lummox is known as The Eternal Chump; Ian, though, is his given name. And that's The Eternal Chimp with him."

"I see." Casting his eyes again over the battlefield, Phillimore found much more to marvel at: a quartet of caped swordsmen, silver ferrules on the tips of their foils, skewered satanic slaves. Close by, a solitary fencer with an enormous proboscis outshone even the pyrotechnic fighting of the foursome. Elsewhere, a young cowboy with a woman by his side whooped and yowped like a desert-dog. They both swirled lassos that cinched their enemies, hoisted and hurled them to the moon.

"That's m' buddies," Mike Fink grinned, his gold tooth bright in the flash of sorcerous light that glinted off sword and shaft. "Pecos Bill 'n' his saddle-pal, Sluefoot Sue!"

"And the *peasant* in boxing trunks?"

"Aww," said Fink, "he got t' fight from now to doomsday. That's The Eternal Champ-peon."

Turning aside from the noisy fray, the professor asked Fink once more how he was so quickly able to summon up such a vast array of heroes and arrive in time.

"Another thing! You say the man in black shot the witch-queen from the bottom of the mountain. . . ."

"Yep, Jimbo, that's right."

"If that's so, then how did he get to the top of the hill almost immediately?"

"Easy!" Fink replied. "I *tol'* ya I got a special pal."

But before he could elaborate, a hurtling figure sped out of the midst of the great battle and flew straight towards Phillimore.

"*Hang on, sonnyevitch!*" Baba Yaga yelled. "I'll save you!" And with that, she plucked the professor off the ground and shot into the air, the witch on her broomstick, the man dangling in the feeble grasp of the incredibly ancient harridan.

"Don't shoot!" Phillimore called to whoever might be listening. "She'll drop me!"

Mike slapped his palm against his forehead. "Sufferin' catfish! Do we gotta rescue him *again?*"

The Russian witch carried the professor to another mountain some ten miles distant. They alighted on a steep slope.

The old woman, much more wrinkled than the last time he'd seen her, wheezed and panted for breath. Phillimore was once more reminded of his late foster mother.

But the sly leer in her eye was anything but maternal. "Nu, sonnyevitch?" she inquired. "Did you find my black sunflower? I've been keeping tabs on you. . . . I *know* you reached the island!"

How'd she find that out? "Yes," he said, "I made a bargain for the flower."

"Then you *got* it?" Her eagerness was uncontainable. "Hand it over! Hand it over!"

"Not so fast," he demurred. "I want my umbrella."

She cast a fretful glance at the lightening sky. "Hurry up, soon it'll be dawn, and my broomstick won't work!"

"The umbrella! I *insist* upon it!"

Baba grinned innocently. "Would I keep you from your precious property, dearie?" She twirled the umbrella by the handle. "*You* hand me the sunflower, I'll give you the umbrella in the same movement."

"Sounds fair," said the professor, digging in his jacket for the folded flower. He drew it forth, smoothing out the curled stem as he did.

When she saw it, the witch's eyes glittered. A trace of saliva foamed at the corner of her wrinkled mouth.

Phillimore held out the flower, simultaneously striving to get hold of his umbrella. . . .

And at that instant, without warning, the sunflower was snatched from his grasp. A blur, some great pale thing passed before his eyes, and the witch crowed in triumphant delight.

Her pink horse-servant, Walter, had dashed up behind, grabbed the flower in his mouth, and trotted it over to Baba Yaga.

"HEY!" Phillimore shouted. "What's the big idea? Give me my umbrella!"

"Sorry," Walter rasped in his deep voice, "but orders is orders, pal!"

And now the witch, clutching the sunflower *and* the umbrella, laughed spitefully. "Did you *really* think, sonnyevitch, that Mama Baba was gonna give you back your sweet little parasol?"

"*You* can't use it! I told you! It's imprinted with my brain-pattern and—"

"And what happens," she crooned, "if your brain don't function no more, bhubbaleh?"

The professor mentally swallowed his Adam's-apple.

"Maybe I'm some kind of greenhorn?" the witch sneered. "Possession of magic is my game, shtupid! Soon's I heard about your little toy, I knew all I had to do was tell Walter to kick out your *f'shimmelte* brains and the umbrella would work for *me!*" She turned to the horse. "And now that the thought occurs to me, Walter-baby . . ."

"But how did you know I reached the island?" Phillimore hastily interrupted, trying to play for time. The first dim streaks of twilight were faintly washing the sky, and while Baba apparently did not lose anything but her powers in the daytime, it *might* be impossible for her to command Walter after sunrise. Anyway, it was worth trying—*what else is there for me to do?*

Somewhere, a long way off, thunder shook the air.

Baba preened herself. She patted Walter's mane. "Tell 'im, mine Waltaleh, tell how clever Baba is!"

Walter shrugged sourly. "When you didn't show up at the bridge, I figured either the Headless Horseman got you or you were hiding in the woods. I snooped around and got on your trail as fast as I could, but when I found you, you were traveling with a lion, so I kept my distance. Then, just when I thought we'd join up, *plop!* You go and get in dutch with the Chief Honcho among the local witches! So I trotted back to Baba and *she* got in touch with the queen and they made tentative plans to let you get to the enchanted isle—"

"Not without a few obstacles along the way," the professor grimly observed.

"They didn't want to make it too easy for you." The horse shook his mane in disgust. "I hope you remember I'm just a messenger in all this. I don't have much choice, it's either do what she says or—"

"*Shah!*" snapped the witch. "Just tell the story!"

The thunder was nearer now. Phillimore felt its rumble shake the ground.

"So," Walter resumed, "I was sent off to spy out the water-route, and when I saw you in the ferry heading out to sea, I let Baba know and she let the queen in on it . . . and all that remained was for her to capture you and whisk you off on *Walpurgisnacht.*"

"Which is why, I suppose," said Phillimore, "she didn't grab me the first time I saw her on the island."

"That," the horse confirmed, "and also because she'd agreed to let you find the sunflower for Baba."

"So it was all a trap."

The thunder was so loud the mountain shivered. "What in the name of blighted blintzes is *that?*" Baba Yaga suddenly exclaimed. "Something's wrong! Enough with the talk—"

But Phillimore persisted. "Then there really *was* no chance of your returning my umbrella, was there? Rimski warned me not to trust you!"

"That buttinski!" Baba howled, her voice thin in the din.

"So you never meant to give my umbrella back. Is that right?" Phillimore pestered.

With a self-satisfied self-righteous nod, Baba Yaga confirmed the accuracy of what he had just asked . . . and then the color drained from her ancient face.

"OY-OY-OY!" she howled. "YOU NO-GOODNIK! YOU TRICKED ME INTO ANSWERING A QUESTION!"

A mighty convulsion seized the witch just as a mighty hand seized the top of the mountain and ripped it off.

A thunderous voice rattled the professor's eardrums. *"HO-HO! FINK! I'VE FOUND THEM!"*

A vast face beamed benignly down on the professor, the startled steed and the violently-shaking witch. Straightening, the colossal figure stretched forth one palm, opened it and out of its center tumbled Rimski and Mike Fink.

"Y' okay, son?" the sailor asked, worried.

"I'm fine!" Phillimore replied, grabbing his umbrella and pointing at the positively stupendous man in overalls who looked down smilingly as the morning sun basked the company in birthing radiance. "Who is *that?*"

"Ah told y'," Fink said proudly, "a special friend he'ped us out tonight, Jim-boy! Lemme innerduce Mistah Paul Bunyan, o' Kennebunkport, Maine!"

The megagiant bowed politely to Phillimore. The motion started up a breeze that wafted over the face of Faërie, waving and fluttering six flags as far-off as that world's equivalent of Texas.

Baba Yaga was in her death-throes.

"I won't survive this one!" she told Walter. "My l-l-l-l-last order is t-t-t-t-to KILL HIM!"

The stallion dutifully raised his hooves to dash in Phillimore's skull, but Paul Bunyan chuckled and picked up the horse between thumb and forefinger.

"*I T'INK I KEEP HIM!*" Paul declared. "*HE GO GOOD IN MY TOY SOLDIER COLLECTION!*"

Next morning, nearly all the champions sat down at a table hastily fashioned and laden in the midst of the ruins of the witches' festival. They ate a breakfast of ambrosia, leosylla-cakes and mellofern-ale, toasting to fortune with clear, sparkling drafts of a heady wine drawn from a nearby stream where (Mike Fink said) it flowed unceasing. The company was served by a sultry, smiling beauty in Egyptian headdress and scanty surplice. According to Rimski, she once danced attendance on none other than great Queen Cleopatra, but now the woman was pleased to wait upon the mighty who labored virtuously throughout the ages, battling the spirits of chaos. Phillimore gratefully accepted a cup of eternal champagne from The Eternal Charmian.

Only Paul Bunyan and Andy's lion refused to stay for the victory feast. The animal had a pressing social engagement and the brobding-nagian lumberjack explained he had to go home and feed his blue ox, Babe. Besides, he preferred his own usual light morning meal, consisting of a jeroboam of cranberry juice, forty tons of flapjacks floating in enough maple syrup to turn the Grand Canyon into a public beach, a billion bacon slabs, three thousand gross of fried eggs (ostrich, if possible) and fifty water-towers-worth of coffee.

Bunyan stooped and sought the pink stallion, Walter, but could not find where he'd put him. Phillimore looked anxiously around the spot where the giant had tethered the horse, but the rope was chewed through.

"NO MATTER!" Bunyan bellowed jovially. "I ALWAYS BE MISPLACING MY TOYS!" With a flick of his comb (an uprooted pine tree), he tossed one unruly cowlick the size of a cornfield into place, waved goodbye and started off, calling a good-luck wish to Phillimore over his shoulder as he went.

The professor sat down with a melancholy sigh, Rimski to his right, Beauty on his left hand. The morning meal was pleasant enough, but he knew he was still in a mess. There was always the option, of course, of employing the umbrella to take him elsewhere, but the last time he tried that, he discovered, to his dismay, that a kind of law of universal economy interfered with his choice of destination and landed him in a world where a similar problem to the one he'd fled still confronted him.*

Nope, I made a bad bargain—and now I'm stuck!

"Hey, give a look!" Rimski suddenly exclaimed. "Company's coming!"

Phillimore turned in the indicated direction and saw, riding along the road, the Beast of the enchanted isle. He was clad in a new morning-coat with matching top-hat. His monocle shone in the early sun. Mounted at his side was a tall woman clad in wedding-dress, sporting flaming red hair and matching whiskers.

"Well," the professor sighed, "I've been expecting them, sooner or later."

The Beast walked back and forth, teacup in one hand, pinky tilted daintily skyward. Phillimore fell into step beside him as the other paced the meadow at the foot of the mountain.

"It's too bad, don't y' know," the Beast commiserated, "but there's no going back, old chap, is there? And didn't I warn you that Beauty is a vapid little bit of fluff?"

"You did. You did. But you see, I was laboring under the delusion that she was entirely different from what you described."

The Beast nodded sagely. "At that time, I could not comprehend, but now you've elucidated. You are the hapless victim of an evil prank. The witch-queen's malice lives after her."

The professor eagerly agreed with the Beast's assessment of the case. "Then you concede that I do not deserve to have to marry Beauty?"

"Certainly!"

"Ah," Phillimore sighed gratefully, "you *are* uncommonly civilized. You know, in my travels in this world, I have learned a bit of a lesson concerning beauty as a marital determinant. It only took me a moment to recognize Beauty's unworthiness of deep affection."

The Beast sipped his tea. "True enough, my good sir. But of course you must marry her, nevertheless."

Phillimore stopped dead. "What?"

"I have already made arrangements for the ceremony. It shall take place within the hour on this very green."

* For details, see Part II of *The Incredible Umbrella*.

"B-but, I thought y-you said I don't have t-t-to wed her!"

The Beast shook his head sadly. "I said you don't *deserve* to be saddled with such a light lass. But unfortunately, the laws governing this world do not permit the shunting aside of bargains, especially when they are pacts that involve spells and ensorcellments."

Phillimore's face grew long. "Then there is no hope?"

"Not unless you find someone else to take her off *your* hands. Otherwise, you are forced to keep your word . . . and recall, you *did* pick the sunflower and you *did* retrieve your umbrella."

"Much good it will do me," Phillimore replied bitterly. "Wonder whether I can talk Mike Fink into throwing over Ella for Beauty?"

But he couldn't.

The ceremony was not elaborately arranged. Mike Fink himself, it seemed, had the authority to conduct the nuptials, due to his position as the captain of a vessel. Phillimore tried to argue that skippers only could marry people on the high seas, but Rimski pointed out that there were different legal traditions on the world of Faërie.

The groom and his intended stood before the ferryman, attended by Rimski, the Beast, a rather aloof Unsleeping Beauty (still a bit insulted by Phillimore's cavalier behaviour toward her some days before), and divers champions, heroes and trusty talking steeds. Neither principal had bothered to change into ceremonial garb; neither had much to say to one another. Phillimore sulked and Beauty clearly was displeased. She clutched her bouquet with nails white with pressure.

Mike Fink began the ceremony.

"We-all is gathered here t'day t' join t'gether these pore sons-a-guns. Does anybody got somethin' t' say agin it?" He shook his head. "I mean, besides *you*, Jim-boy!"

"Well, well," the professor grumbled, "get on with it."

"La, the way you talk," Beauty moodily murmured, "thou mightst be suffering the extraction of thine appendix!"

Rimski softly meowed something sarcastic about gaining a useless part, rather than etc. The animal felt immensely sorry for his friend, the professor.

"Okay naow," Fink drawled, "who-all gives away this here filly?"

"Oh, *I* do, *believe me!*" the Beast exclaimed with a profoundly satisfied sigh.

"Now d' you take this professor-type for yer intended hubby?"

"Do I *have* to?" the maiden wailed.

The Beast's redheaded fiancée remarked that if she didn't say yes, she might sustain a sudden bodily injury.

Beauty said yes.

" 'N'how 'bout you, Jimbo?"

"Well, if there's no way out of it, I suppose I must."

"Uh-oh!" Rimski abruptly said. "I got a all-of-a-sudden that maybe there *is* a way out of this, professor!'

"There *is?*"

"Don't get excited," the cat warned, "but if you don't turn around quick, you'll never make it to the honeymoon!"

Phillimore swiveled and saw, to his dismay, the pink horse Walter thundering across the meadow on a collision course with himself.

The wedding guests scattered left and right. Rimski scooted up a slender tree some yards away.

The professor ran in the same direction, Walter in hot pursuit.

"Hey!" Phillimore yelled over his shoulder, umbrella flailing, "Baba's dead! Leave me alone!"

"Can't!" Walter rasped, steadily gaining on his quarry. "She told me to kill you, and I've got to do it! Nothing personal."

"Help!" the professor howled, dashing toward the same tree Rimski was nestled in. "Fink! Do something!"

The captain's voice sounded far off. "Who you callin' a fink?"

Roundly cursing him, Phillimore leaped for a low-hanging branch, grabbed hold and started to clamber up.

Walter, now directly behind, reared on his hind legs and aimed a powerful kick at the professor, narrowly grazing his down-hanging posterior.

Phillimore yelled and jumped higher, clutching the branch with all arms and legs. It sagged noticeably under his weight; he couldn't manage to climb to the more solid center of the tree.

"Rimski! Help!"

"What on earth can *I* do?" the fat cat mewed. "He's forty times my size!"

"Jump on him! Scratch him!"

The cat nodded at the plan, but somehow could not manage to pry his trembling paws free of the treetrunk to carry it out.

Below, Walter whinnied and slammed his hooves against the bole. The tree shook and Phillimore's branch curved dangerously, just out of reach of the stallion.

Crack!

Mike Fink fired a round at Walter, but the shell went wide, ricocheted off a stone and neatly drilled a hole in four calling birds, three French hens, two turtledoves and a professor in a pear tree.

"Watch it!" Phillimore screamed. "You just punctured my pants!"

"Are you hurt?" asked Rimski.

"No. My wallet stopped the bullet."

"Dawgone it!" Fink swore from a distance. "I hates t' waste them silver bullets! Only got two left!"

Crack!

"Aww, hell! I cain't hit *nothin'* if'n I don't shoot over water!"

Fink wasn't quite correct. His second bullet *had* managed to strike the limb on which Phillimore was suspended. The wood split and cracked, but did not break through totally. But the branch hung lower than before.

"Cut it out!" the professor pleaded. "You're just making matters worse!"

The first shot startled the horse enough to make him trot away from the tree, but upon observing Mike Fink's poor marksmanship on dry land, Walter regained his courage and again drew near to the dangling, helpless professor.

The branch creaked and lowered Phillimore another inch.

"Just about in range now," Walter said, backing up to align himself.

Rimski, regaining some of his nerve, padded along the treetrunk to a spot as close as he could manage to the horse. But now the angle was not as good as before. Still . . .

The cat leaped, vanishing on the way down. He landed several feet short of the horse, looked up, saw the great size of the creature, almost lost his nerve, finally jumped as high as he could, hoping to land on the horse's back. But he was too fat to manage the elevation. Instead, Rimski clumped against Walter's flank, instinctively uncurling his claws to hold on.

Walter neighed in unexpected pain, shook himself and flopped to the ground, rolling onto the side that hurt.

Overhead, the professor heard a high whine of fear.

"Rimski!"

Without thinking, he dropped to the ground to run to the feline's aid.

"I'm all right!" Rimski yelped. "Get back in the tree!"

Too late!

Walter cantered swiftly, interposing himself between the tree and the professor. The horse exhaled noisily.

"Do you *mind* letting me get this over with?" he protested. "You're wearing me out."

"Good!"

"Don't you see, Baba gave me no alternative? I'm under a spell. I *have* to do her dying command."

Out of the corner of his eye, Phillimore saw Mike Fink circling slowly around to the other side of the tree, hoping to get a better vantage before firing his final silver bullet.

Uh-uh, he'll kill me before Walter does! If only he could shoot accurately—

And just then James Phillimore at last remembered a vitally important detail.

"Mike!" he yelled. "Do you still have Snow White's thermos?"

"Why, shore," came the puzzled reply. "Right by m' side."

"Is it filled?"

"With hunnerd proof akwee vitee. But why in th'—"

"Unscrew the cap!" Phillimore interrupted, eyes on Walter.

The horse pawed the earth.

"Okay!" the perplexed captain hollered. "Now what?"

"Fill it!"

Walter lowered his head.

"Y' think m' aim'll be better if'n ah'm drunk?"

"No! Put the filled cap on the ground in front of you!"

With a mighty whinny, Walter bounded for the professor. Phillimore dashed to one side. The animal screeched to a halt, turned and chased his prey.

Phillimore sped to the tree, Walter two yards behind. As the professor ran beneath the dangling branch, it snapped and dropped straight down, smacking Phillimore's skull so hard that his knees crumpled. He fell to the ground, insensible.

The stallion, seeing the accident, checked his pace and stepped up to the recumbent figure. Walter prepared to smash down with all his might.

But Fink suddenly realized what Phillimore had been trying to communicate. Swinging his rifle into position, he aimed over the thermos-cap.

Crack!

Walter roared and toppled over backwards.

True to his legend, Mike Fink was a sharpshooter only when he fired across water.

The professor woke just in time to see the pink stallion close his eyes and expire.

What happened next surprised everyone.

As life left the great body, the horse-form trembled and dimmed and faded from view. Where Walter had been, there now lay a tall, handsome youth with graceful features but newly attainèd to manhood. He was dressed in the fine clothes of a nobleman.

As Fink and Phillimore gazed upon him in awe, his eyelids twitched and opened. His blue eyes filled with tears of gratitude and joy.

"O dear friends," he addressed the professor and the skipper in a voice gentle and manly, "I thankst thou for freeing me with a silver bullet from the witch's powerful enchantment."

"Why, who are you?" Phillimore asked, amazed.

"My name is Florizel. I am a prince whose homeland lies at some distance. Being the youngest of three brothers, I determined to seek my fortune in lands unknown. But on my very first foray into wilderland, I fell victim to the dangerous potions of the witch, Baba Yaga. Yet was my nature noble enough, I thank the fates, that I would not do her bidding to fetch the fabled black sunflower and prolong her evil existence on this globe!

"Such was the nature of the potent magic in which she ravelled me that, so long as I bore the form of an animal, I must do her bidding. Because I refused her in the one favor she could not wrest from me, I was sternly commanded to enact her will in all else.

"But your bravery hath brought disaster to that wicked witch, and now I am free to undo the awful work she made me perform . . . or if I cannot right all the evil my baser form perpetrated, at least may I hope to repent."

Rising then from the dewy grass, the prince resolved to begin his good works with a special favor on behalf of his liberator, James Phillimore.

The professor was overjoyed when he heard the proposal. Swiftly he sought out Beauty and the Beast and put it before them.

Beauty had only to take one look at the elegant Florizel to lose her heart to him.

The Beast shook the newcomer's hand and affirmed that his offer to marry Beauty would quite adequately satisfy the conditions of the curse he'd passed on to Phillimore. To the professor, the Beast merely said, "Congratulations, old man! What fortuity, eh? A convenient prince, charming solution, don't you think?"

The two couples, once wed, said farewell. The champions departed, leaving Mike Fink and the professor alone in the field. Together they searched for the missing philosopher-cat, last unseen near the tree. They had to comb the grass gently for some time before Rimski could be discovered.

With a shaky *purr*, he popped into view. "I must have passed out," he apologized. "That big lummox almost squashed me when he rolled over. I just managed to wiggle free."

"Then he *did* land on you?" Phillimore asked, worried.

"A *bissele*."

Upon examination, they saw that Rimski had sustained a broken leg, the pain of which was responsible for his fainting.

Phillimore fussed over him, binding up the injured limb carefully. Fink administered a small quantity of akwee vitee to deaden the ache in the cat's paw.

"Waal, what's the plan, Jim-bo? Wanna come 'long 'n' see me 'n' Ella tie th' knot?"

"No, I'd rather not," the professor candidly admitted, cradling his wounded friend in one arm. "I think it's time I moved along. This is a lively world, but it didn't work out too well for me, not at all according to plan."

The ferryman shuffled his feet, feeling rather sheepish. "Aww, Jim-boy, ah hope y' don't hold it 'gainst me 'bout Ella. I reckon you *was* a bit sweet on her y'self."

"Maybe a little," the professor admitted, shielding his face from the glare of the noonday sun. The brightness made his eyes sting, or so he told himself. "But we weren't really suited for one another. A good person, though, in her own—ah—colorful way."

Fink shook the professor's hand heartily. "Waal, if'n you say so, Jim, then no hard feelin's, right?"

"Right."

"C'mon back this way sometime 'n' set a spell."

Phillimore shivered. "Don't say 'spell'! I never want to hear that word again!"

Fink uttered a hearty laugh, then ruffled Rimski's fur. "Wanna come 'long with me 'n' Ella, ol man?"

"No"—the cat shook his head—"I'll be all right. Have a good trip home."

The ferryman said a final farewell, then started off on his journey, rifle in hand, filled thermos ever after at his side.

Phillimore frowned at the cat.

"Why didn't you go with him?"

"I didn't want to, that's why. Such a genius you have to be to figure?"

"But damn it, you *know* I'm leaving."

"I know." The cat yawned and licked his paw.

"Well, damn it, I can't leave you behind with a busted leg!"

"I know," Rimski said smugly.

"But I may *never* come back!"

"I know, I *know* . . . what's so great here, anyhow? So long as you don't fly me someplace where there's no milk, everything is okay by me."

The professor shrugged. "In that case . . ."

He pressed the release button on the umbrella and the vast folds of the hood unfurled, blotting out the world of Faërie from their view.

As they disappeared (smile lattermost in Rimski's case), the cat wondered whether his friend really had no regrets about leaving.

"You loved Snow White, Ella, Beauty, or at least you thought so," Rimski meowed. "Do you wish you could've—"

"The only thing I wish," Phillimore yelled to make his voice heard over the roar of the cosmic winds, "is that they all live happily ever after!"

And they did.

Part II

"It's my turn!" Leila declared.

"I *beg* your pardon!" Fleta contradicted, stamping her dainty foot. "It's *my* turn, sis!"

"No, it's not!"

"Yes, it is!"

"Not, not, *not!*"

"Too, *too,* TOO!"

Boris Frankenstein stifled a yawn. The great creature sat beneath an alder, weary beyond recounting. Maybe it was the rarified fare of the fairy forest that depleted his reserves of energy; truly he felt enormously anemic. On the other hand, perhaps it was *not* the food.

"I say 'tis *my* day to serve this quaint gent," Leila insisted.

"Greedy pig!" Fleta spat spitefully. "You served him these three days hence!"

"You say me false!"

"True!"

"False!"

"*True!*"

Into the glade tripped the Fairy Queen, petulantly swishing her magic wand. "Here, here, what manner of disharmony have we, ladies? This behaviour 'tain't seemly, it smacks of mortal fray."

The two fey sisters spoke simultaneously, advancing each her particular claim upon the pitiable monster slumped against the trunk of the alder-tree.

The queen signaled impatiently for silence. "If you do not reconcile yourselves to our customary condition of gentle unanimity of viewpoint and voice, I shall dispossess ye both of service for the nonce, and take up the slack myself!"

Boris groaned at the idea.

Leila and Fleta, who knew their sovereign would use any excuse to steal more time with Boris, smiled sheepishly at one another. As the universal accompaniment sweetly stole over the scene, they warbled and trilled a thoroughly Gilbertian duet of unanimous assent to the will of the queen, characteristically adding a *sotto voce* chorus depicting their cleverness at thwarting the will of their queen.

Halfway through the second verse, Boris sneaked off to catch some sleep. He had a favorite hiding-place within a hollow log, a secret spot he resorted to with increasing frequency as the long summer nights crept by.

Morning. The trilling of a bird. Boris stirred. With a mighty yawn, he stealthily poked his head out of the log.

The first thing he saw was a pair of yellow unblinking eyes staring curiously into his own watery orbs.

"*Vayzmir, boss!*" said a grumbly, somewhat thickly-accented voice. "*This* must *be him! What I call creatively ugly!*"

With a growl, Boris clambered forth . . . and saw none other than this old friend James Phillimore, smiling at him with outstretched arms.

The professor endured a bone-crunching hug of affection.

"Am I *glad* to see you!" Boris happily howled. He did not exaggerate. The last time the professor visited him, the fairies left him alone for several blissful days. "O Mighty Phillimore, regale me with thine latest ventures, *do!*"

"Well, Boris," said the dimensional traveler, "it's rather a *long* story. . . ."

"Thou wert ever the bearer of happy tidings!" Boris exclaimed, tears of relief welling in his eyes.

Before he allowed the professor to begin, the monster hosted him to the central glade, making sure to bring the presence of his friend to the attention of the Fairy Queen. Then he ordered breakfast for all.

Phillimore introduced everyone to his feline companion, Rimski. Then as soon as milk and melon were set before the company, he began his story.

It took all day to tell. Boris languished languidly and listened, hanging on every syllable. Often he stopped the professor to question a point, and once or twice, so enrapt was he with the narrative, that he asked some part to be told again.

But by the onset of evening, the tale was finally unfolded to the last turn. So unusual did the fairies find it that they, too, sat in the circle, taking in the details of Phillimore's amorous quest in the world of Faërie.

During the telling, many of the sprightly sisters vied for the opportunity to pet the shaggy cat, Rimski. They made a considerable fuss over his injured paw, and the queen herself bathed it with healing fey lotions. The animal purred happily, relishing the attention lavished on him that afternoon.

When night fell, Iolanthe rose and hustled up some of the customary delicate grub that Phillimore knew he must tolerate in Arcadia. *Mistcakes are hardly gut-stuffers,* he silently grumped, but considering the enormous spell of talking that he'd subjected his throat to, their blandly moist texture was not without reward.

But they'll never replace a pint of Watney's.

After supper, the professor said he was tired. So he and Rimski stretched out beside Boris (who insisted on their proximity) and the three friends almost instantly fell into the slumber of the virtuous, the innocent, the blameless, the blessed, the redeemed, and those that are just plain pooped.

As the world turns, so does the G&S planet likewise eke out the days of our lives in its own petty pace, and thus did James Phillimore rest for a time, temporarily soured on amatory quests. Meanwhile, Rimski's limb mended slowly, and the professor vainly sought assistance of all the doctors of the neighborhood, but none were acquainted intimately with feline anatomy, so at last the professor decided it was necessary to despatch his friend to a general hospital for animals in London.

The night before they were to go to the city, the guiding light of inspiration again visited Phillimore. Being young and restless, he could not endure the thought of eternal celibacy, and from a sense of duty to a hypothetical posterity, the professor at last hit upon another world where he thought he might discover the perfect mate.

So he called his friends to him and spoke thus of the promptings of his spirit: "As I have but one life to live, and since I have a great love of life, I must set out once more on my connubial search. All my children that yet might be demand it of me!"

Cocking his head, the cat looked quizzically and skeptically at him. "You didn't fare so well looking for her in the world of myth. Have you a better place in mind?"

"Yes, Rimski. My earlier mistake was picking a place solely because of the availability of comely women."

"Beauty ain't everything," Boris grunted.

"True," said Phillimore, "willingness counts for a great deal. Now there is a kind of fairy-tale place popular in my own world that includes both distaff physical attractiveness and a mature attitude towards love and sex upon the part of at least some of its women. In the infinity of worlds that the umbrella may take me to, I assume this fabled spot must also exist."

"And what is this marvelous place?" Rimski asked.

"A world based on what is known in my native country as 'daytime drama.'"

Neither of his comrades had ever heard of such an institution, so the professor briefly explained: "They're also known as soap operas . . . ongoing stories that chiefly deal with male-female relationships. These programs employ some of the loveliest, yet most palpably *real* women on all of television!"

The latter term was also totally foreign to his friends, so Phillimore described to them the mysteries and intricacies of kinescopes and iconoscopes, networks, sweeps, counterprogramming, ratings wars and also commercials.

At first the others attended with wonder and fascination, but slowly their eyes glazed and their heads drooped and when the professor was done, Rimski sighed and squeezed his lids shut tight; Boris stared stonily into space.

"Once, Mighty Phillimore," the monster muttered, "thou saidst that I hail from a world based on the horrors of thine own globe." His lips compressed. "Thou hast always been faithful to me, yet how may I countenance this thing you call television? I never encountered it on mine native planet. . . ."

The professor wanted to delay his umbrella flight till Rimski was all healed, but the cat would not permit his injury to delay the successful conclusion of his friend's quest. At last it was agreed that Boris would accompany the animal to London (the monster was eager to quit the glade, now that he had a satisfactory excuse to offer the powerful Fairy Queen).

"If you return here," said Boris, "I can be your Best Man!"

"Of course I'll return!" said the professor. "I want you and Rimski to be present at the festivities. And we'll go get Mike Fink, too!"

"He may prefer to be Best Man," the cat observed.

"Well, we can quibble about it later," Phillimore answered, privately wondering whether Boris' feelings would be hurt if he asked him to serve as Best Monster.

Rimski pouted. "And what about me?"

The monster patted his shaggy head. "You can be Best Cat."

"Hmpf. We'll see about that," he purred sulkily, but would not elaborate on his meaning.

Boris suggested Phillimore might want to set out at once, but he shook his head. "It's too dark. I don't care to fly by night. Besides, I want to see you and Rimski start on your journey before I employ the umbrella. I can certainly delay my search for tomorrow's necessary business. And now, I think I'd like to wash up before going to sleep."

Boris stood and brushed the grass-stains from the palms of his meaty paws. "O Dearest Benefactor, shall we not toast this night the success of our respective ventures?"

Phillimore grimaced. "Sure . . . if you can persuade the Fairy Queen to conjure up something huskier than that insipid Nectar!"

Winking, the monster said he'd do what he could. A few minutes later, beaming proudly, he returned with a bottle of rye, and soap for the professor's bath.

The three friends drank one another's health, Rimski lapping booze from a saucer.

They finished the bottle and snoozed the better part of the day. Thus it was late afternoon before Boris gently picked Rimski up in his enormous hands and started on his journey to the big city. The professor, despite his unwillingness to travel after dark, could not manage to clear his head and press the button of the umbrella till it was practically the edge of night.

Foggy, stormy evening. Not a wise time to negotiate the hairpin curves of Skyline Drive, but Myra left him no choice. After the things she said, the accusations she made, there was no way they could stay together, and so Brett packed his bags and threw them in the trunk of the station wagon, rain streaming down his face, lightning illuminating the countryside that sheltered the little lakehouse in the folds of a rise of oaks and maples, and all the while Myra stood by the door, shouting, screaming her anger which, he knew, was not a product of her best nature, but the excrescence of poison that Louisa Stone insidiously whispered to poor confused Myra, at a loss to know where she stood with Brett who could *not* tell her, no, that he *dared* not declare his desire to wed her now that she carried his child. . . .

A swirl of remembrance. Old Doctor Tom waggling his finger and head. A thin recollection of sound echoing and reechoing in Brett's tired, taxed brain.

DR. TOM

. . . can't recommend it, lad. You may go into remission, but if not, what then? Should you saddle Myra with a husband who'll rot before her eyes like an over-ripe fruit?

BRETT

And . . . and what about the baby? (ECHO: *the baby, the baby, the baby, the baby . . .*)

DR. TOM

(*SIGHING*) There's no danger. It's not hereditary. But do you want Brett Jr. to grow up with an old man who's a decaying fruit? (ECHO: *fruitfruitfruitfruit.*)

BRETT

No, I guess not.

The last bag in place, the trunk closed and latched, Brett turned to Myra, beautiful Myra, noticing yet again how desirable she was, especially when she was angry.

"If you walk out now, Brett, it's goodbye! And it's still goodbye if you don't tell me the truth."

"Whose truth?" he snapped. "Mine? Or Louisa Stone's?"

She only hoped that Louisa *was* wrong, but if she was, then now was the time for Brett to take her in his arms at last. But would he?

Will he?

"Goodbye, Myra."

"I mean it, Brett! If you leave now, I never want to see you again!"

As he drove off, he heard the word *never* repeatedly slashing him with its awful finality. *I'll never see Myra again. Never . . .*

It was the noblest thing. *But damn Louisa Stone!*

He pressed on the fuel, savagely wishing it was Louisa's lovely, spiteful face. The rain slanted across the windshield in sheets so thick he could not see anything but the white line of the road a few feet ahead of the front wheels.

Shouldn't be driving this fast. Dangerous.

Brett laughed a bitter laugh.

What do I care? Maybe I'll go off the road, maybe the car will burn and I'll die! What difference—

"OH, MY GOD!"

Brett twisted the wheel, shouting.

Myra was inclined to ignore the ringing of the bell, the pounding of the door. But he wouldn't stop, so at last she threw wide the portal.

"I told you never to come back, Brett!" She tried to bar the way, but he pushed her aside.

"I have to use your phone," he declared, his face white and tense. "I just ran over a man. And, my God, my God, I swear he appeared out of *nowhere!*"

Dark clouds swirling behind his closed eyelids confused him. He tried to will them away, but they had their own thoughts on the subject and would not accommodate him—

Him?

Who is "him"? he wondered, wincing from the pain of unaccustomed concentration. He could not manage the resolution of the question, so he returned his attention to the clouds. After what seemed like hours, he found the strength to open his eyes.

The first thing he saw was a poignantly beautiful blue-eyed blonde in nurse's white uniform and cap bending over him. When she saw him open his eyes, she smiled so happily that his heart skipped an entire cadence.

"Can you hear me?" she asked.

His throat was dry, he couldn't make it work, but at least he could nod his head slightly, enough to reply affirmatively.

"That's wonderful!" the nurse exclaimed. "Now you just rest up, I'm going to fetch Dr. Tom immediately!"

She hurried from his limited angle of vision, but in a few moments returned and told him he was under the care of the senior surgeon, Dr. Tom. Her head disappeared again and a kindly, aging male face hove into view.

Dr. Tom was a florid elderly physician with a habit of squinting nervously every few seconds. His features were doubtless once handsome, but age etched a veritable roadmap of secondary highways upon his face. He smiled down, asked a few polite questions, squinted, checked vital signs, then sat down at the side of the bed and patted his patient's hand.

"I realize you are still quite enervated, so I'd rather you don't exhaust yourself asking questions just yet. You had a close call, but we pulled you through the accident. You're in Regatta Heights Infirmary."

With great difficulty, moistening his lips, he managed to ask the physician what accident he was talking about.

"You were hit by a car."

"Ah."

"Though I really insist on your resting, before I leave you to do that, perhaps I should ask whether you have any relatives you want us to call. There've been no inquiries, and I'm afraid someone may be worried at your absence."

The patient wrinkled his forehead. "I . . . I'm afraid," he whispered, "that I can't remember."

Eyes narrowed, Dr. Tom frowned. "Can't remember what?"

"*Anything.* I don't even know my own name!"

The physician turned to the nurse and whispered a few words to her. She nodded, then went to a closet and rummaged through the pockets of the trousers the patient was wearing when he was first brought into Emergency. She returned with a billfold and handed it to her superior.

The doctor examined the wallet and found a neat white identificatory pasteboard. Withdrawing it, he held it beneath the invalid's nose.

"I assume this is your name, lad."

The patient's eyes focused with difficulty. He read the card.

> **J. ADRIAN FILLMORE**
> 38 C Pugh Street
> College Hills, Penna.
> 377-0725

"Sound familiar?" the physician inquired.

"Not really, Dr. Tom."

The older man smiled. "Oh, you doesn't have to call me Tom. You may use my first name."

"I thought I *was*. What *is* your first name?"

"Thomas."

Fillmore regarded him doubtfully as he left the room.

Resting back against the pillow, the patient yawned through a shielding hand, managed a wan smile in the nurse's direction and closed his eyes.

J. Adrian Fillmore, he repeated to himself. *Nice name. Dignified. I like it. . . .*

And, repeating it over and over to himself, he fell asleep.

She sidled into the room, glancing back to see whether she'd been followed. Satisfied no-one noticed her arrival, she shut the door and turned to her superior officer.

The government agent nodded at her and she sat.

"Have you learned anything new?" he asked.

"Yes." She reached into her purse and withdrew Fillmore's calling-card. "This was in his wallet. I really think he's lost his memory."

The agent glanced at the card, then turned it over and over in his fingers, eyes studying a spot on the wall some feet above the blonde's head. "Hmm," he mused, "a man materializes from nowhere. A car hits him and he loses his memory. His name appears to be that of a prominent literature professor. I wonder . . ." Suddenly he swiveled to his telephone, picked it up, dialed.

While he waited on Hold for his field researcher to run down the information, he turned back to the blonde. "How long did you say this 'Fillmore' was in a coma?"

"Five months."

"Hmm." Just then a voice sounded through the wire and he gave his attention to it. After a short time, he hung up.

"Well?" she asked.

"J. Adrian Fillmore is at this moment teaching a class in Shakespeare. Your patient is indeed an impostor."

"Then . . . ?"

"Then either the United States has a new weapon, or we have our first genuine space-traveler in our reach, *tovarich!*" A transitory doubt shadowed his brow. "Unless your source is mistaken. . . ."

The blonde smiled icily. "Brett has never told me a lie."

"Very well," the agent replied, "then we must carefully investigate the scene of the accident in case—"

The lithe woman interrupted by getting to her feet and opening her long coat. "I already have. I found *this* in the bushes. . . ."

She placed a large, garishly-colored umbrella on his desk.

His face fell. "An *umbrella?*"

"That's all I found. Shall I try again?"

"No, no, your thoroughness is a byword in the service. There's nothing else to do except see that the fellow is brought around gradually to remember who he is. And as the clouds of amnesia disperse, you must be there to glimpse through the rifts."

She frowned. "That will be difficult. Dr. Ryan has been assigned to his case."

"Not *Myra* Ryan?"

"The same. Ever since Brett Richards recovered, things have gone downhill with the friendship I deliberately built up with Myra. They're engaged now, and I no longer have her confidence."

"Well," her boss drawled, "I've never known you to be stumped by such a minor obstacle. After all, this bogus Fillmore is in your care. Surely you can think of something."

Louisa Stone licked her lips, the ghost of a smile twitching at their corners. "Something might occur." She rose, smoothed down her dress. "Shall I give him back his umbrella?"

"Not yet. There may be something about it we're missing, a secret message compartment, perhaps. I believe I'd better study it. . . ."

Several days later, when Louisa telephoned the agent to report her progress, she did not get an answer. Worried, she hurried to his office.

It was empty. He was gone.

She checked to see whether he'd been recalled, but the central office could not enlighten her.

It was as if he'd vanished into thin air.

Bells pealed. As the groom lifted the bridal veil and saluted his mate's lips, a soprano of Wagnerian girth cut off the carillon with an imposing slice of her hand that made the balcony on which she stood tremble. Her gesture was a signal for the organist; he played the introductory chords of "Oh Promise Me" and the large woman made an heroic effort to bellow on key.

Below, the couple strode up the aisle, he looking perplexed, she triumphant. Behind them walked Dr. Thomas Tom who, since neither had relatives or friends in town, had consented to give away the bride who, after all, *was* one of his nurses, all of whom he thought of as daughters.

At least Myra and Brett Richards had arrived at the last minute, their teenage son in tow. (Brett, Jr., their sole offspring, only recently had returned from school abroad.) The Richardses were not there because of any consideration for the bride, but each cared about the groom for different reasons. He was, after all, Myra's patient and she wanted desperately for him to regain his memory; never before had she encountered such a complete case of amnesia and her compassion for her subject was intermingled with personal fears of inadequacy because so far she'd had no success effecting his cure. Brett, on the other hand, still felt enormous guilt because he'd hit the groom with his car, thus causing his loss of memory in the first place. He blamed himself, too, for what he regarded as a disastrous nuptial event.

Louisa attempted to hug Brett, but he pulled away, bestowed a limp handshake upon her and drew her husband to one side.

"I hope you'll be happy," he said without much conviction. "I still think you might've waited, though."

"What for?" Fillmore wondered, pumping Brett's hand.

"Don't you feel it dangerous to marry without knowing who you are?"

It'd be damned awkward to wake up one morning and recall you have a wife already stowed elsewhere."

"Louisa was worried about that, too, but I'm positive I'm single."

Overhearing the remark, Myra joined the two men. "What's this? Have you finally recalled some detail of your past?"

"Not really," said Fillmore, running his finger around the inside of his uncomfortably tight formal collar. "I just have a feeling that I never met anyone in my life like Louisa. And I'm *so* worried about saddling her with my problems, Myra! I'm still not well. Time is so *peculiar* for me." He passed a hand across his forehead; his eyes wore a dazed expression. "Ever since I came out of that coma, I've been disoriented. I black out frequently, each time for precisely two minutes. Some days, moments stretch out until, before I know it, the sun is down and I never noticed. Other times, things move so swiftly that though I see the results of some action I performed, I cannot recall ever having done the thing. But the weekends are worst of all!"

"What happens then?" Brett asked.

"Fridays are my most normal days, everything tends to function in real time (always excepting the blackouts). Then all of a sudden, it's Monday! I know I've been asleep all weekend, yet I can't remember ever having gone to bed. And whatever the last thing was that I did on Friday still seems to be taking place. All over again! And yet the calendar has been torn off and it's Monday!" He pressed Myra's palm with fond fervency. "What does it all mean, Myra, what does it all mean?"

"It's a product of your accident," she said, without much conviction. "Eventually it'll stabilize and you'll have your memory back." She restrained herself from adding "I hope." Myra then changed the subject, contributed briefly to the small talk, then, excusing herself, pulled Louisa aside.

"I hope you're aware that Adrian is still recuperating?"

"Yes, Myra. Why?"

"He adores you. I don't want you to hurt him."

A flash of pique tightened the blonde's features, but quickly disappeared. "Myra, I admit you have some reason to think ill of me. So I'm going to confess that when I first paid attention to Adrian, it was for a selfish motive. But it's gone now."

"Are you sure?"

"Ah, yes. Shall we say it, uh . . . *vanished?*" the blonde uttered, a faint smile-line curling her cheek. "And now I am deeply, unselfishly in love for the first time in my life!"

Noting the sparkle of the bride's eyes and the radiance flaming on her cheeks, the psychiatrist said, "Louisa, maybe I'm a damn-fool romantic, but I'm disposed to believe you!"

"Do, please!" Louisa impulsively pressed the other's hand. *"I've never been so happy in my life. . . ."*

Overhead, the Wagnerian soprano leaned against the balcony rail. It groaned rustily and dislodged a great chunk of stone from the side of the mezzanine.

The singer attained C above high C as the big block hurtled downward towards Louisa.

Dr. Brett Richards Jr., staff psychiatrist at Regatta Heights Hospital, doubtfully eyed the bushy-haired gentleman in gray seated in the swivel chair on the other side of his desk.

"The individual you're inquiring about," the doctor explained, "is one of my outpatients. I cannot reveal any of his personal—"

"Please, please," the other interrupted, nervously fingering the straggly whiskers bristling beneath his squat nose, "I wouldn't want you should violate your professional ethics. All I'm asking is for the public facts."

Dr. Richards exchanged a suspicious, furtive glance with the sad-eyed nurse standing behind the gray-haired visitor. Her lips compressed when she heard his foreign intonation of English.

"Could you tell me his name again, doctor?" the man asked.

"J. Adrian Fillmore."

"Hmm," the stranger mused, the ghost of a dour smile shivering his upper lip. "Very good. Now please share the public facts with me."

"Very well," Dr. Richards replied, casting a concerned glance at his nurse. She was biting a knuckle in considerable agitation. "It's a long story. Years ago, my late father hit Fillmore with his car. Dad always claimed he popped out of nowhere. Fillmore was badly hurt, but he recovered. However, the accident caused almost total amnesia. He was in the old Regatta Heights Infirmary, on the ground of which this hospital is built. He and his nurse, Louisa Stone, fell in love and were married. But on their wedding day, she was dreadfully injured by a loose stone block that fell from a balcony. After six months in intensive care, Louisa seemed to die and—"

The man in gray, looking rather distressed, held up a hand to halt the flow of words. "What do you mean she '*seemed* to die'?"

"A sad story. She's a cataleptic. They were going to cremate her. But at the last instant, an attendant noticed the perspiration and knew she was not dead. Eventually she totally recovered."

The other nodded. "Then she's Fillmore's wife."

The physician shook his head. "No, for shortly after Louisa was admitted to the hospital, my father died of an obscure disease that he supposedly had been cured of. That was just before old Dr. Tom was disbarred and went into politics. Now poor Fillmore was so upset at Louisa's accident, he talked over his grief with his psychiatrist, my mother, Myra Ryan Richards. But when my father died, my mother was so grief-stricken that she talked it all out with J. Adrian Fillmore, who'd studied psychiatry in his spare time while he waited for Louisa to recuperate. Well, by the time Louisa appeared to drop dead, Fillmore and my mother were deeply in love and they immediately married when they learned Louisa was supposedly no more."

"Rather hasty behaviour, wouldn't you say?" the chubby stranger commented.

"Well," said the doctor, "considering my mother was several months pregnant, it was not totally reprehensible."

"Then she and Fillmore are the parents of your half-sibling?"

"No. My mother miscarried. That occurred when she learned of Louisa's resurrection. It was a complicated legal tangle, but Louisa finally permitted a divorce and now Fillmore is my patient and . . . well, I can't talk about *that*."

The man in gray mopped his brow. "Perhaps that's just as well. All this *angst* is too much for me to handle, let alone the time factor—"

"Time factor? What do you mean?"

The other waved the point away. "No more. My head feels like it's filled with two-cents-plain! But tell me, where is this Fillmore now?"

"Out of town. I prescribed a vacation for him and my mother. It's connected with the difficulties he's seeing me about."

"When do they return?"

"Soon. I'm not sure which day, though."

"Mm-hmm. And Louisa Stone? How may I locate her?"

"Search me," said the physician. "She left town years ago."

Sighing, the curious stranger rose. "Oh, one last thing," he remarked, hand on the door-handle. "When Fillmore was admitted to the infirmary for the auto accident involving your father, do you know whether he had any—ah—*unusual* object in his possession?"

"You're asking me about an event that took place before I was born," Dr. Richards replied stiffly.

With a dismayed lift of his shoulders, the man left. As soon as he was gone, the thin, sad-eyed blonde nurse collapsed into a chair. The psychiatrist circled round his desk and placed his hands comfortingly on her shoulders.

"It's all right, Louisa, he's gone. But surely you're not going to tell me he's connected with your old secret-agent fantasy?"

"Damn it, Brett, it's not a fantasy! Why won't you believe me?"

"I'm not supposed to," he replied simply. "I'm your psychiatrist."

She pulled away from his touch and spoke aloud to herself. "I always was afraid that sooner or later someone would show up from headquarters investigating my boss' disappearance. Now this man arrives, asking questions about whether Adrian has any odd possessions. That means my superior must have transmitted his suspicions about that weird umbrella to HQ before he fiddled with the contraption and vanished."

"Are you afraid, Louisa? Do you feel you are in danger?"

"Not me, you fool! I'm worried about Adrian."

"Fillmore? You still have feelings for him?" Brett sighed.

She exhaled noisily. "Goddamnit, don't you *ever* pay attention when I'm talking on the couch? What kind of bargain-basement shrink—"

But she was cut off by the sudden opening of the door. In walked an agitated old ex-Dr. Tom clad in pinstripe suit covered with campaign buttons. An unlit cigar dangled from his lips; his face was pale, his jaw set in a stern line.

Brett asked, "What's the matter, old ex-Dr. Tom?"

"I have terrible tidings," he said, squinting fiercely. "Brace yourself, lad . . . your mother is dead."

The psychiatrist promptly collapsed.

"Confound it," old ex-Dr. Tom grumbled, "I *told* him to brace himself."

Louisa grasped his arm. "Then Myra is gone?" He gravely inclined his head. "And what about Adrian? Is he—"

"We-e-e-ell," he interrupted, "I have both good and bad news about our old friend Fillmore."

Louisa sucked in air to control her impatience. *"Well?"*

"The good news is that he got in a fight and nearly had his block knocked off—"

"That's the *good* news?"

"Let me finish. The blow to his skull brought back his memory. Now the bad news: his fight was with a man the police assume was Myra's lover. The authorities think Fillmore shot them both."

At which point, Louisa collapsed, too.

Old ex-Dr. Tom squinted, squared his shoulders, stuck his stogie in an ashtray on Brett's desk, muttered, "Aww, what the hell," and also fell on the floor.

On the opening day of J. Adrian Fillmore's murder trial, the new judge stood in front of the mirror in his chambers, primping. The son of an impoverished linotype operator, the elderly magistrate was proud of finally achieving a lofty civic position.

Not that I haven't worked hard for it! Refusing to learn his father's trade, he'd scrimped and slaved and saved until he could afford to enter college and study medicine. After graduation, he rose slowly but steadily to the exalted post of senior surgical resident at Regatta Heights Infirmary, later becoming chief surgeon at the hospital of the same name. And then . . . a meteoric rise in the political sphere, which he'd entered after his "retirement." His services with the county election machine led to nomination to a slot on the revenue review board which, in turn, paved the way for his honorary law degree. After that, it was a simple matter of high legislative redaction to clear the statutory path toward attaining the state supreme court judgeship.

He chuckled to himself. *Pretty neat accomplishment for old Tom Tom, the typer's son!*

Adjusting his black robes, he stepped into the corridor with his sternest no-nonsense squint to show he was an arbiter to be reckoned with; nodding at the bailiff, he strode into court and seated himself at the Bench.

In the front row sat Louisa Stone, looking worried and sad. He bestowed a slight nod and subtle wink in her direction.

Damn, thought Louisa, *the wages of sin and all that stuff!* But she knew she had to go through with it, for after all, she was not proud of the evil, spiteful things she once did in her youth and now that Adrian was in danger, no course lay before her but to sacrifice herself for his salvation.

Well, she mused bitterly, *I always said security counted more than love.* . . .

Just then, out of the corner of her eye she caught a glimpse of gray. Turning anxiously, she saw, there in the first row of the spectators' section on the opposite side of the central aisle, the chubby foreigner in the old-fashioned Mad. Ave. suit. Perhaps sensing her scrutiny, he hunched back on the long bench so he was hidden by a bald, bearded tall man to his right. As she continued to stare, the nearer individual turned and smiled rakishly at Louisa.

She looked away, having seen enough. She knew what the man in gray had been staring at intently before he realized she was watching him.

He'd had his eyes riveted on an object resting on the prosecutor's table . . . a large, garishly-colored umbrella too big for street use, yet too small for beach employment as a sunshade.

The thing was clearly labeled STATE EXHIBIT A.

(THE COURTROOM. THE ASSISTANT PROSECUTOR IS IN THE MIDDLE OF HIS OPENING REMARKS).

ASST. D.A.
And the State concedes that this must have been the unpremeditated act of an irrational man, the crazed consequence of both physical and psychological shocks to the psyche of a person whose mental health has not been stable since he arrived in—

FILLMORE
(OUTRAGED, HE JUMPS TO HIS FEET) I object! The competency of the defendant has not been proven or disproved at this stage.

THE JUDGE
Don't act like a nut, lad. You know you've been out of your gourd for years.

FILLMORE
May we approach the Bench, Your Honor?

THE JUDGE
(SIGHING) If you *have* to. . . .

(FILLMORE AND THE ASSISTANT D.A. SPEAK TO THE JUDGE IN WHISPERED COLLOQUY).

THE JUDGE
Why make such a fuss, lad? The best way to let you off light is to prove you're a Hoo-Hah Loony!

FILLMORE
But I didn't murder him!

THE JUDGE
Well, maybe Jack here can cool it for the time being?

ASST. D.A.
I'll outline the facts of the case as we see them, then I'll be finished.

THE JUDGE

Good. I've got a lunch date I want to spruce up for.

(FILLMORE EYES THE UMBRELLA ON THE PROSECUTOR'S TABLE).

FILLMORE

(SLYLY) If you'd just allow me to examine the umbrella in your chambers, Your Honor, I could clear this whole thing up one-two-three.

THE JUDGE

Nothing doing! This is my first big case!

ASST. D.A.

No soap. That's State's evidence. I can't permit you to put your hands on the bumbershoot.

(FILLMORE, LOOKING EXASPERATED, RETURNS TO THE DEFENSE TABLE. THE JUDGE NODS HIS HEAD AND THE PROSECUTOR AGAIN ADDRESSES THE JURY).

ASST. D.A.

What apparently occurred that evening is that the defendant went out to buy some food at a local diner. He and his wife, the dead woman, intended to have dinner in their motel room. When Mr. Fillmore returned, what he evidently discovered was his wife in the arms of another man. There was a struggle, during which the defendant freely admits he was bashed over the head with an umbrella. He claims to have lost consciousness and says that when he revived, he found both his wife and his assailant dead. The State contends that what really happened is that the defendant shot and killed both Myra Ryan Richards Fillmore and the as-yet-unidentified second man during what he has termed a "blackout." The State means to show that the defendant has a history of such psychologically peculiar incidents, and that during one, J. Adrian Fillmore was capable of, and indeed did murder two persons.

(THE PROSECUTOR SITS DOWN).

THE JUDGE

The Defense may present its opening argument. (HE GESTURES FOR THE ATTORNEYS TO APPROACH THE BENCH). Are you sure you don't want me to appoint an attorney for you, lad?

FILLMORE

No, dammit! If you would allow me to show you a peculiarity of that umbrella . . .

ASST. D.A.

I already told you—no tampering with State's evidence!

THE JUDGE

Well, lad? Shall I get you a competent lawyer? (FILLMORE SHAKES HIS HEAD) Very well. But you're a pigheaded fool. (TO COURT STENOGRAPHER) Don't put *that* in the record, stupid!

THE CLERK

How do you spell "stupid"? One *P* or two?

(THE JUDGE SIGHS AND DISMISSES THEM. THE CLERK AND THE PROSECUTOR SIT. FILLMORE GLANCES AT THE JURY, GRIMACING WITH DISGUST).

FILLMORE

Look, the only mental problem I've had is years of amnesia. That night, when I came back with food for my poor late wife, Myra, I found a strange man holding her at gunpoint. He swung around. I ducked. Maybe he didn't want to fire in a motel room where the shot could be heard. Instead he swung an umbrella at me, knocking me on the head. I passed out. When I came to, I finally remembered who I am. And I knew the umbrella I'd been hit with belongs to me. I opened my eyes, but the stranger was sprawled across the bed, dead. So was my wife. I searched for the umbrella, saw it underneath the bed. Just as I was reaching for it, the door burst open and police entered and arrested me. That's all I know.

(FILLMORE SITS DOWN).

THE JUDGE

The State may call its first witness.
(SHAKES HEAD: VOICE-OVER OF HIS THOUGHTS)
Worst excuse for an opening argument . . . the lad's doomed. . . .

During the testimony of the police witness, J. Adrian Fillmore slouched low in his chair and silently groused.

Well, here's another fine mess I've gotten myself into! He'd been so intent on securing for himself *la dame juste* that he'd neglected to analyze the probable dangers of a world that operated on the underlying plot devices and traditions of TV soap operas. *Such as a high percentage of melodramatic misfortunes: accidents, rare diseases, amnesia, & c.—as they say in D'Oyly Carte libretti.* . . .

ASST. D.A.

And then what happened, Officer Horton?

POLICEMAN

I read the suspect his rights and affixed handcuffs to his wrists.

And what about the time factor? the professor worried. *There's nothing constant on soaps, except when they mention something will happen on Friday, and then it's sure to coincide, just to "cliffhang" the viewers till the weekend's over. Otherwise, soap opera time is illogical and unpredictable, the whim of the writers. Kids go away at age five and return three years later as college sophomores.* . . .

ASST. D.A.

And is that suspect in this courtroom?

POLICEMAN

I see him there.

THE JUDGE

Let the record indicate that the witness pointed to the defendant.

ASST. D.A.

No further questions, Your Honor.

THE JUDGE

Lad?

FILLMORE

No questions at this time, Your Honor. The Defense will recall the witness.

THE JUDGE

(STARTLED) What the hell for?

FILLMORE

I'd rather not go into that now. . . .

(SUDDENLY, HIS HEAD SLUMPS ONTO THE DEFENSE TABLE).

Two minutes later, after Fillmore came to, the prosecutor called his second witness, the motel clerk. While that individual went through the business of identifying the suspect as the man who signed his register that night and also recounted the sounds of struggle and gunshots from that room unit, the professor drummed his fingers impatiently and thought about the subsumption problem. *According to Holmes, there oughtn't to be one.* . . .

The Great Detective once theorized to Fillmore that his incredible umbrella responded to the thoughts of its user and therefore ought to do whatever was expected of it. Certain principles of energy conservation governed its employment, so that one could not ply it again immediately after it made an universal hop, but Holmes contended there was absolutely no logical reason why the professor should have to "finish a sequence" before escaping any given world. Nor should it be possible to become "subsumed," a concept which the sorcerer who manufactured the parasol once defined as the wholehearted mental acceptance of the axioms and tenets on which any given planet was formulated. Subsumption meant that if Fillmore participated too heartily in the soap-opera world, he might find himself permanently stuck there—a prospect that was extremely unappealing, considering . . . but he couldn't even bring himself to think about *that* problem at the moment.

The monkey-wrench, he supposed, was his own sense of literary form. Something within was extremely reluctant to allow him to escape the world he was on without somehow rounding out his adventures in a manner befitting the style of the place as he induced it. Of course, the fact that he immediately lost his umbrella upon arrival on the soap-opera planet precluded his putting his suspicions to the test, but the fact that he blacked out frequently—*right where the commercials would be liable to come*—profoundly disquieted him; it strongly suggested he might be so deeply enmired as to be incapable of extricating himself.

I'm just lucky the umbrella popped up again. How the stranger holding Myra at gunpoint managed to have it in his possession, Fillmore did not know, but he theorized that he was some kind of villain who, by chance, happened on the device and learned something of its usage. If he was aware it once belonged to the amnesia victim at Regatta Heights Infirmary, he might well wish to interrogate him abouts its properties and origins. *But why'd he wait so long? Did he use it and get stuck on another world? That would fit. And there'd be two factors that might well make him show up right in our motel room: his own mentally communicated desires, and also the preponderance of coincidence in soap opera plots.* . . .

ASST. D.A.

No more questions, Your Honor.

THE JUDGE

Does Defense wish to question the motel clerk?

FILLMORE

No, thanks. I'll probably recall the witness later.

THE JUDGE

Will Counsel approach the Bench?

(THEY DO SO).

Are you trying to get off, lad, by acting like a nut?

FILLMORE

(STIFFLY) I beg your pardon?

THE JUDGE

(WEARILY) Oh, never mind. Let's get on with this. I've got a lunch date.

The thing to do, Fillmore mused as he sat again, *is find the fine line between participation and subsumption and never stray over it. Now that I know the world I'm in, I can manipulate its premisses and get myself acquitted. But—will the umbrella still work for me?*

He glanced over his shoulder at the spectators, wondering why one of them looked vaguely familiar. *Well, if I'm permanently stuck here, at least there's Louisa . . . funny how she reminds me of Cinderella!*

But there was still his *problem,* the one he was going to Brett Jr. about. Could he solve it? Could he ask Louisa to countenance such an humiliating thing? Was it fair?

Damn it, there I go again! Too much participation!

Louisa saw Fillmore look at her, and she smiled wanly. *I have to save him!*

She leaned forward and casually checked up on the man in gray. Again he hunched back in his seat and the big bald man with the beard hid him from her view. Again the tall, hirsute stranger flashed a disquieting smile in her direction. . . .

The assistant district attorney cleared his throat and called his final witness. Louisa's brows knit. She turned to see whether it was a surprise to Fillmore as well.

It was. The professor blacked out again.

THE JUDGE

(SOURLY) If the defendant is awake . . . ?

FILLMORE

(NERVOUSLY) I'm not asleep.

THE JUDGE

Goo-oo-ood! (TO PROSECUTOR) Your witness.

ASST. D.A.

State your name and profession.

BRETT JR.

Brett Richards Jr., chief psychiatrist, Regatta Heights Hospital.

ASST. D.A.

Are you acquainted with the defendant?

BRETT JR.

(NODS) He's my patient.

ASST. D.A.

What precisely are his problems?

FILLMORE

(LEAPING TO HIS FEET) I object!

THE JUDGE

Overruled.

FILLMORE

(FURIOUS) Why?

THE JUDGE

I don't have to tell you.

FILLMORE

May we approach the Bench?

THE JUDGE

There's nothing to discuss. Request denied.

FILLMORE

The witness cannot be permitted to answer.

BRETT JR.

I don't mind.

THE JUDGE

Look, lad, I'm in a hurry. Sit down and let's get this turkey done with.

FILLMORE

But he's asking him to violate a professional code of privileged information. (TO BRETT JR.) You *know* you should refuse to reply.

BRETT JR.

(SHRUGS) So sue me.

THE JUDGE

Defendant will kindly sit down, or I'll hold you in contempt.

FILLMORE

The feeling's mutual. I move for a mistrial.

THE JUDGE

Petition denied.

FILLMORE

(SITTING) If I lose, I'm appealing.

THE JUDGE

Win or lose, you're repulsive. (TO CLERK) Read the question to the witness.

THE CLERK

"What precisely are his problems?"

BRETT JR.

He's an amnesiac. Or was. He blacks out for precisely two minutes at a time.

ASST. D.A.

As has been observed in this very courtroom, Your Honor.

THE JUDGE

I saw, I *saw*.

ASST. D.A.

Are there any other psychological problems, Dr. Richards?

BRETT JR.

Oh, yes. The main one he came to me for in the first place.

ASST. D.A.

Its nature?

BRETT JR.

Sexual.

ASST. D.A.

Describe it.

FILLMORE

(SCREAMING) *I OBJECT!!!*

THE JUDGE

Overruled. (TO WITNESS) Go ahead, lad, get to the hot stuff.

BRETT JR.

Mr. Fillmore has a strange sexual problem. Whenever he attempts to engage in romantic endeavor, he blacks out.

ASST. D.A.

You mean the way we witnessed earlier?

BRETT JR.

No. This is an entirely different kind of blackout.

ASST. D.A.

Please describe it.

FILLMORE

(HOARSELY) I object.

(NOT DEIGNING TO REPLY, THE JUDGE NODS AT THE WITNESS)

BRETT JR.

His two-minute blackouts are true bouts of fainting. When those spells occur, Mr. Fillmore loses all consciousness and his body falls into a sleep mode. But the blackouts he undergoes at intimate moments are sheerly a mental phenomenon. Bodily, he apparently functions as expected. But his mind blanks. It's like a curtain was drawn between him and the scene in progress. (PUZZLED) It's very odd. It's almost as if he felt he had to censor himself from seeing what takes place.

(A BLONDE IN THE FRONT ROW GASPS).

ASST. D.A.

I see. Now, doctor, answer this next question very carefully, after giving it proper weight and consideration.

BRETT JR.

I'll do my best.

ASST. D.A.

Is it conceivable that, under extreme stress, this "sexual" type of blackout might occur to the defendant in a nonromantic moment? That he might see something so shocking that his mind quits while his body still performs some action or other?

BRETT JR.

Oh, yes, it's possible. If he saw, say, another man making love to the woman he himself—

FILLMORE

I object to this entire line of questioning!

ASST. D.A.

Your Honor, the State has been attempting to prove the defendant might have shot the two victims during one of these mental hiatuses. . . .

THE JUDGE

(NODS) Sounds plausible. You may proceed.

ASST. D.A.

I have no further questions.

THE JUDGE

Well, lad? Do you intend to recall this witness as well?

FILLMORE

(RISING) No. I have two questions I want to ask him.

THE JUDGE

Go ahead.

FILLMORE

Dr. Richards . . . are you in love with Louisa Stone?

(ANOTHER GASP FROM THE BLONDE IN THE FIRST ROW).

BRETT JR.

Your Honor, am I required to answer?

THE JUDGE

(TESTILY) Yes, damn you!

BRETT JR.

Very well. The answer is—yes.

(GENERAL CONSTERNATION. THE JUDGE RAPS FOR ORDER).

FILLMORE

In that case, haven't you broken your professional code by revealing aspects of my personal life merely to make Louisa think twice about marrying me again?

BRETT JR.

(SOFTLY) Yes.

FILLMORE

Therefore your testimony concerning my condition is extremely suspect.

BRETT JR.

But my mother's files verify you've had the same problem for years!

(HUBBUB. THE JUDGE RAPS HIS GAVEL).

FILLMORE

(BLUSHING) No further questions.

ASST. D.A.

No questions, Your Honor.

THE JUDGE

The witness may step down.

(BRETT JR. LEAVES THE COURTROOM).

ASST. D.A.

That concludes the case for the Prosecution.

THE JUDGE

There will be a two-minute recess. When the defendant wakes up, we'll hear the case for the Defense.

Well, this is it, Fillmore thought. *Friday afternoon in soap opera land and it's my turn.* "A crisis now affairs are coming to!"

He rose and approached the Bench. The prosecutor, looking rather curious, joined him.

"*Now* what?" Judge Tom rasped. "You haven't done anything yet, how can you have a question?"

"I want permission," said Fillmore, "to call more than one witness at a time."

"And what do you intend to do with more than one witness on the stand?" Hizzoner inquired sarcastically. "Elicit antiphonal responses? Or stage an orgy?"

Inhaling slowly to maintain his equilibrium, the professor answered, "I'll be done sooner if you'll just say yes."

"Okay by you?" the judge asked the prosecuting attorney. That worthy shrugged eloquently. "In that case, lad, you go right ahead and make a fool of yourself."

Fillmore turned to the bailiff and told him to recall the police officer and the motel clerk. A moment later, the pair stood in the witness box, jostling each other for space.

Said the professor: "Gentlemen, earlier you positively swore that I am the man you met on the night of the tragedy. Do you still maintain that position?"

THE CLERK

Of course.

POLICEMAN

Absolutely.

FILLMORE

You couldn't possibly be mistaken?

THE CLERK

Positively not.

POLICEMAN

Impossible.

(*Whoops. Don't participate so freely, straddle the fine line!* In an attempt to back away from the subsumption threat, the professor paused and sipped some water. Then he told the bailiff to summon the sole remaining witness for the Defense.)

THE JUDGE

Another witness?

POLICEMAN

There's no more room in here!

Fillmore tried to ignore the impulse to play the melodrama for all it was worth. Just then, the new witness walked into court. The buzz from the spectators waxed to a loud drone and the judge had to pound for silence.

The witness was slightly below medium height, wore academic garb but sported a colorful ascot about his full neck. Fillmore instructed him to state his name and occupation.

"J. Adrian Fillmore, literature professor, Parker College, Pennsylvania."

(A GREAT HUBBUB. THE JUDGE RAPS HIS GAVEL FURIOUSLY).

FILLMORE

(POINTS HISTRIONICALLY AT THE CLERK AND THE POLICEMAN) And now . . . can either of you swear which one of us you actually saw that night?

THE CLERK

(AFTER A BRIEF SILENCE) I can't tell the two of you apart.

FILLMORE

And you, sir?

(THE POLICEMAN EXAMINES EACH FACE FOR A LONG TIME BEFORE SPEAKING).

POLICEMAN

No way I can distinguish between the pair.

FILLMORE

Defense is prepared to submit documentation attesting to the truth of the witness' identity. Also we are prepared to undergo fingerprinting to show we both possess the identical patterns. If the State does not so insist, I have no further questions.

But the prosecution did so insist, and the business proceeded for several minutes more until the judge ascertained that there were, in fact, two identical J. Adrian Fillmores bearing no relationship to one another.

THE JUDGE

The case for the Defense being completed, I will instruct the jury to—

ASST. D.A.

Excuse me, Your Honor, but the State has not cross-examined the witness for the Defense.

THE JUDGE

(LIVID) Will it take long?

ASST. D.A.

Only one question. (TO FILLMORE II) Do you suffer blackouts while making love?

FILLMORE II

(OUTRAGED) I certainly do *not!*

ASST. D.A.

No further questions.

Well, the professor groaned, *that's that! The fancy footwork failed. I'm doomed. Unless . . .*

Unless he could grab the umbrella. IF it would work.

He prepared to lunge towards the State exhibit table. But just at that moment, Louisa Stone stood up and spoke in a ringing voice that all could hear.

LOUISA

Stop the trial! This man is innocent!

(GENERAL CONFUSION. BROUHAHA).

THE JUDGE
(PEERING AT HER IN ASTONISHMENT) *Louisa?*

LOUISA
Yes, Tom. I know this is irregular, but I have important information that will—that MUST—affect the outcome of this trial!

Gazing fondly on his former wife, Fillmore totally forgot to resist participating in the soap opera world-set. *Gad, she's beautiful! Just like Cinderella!*

Neither attorney objected to hearing her testimony, so the judge permitted Louisa to enter the witness-box and take the oath.

LOUISA
As soon as the newspapers ran the photograph of the dead man, I recognized him. He was a Russian spy. I know because I once worked for him.

(ENORMOUS REACTION IN THE GALLERY).

I still have documents hidden in my room to prove what I say is true. I've brought a few here. (SHE OPENS PURSE) You'll see that one of them is a photo showing the deceased and myself at a party rally. (LOOKING SORROWFULLY AT FILLMORE) I hate to say this, but I have no choice . . . the deceased was my husband.

FILLMORE
No!

THE JUDGE
Louisa!

LOUISA
(CRYING) It's true! It's true! But it was inconvenient for us to appear as man and wife, he needed me to use my . . . oh, I can't say it! He was a beast!

Louisa broke into uncontrollable sobbing that lasted precisely the 120 seconds that Fillmore suddenly napped. After he woke and she gained control of her emotions, she told about her late spouse's speculations concerning the umbrella.

The judge eyed Fillmore with considerable curiosity and suspicion.

LOUISA

I believe my husband accidentally activated the mechanism and it took him somewhere from which he could not manage to return for several years. When he finally found a way back, he traced Adrian, arrived while he was out, tried to elicit information at gunpoint from Myra, then, when Adrian returned, they struggled and that's when he hit Adrian with the umbrella.

THE JUDGE

But he wouldn't go shoot himself and Myra while Fillmore was unconscious!

LOUISA

No, but *another* enemy agent would! My husband was a loner, he was always being reprimanded by headquarters for keeping things to himself till he could be sure of garnering all the credit. It's my contention that a spy from the central office entered the motel room while Adrian was out cold. They argued and who knows what took place? Perhaps shooting Myra was accidental. But I'm sure—

THE JUDGE

Now, now, Louisa, this is all quite ingenious of you, but after all, you're merely speculating there might be another secret agent. You don't know it for a fact.

LOUISA

Oh, yes I do! I know because that very person, that spy, that MURDERER is sitting here right in this courtroom! (RISING TO HER FEET, LOUISA POINTS DRAMATICALLY AT A SMALL, CHUBBY, BEWHISKERED INDIVIDUAL IN GRAY IN THE FRONT ROW OF THE SPECTATOR GALLERY) *That's him!*

The crisis happened swiftly and unexpectedly.

As soon as Louisa pointed, up leaped the tall, bald, bearded stranger next to the little man in gray. Screaming a Russian imprecation, the tall man withdrew a pistol and fired at Louisa.

She screamed, clutched her side and slumped to the floor.

FILLMORE

Louisa!

THE JUDGE

Darling!

The spectators, shrieking, scrambled to their feet and pushed and shoved to clear the courtroom. The clerk ducked. The bailiff yanked out his gun. But he lowered it without firing.

The bald assassin was flailing about blindly, yowling in pain. On his back, the man in gray clung with arms and legs and raked his long fingernails along the cheeks and temples of his prey.

Bounding over the railing, Fillmore seized the spy's gun hand and prized the weapon free. As soon as he did, several spectators turned about and tackled the big man, bringing him to the floor. The bailiff hurried over to his side and rapped his skull with a nightstick.

During the confusion, the little man in gray dashed to the exhibit table, snatched up the umbrella and disappeared through the first open door he could find.

In the judge's chambers, Louisa sat up groggily.

"Luckily," proclaimed His Honor old ex-Dr. Tom, "it was only a flesh wound." He lowered his voice and, anxiously squinting, said to Fillmore, "Don't let the A.M.A. find out I treated her without a license. . . ."

Fillmore regarded him with an expression of numb, hurt bewilderment.

"You called her 'darling.'"

"Yes, lad. Louisa and I are betrothed."

"Is that *true*, Louisa?" Fillmore searched her face anxiously.

"I'm afraid so," she replied wanly. "He took advantage of me several months ago. I'm carrying his child."

The professor squeezed his eyes shut tight.

"Well, I hope you'll be very happy together."

"Thanks, lad," the judge beamed. "I suppose you're free to go now. Sorry your umbrella was stolen."

Fillmore nodded without replying, shook the proffered hand, kissed Louisa lightly on the cheek and left.

Outside, on the courthouse steps, J. Adrian Fillmore sighed sadly and considered his options.

No choice. I'm stuck here now. I suppose eventually the umbrella might cross my path again. For that matter, if I wait long enough, perhaps Louisa will be free once more and I can marry her.

"But what about the baby?" he asked himself suddenly, aloud. The vaulting edifice behind him picked up the sound and made it reverberate in the wind . . . *the baby, the baby, the baby* . . .

In a soap opera world, the child would probably be full-grown in five or six years. He might resent Fillmore taking his father's place. There'd be friction in the household. Louisa and the kid would become estranged from the professor, the rotten brat would play them off against one another, and *who knows? He might even try to kill me!*

No, all in all, it was a lousy world to be trapped in. Fillmore swore to himself that if ever he got free, he'd be much more careful about where he'd travel next. But he was too honest with himself to really buy his own assertion. *Man can engender what he is himself. Nothing more.* He twisted his lips in a self-mocking smile. *There I go, quoting literature again, even when I'm thinking! Miserable, asocial pedant, that's what I—*

Just then, someone plucked at his sleeve. Turning, he was astounded to see standing just below him on the courthouse steps the small round man in gray.

"I figured you'd be missing this," he said, handing the umbrella to Fillmore. "I only grabbed it because I was afraid the State might latch onto it and refuse to let it go after that blonde dish described it so accurately."

"Much obliged," said Fillmore, narrowing his eyes, "but how do *you* know she was correct? Who *are* you?"

The other grinned. "Some difference, huh? You really don't recognize me?"

"Should I?"

"I'll give you a hint." With that the man in the gray suit slowly faded from sight, his smile the last thing to hover in the air. Then he popped back into view. "How's that, boss?"

"*Rimski!*" the professor yelped in delight, hugging his friend the former cat.

Rimski unlatched the door and ushered the professor into his living-room. "I rented this place, boss, while I was trying to track you down. It's not the fanciest neighborhood in Regatta Heights, but I didn't figure to stay forever. Anyway, once you've been a cat, you get used to sleeping practically anywhere. Can I get you a beer?"

"By all means," said Fillmore, easing himself into an overstuffed armchair, "and please proceed with your tale."

His friend, looking puzzled, glanced behind himself, then grinned sheepishly. "Force of habit," he murmured, and went into the kitchen for a bottle of Carlsberg Elephant and an iced milk for his own palate.

"So," said Rimski once he was ensconced upon a couch (he curled up on it in a decidedly feline fashion, the teacher noted with some amusement), "after I got my busted paw fixed in London, me and Boris went to the shop of this sorcerer you mentioned."

"John Wellington Wells. He manufactures interdimensional umbrellas just like mine."

"Not quite," Rimski grinned, "he's worked up some fancy new improvements."

"Such as?"

"I'll come to that. But the first time I visited his shop, it was to ask him to remove the witch's spell that once transformed me into a cat."

"I thought you preferred that shape to being a tax collector."

The chubby man lapped at his milk, prior to replying. "In my native world, sure, I had no choice but to go back to my old job. Employment's scarce there. I really wanted to be a bum, but the I.I.I. has that field all sewed up, so—"

"The triple I? What's that?"

"A union. Itinerants & Idlers' Internationale. Anyway, on the G&S world, I could see lots of advantages to shifting to mortal shape. Boris pointed them out to me."

The professor's mouth twisted in a sardonic smile. "I'll *bet* he did. So then what happened?"

"Wells took off the spell and I became the way I am now. Me and Boris returned to the fairy glade and a lot of time passed. . . ." Rimski sighed pleasantly. "But eventually we wondered where you were, why you hadn't come back yet with a fiancée."

The professor frowned worriedly. "How *long* before you began to worry? I've lost all track of the time I've spent on this crazy world."

The ex-cat calculated on his fingers. "Let's see . . . maybe six or seven months before we started getting anxious. Another three or four months while we tried to tell ourselves we needn't be concerned, that you could take care of yourself. Boris would suggest something, I'd nix it. I'd come up with a plan to find you, he'd agree but the Fairy Queen would pick holes in it. . . . All in all, a little over a year before I actually set out to track you down. I went back to London and bought an umbrella from Wells. There it is, over in that corner."

Fillmore rose and walked to the instrument. He picked it up and examined it carefully. "What's this subsidiary shaft and button?"

"One of those improvements I mentioned. It's a kind of searchlight."

"You mean a *flash*light?"

"Nope. A searchlight. It helped me search for you throughout the cosmos. After all, I couldn't program my umbrella too accurately with a description of the world you were on. I had to give it a rundown of *you*, boss . . . and even then, I had a lot of parallel Philli-Fillmores to sift through before I ended up here."

"A searchlight," Fillmore mused. "Sounds familiar."

"Wells claims he got the idea from some wizard he once met." Rimski eyed his friend curiously. "Nu, so are you ready to go?"

"You bet I am, Rimski." The professor got to his feet and handed the newfangled bumbershoot to his friend, then reached for his own umbrella.

"By the way, boss, what do I call you from now on? Fillmore? Phillimore? And how come you changed your name in the first place?"

"It was my original name. While I had amnesia, Louisa found an old Fillmore name card in my wallet. The funny thing is I like 'Fillmore' now, but I used to hate it."

"Meaning?"

The professor shrugged. "Beats me. Maybe it's because I got used to hearing Louisa say it with a special kind of caress in her voice. That was in the early days before she started calling me Adrian." He winced. "Well, I think I still prefer 'James' or 'Jim,' but I've decided to go with the name I derived from my father: 'Fillmore.'"

"Okay, Jimmy," Rimski purred affectionately, "so now let's go visit Boris and let him know you're all right."

They positioned their thumbs on the release catches and prepared to press them. But suddenly the professor stopped.

"What's the matter?"

"Better let me push my umbrella's flight-button first. I'm worried it might not work."

"Why not?" the chubby man in gray asked anxiously. "You think it's busted?"

"It's more complicated than that. I'll explain later." Fillmore pressed the catch.

It did not open.

"I'm stuck here," he groaned. "Subsumed."

And then he passed out, right on schedule.

"*Vayzmir*, boss!" Rimski wailed once the professor woke up and detailed his plight. "What are we going to do?"

Fillmore shrugged. "There's not much that can be done. You're free to go. I have to stay."

"Maybe if we exchanged umbrellas?"

"I doubt it. They tend to become imprinted with the owner's brain-patterns and can't be operated by someone else. Still, I suppose we can try."

They handed one another their umbrellas, but again Fillmore cautioned Rimski to allow him to go first. "If you vanish, Rimski, it'd be a long time before you could return. It takes a while for the umbrella to cool off after any flight."

He depressed the button on Rimski's umbrella, but nothing happened.

"You see?" Fillmore remarked gloomily. "I'm stuck."

Rimski sadly shook his head. "All that *tsooris* for nothing. What I call ironic."

Fillmore nodded. "Yes, I might as well have remained at Parker College on my native Earth for all the—" Abruptly, he stopped talking. His eyes widened. His jaw dropped.

Rimski clutched his arm. "You're maybe thinking something good?"

"Yes! *Yes!* You just told me how I can escape this world!"

"I did?" Rimski asked, puzzled.

"Absolutely! Listen: every world has its own peculiar governing principles. Once I was on a planet derived from popular horror literature. Finishing a sequence there, I was morbidly certain, would mean my death. I tried to get away by umbrella, but the damn thing wouldn't open. It *knew*."

"So what did you do?"

"I jumped out a window."

"*What?*"

"There was no way I could survive the defenestration. It was an immense drop, and I was as good as dead, anyhow, so the umbrella finally opened and took me away."

"Whew! But how does it apply here? Are you going to hop off a cliff, maybe?"

Fillmore shuddered. "Hardly. On a soap opera world, a physical suicide attempt might result in some lingering horror . . . brain damage, coma, hospitalization encased entirely in bandages, all bones broken. No, there's only one surefire way out of a soap that I've ever witnessed."

"And that is?"

"Give you an example. Once, on a show called 'Days of Our Lives,' this sweet redhead, Maggie, said words to the effect that it was the happiest moment of her life. Practically immediately afterward, Mike —her husband Mickey's son by a former marriage—got pinned under a wagon. He lost so much blood he needed a transfusion. Which is when Mickey learned, to his horror, that neither he nor his former wife had Mike's blood type. Mike was the offspring of Mickey's brother, Bill. Mickey went dotty, shot Bill, had to be stuck in an asylum. Later, Maggie became an alcoholic, had her adopted daughter taken away from her by the courts, and one day invited her friend, Julie, to her farm; the stove blew up, burned Julie hideously. Julie finally lost her husband because of the accident . . . and Maggie blamed herself for Julie's troubles. All because poor Maggie tempted the Fates by saying how happy she was. Get it?"

"Mmm-hmmm," Rimski mused, fingering his whiskers, "soap operas operate on a system of melodramatic irony."

"Precisely. When you used the word 'ironic,' I realized immediately what I must do to ensure the termination of my role on this planet." Hefting the umbrella, he placed his thumb against the catch. "And now, Rimski, do me a favor?"

"You name it, boss!"

"Ask me how I feel."

The ex-cat grinned. "Nu, Jimmy, so how's by you?"

FILLMORE
(BEAMING) Old buddy, *I never felt better in my life.* . . .

With a sudden, violent, phthisic cough, J. Adrian Fillmore pressed the button and the umbrella snapped open with a profoundly satisfying click.

FADE OUT

Part III

"Brightly dawns the wedding day," trilled the Fairy Queen, smartly rapping the men's feet with her magic wand. "Wake up, you three! Our troupe must bless a multiple nuptial, and there's many a mile to go ere we reach our destination." She placed her hands on her ample hips and, with compressed lips, shook her head. "If you weren't so stubborn, I could induct you into our immortal band, then you'd all grow wings and we wouldn't have to rush. We could all fly to Castle Bunthorne."

The professor, first to rouse, demurred. "The prospect of life without foreseeable cessation is not without attraction, but I should prefer not to flit through it."

The Fairy Queen shrugged tolerantly. "Well, I shan't force you. There's nothing so dismaying as an unwilling fairy, they do not contribute cheerfully to the communal gaiety. Well, do as you will, but get your lazy companions ready to leave directly after breakfast." She fluttered off to the central sylvan glade to supervise her people's preparations.

J. Adrian Fillmore rubbed the sleep from his eyes and poked gently at a chubby little man in a gray suit curled up by the foot of a maple. His friend Rimski opened his eyes, yawned, stretched in a decidedly feline fashion, then trotted off on all fours to wash himself in a nearby creek. Fillmore smiled to himself. Rimski once was under a witch's spell and spent several years in the guise of a cat. *And he hasn't quite got it all out of his system as yet.*

He really hated to disturb his other friend, Boris, the Frankenstein monster. The hapless favorite of all four-and-twenty adorable members of the Fairy Queen's fey company, the hulking creature simply could not cope with the unceasing demands upon his affections. In the year-and-many-months since Fillmore last set eyes on his huge friend, Boris' Shelleyesque appearance had grown more pronounced, even alarmingly so. His watery eyes were as baleful as ever, his black lips neither more nor less shriveled, but there was no doubt that he was thinner, gaunter, and his sickly yellow skin faded to a wan ivory hue.

Fillmore could do little for him. The sprightly sisters frankly regarded Boris as their personal property. They treated the professor with considerable respect, but that was the full extent of their treats. Only the diminutive Rimski was able to compete for their attentions, and he positively basked in the glow of their distaff delight in him. *Good thing we got back when we did! I fear for Boris' health. . . .*

Gently, Fillmore nudged the monster's shoulder. "Time to travel, Boris. The weddings, remember?"

One watery eye trembled open, then the other. Boris sighed deeply. "I have blessed this day already. A moment more and I shall rouse me sufficient to perform mine ablutions."

"The Fairy Queen says to get up now. Sorry."

Groaning, the monster lumbered to his feet.

They arrived in time to witness the last in a series of unexpected, typically-Gilbertian reversals in marital status of the principals of the rites in question. The invitation had specified Reginald Bunthorne, lord of the adjacent castle and a fleshly poet of vast pretensions, would wed a village milkmaid, Patience, but by the arrival of the nuptial morn, Bunthorne's fortunes twisted and dipped until he had no prospective mate left to marry but a stout cellist by the name of Lady Jane.

But no sooner did the skinny, black-velvet-clad poet proffer his hand to the large woman than a blare of trumpets silenced him. A splendidly-garbed nobleman, the Duke of Dunstable, strode forth on the greensward and himself proposed to the same massive damsel.

Lady Jane dropped her cello on Bunthorne's foot, threw wide her arms (incidentally bashing the poet in the face) and thundered over to the Duke, whom she accepted with simpering glee.

"Fickle frump, ain't she?" whispered Rimski to Boris and the professor, all three of whom stood a little to one side in a grape arbor watching the goings-on of the assembled cast of Gilbert and Sullivan's operetta, *Patience*.

"Don't be too swift to judge," Fillmore cautioned. "Actually, Lady Jane's doing the right thing. Bunthorne is an aesthetic *poseur*. He goes around pretending that his only passion is for the pure, chaste form of a piece of aspidistra or perhaps a poppy . . . and all the while, out of the corner of his eye, he studies the ladies' legs. No, to Bunthorne, women are playthings at best, at worst the necessary reflectors of his own sterling worth. He's vain, conceited, cantankerous, egotistical, self-centered and enormously selfish. He's taken Lady Jane for granted for quite some time. No, no, she definitely deserves a better husband than him!"

Boris regarded him in amazement. "But how dost thou know aught of either of these strangers?"

With a sour smirk, Rimski spoke before his friend could say it. "Bit of a fey quality, he fancies."

Boris nodded sagely. "I had forgot! Mighty Philli—" He corrected himself. "Mighty Fillmore's puissant practices!"

The professor emitted a sigh of long-suffering acceptance of the minor, uncorrectable fault. *Won't Boris* ever *learn to pronounce that word?*

The universal accompaniment struck up and the Duke of Dunstable joyfully proclaimed his marital intentions in song.

Duke.   After much debate internal,
                  I on Lady Jane decide . . .

Pointing toward two other couples awaiting the notary's official administrations, the Duke completed his quatrain:

                Saphir now may take the Colonel,
                Angy be the Major's bride!

The drearily-dressed poet sneered, then, clutching to his bosom a demure representative of the vegetable kingdom, Bunthorne echoed the Duke's melodious statement.

Bun.   In that case unprecedented,
                  Single I must live and die—
              I shall have to be contented
                  With a tulip or li*ly!*

"That," said Fillmore to Rimski (who had a better grasp of the principle of parallel worlds than Boris did), "is a thoroughly Gilbertian rhyme-joke. What's more, there's a delicious irony to an operetta subtitled *Bunthorne's Bride* which ends with everyone *but* Bunthorne hitched to one another!"

"Aww, who cares?" Rimski yawned. "When do we eat?"

Just then, the company of maidens and dragoons chanted a finale to the stanzas of the Duke and Bunthorne.

All.　　　　　　Greatly pleased with one another,
　　　　　　　　To get married we decide.
　　　　　　　Each of us will wed the other,
　　　　　　　　Nobody be Bunthorne's Bride!

At that, everyone broke into a decidedly dithyrambic celebration and even the professor joined in the dance.

"First solid meal I've had in weeks," Fillmore said to himself, putting down the beef-bone to refill his beer-mug. He wiggled his bare toes in the grass and inhaled the sweet air of summer. Though he knew it was, at best, a transitory state brought on by the food and brew, he could not help but feel at peace with the worlds.

Nearby, Rimski reclined by the side of a coquettish redhead, Daphne, a member of the Fairy Queen's immortal ring. The two indulged in light amatory games; Fillmore saw them and sighed.

And there goes my contentment, he told himself, feeling like Lazarus at the Feast, observing everywhere romantic companionships and the tang of dalliance without, however, being able to partake of the tiniest morsel.

An immense shadow suddenly interposed itself between Fillmore and the sun. Looking up, he spied the homely but honest countenance of Boris Frankenstein. Quaffing deeply from a flagon of mead, the monster wiped his mouth with the back of one great hand, burped, observed of the drink that it was "Good stuff!" and plopped heavily onto the grass beside the professor.

"Thou hast about thee, Dear Benefactor, an air of indescribable melancholia."

"Foolish, isn't it?" Fillmore mourned. "This is supposed to be an occasion of mirth and pleasure."

"Yet," said Boris with a sage wag of his head, "as a great poet once remarked, ''tis agony to recall joy in adversity,' and, in like manner, I perceive it pains thee to perceive plenty when thou art wracked by privation."

"You're marvelously percipient, my friend," Fillmore replied, draining his mug and mentally admiring the creature's self-taught literacy.

"O well," Boris said, patting the professor's hand, "he who suffers is sensitive to the symptoms in others."

"True. You did have a hard life where you came from."

"Aye. Yet I bethink me it be grand irony that I suffer now from a surfeit of the very commodity whose absence I once sorely lamented."

"Yes, Boris," said the professor, feeling cosmic (a mood in him that was concomitant with slight tipsiness), "there is always danger when one attains one's dreams." He refilled his beer-mug. "Take, for example, 'das ewig-weibliche' that I have sought in other climes. The Eternal Womanly is as chimerical as her opposite, which I certainly do *not* embody. Yet, though I grant myself unworthy, still I seek, even though I know it's a quest impossible of fulfillment."

"And yet," countered Boris, "I see a restlessness that waxeth in thee of late, and Rimski hath confirmed mine observation with the witness of his own orbs."

The professor shrugged. "I have little enough here to entice me to stay. Perhaps I do dally with the notion of having another go at seeking a mate. Yet I'm almost disposed to believe nothing will come of it if I do."

The monster leaned forward, intensely interested. He lowered his voice to a whisper, afraid the Fairy Queen might overhear. "And hast thou selected a new world to conquer, O Professor of Probity?"

Fillmore smiled at Boris' hyperbolized esteem. "A notion *has* occurred to me, as a matter of fact. And yet, I don't know . . ."

"A world, perhaps, of great risk?"

"One might say, 'who chooseth it must give and hazard all he hath.'"

Boris' brows contracted; he shut his eyes and rocked in fierce concentration. "Certain I am that once I heard or read that phrase—or one with a similar ring." Suddenly, his eyelids opened wide. He regarded his friend with mingled respect and doubt. "Friend Fillmore, I believe I perceive your plan."

"At this stage, it's hardly a plan. Only a notion."

"An heroic one! A planet of high adventure, colossal danger—"

"And potential reward," Fillmore added. "Think of the *women!*"

Boris inclined his enormous head. "So you consider a flight unto a land populated by the characters of The Bard?"

"To the world of Shakespeare, yes."

Standing, the monster grasped the professor by an elbow and helped him to his feet. "Come, Benevolent Leader, let us turn our steps toward yon inviting wood and, as we ramble, bethink us of the virtues and perils which your scheme portendeth to us twain."

"To us?" Fillmore echoed, slipping on his shoes. "You mean you'd like to come along with—?"

"*SHHH!*" Frankenstein interrupted, darting fearful glances all about lest their counsel be heard. But he noted the Fairy Queen at some distance flirting outrageously with Reginald Bunthorne. The poet did his best to keep his attentions centered on the limp *flora* in his limp hand.

Boris steered the teacher to a small copse, then, casting frequent glances about to ensure their privacy from the jealous ears of the fey sisters, he reopened the discussion.

"Forgive me, O Sire, for dwelling on that which is doubtless painful to remember, but save for the friending of Rimski, thine earlier amorous searches were fraught with disappointment and dire event."

"You're telling *me?*" the professor agreed, reflectively running his finger along the garish folds of the umbrella-hood. "I didn't even get close to marrying the woman I wanted in Faërie, and as for the day-time-drama planet, I found someone I cared for dearly, only to lose her."

"You refer to the ineffable Louisa?"

Fillmore sighed. "Yep. Angelic features. And I guess I've got a thing for blondes. But—" Another sigh. "*But* there are some women, I guess, that are never meant for anything other than my distant admiration." His mouth quirked sideways. "Funny how she resembled Cinderella."

Silence. Recollection drained the professor of the wish to converse further on the subject, and Boris seemed lost in thought. But after several still moments, the monster began to muse aloud.

"Long and long ago," he said in a low voice, more to himself than his companion, "I haply found a set of Shakespeare's plays. How I reveled in their heady verse, the sweep of heightened prose. Even when I read the appendices and learned he'd borrowed his plots from other sources, still I thrilled at his vasty projects and reversals, marveling how his genius wrought sea-changes on the crudest of stories." Boris sighed, he could not tell why. Then a comical expression suddenly lit his face. He prodded Fillmore with one long, bony finger. "Those were early days when my soul might have inclined this way or that, but for your beneficence. 'Twas then I had an odd notion. Wouldst hear?"

"Of course. Something concerning Shakespeare?"

"Aye. I perceived what I thought to be a sole flaw in his tales."

"And that was?"

A scowl appeared on the monster's countenance, a look so concentrate with murderous fury that the professor started and involuntarily drew back. He'd been friends with Boris for so long, he'd almost forgotten the towering, menacing rage that once grew within that manufactured breast. "Thou must recall, O Professor, how I was, in those incunabular days of mine birthing spirit, a creature shunned and stoned where'er I roamed. How should I not wish the worst to creatures of the light of day when I seemed doomed to haunt the night with ghouls, predators and murtherers?"

"Yes, yes," Fillmore nervously agreed, attempting to soothe the other's sudden anger, "but what has this to do with Shakespeare?"

The mood passed, and Boris smiled once more. The professor exhaled. "I but mentioned mine early state," said the giant, "to show why I might peruse the plays of the Immortal Will and wish the villains all success."

Fillmore laughed, more in relief than appreciation. "You mean, you wanted the Claudiuses and Iagos and Aarons to *win?*"

"Aye," Boris chortled, "and for a time I had a scheme to re-pen the plays myself, redistributing the villains so they'd stand a better chance elsewhere."

"Huh?"

"Take, for instance, that Cassius, he of the lean and hungry look! Couldst not, Sage Pedagogue, perceive him working his wiles on Laertes, Polonius and the like, just as he did when he plied honest Brutus to join the assassins of Caesar?"

The professor smiled. "You have a cute idea there, Boris. Cassius might well have brought it off, where Claudius ultimately failed to snuff out Hamlet soon enough." He frowned. "But this idle talk isn't helping me make up my mind. How do you think I should proceed, Boris? Ought I risk the world of Shakespeare? The women, I admit, are tempting, indeed: Cleopatra and Juliet, Portia and French Kate. . . ."

"Apace, apace!" Boris cautioned, holding up a forestalling palm. "Forgive me my boldness, Dear Professor, but wouldst thou truly court treacherous Egypt or seek out Capulet, green in years?"

Fillmore sighed, but nodded his head somewhat vigorously. "You're absolutely right. I always set out too quickly before I think things through." He rummaged in his pockets for pencil and a small notepad. "I'll make a list. . . ."

"Another thing," Boris said warningly, "did I not read that the women of Shakespeare's plays actually were portrayed in those times by young boys of the company?"

"Yes, but that is *not* a factor to worry about, Boris. These worlds I visit are presumably the places from which authors with which I'm familiar derive their root-notions. Shakespeare may have had to employ boys to play his distaff roles, it was the custom of the time. But in his imagination, he *surely* saw real women when he created his great female characters. . . ." The professor's face darkened. "Still, I wish you hadn't brought that up."

"Why not?"

"There's a kind of universal economy that functions when I use the umbrella. Call it energy conservation, if you will. The umbrella mechanism, responsive as it is to my thoughts, appears to fetch out every subconscious fact relating to the proposed destination. If it's possible to fly to a world which matches the general mental specs, but also embodies the irrelevant facts—and if *that* world's easier to reach than the planet that doesn't include the unwanted extras—the damned umbrella always seems to travel the route that costs the least energy." He shook his head. "Well, never mind, it's too late now. When I go, I'll just have to concentrate as carefully as I can on the proper coordinates."

"Then you are determined that you *will* go?" Boris asked eagerly. "And may I accompany thee?"

"Sure you can!"

The monster leaped up, crowing with happiness. He threw his arms about the professor and nearly choked the life out of him in his enthusiasm. "O Convenient Saviour, thou hast always been mine guardian angel! Thou protectest me like a father!"

"Fine," Fillmore wheezed, "just don't call me Daddy."

Boris gave him another affectionate squeeze before releasing him. When he did, he was astonished to see Fillmore collapse in a heap. The monster, immediately contrite, dropped to his knees and anxiously prodded his friend.

"I'm all right," the teacher groaned, "but if you don't control your elation, you're going to tip off the Fairy Queen."

A look of pure terror passed over Boris' face. Helping Fillmore to his feet, he murmured, "Shall we not depart on the instant, ere she discovers our intent?"

"No, we ought to say goodbye to Rimski. Besides, he might want to join us. And I need more time to think. I'll fly tomorrow."

The next morning, just before dawn, the three friends crept to the copse by separate routes. Meeting in the central glade, they exchanged farewells in whispers.

"Sure you won't come, Rimski?"

"Naah, boss, I like it here fine. But you watch out for yourself, hear?"

"Don't worry," the professor said. "This time I've thought things out quite carefully."

Boris and Rimski exchanged a significant glance, but said nothing.

Fillmore consulted a bit of paper scrawled with various notations. "I've gone over the entire Shakespearean catalogue painstakingly. There are only a handful of women in his plays that I perceive might be fitting companions for my future."

"For example?" Boris prompted.

"The ones with the best minds and wit, the women who refuse to sit back and play passive pawn-roles in their male-dominated society."

Boris interrupted. "Well, I, on the other hand, would have imagined the fair, innocent Miranda just the sort of lass thou wouldst elect to pursue."

Fillmore shrugged. "Well, I considered her. But I had an unpleasant experience with another sweet young thing. Remember Snow White, Rimski?"

The chubby man winced.

"No, no," the professor expounded, "those whom I most admire in Shakespeare are his Portias and Rosalinds, Violas and Isabellas. They are more than a match for their Bassanios, Orlandos and Prince Hals, you name them. Actually, the one woman in all the plays whom I suspect might be the most interesting of all is—don't laugh!—none other than—"

"The Fairy Queen!" Boris howled.

"Huh?" Fillmore blinked foggily. "Titania? Hardly. No, the character I meant—"

"*I* meant," yelped Frankenstein, "that the Fairy Queen is coming! And she seemeth passing fierce!"

Fillmore looked up and saw the magical monarch swooping down upon them, her diaphanous wings buzzing angrily. The professor grabbed Boris' hand, wrapped it tight round the haft of the umbrella, then stabbed the flight button, leaving Rimski behind to tender their regrets.

ACT I.

SCENE. – SCOTLAND.

SCENE I. – *An open place. Thunder and Lightning.*

Enter two Witches.

1 Witch. What work's afoot? What's to be done?
I fear our battle's lost and won.

2 Witch. Our sister Hazel's set her lure,
The Duke shall perish by the Moor!

Enter third Witch.

3 Witch. Our prey hath 'scaped! Pursue we must!
That stupid Moor's a foolish bust!
Be quick, make haste, we'll track 'im down
Before he hides in yonder town!

1 Witch. Bestir thee, Hilda! Wake! Ne'er mope!
Come shake a stick, thou arrant dope!

2 Witch. Have done, thou drab, with apish jibes!
Dost thou not sense peculiar vibes?

Ye 1 Witch sniffeth.

1 Witch. I'sooth, 'tis true! Och, what's amiss?
Disturbance in the ether, sis?

2 Witch. A mage?
1 Witch. An imp?
2 Witch. A sprite?
1 Witch. A wight?
2 Witch. Some ghoulish flotsam of the night?

Ye 3 Witch peereth.

3 Witch. I see a fiend a ghoul might fear!
He's pierced the veil, he's flying here—

His dreadful face gives *me* a wrench!
And with him hies a dour *mentsch*. . . .
  2 Witch. What doth this mean?
  3 Witch.   I do not know.
  1 Witch. It matters not! Bestir! Let's go!
Our prey escapes! We must not gab!
The Duke, the Duke's the one to nab!
  3 Witch. She's right; we must forget this pair
That ply the worlds and filthy air. . . .

                                    [Witches *vanish*.

SCENE II. — *A blasted heath. Thunder.*

Enter FILLMORE & BORIS *from above.*

The rain swept in sheets upon the moonless plain. Boris and the professor floated gently downward, but as their feet touched the ground and Fillmore's eyes opened, the umbrella snapped shut and the torrent instantly soaked them to the skin.

The teacher uttered a terse, terrible curse for the umbrella's special behest, but the thunder raged and the wind snatched the words from his mouth, so neither Boris nor the bumbershoot heard.

Being a good foot taller, the monster commanded a better vantage of the dreary countryside. Peering every which way for shelter, he squinted in the direction of a low hummock in the middle distance. A livid talon of lightning split the sky, limning the small hill against the firmament. Thinking he spied a deeper shadow in the slope, Boris tucked the professor under the crook of his arm and slogged toward the mound, shivering in the icy wind and driving rain.

An occasional flicker of heavenly fire gave Boris his bearings, but in between flashes, he could not accurately gauge the distance in the dark, which is why the hill loomed up faster than anticipated, and he came to a stop when his friend's pate smartly smacked the side of the slope.

"Dammit, you lummox, do you think I'm a battering ram?" The professor's shrill voice sounded loud beneath the overhanging rocks that somewhat hushed the fury of the tempest. "*Put me down, you big jerk!*" he snapped with uncustomary pique.

Feelings somewhat injured, the monster instantly obeyed, depositing the teacher in the middle of a mammoth mud-puddle. "Methinks," mused Frankenstein, "this adventure hath not got off to an auspicious start."

"*Do* tell," Fillmore growled, poling himself to dry land with the aid of the umbrella and squelching to his feet. He glowered at Boris, but said nothing further, busying himself instead with the futile task of trying to wring the excess moisture from his trouser-legs.

They stood beneath a low stone outcropping sheltered from the rain, though not from the wind's stiletto-edge. The professor trembled in the wet and cold and cursed the capriciousness of his infernal umbrella.

"Where, O where," Boris groaned, "didst thou command it to deliver us? What portion of the globe that's patterned on The Bard? What clime?"

"Certainly not here," the professor rumbled. "I expected to alight in Italy, probably Padua."

"Padua?" Boris echoed, amazed. "*Really?*"

"Sure." The professor shrugged. "There's a maiden there with a quick wit."

"Aye," the monster agreed, "and a quick left to the gut if any male is witless enow to tackle her."

"Bah, the only reason Kate's so unruly is that she's a woman of intelligence trapped in a society that circumscribes woman's role." Fillmore spoke in his stiffest classroom manner. "I considered Beatrice for a time, there's some similarity in her talent for repartée."

"Aye, but Beatrice is a winsome lass, whereas—"

"Whereas Kate is, by the very title of the play in which she appears, a shrew. Which is probably because she knows she has a lot to offer a man, if only there were one worthy of her mettle."

Boris put a hand to his forehead and rocked from side to side, but said no more to contradict his benefactor. "Well, then," he asked at last, "is't your intention to tame the virago? For sure she will not lightly list to protestations of ardor."

"Well, I don't plan to rush into it quite so fast, Boris. I'd like to cultivate her acquaintance, turn aside her rapier-wit with the gentleness of true understanding."

Boris sighed. "And if you can't manage it?"

"Why, then, I'd just move on to another Avonian maiden." He waved it away, the corners of his mouth downturned as if he smelt a spoiled egg. "Anyway, what's the use discussing it? As usual, the umbrella fouled up. We're nowhere near Italy."

"Where thinkst thou we've been untimely ripped?"

"My guess," said the professor, disapprovingly eying the terrain, "is that we're either plump in the middle of Lear's storm, or else we've fetched ourselves Scotland."

Boris grimaced horribly. "*Macbeth*, you mean?"

"Sure looks it."

They huddled against the damp earth, shivering from the wind's slicing sting. Neither spoke for a time. Each was preoccupied with thoughts of murder, diabolism and bloody vengeance, the plot appurtenances of Shakespeare's starkest tragedy.

"Ah, well," Fillmore sighed, breaking the silence, "maybe being in *Macbeth*'s better than trying to teach it to a lumpish collection of unwilling sophomores. . . ."

"Doubtless these sentiments intendeth comfort," quoth Boris, "yet I have nothing with this answer. These words are not mine."

"No, nor mine now," Fillmore replied melancholically.

Time passed, but the storm did not slacken.

Suddenly, Boris remembered that he thought he'd seen a cave in the hillside when he regarded it from a distance. He communicated this new bit of data to the professor and asked, "Thinkst thou that we should search for it and seek shelter within its recesses?"

"I don't know, Boris. It might be the lair of some wild animal. Or worse, considering where we are. Which way does it lie?"

"To the left, I do thinkst."

"Well, we might as well have a look at it. But be on the alert. It might prove dangerous."

"There's little *I* fear, Mine Friend." Boris smiled grimly. "Come on, I'll go first."

"Want to borrow my umbrella?"

"What for?" the Frankenstein monster asked, mystified.

"You can wield it like a club."

"Nay, keep it for thine own protection. But I spy up ahead a pile of kindling. There will I select me a spruce stock."

"Okay, Boris, let's go. But step softly."

"Aye; and I shall carry a big stick."

Cautiously, they approached the mouth of the lightless cave.

SCENE III. — *A cavern, within. Total darkness.*

BORIS *thrashes with stick.*

Fil. Good Gad, it must be big. But I can't see.

Bor. Nor I. But sure, this cave's a vasty thing,

Fit to harbor Death's fell brood, a throng
Whose lightest thought's enough to make a corse
Of him who, hapless, hears such filth unclasped
Unto the skinless air. But list, O list,
Good Sire, my cudgel flaileth wide and near
And far, and yet nor roof nor wall I hear.

    Fil. The portal's here, but then the sides give way.
I feel a wall, and now I'll pace it out.

    Bor. Hast done?

    Fil.   Some forty feet from side to side.

    Bor. Now mark me: though I stand so wondrous huge,
That in the catalogue of men—of which
'Tis said I *am* a very catalogue
Of men—I am assessed quite monstrous tall,
Yet cannot I, with twig outstretched above,
Effect to tap this cavern's lofty top!

                                          [Thrashing.

    Fil. Rest, rest, perturbed spirit. —Let's sit
Upon the ground and tell dull tales so dry
That we might shake this all-pervasive wet.

                                          [They sit.

    Bor. Hsst! Methinks that I did hear a stealthy sound.

    Fil. Relax, relax. The cave is surely full
Of mice. We'll hide in here till all our clothes
Be dry, and then, when the firmament shuts up,
Perhaps we can fly away from here.

    Bor.   How's *that?*
And can it be?

    Fil.   It can. Not likely, no,
That we could leave this world behind yet,
But, Boris, do you not recall one time
When you and I flew *overland* by virtue
Of this same umbrella?

    Bor.   Aye, I do. But hush!
Again I hear a sussuration like
The sibilance of richly Eastern silk. . . .

                                          [They listen.

    Fil. It's just an echo, sure. These caves possess
Such eerie tricks. There's no one here but us.

    Bor. And yet—

Fil. AUGGHH!

Bor. What? I did not catch—

Fil. AUGGHH!

Bor. Master, *what is't?*

A Voice. Budge not, or else he's dead!

A struggle, quickly cut short. A light is struck. BORIS, *on his feet, has cudgel ready to strike.* FILLMORE, *on ground, is held by a small youth all cloaked and hooded. This nameless figure has one arm round the professor's neck and a dagger bladed at his throat but nearly drops it when the light first reveals* BORIS. *Holding the lantern and a little way off is he who spoke: a richly-dressed patrician of early middle years, tall, sinewy, brown-bearded. He is* VINCENTIO, *Duke of Vienna, and he, too, starts upon beholding* BORIS. BORIS *lowers stick.*

Duke. O'ername thyself, fiend, before my lad dispatch him.

Bor. How dast thou threaten? Who are you that demand aught of those who've done no harm to thee or thine?

Fil. Boris, don't argue!

Duke. Good words, and well pronounced. Do not make me ask again. His life's forfeit if I do.

Bor. I'm Boris Frankenstein, you know me not. I'm new to these parts.

Duke. And he?

Bor. I shall not say.

Fil. Boris!

Bor. Master, I dare not reveal thy true name. The Mage who does, 'tis said, forfeiteth the greater part of's power.

Fil. [*Groans.*]

Duke. 'Tis as I guessed. A sorcerer, doubtless leagued with those fearful hags that chase me. Though the Thane's plan miscarried, and I 'scaped, I'm followed by wights and frights. I'll tend to thee, at least, and when you're despatched, sure that beast-with-the-club-who-must-be-your-Familiar will vanish, too, into the pits of Hell.

Fil. But damn it, you've got it all wrong. Tell him to take away his knife for a moment and I'll tell you who I am. Not only don't I wish you any harm, but I might be able to help. Who knows?

Duke. You'd coin me counterfeit to credit thee guiltless. Have done, I am no jade, no gull. Lad, what thinkst thou?

Youth. [*Shrugs.*] He *may* be harmless.

Duke. Well, well, I wish none injustice. I'll hear thee ere I judge.

Retire to a further recess of this tunnel and there my man shall watch
that you conjure not further infernal aid.

Fil. Prejudging a bit, aren't you?

Duke. Thy thing must not come with's.

Fil. All right, all right! Boris—*stay!*

Duke. Each dog shall howl, each spy shall have his say.

[*Exeunt;* BORIS *manet.*

SCENE IV. — *Another part of the cave.*

Enter FILLMORE, DUKE, YOUTH. DUKE *sets down lantern.*

Fil. So. Now have I satisfied you?

Duke. A wilder tale mine ears hath never heard.

Youth. Sire, if what he says is true, he'd be
Great use in thy escape!

Duke.   'Tis true. But can
You really speak me sooth? My Fate?

Fil. More or less. Like I said, I know you from a play penned in my
home-world. It's called (the play, not the planet) *Measure for Measure.* In it, you, Duke of Vienna, announce you mean to spend some
time in travel and study. So you appoint a deputy to govern in your absence.

Duke. Quite true.

Fil. But the truth is that you've grown worried that your country's
morals are slipping and that the law has not been properly upheld. So
instead of leaving the country, you disguise yourself as a poor friar and
sniff around, especially checking up on how your appointed deputy's
running Vienna. He begins well, but soon is lured into corruption by
the paradoxical chaste offices of a woman, Isabella—

Duke. Pause, friend. To a point, what you said's true, but now your
tale hath veered from mine.

Fil. I was afraid it might. In what particulars?

Duke. Give ear to mine history:
Be absolute in the firstlings of your tale:
I *did* intend, at first, to pry and peer
When everyone did think I was not here
But shipped abroad to visit kingly friends,
To mark the springs and styles that fellow dukes,
Or kings, or thanes, or earls, or other chiefs
Employ to wind the clockwork State and see
It tick those tunes that are the hour-tithes

That rulers seek to shape whene'er they rule
The shape of Time. But hear me now, what happed:
This deputy I appoint me somehow learns of my real plan.
He seeks me out and says: "Vincentio,
Your scheme is mere corruption, you wrong
Your people and your State to make of me
A puppet-surrogate, a bastard-Duke,
A jester deputy who, sceptreless,
Shall be but mock and butt when all the facts
Are known, as e'er such tricksy deeds shall out."
Well, well, I heeded his counsel, and spake I should
Truly go abroad. My deputy, wily,
Suggests I sail to see the newly-crownèd
King of Scotland. But unbeknownst to me,
This false deputy sends forth secret notes
Unto that fledgling king, a man who stole
His throne, I hear. "The Duke, Vincentio,
Approacheth thy shore," so runs the traitor's
Letters. "Immure him in deepest dungeon,
Or have his head at once, and thou hast won
Vienna's favor, Vienna's lasting debt!"
　　Fil. What in hell? Your deputy, Angelo, pulled that old Rosen-
crantz-and-Guildenstern number?
　　Duke. I beg thy pardon?
　　Fil. Never mind, I've got the picture. Angelo—
　　Duke. The second time you've said that name? But who's he?
　　Fil. He? Who?
　　Duke. Angelo.
　　Fil. Your deputy!
　　Duke. Nay. I know no such man.
　　Fil. Uh-*oh* . . .
　　Duke. Pale, art thou? But nay, the deputy of whom I spake is a na-
tive of Britain, an expatriate noble of the Plantagenet line. Now to the
latter turnings of my history: shortly before I set sail for Scotland, this
lad here puts into Court, beseeching me a place. His nature's sweet, his
need's desperate, I sensed he fled some secret of's past. (Nay, blush
not, lad, I'll ne'er inquire what 'tis.) So I took him on and the two of
us come to Scotland. The Moorish king all too readily doth my foul
deputy's bidding, shuts me up—but look you, thou'rt ghastly pale, indeed!

Fil. What do you mean by "Moorish king"? Isn't the Scottish usurper a native named Macbeth?

Duke. Thou'rt befuddled still. Macbeth's in Rome, third member of the triumvirate. The Scot's ruler's Aaron the Moor.

Fil. [*Aside.*] Why in all good hell did I discuss things with Boris? Macbeth in Rome! Aaron at Dunsinane!

Duke. You've heard, then, of the Moor?

Fil. *Have* I! He's one of Shakespeare's bloodiest, most treacherous villains. From *Titus Andronicus*.

Duke. These names portendeth naught to me. But aye,
This Aaron is a fiend. He chained me up
And meant to stock his larder-store against
The coming cold by slicing off from me
Each day a single filament of flesh.
But this, my servant-lad, hid him away
And steals me the key to Aaron's charnel-vault.
But for his grace, I'd grace this night or morn
That ogre's festive board. Scarce three hours since,
We fled, though Hell itself sent hounds to chase
Us down. We refuged in this chilly cave,
Pursued by awful sprites and hags of Doom
Who wouldst enforce their compact with the Moor.

Bor. [*Within.*] O Mighty Fillmore!

Duke. What's this, what's this? Your man (if man he be)
Hath broke his word, which was to leave thee
Unattended here. He comes.

Fil.   Will you calm down?
Boris won't hurt either of you. Relax.

Enter BORIS.

Bor. I thought you'd wish to know, outside hath come
A nasty band of nasty things; they seem
To do the will and bid of biddies three,
Three crones that hath a mean and hungry look.

Duke. They've found us out, Aaron's vile mentors!
[*Drawing sword.*] Defend us, if thou truly hast
Good will to mine estate. If not, die, foe!

Fil. Cool it, Duke. Are you forgetting my plan?
Boris, c'mere a minute. . . . [*He whispers to* BORIS.]

Duke. How may I know whether they plotteth aught
Against us now?
    Youth.   O Sire, I *think* they're true.
    Fil. All right, Duke, now listen. Here's my plan. . . .

Whilst they converse apart, the YOUTH *cowers in a corner waving a
dagger in* BORIS' *general direction.* BORIS *deigns to smile benignantly
at the frightened aide . . . an unsettling spectacle.*

    Bor. Nay, lad, ye've naught to fear from me this night,
And I will rout these things without, or fight.

                                   [*Tableau.*

SCENE V. — *Outside the cave. Thunder and Lightning.*

Enter three Witches.

The storm split the paling sky. The First Witch, suspiciously
sniffing, said, "I tell thee, Hazel, I don't like it."

"Bah," scoffed Hazel, studying the East. "No time for vague por-
tents. Rather, perform your requisites. See not how the dawn marcheth
swift out o' th'East? If we don't capture this Duke straightway, he'll
win a full day's flight."

"So what?" the First Witch countered. "From dawn to dusk he may
flee and not reach the border (beyond which our power's much weak-
ened, save for certain delimited places further south). But I tell thee,
sis, there still be something ill within. I like it not. I smell a kind of
death that's yet won'drous quick."

Hilda, the Second Witch, cackled, "But if we send our *leetle* pet inside, he'll roust all out quick enow."

"A good idea," Hazel agreed, ignoring the First Witch, who still
shook her head skeptically. She signed to Hilda, who stomped into the
mud and pushed her way through the massed pack of miscellaneous
hounds, beasties and diabolic vermin that the weird sisters had brought
with them. She returned a moment later accompanied by a slavering,
vile-smelling cacodemon principally distinguished from others of its
foul breed by a bright green horn growing from its forehead. It smiled
crookedly and perched on its hindmost limbs, croaking, "Eat? Eat?"

"Aye, Rover," Hazel nodded, indicating the cave. "In there."

Even the Witches stopped their ears at the hideous sounds which
soon emerged from the dark gaping mouth of the cavern. After several

minutes, all within was silent. Smiling at one another, the Three Witches agreed the whole affair had been handled admirably.

"Well," said Hazel, "let's go in and collect a few relicts for our pains."

With a jaunty shrug of her gnarly shoulders, she started to enter, Hilda right behind. Their sibling was not so quick to follow. Which was just as well for her since she would have been trampled by the others suddenly spinning on their heels and running out of the cave, shrieking at the top of their wizened lungs.

From the Stygian blackness that was the mouth of the subterranean channel emerged an enormous man in a heavy cloak and hood that for the moment hid his features. In his arms he carried the broken remnants of what was once the horn-skulled cacodemon.

Scornfully, he dropped the twisted thing, brushed off his hands, then, throwing back his hood, grinned malignantly at the Witches.

"Keep your pets to yourselves," Boris warned, then, turning toward the rest of the Hell-pack, uttered a triumphant howl so malignant that the entire demon-band, yelping hideously, instantly fled away across the heath, committing innumerable nuisances in the process.

Frankenstein faced the hags who, though they seemed dismayed, had not quit the spot. Hilda and Hazel hunkered behind their bolder sister, prodding her to speak on their behalf.

But Boris did so first. "Begone, vile insects!" he commanded, pointing at the sun. "It lacks but a few moments till the dawn doth peep its round above those bleak pinnacles. Thou canst not further impede us!"

"Y'wanna bet, you warehouse retread?" the First Witch sneered. "We won't go till we bear away the Duke."

"You shall not have power of me," a new voice proclaimed ringingly. Vincentio emerged from the cave, Fillmore close behind, umbrella in hand. The youth who'd loaned Boris the cloak kept to the rearward shadows. "Bid thee tell the Moor that the Duke, his better, hath 'scaped the stays of shackles, bolt and locks."

Fillmore eyed the Duke with considerable respect. The outcome of the nefarious battle was not yet certain, but Vincentio's nobility rose above fear, it appeared. He stood tall and proud in his wine-hued tunic, jeweled fingers clasped against the hilt of his burnished sword, his silken brown beard none the worse for the pelting it took in the rain.

"I am a free spirit," the Duke retorted. "You can do nothing to stop me from leaving this cursèd Scotland."

"Maybe *I* can't, dearie," leered the First Witch, "but *he* can, I'll wager." With that, she pointed a willow-wand at the broken heap that had been the cacodemon.

Instantly, each part lurched up on end and from every section grew a new fiend identical to the first.

Boris snarled and prepared to fight them, one and all, but the professor commanded him to stop.

"She'll reanimate them," he said grimly, "and every one you tear apart will reknit. You can't fight an army of them."

"Can *try*," Boris growled.

"Enough chatter!" the First Witch shrilled. "Our time is short. Either surrender the Duke at once, or they attack!"

Fillmore tapped the nobleman's shoulder lightly. "Okay, time to work my plan. *Hop to it.*"

Before the hag could wave the cacodemons into service, Fillmore thumbed open the umbrella-catch and as the hood spread, Vincentio grasped the handle with one sinewy hand. The other he kept on his sword.

Instantly, the two arose high in the air. Below, the witches gaped stupidly at the men as they ascended far into the stratosphere.

"*Damn it all!*" Hazel muttered at last, "*if that don't beat broomsticks!*"

When the evil trio finally turned their vengeful eyes toward Boris, they were too late. The storm had stopped, the sun shone bright. In the first flush of dawn, the cacodemons melted mumpishly into the earth, leaving behind a stench that was swiftly dispelled by the cleansing breeze of morning.

Now Boris leered at the sisters and stamped his foot. Howling, they bumped into one another in their haste, quickly sorted themselves out and sped off across the blasted heath, fingers in ears to avoid hearing the monster's triumphant bellowing.

When they were lost to sight, Boris stopped yowling and turned around. A worried look crossed his face. The Duke's friend had fainted dead away.

With a sigh, the monster removed the cloak he'd borrowed to mask his visage till the proper dramatic moment. Wrapping it about the youth's shoulders, he gently rocked the sleeper awake.

"Nay, wee one, fear me not. Though I be cursed with a face that only the sightless can stand before unshaken, I have no hatred in my heart for good things. Calm thyself till my Master returneth and fetch us from this inauspicious spot."

"He *will* return, then?"

"Aye. He took first the Duke, for it was he they most desired. Your principal's tall and muscle-heavy, so I was left to protect thee till Mighty Fillmore reappear. When he does, I doubt not thou mayst cling to me and all may go together to rejoin the Duke. And now, sith we must needs endure the passage of some little time together, shall we not know one another better?"

"Aye, 'tis seemly. You may call me Baptista."

"And I am Boris. Come, let's sit in the cave where 'tis warmer and there I'll tell mine tale. 'Tis a strange one, I warn thee, that well might set thine youthful hair to stand up like the fretful quills of porpentine."

"I've known a mundane horror or two myself." Baptista smiled grimly. "Come, let's away."

When the professor returned by himself an hour later, he found the pair engaged in sober conversation. No longer did the youth fear Boris. The two had become fast friends.

As Frankenstein predicted, it was easy for him to carry Baptista on his back, and no great strain on the umbrella to bear all three aloft.

SCENE VI. — *Another part of the heath.*

Enter three Witches.

2 *Witch*. That cursèd pair hath robbed us all,
Hath ta'en our prey, hath dared our power.

3 *Witch*. [*Peering.*] I see them now. They've crost
The country's southern edge.

2 *Witch*.   Then all
Is lost, we cannot chase 'em there:
Our union cards ain't good below
The border of these northern lands.
That's Local # 1984,
They don't got reciprocity.

3 *Witch*. But we've got spies who'd do our bid
Even down in England, kid!

2 *Witch*. That's very true. Let's think this out;

Is't worth the risk to use them 'gainst
The Duke?
 1 Witch. Forget that paltry knave.
A token hurt's enough to quit
That score. But shall we brook that pair
Who interposed their will betwixt
Ourselves and our prey?
 2 Witch.   Ah, nay!
 3 Witch.   Ah, nay!
 1 Witch. And I say nay until I'm hoarse!
Now mark me as I map our course:
Let's lure them south unto a clime
Outside the union's temporal sway.
Wilt thou be ruled? Art game?
 2 & 3 Witch.   We are!
 1 Witch. Then we must travel, near and far.

           [Exeunt severally.

ACT II.

SCENE. — ENGLAND.

SCENE I. — EASTCHEAP. *A room in the Boar's Head Tavern.*

The time is out of joint, J. Adrian Fillmore groggily told himself, studying his watch. *But how does one keep a contemporary Earthly chronometer accurate across the interstellar continuum?* He had no answer; at the moment, he wasn't even sure what properly could be called contemporary.

Never one, however, to modify his cosmic perceptions by the merely relative, the professor rallied his spirits and sat up in bed. He pushed the rough ticking off his bare legs, swung them to the floor and began to clothe himself.

Far as I can figure it's been the better part of two days. The combination of inclement Scottish weather and three long-distance hops over a huge chunk of British mainland greatly wearied him. The Duke, too, was tired from his ordeal in Aaron's dungeon and the subsequent flight across the storm-swept moors.

But before he retired, Vincentio insisted on treating the group to new garments to replace those spoiled by the rain. Boris, less tuckered than the other men, accepted a quantity of ducal ducats and went off shopping with Baptista. Together, they gathered a creditable wardrobe for all concerned, and for surprisingly little expense. The merchants Boris patronized displayed an astounding lack of avarice when debating price with him.

Both Fillmore and Vincentio slept one full day and the greater portion of a second. When the teacher finally quitted his bed, extremely hungry, he found the others, the Duke included, just sitting down in an antechamber to a supper of boiled beef, partridge, fresh greens, thick slabs of brown bread and strong beer.

Looking up from the table, Boris beamed at the professor. "And have you enjoyed your rest, Master?"

"Sure did," Fillmore yawned, stretching. "That grub looks marvelous."

"Thou puttest on a good face," the Duke said, biting into a slab of beef, "but I feel keenly the lack of grandeur I should have treated you to, had we been in my native Vienna." He paused, swallowed, then raising his beerstein, rose to his feet. "I owe thee a debt, sir, which I know not how to repay in this makeshift position which you discover me in. But wouldst permit me to toast thee in good fellowship?"

Fillmore felt his cheeks burn with pleasure and embarrassment. Though his democratic origins did not permit him to evidence obeisance toward those of rank and title, yet in the presence of the Duke's easy courtesy, the professor felt inclined to duck his head.

"You honor me too much, sir. To aid a fellow in distress is a duty which none should use as claim to extra honors. And as for the board that's set here, I could not ask for grander fare, sharing it as I shall with one of the nicest rulers in all Shakespeare."

Vincentio changed a puzzled look with Baptista. The pair shrugged, as who should say, *well, well, these foreigners are strange, yet's plain they meaneth well.* . . .

Little was said during dinner. After the tapster refilled the mugs a second time, the teacher pushed back far enough to allow his stomach freedom from the table-edge. Taking another draught of the strong, sour brew—*probably unsanitary, but I sure could develop a taste for this stuff!*—Fillmore studied at a more leisurely pace the features and mien of his host.

Vincentio was a tall man whose sturdy spirit belied his years; he seemed a good ten years younger than his position and probity proclaimed him to be. His ascetic features were cut fine and surmounted by a scant fringe of curly brown hair, mirrored below in a well-trimmed beard. His brown eyes, when not actually engaged in converse, had a deep-set brooding cast, as if their owner were preoccupied with the weightiest of issues (as indeed he was). Yet when they rested on another in talk, common or lofty, these same orbs shone with keen attention and sardonic wit. In clothing, the Duke's tastes ran to sober understatement. Though the cloth was costly and the style precisely tailored, he did not affect to bruit his rank in gaudy finery; his suit was quietly dignified in keeping with his characteristic manner.

Fillmore regarded the youth seated to the right of the Duke. There was something curious about Baptista, a familiarity that, till now, the professor had been too preoccupied to analyze. But now he examined the delicate mouth, the upturned nose, the corntassel hair, the eyes bluer than star sapphires . . . and suddenly a pained expression contorted Fillmore's face.

Oh, damn! he cursed to himself, snapping his fingers at the realization, *now I've* GOT *it!*

Misunderstanding the professor's gesture, the tapster bustled to the table and freshened his patron's mug. Draining it in one gulp, Fillmore glared at Boris, who was obliviously engaged in idle table-talk with Baptista.

After dinner, Vincentio sent his young companion out to procure tobacco for his pipe. While he waited for Baptista to return, the Duke took up a spot by the great stone hearth in the corner, rubbed his hands in the fire's glow, and began to discuss his plans:

Duke. As I no longer trust my deputy,
I can't return unarmed, 'twould folly be:
One taste of power's enough to taint
The wills of lesser men, and he hath shown
A crooked bent that speaks a mind as wracked
And warped as he himself is crooked bent.
Fil. Uh-oh . . .
Duke.   Didst speak?
Fil. [*Waving a hand.*]   No, no, go on.

[FILLMORE *glareth at a blithe* BORIS.]

Duke. When I return unto mine native land,
It shall not be alone; I'll seek me here
Some band of hardy men who'll fight for pay,
And I and they shall storm the capital.
O Fillmore, friend; O Boris Frankenstein,
I have no hold on either one of thee,
But wouldst thou think to throw thy lot with me?
Art apt to holp me wrest away my throne
From he who stole the precious diadem
And put it in his pocket?
Bor.   Aye, I'd fight

On thy behalf, O Gentle Duke. But what
Doth Mighty Fillmore say?
   Fil. [*Sighs.*]   Oh well, I guess
My plans will wait; we'll help what way we may.
   Duke. For this, much thanks. And wilt thou swear, good sir?
   Fil. Before this venture's done, I'm sure I shall.
   Duke. From this time forth, I'll count thee both a pal.

                               [*Exit* DUKE.

SCENE II. — EASTCHEAP. *The public room of the Boar's Head Tavern.*

Enter PRESTON *and* BAPTISTA *from opposite doors.*

Bob Preston, veteran tapster at the Boar's Head for more years than he cared to consider, shook his grizzled pate and wondered at the strange customers on the upper floor. Nobility was not uncommon, *but the foreign Duke's friends! The giant, doubtless a mercenary, has the vilest visage that sure shouldst make Mother Moll drop her bairn before full time! Good he keeps to's rooms and shows not his baleful front in here; 'twould empty the common-room!* He chuckled to himself. *Or else our liquor sales'd triple.* . . . As for that other companion of the Duke, the dour-faced fellow with the great capacity for beer, *how oddly was he suited when they arrived! And speaks an idiom like none I've ever 'eared!*

"Mr. Preston, sirrah!"

The drawer turned. "Aye? Who hails?" He saw a slip of a youth approaching and recognized the Duke's other friend.

"Ah, what's that, laddie?" the tapster asked. "Good tobacco? Aye, there's longbottom leaf in th' cellerage. Sit ye down and patient be; I'll fetch a plug anon."

Preston bustled through the public room, bestowing a greeting here, a wink of the eye there. Pausing long enough to slap the shoulder of a wizened chap playing draughts with *that rascally Bardolph*—"Take care the whoreson rogue don't cheat ye when tha' blinkst."—the drawer finally clumped down a flight of sturdy oak stairs leading to the basement.

Baptista sat and watched the noisy revelry in the pub with keen interest. Suddenly, someone tapped the shoulder of the blonde-haired youth.

Turning, Baptista saw a darkly-handsome, well-muscled man of early middle years. He wore an Italian doublet and cloaked himself in honest homespun, yet appeared to be a person of some substance and character.

The stranger's face was broad, open and honest, but it wore a troubled expression as it faced Baptista. "Lad," the newcomer said in a low tone, "art thou the man o' Vincentio, Duke of Vienna?"

Baptista's brow contracted in an expression both puzzled and guarded. "I am. What's your business with me?"

The stranger sighed, seemingly relieved. "My business is but to take a vital word unto the Duke. 'Tis good I found thee. There's matter crucial to his peace of mind and future State."

"Then I'll convey thee to my Master at once," said Baptista, rising and taking a step toward the staircase leading to the higher reaches of the tavern.

"Nay, lad," said the stranger, shaking his head, "first I must fetch certain packets of documents that must be hand-delivered to your principal. They're cased in a chest of some considerable heft. Wouldst think to take an edge and aid me in carrying it?"

"Of course! Where is't?"

"By my horse in the stable. I hid it in the straw. Come, boy, and help me bring it to the Duke."

He hastened toward the door and Baptista followed him through it and out into the night.

SCENE III. — EASTCHEAP. *A room in the Boar's Head Tavern.*

BORIS *studies* FILLMORE's *face.*

Bor. Is't possible that I have done some wrong?
Thou glarest at me as if I owed thee cash.
Fil. I *know* it's not your fault, but still I'm ticked.
I never should have talked with you about
The world I planned to visit next.
Bor.   Why not?
Fil. Because, although you could not know, that chat
I had with you about the Shakespeare plays
Stuck in my mind; and when we flew, your words,
Ensconced within my brain, got mixed up with
My thoughts about our destination.
The universal economic rule

By which the bumbershoot is ruled
Has snapped us to a place not *quite* the place
I had in mind.
    Bor.   What's wrong with it?
    Fil.   You're blind?
You haven't seen—but no, of course, you were
Not there. Or there.
    Bor.   Not where? Or where?
    Fil.   The world
Of Faërie, and the world of "soaps."
In each I met a lass that I did crave:
And both resembled one another, too;
Louisa Stone was one, the other was—
    Bor. The princess Cinderella. Yes, you told
me so.
    Fil.   I thought there'd be a woman here,
An analogue of that complexion that
I seem to love. But you sure put the botch
On that.
    Bor. I have? And how?
    Fil.   And how! You spoke
To me about the way, in Shakespeare's day,
The women's roles were played by boys.
    Bor.   So what?
    Fil. So: this: the Duke's lad, Vincentio's aide—
    Bor. Baptista?
    Fil. [*Nods.*] Is the spit and image of
Louisa Stone and Ella that I loved.
    Bor. Oy!
    Fil.   Yeah, and that's not all. You also talked
About the villains in the plays and how
You'd switch them 'round about, to help them out.
And so the Moor's in Scotland and Macbeth's
In Rome. And do you know who's waiting for
The Duke at home?
    Bor. [*Nods.*]   I picked that up. "A noble
Of the Plantagenet line." And one who has
A crooked frame: the Duke of Gloucester is
His name; Humpbacked Dick.
    Fil.   Uh-huh. Instead

Of Angelo, the deputy that rules
Vienna's Richard the Third!
                    [*A knock.*]
                                        Who's that?

Come in!

Enter PRESTON *with a packet.*

Pres.   'Tis me. I bring the Duke tobacco.
Bor. [*Puzzled.*] But where's the lad he sent?
Pres.   I do not know.
I bade him wait within the public-room,
But when I came again, I could nor hide
Nor hair of him espy. I thought he thought
No need to pause below, and so I came
And now I press this plug into thy care
And so I've done.

> [*He waiteth for a tippe, which, when
> not forthcoming, causeth him to exit
> with some little pique.*]

Fil. Hmm. I wonder where Baptista's got to.
Bor. This likes not me.
Fil. Me, neither. The kid may just have gone to take a walk, and
yet it's late, and London after dark is not the best place to perambulate
in Elizabethan times (or whatever time it is now, I can't figure all the
anachronisms). Where on earth could the boy have vanished to? I'm
worried that—

A stone crasheth into the room.

Bor. [*Howls with surprise and anger.*]
Fil. What the hell—!!?

Enter the DUKE.

Duke. What noise is this? Are we attacked?
Fil. Someone threw a rock right through the window there!
See? It's in the middle of the floor.
Duke. Some street beggar, a rascal unworthy of note.
But where's my man?
Fil. He went for tobacco, but didn't get back. The tapster brought
the order a moment ago, but Baptista—
Bor. HA!

Fil. Huh?

Duke. Hm?

Bor. A note is tied about the stone!

　　　　BORIS *unwraps the paper, readeth and frowneth.*

Duke. Why, what's the matter?

Bor. The matter which I read's the matter with me, Duke. But note the matter of this note, and sure thou'lt note what matter pulls my face awry. 'Tis for thee, Duke, that matter you will instantly denote.

　　　　DUKE *accepteth the paper and readeth therein.*

Duke. "Vienna-laid-low, list: if thou wouldst see thy lad alive again, immediately come alone to th'alley one block south of the tavern-door; thou hast but five minutes ere the boy be dead."

　　　DUKE *throws down the paper, claps hand on's sword and strideth to the door.*

Fil. No! It's you they want! You mustn't go!
They've set a deliberate lure.

Duke. That's obvious as the grossest thing to sense,
And yet I have no choice except to do
Their bid. Baptista saved my life, I shall
Not pause to reckon up my State against
His tender loyalty. Have off thy hands!
Whilst we stay jawing here, his time doth lapse!

Fil. We'll come with you then! Right, Boris?

Bor. 　　　　　　　　　　　　　Yes, we will!

Duke. Alone! The missive specifies *alone.*
By heaven, I'll make a ghost of him that lets me.
[*Drawing sword.*] Corragio, lad! I follow!

　　　　　　　　　　　　　　　　　　　[*Exit* DUKE.

Fil. We can't let him go alone.

Bor. 　　　　　　　Nay, let's follow!

　　　　　　　　　　　　　　　[*Exeunt* FILLMORE & BORIS.

SCENE IV. — EASTCHEAP. *A street and an alley.*

　　　　Enter BAPTISTA, *bound, and* IAGO.

No moon relieved the darkness of the narrow street. Offal cluttered the walkways and in one corner just within the entry to the alley, a huge mound of some spherical stuff all but choked off pedestrian access.

Into the deserted thoroughfare came two figures, one kicking and struggling in the burlap sacking bound about the unfortunate's head, tethered with stout cord. The other impelled the prisoner along, half-dragging, half-carrying his victim. When they reached the alley, the captor withdrew a thin, sharp dagger from his doublet and prodded the point into the place where the other's neck dwelt inside the sacking.

"I'll slice your throat in twain unless you're still," Iago hissed in Baptista's ear. "You feel my poignard?"

"Aye," the answer proceeded, muffled, from within.

"Then have done with your struggling. I shall not harm thee, you're but the bait for bigger fish. Now brace thyself, egg, for you must fall."

With that, the villain shoved the youth smartly in the midsection, tipping balance so that backwards fell Baptista into the alley, landing atop the roundish mound and headfirst flailing to the further side within the narrow passage. A deep, mournful groan arose; Iago shushed with vehemence.

"The Duke's coming, I see him. Peace, or else I'll rip thy entrails out! If thou wouldst save thy life," Iago lied, "best hold thy tongue!"

Silence, save for approaching footsteps.

"Put up thy sword, Vincentio," Iago called, "or else the pup's dead."

Vincentio reluctantly sheathed his sword. "What do you want? I knew thee once, traitor. Art now in Gloster's employ? Or Aaron the Moor's?"

Iago grinned. "Nay, Vienna, I've fairer employment. Three comely dames I bet tha'st met in thy travels."

"The weird sisters? They pursue me here?"

"Aye," the other said, not wholly truthfully. "I'm fee'd to settle a score on their account. Wilt cross me, Duke, in dagger-play?"

"I have but the longsword you see."

"Ah, but I can loan thee a weapon." Iago reached within the folds of his jerkin and withdrew a second stiletto. Smiling, he held it, half outward, for the Duke to take.

Vincentio reached for it, but Iago withdrew a step toward the alley, waving the weapon just out of his foe's reach.

"Give it me, churl!"

"Come get it, Vienna," Iago laughed. He tempted Vincentio like a wayward child who steals the possession of a weaker lad and proffers it tauntingly beyond his reach.

Suddenly, Vincentio lunged at Iago, but it was what the Italian had planned. Ducking to his knees, he made a pass with his first and forward-pointed poignard (on which he'd maintained a grip since loosing it to threaten Baptista). The Duke uttered a terse cry of pain as the steel sliced deep within his thigh. Iago scuttled sideways to clear the alley and Vincentio pitched prone upon that same great mound behind which lay his friend.

Smirking wickedly at the loud groan he heard, Iago approached the Duke's helpless figure, weapon ready to plunge into his enemy's back. "Hear me, Vienna," said he, "the sisters only hired me to wound thee, but I have some wrongs of memory, methinks, which now to claim my vantage doth invite me." He raised his knife.

And then the vast thing on which the noble lay—a pile that Iago thought must be a mountain of refuse—tilted and heaved like a storm-tossed sea, gently rolling Vincentio down its further side. Rearing up like an amoeba that somehow learned to stand on end, the dreadful entity balanced on lower limbs as thick around as tree-boles. It stretched two fleshly appendages out on either side and, muttering unintelligible noises vaguely akin to civilized speech, began to shamble towards Iago.

The terrified ancient held out his dirk; the creature ran upon it, the point driving in easily enough, but apparently inflicting no pain. The huge pile still shuffled toward Iago, who strained his eyes in the darkness to make out what manner of monster it might be. He tried to free his dagger, but it seemed stuck in the beast's hide; he wrenched with all his might and it came out. Where it had stuck, there spurted forth a dark stream of strong-smelling liquid. As soon as the weapon emerged, the ponderous creature slapped flabby paws to the bleeding hole and roared with rock-shattering force and unmistakable rage.

Iago screamed and spun upon his heel, blinking at a sudden burst of light. He ran, but only a few steps, for he was halted by the outstretched arms of Boris Frankenstein, who folded him tightly in his powerful embrace. It was more than Iago could stand; he took one look at his captor, then his eyes turned up, his knees buckled, his shoulders sagged, his knife clattered to the ground, and he sank, unconscious, upon the cobblestones.

Adjusting the catch, Fillmore held the dark-lantern aloft, starting when, in its glare, he beheld the enormity that terrified Iago.

The monster, dazzled by the illumination, screwed up its massive face and bellowed anew.

"WHAT WHORESON BULL'S-PIZZLE HATH PUNC-
TURED MY SACK O' SACK?"

The professor saw a tall, white-bearded man of such great girth as to
be a veritable Everest of avoirdupois. The man-mountain noticed Fillmore and, clutching the ruptured wineskin, whined, "O, who wouldst
dash away the cup from a supplicant at Sunday reck'ning? Quick,
friend, fetch me a chalice, a bowl, a soldier's brassy family protector, O!
a chamberpot if there's naught else, but let me not lose one precious
drop o' this divine Ichor!"

And thus (to use a worn, but enormously apt phrase) did J. Adrian
Fillmore first meet Sir John Falstaff in the flesh.

SCENE V. — EASTCHEAP. *A room in the Boar's Head Tavern.*

Enter PRESTON *with a flagon of sack.*

"Aye, Bob," quoth fat Jack, seated at the table, "go the rounds once,
but leave the residue by my place, here where the cold fowl's bones
rest uninterred. Hast aught wee morsel left in larder to stay me?"

The drawer unstopped the wine and splashed some in the waiting
vessels. "There be a remnant o' beef, Sir John. And shall it be upon
thy tab?"

Falstaff leaned back in his chair, and both he and it wheezed at the
effort. "Nay, laddie," he demurred, merry eyes crinkling at the corners,
"this foreign Duke's that grateful that I saved 'im, he's bade me eat and
guzzle what I want here in's antechamber. All's at his expense."

Bob Preston put the container of sack next to Falstaff and headed for
the door, shaking his head. "A gratitude untaught, to 'quite the saving
of's life with ruination of's State. An if thou takest him at his word,
why then by morn Vienna's bankrupt."

Falstaff boomed with laughter. "Thou'rt unparalleled 'mongst seers!"
Draining his goblet, he called to the tapster's retreating back, "O Bob,
good Bob, Bob of all Bobs, these gents within may have an hearty
thirst to slake, and beef that goes down dry's as vile a thing as bussing
virgins in church; best bring another measure o' sack."

The drawer soon returned with the meat and additional wine and
set them on the table, leaving the gross knight alone to enjoy the
repast. Falstaff fell to with an appetite.

Midway through the meal, the inner door leading to Vincentio's bed-chamber opened. The physician came out and departed. Behind, Fillmore and Boris emerged and took up seats at the table with Falstaff.

"Drink up lads!" the fat man invited. "And how's our host?"

"He'll be all right," said the professor, "but it'll take a while for his leg to heal, and till it does, he'll have to stay off it. It means a delay in his plans, I'm afraid. Ditto, mine."

"Plans?" the knight echoed, chewing a great morsel of gristle. "Why, what's up that may be sped?"

"It's a long story, I'm afraid," said Fillmore.

"No matter, lad," Falstaff majestically shrugged, smacking his lips, "we'll summon up more sack to moisten thy teeth and tongue and make the telling run more smooth."

And so the professor outlined the pertinent details of both his and Vincentio's histories, pausing once only when Baptista joined them and said the Duke was sleeping peacefully from the pain-draught administered to him by the doctor.

When Fillmore's tale was finally done, the elephantine knight leaned back from the table, belched comfortably, and clasped his great hands about the continent which was his belly.

Fal. [*Wheezing.*] Well lad, there's stranger things, I see, than e'er I dreamed of in my philosophy. But touching on this Duke, why there's nothing that need stay the swift instatement of Vincentio at the helm of's State, where he ought ne'er have budged. While he heals here, we four shall go depose this crumpled deputy! I hath at my dispose a doughty crew o' picked warriors who'll sail with us in two days' time and battle do in Vienna's cause. What thinkst thou? mayn't we sweep foul Gloster from his borrowed throne and then pen the news to this royal invalid to return triumphant to his native land?

Bap. But I can't leave my Master here! That man
We threw in jail may only be the first
Of many wretched hirelings that might
Be fee'd to end the work the witchly crew
Hath broached: to murther the good Duke.

Bor. 　　　　　　　　　　　　　　　'Tis all
Too true: the convalescing Duke can ill
Defend himself, nor is that office apt
Alone for this small lad.

Fil. 　　　　　　　I know, I know.

And yet, each day that Dicky Three's in charge
May swell the sufferings the citizens
Endure, might mean the loss of lives, for all
We know.
    Fal.   If thou'lt be ruled by me, Fillmore,
Tomorrow morn I'll call my men, and I
And they and thou shalt sail the after-dawn.
Behind we'll leave this loyal lad to soothe
His Master's malady, and with him, set
This tree-trunk of a man to guard them both.
    Fil. Hm. What do you think, Boris?
    Bor. It shall be so.
Weakness in great ones must not unwatch'd go.

                                            [Exeunt.

ACT III.

SCENE. — ENGLAND *and* ITALY.

SCENE I. — LONDON. *The stern of a docked ship.*

Enter FILLMORE *and* FALSTAFF.

Two dawns after the Duke was wounded, J. Adrian Fillmore stood near the taffrail of the *Hamilton* and wondered whether it would survive Sir John Falstaff leaning on it.

"So that's the grammarye-device of which thou toldst me?" the knight inquired, staring wide-eyed at the professor's umbrella. "And thou claimst it hath power to waft me to the very antipodes?"

"It *does* have its limitations," Fillmore admitted, dubiously eying Falstaff's paunch. "I wouldn't care to put it to that test. No offense."

"There's none ta'en," the other laughed, belly a-jiggle. The rail groaned, but held up under the strain. "Why, lad, I worked long years at my hemisphericality, as 'twere; this girth denoteth a large character; give old Jack Falstaff, fat Jack his due, though he may love tippling better than prancing in fields waving edged wands, yet is he of generous denomination, stamped with toleration of all the huggermugger earthly state that lesser men chaff at withal. I had as lief cheat the worms o' nine years' sup with preservation of this continent of cells in sack than dressing up like popinjay to tilt at arduous swiving. Say what ye will, a fat man's never hated, it is nor sin nor temp'ral breach; here's room in this plump planet for love of all the world and fat Jack, kind Jack, true Jack forgives his fellows' faults and banisheth them not, a courtesy I hope shall lovingly be returned to me."

At the latter words, Fillmore remembered Falstaff's bleak fate at the mercy of the ungenerous Henry V. He gently laid a hand on the knight's meaty shoulders. "Well, Jack, here's one friend who loves you, vices and all. But take a tip: don't put much trust in kings."

Falstaff waved away the advice. "Oh, Dick's a goodly chap, I'd trust him as much as any monarch, which says little enough, i' truth. But what with's hangers-on, I was but another member o' th' gang. Courtiers there be enow, but *not* Jack Falstaff! Truth to tell, though, I made a pallid bust o' palace life, and—"

"Hold on, I'm thoroughly confused," said Fillmore. "You just threw me a powerful curve."

"Interesting idiom," Falstaff remarked.

"I assumed Henry was king."

"Henry? There's not been a British Henry for some time."

"The hangers-on you mention . . . are they cronies of the king with the names of Bushy, Bagot—"

"And Green. Aye. What are they to thee?"

"Then Richard II is the ruler?"

"Well, of course he is," Falstaff replied, perplexed. "What *is* the trouble with ye, lad?"

"Never mind, it's too complicated to explain." The professor put a hand to his head, feeling a trifle dizzy. Of course, Shakespeare's character Falstaff made reference to being present during the court of Richard II, but he must have been a young man at the time, *and here he is in his sixties, at the least. No mention at all of Henry Bolingbroke or Prince Hal—which is just as well, considering how Falstaff fares at their hands. On top of the other anachronisms, Richard of Gloucester, later Richard III, is old enough to manage the government of Vienna!* Fillmore sighed, unable to bring it all into focus. *The time IS out of joint.*

He wished they'd set sail already. The voyage south past Portugal and through the straits to the Mediterranean would consume a good deal of time. Eventually, the *Hamilton* intended to put into port at Venice, after which their journey must continue overland to Austria.

For the fortieth time, Fillmore took out the ruby ring to make sure it was still safely in his pocket. Its gold-worked seal would identify him to Vincentio's advisory council as a true and reliable emissary from the Duke. Then he'd deliver instructions to unseat Richard and imprison him pending the rightful Duke's return. . . .

Just then, the captain of the vessel hailed Falstaff. Excusing himself, the knight joined the seaman and spoke for a few moments. When he returned to the taffrail, the fat man's normally cheery features were drawn down in worried thought.

"What's the problem?" the professor asked. "Is our departure delayed?"

Falstaff shook his huge, bearded head. "Nay, the tide waxeth and there's a breeze shall help us swiftly scud."

"Then what's eating you? You look green around the gills."

Falstaff nodded. "A pretty idiom, that, and apt. Hear me, James, my news: a ship is lately put into port with news from the continent that distresseth me full sore. Tidings of the State whereat we tilt; I like them not at all."

"Specifically?"

"That crooked Richard's ambition hath swoln so that he's fitted out a company of mercenaries to do his bid, and yestermonth, this force, augmented by glory-drugged private citizens, marched forth and did battle in all the neighbor-states to Vienna. They've won, and all victories but greater swell his standing-army. The short of it, then, is that Richard's no more merely th' Viennese Duke-deputy, but calls himself king!"

"King? Of *what?*"

"All Austria. He's bound them to his sway; the country groans with tax and arbitrary laws, and now his neighbors quake lest he try to push the borders further."

"This *is* serious!" Fillmore agreed. "Dictatorship certainly's within Dicky Third's psychological makeup. Now it's no longer a matter of you and me assailing a minor municipal official. He'll be harder to get near, much harder to depose."

"What thinkst thou we ought do, then? Return to Vincentio and holp him compose's mind t'accept the drear fate o' one in exile?"

"Positively not!" Fillmore protested, surprising himself by his own vehemence. "We have to stop Richard before he grows any stronger. Let's see," he mused, "what do I know about his methods? He manipulates people with hypocritical false candor. He—"

"Lad, lad," Falstaff broke in, alarmed, "what madness is this? He's already too powerful. What may *we* do, who are but thee and me and a scantling o' warriors?"

"Well, as for that," the professor said, "the first thing might as well be to dismiss your men, they'll no longer be of any use. We'll have to rely, instead, on strategy, not force of arms. Incidentally, where *are* they? When did you tell them to show up today?"

Turning away red-faced, Falstaff looked over the taffrail and watched a dockside crew loading a barrel of pickles on a dray with uncommonly keen interest.

"I asked where your men are," Fillmore repeated, suddenly suspicious.

"Ah, well, they're here already," the corpulent gent muttered.

"They've stowed their gear below deck and wait, like us, the casting-off. I'll just step around and see 'em. They'll be that sorry, but there's no help for't, I must dismiss them with but a moiety o' what was promised for this venture."

Fixing Falstaff with a frosty eye, the professor informed the knight he would come with him.

"If thou must," the other said unhappily, looking like a small boy caught with his hand in a cookie-jar.

Just as I suspected! Fillmore pressed his lips tight and surveyed a small group of the runtiest, skinniest scarecrows that ever tottered along on breadstick legs. *Fight? They look like breathing's a conscious effort of the will!*

Calling one of Falstaff's "handpicked doughty warriors" over, the professor questioned him briefly, then, letting him go, watched while the knight paid each and sent them all on their way. When the business was completed, Fillmore sharply summoned Falstaff.

"Wilt keep me stumping about all morn, lad, on these poor o'er-worked legs?" he wheedled and whined. "Standing up's a business I have scant stomach for; that organ's more properly reserved for the full-time occupation o' stomachs. . . ."

"Don't try to charm your way out of this," Fillmore snapped. "Hand over the rest of the Duke's money."

Sheepishly, the knight reached within the capacious folds of his doublet and took out the bag from which he'd given his crew their severance pay.

Snatching it from him, Fillmore warned, "See here, Sir John, I'm quite fond of you, but I won't tolerate any more of your nonsense or tricks on this voyage, understand?"

"Trickery?" Falstaff wheezed, a caricature of offended innocence. "What crimes dost accuse me of?"

"Of informing the Duke you needed X amount of money to pay each soldier with, then rounding up the sorriest batch of feeble factory-rejects that any baby could wrestle to a fall. Of promising those shambling wrecks a fraction of what you told the Duke you'd give each man. Of intending to pocket the difference."

"Ah, well," Falstaff reflected philosophically, "no one's perfect. . . ."

"And that's not all. I expect you planned to stay to the rear while your skeleton crew destroyed themselves attempting to manage whatever work there was to do."

"But Jim, good Jim," the other argued, eyes wide, "a good commander's ne'er found in the thick o' th' fray!"

"Hmph."

"O, that such fearful travails shouldst assail one o' my advanced years," the knight complained, emitting a windy sigh. "Probity better suiteth white hairs than mortal combat."

"I'm not buying it, Sir John," Fillmore said, though not without the hint of a smile at the corner of his mouth. He hefted the money-bag in his hand. "Just remember for the duration of this trip who's paying all your bar-bills."

Falstaff shrugged. "Ah, well, as thou prescrib'st no remedy else, there's naught but to store up sweets 'gainst the coming bitter."

A shrill whistle blasted from the foredeck. Crew members bustled about on last-minute tasks: securing of rigging, unloosing of lines, weighing of anchor.

"Well, lad," the knight inquired, bestowing a broad wink on the other, "wouldst break thy fast with an arrant blackguard?"

"I believe I will," Fillmore laughed, slapping his fat friend good-naturedly on the back. The pair stepped off toward the galley.

Neither noticed a furtive figure who had been watching them from an alley near the ship's stern move out into the middle of the dock and question one of the sailors busy with the taking up of the gangplank.

[*Exeunt.*

SCENE II. — LONDON. *A dark parlor.*

Enter 1 Witch *and* SPY

"Be brisk," the weird sister told her hired underling, "I must not stay out o' my licensed territory lang lest sair pain I maun bide. What hast?"

"The fat one and's umbrella-friend," said the bandy-legged rascal, "set sail this day aboard a ship called *Hamilton*."

"Where bound?"

"O, many ports, but this pair intends to disembark upon Venetian soil."

"That suits well," the old woman murmured. "Now hark'ee, I must thee use again. An urgent task—"

"I must tell thee, madam," he interrupted, "your business is something else than my usual. Couldst not thou employst me in my more normal custom? We're citizens of th' wide world, are we not?" He winked and ducked his head in studied servitude.

"Have done, Pandarus," she scowled, "I can conjure up those who'd put thy plaguey stable to shame."

"But—"

"Peace, bawd! I have no need for hold-doors! Now ready thee to travel faster than Phaëthon's chariot ever clipped."

"Where? To what purpose?" the crestfallen Trojan asked.

"To Austria. Warn Richard of his impending guests, describe all ye've said to me, their looks, appurtenances, and all dependent matter."

"And when shouldst I depart?"

"Now," said the Witch, gesturing.

[PANDARUS *vanisheth. Exit 1* Witch.

SCENE III. — VENICE. FILLMORE's *cabin in the* Hamilton.

FILLMORE *discovered, asleep. To him,* FALSTAFF.

Fal. Wake, lad, wake! We must depart! Awake!

[FILLMORE *snoozeth still.*]

Ah, what shall we do? This Duke's safe in London, but good Jack Falstaff risketh his ponderous butt in an hopeless cause. Whew! Danger's hot work; it lacks malt t' clear the palate and cool the blood! Yet here's no malt . . . shalt make do, then.

FALSTAFF *hauleth out his wineskin and sitting on* FILLMORE's *bed, begins to drink. But the frame gives out beneath his great weight and bed, knight and professor crasheth to ye floor.* FILLMORE *sitteth up and gripeth.*

Fil. Can't you find some simpler way to wake
A person up?

Fal.   O hush thee, Jim, be still!
There's danger that we did not count upon:
Whilst we did slowly sail us past the Rock,
The villain-king invaded Italy
And with his brutish mercenary band
Hast torn the northern lands away from Rome.

Fil. Oy! And how far south has Austria pushed?

Fal. He claimeth all the land above the boot.
Venice is his, and I have seen upon the docks a fell
And fiercely gang ringed up to board us when
We dock!

Fil.   You think they're after us?

Fal.   'Tis best
T'assume the worst. But may we 'scape, dost think?
　Fil. It sounds as if there only is one way.
　Fal. [*Swallowing hard.*] Umbrella-flight?
　Fil.   Mm-hmm. But I don't know
If it can lug us both.
　Fal. [*Holding his stomach.*] I don't feel well.
　Fil. Well, there's no choice. We'll have to try it, Jack.

          [*He riseth from what was once the bed.*]

I'd better think this through. Have you a map?
　Fal. I have one here. What wouldst?
　Fil.   Where may we fly
To hire some manner of conveyancing
Us to the capital of Austria?
　Fal. The closest possibility I see
Upon this map is Padua. Yet it
Is in the villain's gripe.
　Fil.   But that's a place
I meant to go. What luck!
　Fal.   I prithee, jinx
Us not with talk of luck. I'll count us not
Among the lucky-born until we're quit
Of this vile mess. To Padua we fly,
And I shall pray th'umbrella bears up brave
Beneath my weight.
　Fil.   Let's go on deck, come on.
We have no choice, we've got to risk it, man,
And hope we each don't end up on our can!

                                    [*Exeunt.*

          SCENE IV. — VENICE. *On deck of the* Hamilton.

                Enter FILLMORE, FALSTAFF.

　The pair peered over the rail cautiously. It was night. Below, torches
flickered, lighting up stone gargoyles leering on the ledges of the surrounding buildings.

　No Gorgon, though, instilled fear in Falstaff's and Fillmore's hearts
like the grim company of silent sheriffs below. They were the ones
who held the torches patiently till the *Hamilton* should set down its'
gangway.

Fillmore plucked his friend's sleeve and led him into the shadows.

"Aye?" Falstaff whispered.

"They haven't seen us yet, Sir John. Let's hope we can gain sufficient altitude to fly free before they fire at us. At least the darkness ought to ruin their aim."

The knight's knees knocked together. "I dread this thing that we must do, James. Instruct me; must I ope my eyes when we're aloft?"

"All you have to do is hold tight to the umbrella's clasp and keep your mind free of thoughts concerning direction or destination."

Falstaff frowned. "I might as well count off twenty without considering armadillos!"

Fillmore winced. "I guess I should've put it some other way. Sorry!" He shrugged. "Well, too late now. Grab hold and let's see what happens."

Wobbling alarmingly, the umbrella rose into the night-sky at a much slower rate than usual.

As soon as they saw their prey escaping, the members of Richard Gloucester's police force shouted ferociously. Their leader barked an order, and all fitted arrows to strings and shot volley after volley.

Evasive action! Fillmore thought, and the umbrella began to zigzag, much to Falstaff's discontent. He moaned piteously.

"O, this is more than flesh can withstand. No more, lad, I'll take my chances on the ground; a patch of brown furze beneath my heels!"

As if in answer, the umbrella suddenly tilted to one side and sank a few feet.

"Sir John," the professor yelled, "get hold of yourself, you're affecting my directional control!"

"Put me ashore, lad! I'm not a ruddy hummingbird! I'll take what Crookback Dick disheth out; can be no worse than *this*."

"Like hell it can't! Now *knock it off!* We're losing altitude."

"Thank'ee, Jim!"

"I'm not *trying* to, damn it!"

The umbrella plummeted toward the deck at a sickening speed. Biting his lip and squeezing his eyes tightly shut, the professor furiously concentrated on willing the device to tune out Falstaff and listen only to its owner. Slowly, tossing as if buffeted by a mighty wind, the umbrella righted itself and climbed once more.

But just as it changed direction, an arrow whizzed by so close to Falstaff's bulbous nose that the man-mountain instinctively flung out both hands to protect his eyes. Instantly realizing his catastrophic mistake, Falstaff grabbed frantically for the umbrella, missed, and plunged down, down, bellowing in terror.

High above the ship, Fillmore flinched as Falstaff hit the deck of the *Hamilton* with a devastating crash. Looking down, the flier could not distinguish the knight's figure, but he had no trouble at all making out how the entire vessel distinctly listed to one side.

The professor tread air and waited to see what damage Falstaff had sustained. The ring of torches reshaped into a line and the sheriffs moved up onto the craft. *The gangway's down, then. . . .*

An indeterminate wait. Fillmore's heart beat dully; he felt cold and numb. The same words throbbed in his head, a melancholy litany he could not face nor ignore: *what if he's dead?* At first, he thought it astonishing that he should have grown to care so deeply for the fleshly rogue in so short a time, but on reflection, Fillmore realized his feelings were logical enough. *Ever since I read the first part of* Henry IV, *I've loved Falstaff—and ever since I read the second part, I've pitied him.* He began to brood on the character of Henry V, but just then, the torches began to move again and all other considerations fled.

Deciding to risk a closer look, the professor dropped behind the masking architecture of a massive cathedral, then worked his way across alleys and parapets till he came to rest upon the balcony of a banking establishment on the border of the quay.

Six groaning sheriffs carried Falstaff spreadeagled off the ship, dropping him on the stone paving of the docks. Their chief came up and said something, and two of them peeled off to execute some errand.

Keeping one hand clutched upon the handle of the hovering umbrella, Fillmore tried to hear what the head sheriff said, but could not. The nasty laughter of the others, though, did nothing to reassure him.

He briefly considered swooping down to rescue Falstaff, but quickly rejected the idea as hopelessly quixotic. *Too many of them, too well-armed. Besides,* he told himself, *Falstaff probably broke some bones in his fall. His injuries might worsen if he's moved . . . and what the hell could I do, anyhow? Toss him over my shoulder and fly off? He's no bag of feathers!*

An ominous rumble.

The two sheriffs returned from the shadows, rolling with great difficulty an enormous wooden barrel which they brought to rest by the side of the wounded knight.

"An appropriate gallows," their chief ironically commented. "Is't full?"

"With malmsey. To the brim."

Fillmore's eyes bulged from their sockets. He suddenly knew the hideous thing about to take place. *And there's nothing I can do to stop it! If I act like Errol Flynn, we're both dead . . . and the monster, Gloucester, goes unchecked!*

Josephine Tey notwithstanding, that Richard who stole Vincentio's throne was identical to Shakespeare's bloody king of that name. *And villains may change place in this world, but their methods stay the same. . . .*

Thus, the cask of malmsey: prior to attaining the crown, Richard murdered, among others, his own brother, the Duke of Clarence, accomplishing the deed by hiring assassins who drowned Clarence in a butt of malmsey-wine.

"Grab the old man's heels!" the head sheriff raucously ordered. "Tip 'im up and pickle his suet-guts!"

The teacher watched in fascinated horror as one ruffian removed the barrel-lid and several others, puffing and heaving and straining, jack-knifed their victim into the waiting receptacle, head downward. Falstaff screamed once, then the sound was cut short; he kicked wildly, causing some of the liquid to spill over the top and stream down the sides. Hooting, laughing, swearing, cursing, jeering, the unholy crew dabbled handkerchiefs in the overflow and wrung them dry inside their mouths. One even licked the wood and caught a splinter in his tongue; the other sheriffs roared with merriment at his predicament. Meanwhile, just above their heads, the fat knight's thrashing dwindled and finally ceased.

The chief sheriff, borrowing a boot from one of his men and a boost from another, put back the lid and hammered it down, sealing Falstaff's body in the cask.

Stifling a sob, Fillmore waited several minutes for the killers to leave, forlornly hoping he might somehow still revive Falstaff with mouth-to-mouth resuscitation. But the sheriffs showed no inclination to hurry off, and realizing at length there was nothing else he could do, the professor finally allowed the umbrella to carry him away from there.

Salt tears stung his eyes, but in his breast there burned a desire for vengeance of such terrible intensity as might only be equaled in the heart of some embittered liberal of postpubescent years.

[*Exit* FILLMORE, *above.*

ACT IV.

SCENE. — ENGLAND; ITALY; AUSTRIA.

SCENE I. — LONDON. *A street.*

Enter BORIS *and* BAPTISTA.

Bor. Thou wouldst not jest with me?
Bap.   O, no, 'tis true!
I trust thee so, I've told thee full my tale;
Then why distrust this wish I hold, most dear?
    Bor. My mind's as thine, and yet I'm scored with scars
Upon my soul; my psyche suffered them,
As I have told, when I was young—
    Bap.   O, hush!
The past is dead, your pains are o'er; and though
That one who gave thee life didst spurn thee from
His company, must mind it not; no more.
Who's lost thine hand in loyal friendship's band
Is far the worse. Nepenthe, friend; O, balm
Of Gilead! affection's everywhere,
And we who have the wit still seek it out,
And he who lacks't is damned to die unwept,
Unhonored and unsung; no minstrel-lay
Or any other kind inspireth he.
But Boris, friend o' heart, why dost still sigh?
    Bor. I think on Fillmore, fearing how he fares.
    Bap. [*Gently.*] Shall I be vex't? Must mope? Canst feel no joy?
    Bor. I cannot help but feel for him; some guilt:
I should be there and Fillmore here.
    Bap.   The news,

I must admit, is ill, if tars tell true:
This Richard-villain's grown too strong.
    Bor.   A word
I further rue, this news from Austria,
'Tis ill. Best hurry home and tell the Duke.
    Bap. Yes, let's.
    Bor.   I do not doubt 'twill make him puke.

                                                  [Exeunt.

SCENE II. — PADUA. *A tavern.*

FILLMORE *discovered, drinking.*

In a corner of the nearly-empty saloon, the professor squatted on a wooden bench somberly sipping sour *grappa*, a potion apologized for by his host, who said the best vintages were tribute to the new emperor. "He bleeds us dry," the bartender mourned.

Only a few patrons remained in the tavern. Each drank alone, eyes averted, lest an innocent glance offend some imperial spy.

The country's scared, Fillmore observed bitterly. *Richard's new laws are oppressive and arbitrary. The people groan.*

A morose quintet of musicians played melancholy madrigals. Some other time, the professor would have found their name (enscrolled upon the side of the percussionist's tabor) mildly amusing: Ye Fulle Fathom Fyve. But now nothing raised Fillmore's spirits.

One thing to read about tyranny, quite another to witness it first-hand.

Just then, the round little pubkeeper returned with a long, thin wrapped package. Setting it at the professor's feet, the man plumped down next to his customer on the bench and murmured in his ear.

    Pub. I've wrapped th'umbrella neat, as you did ask;
Can do ye no more handsome, but ne'er let
On that I knew this thing, I beg, or else
They'd close me up and cart me off, what's worse,
Unto the sheriff-camp, from which but few
Return, and those nor whole nor hale.
    Fil.   My thanks,
And never doubt my faithfulness. But have
You found a coach for me?

Pub.   I tried, good sir,
But just before I asked, a lass engaged
The lastly cabriolet available
Tonight. See her? She's over there.
Fil.   Uh-huh.
The dark-haired gal in green, the one who sits
Like there's a poker up her back?
Pub.   The same.
Fil. I wonder who she is?
Pub.   A saintly lass,
A foreigner but lately come from Rome,
Although she's Viennese by birth. Her name
Is Isabella, and she hurries home.
Some tragedy, I'm told, impels her north
To 'seech the vile oppressor at's court.
Fil. Y'don't say? Isabella, hey?
Pub. Tha'st heard of her?
Fil.   Uh-huh, I surely have.
[*Aside.*] The major female character that's in
Vincentio's play, *Measure for Measure*. Hm.
She has a brother, Claudio; I'll bet
My boots he's in a mess of trouble now.

The door of the pub crashed open. A powerfully-built youth with close-trimmed black mustache and beard staggered in.

"A portion o' your finest wine!" he roared, planting himself before the bar. "Don't make me ask again!"

"Oh, here's one I'd hoped would not trouble's again," Fillmore's host grumbled, rising and bustling to the bar. "'Twilt be a short one," he warned the newcomer. "It's nearly closing-time."

"WHAT?" the young man shouted. "There's ample night yet for quaffing deep! The joint's not out of time!"

"Thou forgetst the curfew," said the barman, placing a half-measure of wine in a cup before the rowdy.

"Curfew," he growled. "I count myself a free man, to come and go as I like. Tell me not o' curfews."

"Shhh! Petruchio, hush! If they catch you out past eleven, they'll throw ye in sheriff-camp."

"O, damn the sheriffs," Petruchio raged, shaking a menacing fist. "Damn the curfew, damn all dams, and *damn the emperor!*"

The publican's face went white. Of those five customers remaining, two immediately drank up and scuttled off, casting frightened glances at Petruchio as they departed. The band, too, quickly packed and left.

"Lack-wit!" the host snapped. "Get out!"

"I ha'n't done this rotgut!"

"Try me no further; two minutes, then *out!*"

Leaving the roisterer to curse in his wine-stoup, the bartender apologized to Isabella, then hurried to the professor and did the same.

"I pardon ask for this sottish blow-hard, sir. I pray he's signed none death-writ but his own with's bootless, imprudent subversions i' public. Yet word o't may draw down on us th'emperor's ghastly sheriff-gang. Best take up thy bundle and be off."

"Guess you're right," nodded Fillmore, grabbing the wrapped umbrella and getting to his feet. "By the way, did you call him Petruchio?"

"Aye. A loathely lad, a braggart and a bully. Who blames his wife (though Kate, she was counted a shrew until she met her match in him), who blames her that she quits her husband's estate i' the dead o' night, runs off and leaves 'im to his brutish ways alone?"

"She skipped, huh? Good for her!"

"CHURL! REMOVE THY HANDS! LET GO!"

Fillmore and the publican spun around and saw Isabella struggling in Petruchio's arms.

"Release me! No gentleman art thou!"

"Nor lady, thou," he laughed, planting a sloppy kiss on her lips.

"Faugh!" she grimaced. "Thou'st vile breath!"

"O, monstrous!" the barman chided. "Petruchio, desist! She's done naught t'offend thee!"

"Nay, but she hath: she jigs, ambles, lisps, promiseth much, delivereth little, like all her dissembling sex. Be she a wench, she o'erpainteth her blotches, stuffing sweetmeats in her face. Winning what she'd have, contains herself all else, unless she play the shrew and have's lick her placket-hem!"

All the while he raged, he clutched the squirming woman close, assaulting her maidenly parts with gross license. At last, Isabella wrenched one hand free and raked her long nails down her assailant's face. Howling, he stuck her fingers in his mouth and bit hard. She shrieked.

"Abominable man, have done this disgraceful pother!" the barman bawled, tearing at Petruchio's arms. The youth merely smiled and shoved the older, weaker man away.

"Bewitching bitch," swore the misogynist, "unloose thyself; I'll have thee here and now." He ripped at her bodice.

"Horrible, O horrible!" she sobbed. "Wilt none deliver me from this insuff'rable beast?"

"How's this?" the professor asked, swinging the umbrella two-handed as hard as he could against the attacker's skull.

With a curious sigh, Petruchio let go of Isabella and folded up into a pile on the floor.

Isa. I stand within thy debt.
Fil.   Then will you do
Me a big favor?
   Isa.   And if it be within
The scope a maid may freely grant, freely
Is it ceded thee.
   Fil.   I'd like a ride
To Vienna.
   Isa.   Yes, that's good; thou hast it now,
And I'll the better feel to have thee handy
On the long and lonely road; there's talk about
These parts o' highwaymen and brigandry.

Oh, swell, thought Fillmore. *I look for a mate, but all I find is trouble.* He glanced curiously at Isabella, but put the thought aside. *Too priggish.*

"The carriage comes. Bestir!" said the publican.

As they started toward the door, the professor heard Petruchio groan. He turned and saw the young man on his knees, clutching his head and scowling at him.

"Well, anyway, I'm glad I didn't hit him *too* hard."

"Hmph," Isabella sniffed disdainfully. "I'm sorry thou didst not."

                     [Exeunt.

SCENE III. — OUTSIDE PADUA. *A road.*

Enter three Brigands, *bearing darkened lanterns.*

1 Brig. But who did bid thee join with us?
3 Brig.   Big Boss.
2 Brig. He needs not our mistrust; since he delivers

Our offices, and what we have to do,
To the direction just.
   1 Brig.   Then stand with us.
The night yet glimmers with some beams of moon:
And anyone who trav'leth now's a goon.
Now spurs these lated passengers apace,
To gain far-off Vien; and near approaches
The subject of our watch.
   3 Brig.   Hark! I hear horses.
   Fil. [*Far-off.*] Go faster, dammit!
   2 Brig.   Then 'tis they: the last
O' cabs this night to pace this darksome road.
All ready?
   1 Brig. Aye. How far's these horses, say?
   3 Brig. Almost a mile; but he does usually,
From there to here, eat up that space in half
A trice.
   2 Brig. A light, a light!
   1 Brig.   'Tis time! Stand to't.

        Enter coach with FILLMORE, ISABELLA, Driver.

Driv. Whoa there, whoa!
Fil.   What's up?

The coach halteth and the Driver *gets down.*

Driv.   Alight, alight.
   2 Brig. [*Aside.*] That's what *I* said.
Fil.   Hey, what's the big idea?

The Driver *withdraweth a sword and pointeth it at his passengers, motioning them to dismount. The three* Brigands *open lanterns, illuminating road.*

   Driv. Get down, I said.
   Isa.   O, treachery!
   Fil.   Aww, hell!
   1 Brig. A good night's work. Let's take 'em to the Boss.
   Driv. [*Nods.*] And whilst you tell how much is done, the loot
I'll bring: it's in the boot.
   3 Brig.   Hands up! I'll shoot!

The third Brigand *hath withdrawn an handsome pair of pistols, and aimeth at the* Driver *and other* Brigands.

2 *Brig*. Art daft? The Boss will be displeased.
3 *Brig*.   I serve
No Boss of thine, thou scurvy swine; a Boss
Who's bigger's mine.
   2 *Brig*. [*Sarcastically*.] "He needs not our mistrust."
O ass! O boob! O cream-faced lout! Thou dolt!
   1 Brig. [*Shrugging*.] Go know. So hit me with a thunderbolt.

The third Brigand *driveth off the horses, then addresseth* FILLMORE *and* ISABELLA.

   3 *Brig*. Both follow me. Collect thy gear.
   Fil. [*Groans*.]   What *now*?
   Isa. I cannot brook delays, my brother lies
In mortal fear. I'm wroth! And thou?
   Fil.   And how!

                [*Exeunt* FILLMORE, ISABELLA, *third* Brigand.

SCENE IV. — OUTSIDE PADUA. *A cabin in the forest.*

The third Brigand *leadeth in* FILLMORE, ISABELLA.

The robber set his lantern on the rough-hewn table which, except for a handful of chairs and one enormous tree-stump covered with a quantity of blankets, comprised the sole furniture in the chilly room.

"Wait here," he said, then left them all alone. They waited in worried silence for a short time, then the brigand reentered, holding the door wide.

"Here's the Big Boss," the grinning highwayman announced. "He's been expecting you."

Stepping aside, he made way for the entry of a large man. A *very* large man. He was so immense that he had to squeeze through the entranceway with much huffing and expenditure of effort.

Isabella, who'd never seen anyone so staggeringly gross waddling about on two legs, stared speechlessly, mouth agape.

The professor's jaw dropped even further. "Good Gad!" he exclaimed exultantly. "It *can't* be!"

"O Jim, sweet Jim, this is, indeed, the happiest o' hours!" boomed Sir John Falstaff, clasping his friend within his fleshy arms and hugging the breath out of him.

The brigand, Peto, served cold supper and wine to the professor and his distaff companion. The fat knight sat upon the upholstered stump

(the only perch available that was wide enough for his ponderous
butt) and swigged seas of sack.

    Fal. And so you see, dear James, the only place
I thought to come was Padua, in hopes
I'd find thee here. By chance, I chanced upon
My sometime pal, this Peto, and the times,
Consid'ring what they are, suggested we
Make shift to swell our purses how we may.
    Fil. [*Nods.*] Meaning: highway robbery.
    Fal.   O, call
It rather mimic reenacting of
An hallowed English way of life; and I
Am Robin, and this Richard knave's both John
And Nottingham.
    Fil.   Hmph. Well, go on.
    Fal. Instructions I did give; I said to him,
"Good Peto, keep a watchful eye and ear
For any stranger who doth bear a thing
Most like a bumbershoot, and yet not quite. . . ."
    Peto. Ay; and I'm not alone, I found, in search
For thee, Sire Fillmore, for the men—
    Fil. [*Impatiently.*]   I know,
I'm down on Dicky Three's Most Wanted list.
But, Sir John, you still haven't told—
    Fal.   How Peto found you out?
    Peto. I lay conceal'd beside the tavern-door
And saw you there converse and brawl. The dame
Beside thee here invited thee inside
Her coach. I knew the *modus operand'*
O' that driver and's fellow-thieves and took
Advantage o' their ignorance.
    Fil. [*Impatiently.*]   All well
And good, Sir John, but damn it, man, I saw
You drown!
    Fal. [*Guffaws.*] In malmsey-wine? M'lad, 'twas naught:
I simply slurped it up.
    Fil.   A *BARREL-full?*
    Peto. Why, once he drank so deep that, for a lark,
'a piddle-gushed a pond t' grace a park!

Fal. Tosh, bawd! Curb thy tongue's too lib'ral bent!
How dar'st this tale before this dame and gent?
Fil. Oh, never mind, but tell the rest: how did
You get away?
Fal.   With mighty mournful moans,
With ghastly graveyard groans, I quit the cask;
The craven constables did choke and spew;
They thought me dead, that superstitious crew,
And ev'ry man o' them took to's heels!
Fil. I hope they died of fright, those damned *shlemiels!*

Peto cleared away the supper dishes. Isabella rose, curtsied formally
to the still-seated knight, and addressed him thus: "I thank thee, sire,
for delivering us from the clutches of the brigands, but now I must beg
thee t'escort us safely to the coach and round up the team your man
scattered. I am broached upon a dire business, and every second I delay
may mean my brother's death."

"Why, what's the matter, lass?"

"This monstrous tyrant, Richard, passed a law that states that all
who flirteth, leer, or wink (Unless connubially linked), shall forthwith
Be beheaded."

"Monstrous!"

"The report's come to me that my brother was ta'en in amorous embrace with's fiancée. And now he languishes in jail and soon shall die
unless I find a way to plead for's life!"

Falstaff smashed one great ham-sized fist upon the table. "Shall this
be borne? Since when's romance a crime?"

"Well, Sir John," Fillmore interposed, "if the deputy had been
Angelo, the law would have been more strictly confined to the procrea-
tive act itself, but now Richard Gloucester's king and he, you must
know, fears he has nothing to attract a woman unless he play upon her
gullible nature and manipulate. Such a frustrated man might well seek
to make all lovers suffer for his pangs."

Isabella sighed. "And must this extend to my poor brother Claudio
who fully meant to wed? What can be done? I freely own I'm proud,
but if I must bend my knee to move this king to look more kindly on
this purely technical infraction, then must I do't!"

Fillmore said nothing. In *Measure for Measure*, he recalled quite
well, Isabella did indeed beg for her brother's life. Up till then, the
deputy, Angelo, was an honest official—*though a merciless cold fish—*

but meeting the chaste Isabella corrupted him; conceiving a passion for her, he tried to trade Claudio's life for her virtue, but she would not accede to the proposal. *I remember now why she's an unsympathetic character to most of the kids I taught the play to. They always think she's a lousy sister.* A passing reference to a line in Hochhuth concerning women's honor occurred to the professor, but he put it aside, the vague firstlings of a scheme to overthrow Richard having occurred to him from thinking about Shakespeare's Angelo-Isabella plot.

Just then, a heavy knock sounded at the door. Peto, startled, took out his knife, but Falstaff waved away the weapon.

Addressing the professor, the knight said, "There's one without who may help us. He comes most carefully upon's hour. Peto, let him in."

Gapping the portal, the brigand admitted a corpulent graybeard. Richly, though soberly dressed, he wore a black skullcap on his balding pate and a lettered prayer-shawl about his broad shoulders. His heavy-lidded eyes took in everything in the room with a keen appraising glance.

Despite his girth, Falstaff rose and shook his guest's hand, though the engineering feat cost him much energy. Plopping down again, he waggled a finger at Peto and the highwayman poured some wine into a goblet and set it before the old man. A health was drunk, then Falstaff introduced Isabella and Fillmore.

Fil. Excuse me, did he say your name's Tubal?
Tub. [*Gravely inclines his head.*]
Fil. Are you, by chance, Venetian?
Tub.   I am.
Fil. What do you do?
Tub.   A moneylender, I.
Fil. That's what I thought. You have a friend, Shylock?

TUBAL *pusheth out his thick lips in expression of pity and scorn.*

Tub. Well, I knew Shylock many years, and am
The poorer now by full a thousand ducats.
Fil. The which he loaned a merchant of your town?
Antonio?
Tub. Pfui! That swine! Indeed,
He writ a deed with Shylock for a sum,

A goodly part o' which derived from me.
The bigot forfeited, it came to court;
A case well-known, and dire it did turn out;
How Shylock suffereth; and yet I'd said,
"Get thee t'attorney, ere thou craftst this deed."
O, if he'd but heed, but nay! so stubborn, he;
Had it been *me*, the phrase had run this way:
"*Approximate: one pound o' flesh and blood.*"
But Shylock would not hark. [*Shrugs.*] Go, give advice!
   Isa. Forgive me, must be brisk: Sir John hath said
That you may aid us in our common goal.
     Tub. He did? And who are you, lady?
     Fal.   O, friend
Tubal, thou needst not peer suspiciously.
We're all friends here, united in a hope
I told thee of. Rememb'rest not?
     Tub.   May be.
Forgive me, knight, that I maintain a while
A certain circumspection. We Jews
Are not accorded status in this land,
Cannot obtain our cit'zenship, cannot
Own land, so we are forced, to live, to loan
Our wealth, the which I have full-store. It needs
But small excuse t'entrap one o' my means
And leach my cash t' th'envious State.
     Fil.   Okay.
I know just where you're coming from. I'll say
It first. We all would like to overthrow
This deputy that stole the throne. Sir John
And I are leagued to help restore to power
The rightful Duke. This lady's kin's in jail,
Condemned to death by Richard's rotten laws.
   Tub. Well, then: I have, perhaps, more pressing cause
Than all of thee. The tyrant's men each day
Doth grow in bold and bloody deed; and to
My clan's the danger's worst. Now what's to do?
If thou'st a plan, unhatch it here; my friends
And I shall back it to the full.
     Fil.   All right.

I've got a way to work this thing, if we
Can iron all the difficulties out.

Falstaff agreed immediately, even adding a suggestion from his own past experience. Tubal, too, concurred, pledging money and means.

"Well?" Fillmore prompted, looking at Isabella. "It's up to you."

She considered it a long time before making up her mind. "Some doubts I hold concerning the propriety of the role thou'd have me enact," she said primly, "yet to rescue Claudio, I *think* I might act with greater scope than custom might otherwise dictate."

"Believe me, no shame's attached," the professor said. "Now the first time you see Richard, don't be too obvious, he's no dope. The second time, wear a low-cut dress. That's not overstepping modesty too much, is it?"

"I look quite nice in red," Isabella replied.

It took two hours to find transportation; the robbers' carriage was gone. But Tubal pulled a few strings and secured a comfortable conveyance. Just before they left, the old man gave Fillmore many instructions for safe travel and provided him with a long list of names, together with their respective prices.

[*Exeunt.*

SCENE V. — VIENNA. *A room in a private house.*

Enter FILLMORE *and* FALSTAFF.

Fal. Art worried, lad?
Fil.   Damn right I am. What if—?

Enter LABAN, *cousin of* TUBAL.

Lab. She's back! She's met the King!
Fil.   She's safe?

Enter ISABELLA *with flushed face.*

Isa.   O, yes,
I'm safe, and could not safer be. Is't hot
In here? I feel so flushed!
Fil.   What's up? What did
He say? Is he allured? And will you meet
Again?
Isa.   We will, tomorrow morn. He let

Me see my brother's safe, though Claudio
Didst see me not. [*Sighs.*] A most unusual king,
Not what I thought he'd be.
   Fal.   Indeed? You mean
He's e'en more warped than rumour paints?
   Isa.   O, fie!
Should Christian knight berail a fellow man's
Infirmities? Have charity, Sir John!
   Fal. O, grant me grace to draw a breath!
   Fil.   Oh, cut
It out, you two! Now, Isabella, tell
Me what you think: is Dickie handing you
Red tape, or is he really interested?
   Isa. This much I'll tell: tomorrow morn I meet
With him, not in the Hall of State, but in
Less formal rooms within the Palace.
   Fal.   Haw!
Ye've hooked the fish! Now needs must reel him in!

Not deigning to reply, Isabella swept haughtily from the room, glancing coldly at the fat man as she went.

"I don't like this," said the professor. "I forgot how persuasive Dicky Three can be with women. He seduced his wife, Anne, literally over the dead body of her father-in-law and king, whom Richard killed."

"What art babbling?" Falstaff complained. "I beseech thee, temper thy tendency to wax fey. Plainer, sirrah!"

"Okay, here it is in a nutshell: we can't trust Isabella, Richard's playing on her."

"Impossible! That rigid ramrod in a skirt?"

"Sir John, trust me, Isabella's pride's what makes her vulnerable to Gloucester. I can just imagine how he'd work on her, molding her like putty while she thinks *she's* got the upper hand." The professor turned to Laban, still waiting in the doorway. "Is there some way to sneak me into the Palace tomorrow?"

The pale-faced youth pushed aside his skullcap and scratched his head. "Hmmm . . . hast ever cleaned an arras?"

"No," said the professor, "there's not much call for that sort of thing where I come from. But now's the time to learn. . . ."

                                   [*Exeunt* FILLMORE *and* LABAN.

SCENE VI. — VIENNA. *An Apartment in the* DUKE's *Palace.*

Enter FILLMORE *in laborer's dress.*

Fil. It's almost time for her to meet with him.
I'd better hide.

[FILLMORE *goes behind the arras.*

Ah-CHOO! You'd think they'd dust
Some time! I hope that I don't sneeze again.
Ah-CHOO! Oh, damn! I hear him coming now.
Ah-*mmmf!* I'd better hold my nose. . . .

Enter RICHARD *the usurper, soliloquizing.*

Rich. Ere dawn doth creep astern night's murky cape,
This rebel's blood shall stain the steely blade;
And at his fall, a sister's name shall join
That dust to which the sibling's gore shall run.

Fil. [*Aside.*] I knew we couldn't trust this louse! Ah-*mmf!*

Rich. Plans have I laid, that from my falsest art
She cannot choose but fall; but soft, she's here:
Sink, thou slimèd light, below the scope of sight!

Enter ISABELLA.

Isa. Dread lord, with fear I greet thy sober self,
To know thy mind: if thou wilt countenance
Recourse of form, of show, of stern decree?
If it be meet to search thine fearsome brow
For aught of mercy, then I scan it now.

Rich. Nay, do not give thy graceful self the lie
With base affect of suppleness of spine,
To see an thou can shame my granite heart
To spewing forth some half-regretted "yea."
Such grov'ling whines are not thy powered art:
For I will split the gore of twice a score
O' brothers, ere I'll brook thy hollow prayers.
Thou wast not born to kneel to man, fair maid:
Thou shouldst command, proud Isabel!

Fil. [*Aside.*]   Wormwood!

Rich. Thy head erect, thine eye ablaze doth suit

Thee best; and when thy tongue proclaims thy will,
That brooks not opposition, then sure
As death doth follow life, all else must check;
Nor writ, nor law, nor silver sceptre's swing,
Nor thoughts or words or deeds or any cloak
Of action shall dare to stir a breath
To say thee aught except that which thyself
Thine sov'reign statute stands.

Isa.   Thou flatt'rest well;
But dost thou mean that I, unfettered, free,
May freely strike the fetters from my kin?

Rich. I mean there is a way.

Isa.   A way, I trust,
A maiden chaste may chastely tread.

Rich.   O, no.

Isa. Why, what a wanton thing thou mak'st of me!

Rich. Yet they who love dare much.

Isa.   I dare do all
That may become a maid; who dares do more
Is none.

Rich.   Proud Isabel—

Isa.   I'll hear no more,
Unless it be to free my Claudio;
And if—

Rich.   Nay, hear my suit!

Isa.   And if a chance
There still may be to make thee change thy mind,
Then neither shifting sand, nor rank, nor place,
Nor precedence, nor conduct o' the times
Allow me e'en a wayward word to waste!

Rich. O Isabel, yet hear me, sweetest soul!

GLOSTER *kneeleth.*

Isa. E'en so? Say on.

Fil. [Aside.]   Oh, hell! The same old trick
He used on Lady Anne in "Richard Third"
Is having like effect on Isabel. . . .

Rich. Then know, proud dame, that it is yet my fate
To stand and brace the sliding structure of

The law 'gainst blows and flames of fire, and worms
That work within; and I must do't e'en to
This sternly crush o' good gone once astray,
Deflowering of innocence deflowered;
But see, O see what now hath hap't: there steals
Into mine all-too-mortal heart a smile
That sits in fleshly ice upon thy lips.
O, such a cross-grained join o' law and love
Can ne'er unite to form a peaceful soul.
Then tell me, maid, if aught of remedy
Thy nimbler wit espies, that lying thus
Within my grasp, I may apply.
    Isa. [*Smugly smiling.*]   O, free
My brother Claudio, my most dread lord,
And, by this hand, I'll love thee well.
    Rich.   The law
In mighty majesty proclaims: "This man,
This Claudio, must die"; and yet my most,
My very secret self doth say, in whisper'd
Colloquy: "O, show a front o' mildness,
On him bestow the tender touch o' life,
But not so much for thine own soul's content;
Let this proceed, despite decree, for his
Sweet sister's self." And thus thou seest me now:
A man to double bus'ness bound; I stand
In pause where I shall first begin, and both
Neglect. What if I choose to fell the axe
That like the hurricane shouldst sweep, swoopstake,
Thy brother's head, his very life away?
But then the fear of thine concentrate
And time-enduring hate must give me pause.
'Tis well, he gains his years. And yet, now see
What now proceeds: that tiger, Duty, shall
Bare his reeking teeth, and if the breach
The light o' day e'er view, O still
The bitter gall o' conscience set awry
Shouldst raven me with rank and rav'nous claws!
    Isa. What tongue, what voice, may sway thee for his life?
If thou dost care for me, as now thou spak'st,
Then shall my tongue, my voice command him free!

Rich. I fear thee, dame, I fear that this demand,
Giant-like in thy affections,
Shall spur thee on to use thy powers, charms,
Thy wits and arts, to wheedle me, to force
Mine all-too-spineless resolution
To cast away my sober caution;
Thus, profiting from my weakness, thus to damn me
To commit that which cool reflection shuns,
Only, upon gaining thy keen desire, to laugh
And toss aside and scorn my panting love.

   Fil. [*Aside.*] Oh, bull! She can't be buying this, can she?

   Isa. Try me, sweet lord, but grant this boon, I pray,
And all thy ardent hopes shall come to pass.

   Rich. I tremble, I sway, I fear I'll be undone.

   Fil. [*Aside.*] A ham, a ham, a very palpable ham.

   Isa. If thou profess to love so well, then list:
Thou'lt promise not what you are loath to give;
Deliver Claudio to safety's shore,
Then live our love, my love, forevermore.

   Rich. Beloved star! thou soar sublimest songs
Unto mine ear, they grace the fragile shell.
But mark you well, some risk attends unto
This breach of mine own solemn law, to which
We needs must both together brave the lets
That I've imposed; to pardon Claudio
Undoes the many goods my law hath wrought
O'er vice in this fair land. Then needs we seek
To hide thy kin, as if he 'scaped from bars,
From bolts, from shackles, chains, and cells, and locks.

   Isa. I'm yours t'instruct.

   Rich.   Then meet me, dame, tonight,
Beyond the prison walls, where, presently,
At thine abode, my man shall lead thee thence
To me.

   Isa.   And whither shall we go from there?

   Rich. I have a private home where, safe from spies,
Our plans we'll shrewdly lay.

   Fil. [*Aside.*]   I'll bet!

   Isa.   I'll go.

Then, till thy messenger, by mercy sent,
Shall teach me where to roam, farewell, sweet gent.

[*Exit* ISABELLA.

Fil. [*Aside.*] Whew! I wonder who has got the best
Of whom? I'll bet that each must think the other
Lost that round.

RICHARD *laughs nastily to himself.*
See? That's what I thought.
Rich. [*Solus.*] Thus well my crafty ruse doth go. Ere dawn
Shall peek its golden round above the rim,
This wench I'll rudely force unto my will;
Her brother soon soars high or plunges deep,
And sure, her lily lips shall greet his shade.
To glut my soul with foulest lies I choose,
That she, to conquer, stoops, and yet shall lose.

[*Exit* RICHARD.

Fil. Ah-CHOO! Oh, boy, we're in a pretty pickle!
Move fast! or Claudio's life's not worth a nickel!

[*Exit* FILLMORE, *running.*

SCENE VII. — VIENNA. *A room in a private house.*

Enter FILLMORE, ISABELLA, FALSTAFF.

Isa. I tell thee, churl, I've got that crookback'd king
Enwrapt about my thumb! He'll do *my* bid!
Fil. Like hell he will! If we don't act right now,
Your brother's dead, and you can say goodbye—
Fal. Unto thy maidenhead!
Isa.   O, bawd! O, fat
And foul-mouthed bawd!
Fil.   Oh, well, he's right. Now, look,
This thing has got beyond you, Isabel.
You're staying home. Sir John—
Isa.   I take command
From none else but the dictates of my heart!
How dar'st thou think that I'm not in control?
And wast thou there?
Fil.   You're goddam right I was.
Behind the arras.

Isa.   O! And heareth all?

Fil. You bet I did.

Isa.   O, lowly-crawling knave!
O, shame!

Fal.   O, peace!

Fil.   Oh, crap. We're wasting time.

[*A rapping within.*

Fal. Hark! Who's there?

Laban. [*Outside the door.*] It's me. The king has sent
His messenger. He waits for Isabel.

Isa. I come!

Fil.   Oh, no you don't! Let's grab her, Jack!
Sorry, kid, we have no choice.

Isa.   LET GO!

FILLMORE *and* FALSTAFF *struggle with* ISABELLA, *eventually subduing her.* FILLMORE *gags her, ties her arms and signals* FALSTAFF *who hauls her, still kicking, into her bedroom.*

Fil. [*Calling to* FALSTAFF.] Grab some of her clothes.

Fal. [*Off.*] OOF! I'd best secure her feet, she kicks fierce.
What said'st thou, lad?

Fil. I said, take some clothes from her!

Fal.   There's time
For that?

Fil. No! I mean some things that she's
Not wearing now.

FALSTAFF *reenters with an assortment of* ISABELLA's *garments.*

Fal. What next?

Fil.   A change of plans.
We have to separate. Now listen well:
There's not much time. Here's what I have to tell. . . .

[*They whisper together.*

SCENE VIII. — VIENNA. *A room in the prison.*

CLAUDIO *discovered.*

When the rusty lock rasped, the condemned man turned to see who turned the key. He prayed the time of his execution had not arrived.

The first thing that entered the room was an enormous laundry-cart.

"O, I see it's only you, Solomon. What make ye here? I'll little usage have o' clean linen if the rumor's true that I'm to die this day."

A strange voice answered him. "Solomon is feeling poorly tonight. I'm his cousin, Laban, taking his place."

The speaker pushed the cart further into the cell and appeared to Claudio. The youth's eyes popped. He'd never seen anyone so fat as the clothes-washer, Laban.

"Funny," said Claudio, "you don't look Jewish. . . ."

"*Shh,*" the other whispered, "I'm not. There's little time! A friend am I o' thy sister."

"Isabella! Where is she? Here in Vienna?"

"Aye. But rather tied up at present. Hark: we must work fast to save thee. Hop in th' laundry cart, and pull th' linens o'er thy head." Falstaff chuckled. "A trick I learned once in Windsor."

Claudio did as he was told. Falstaff pulled the cart back through the cell-door, locked it, and did his best to make haste slowly, lest his anxiety to scoot attract the suspicion of the prison guards.

[*Exeunt.*

SCENE IX. — VIENNA. *The Bedroom of* RICHARD's *private home.*

Enter RICHARD.

When the messenger stepped in and told him the maiden had arrived and was bestowed in the sleeping-chamber, Richard permitted himself a tight grin. He sent his man away and spent ten minutes soliloquizing before scuttling upstairs.

"I'll play this game a trifle longer still," he muttered, tapping on the closed door.

"O, is't you, my lord? I'm here within," the high voice giggled.

"How strange she sounds," he said, pushing the portal wide. "She must feel nervous, shy."

The room was dark, save for the pale moonbeams streaming through the wide french windows. He barely was able to make out her dim form seated on the edge of the bed. Richard began to light a taper, but a forestalling hand fell upon his wrist.

"I'm bashful, Dick. Let's keep it dark."

The king plumped onto the bed, scowling. "I see. Thou canst not bear to see this beastly shape I bear."

"Not it at all," the other whispered, falsetto.

"You sure sound diff'rent."

"I caught a cold."

"Well, let's to work." Richard tried to put one arm about his companion, but "she" slid away, wily-shy.

"Not yet," the high voice piped. "Come see the view!"

"Games she plays?" the king grumbled, watching her silhouette as she stood in pale blue relief, framed in the windows. "I thought her taller!"

"O, come, admire the night!"

"O, hell!" Richard got up and stumped over to her side. "I hope this won't take long."

"Not long at all. Wouldst do me a favor, pray?"

"What?"

"Nay, thou'lt be angry. . . ."

"I'll be angry, wench, if thou dost not say. *Swiftly!*"

She tittered nervously. "Wouldst turn and let me rub thy hump for luck?"

Richard counted ten, considered ripping off her dress and having her without further preamble, decided he'd rather have her cooperate, at least at first. "O, go ahead," he snapped, turning his back to her.

"Thanks, Dick!" a deeper voice sounded at his shoulder. An arm circled his neck and tightened. The other held the point of a knife an inch or two away from his left eye. *"One move, one word, and you're dead!"*

Richard did not flinch, nor move a muscle.

The arm about his throat lowered as far as his waist and clutched him tight about his middle.

"Bend, damn you, bend!"

Richard leaned forward; the arm about his midriff lifted him up. And up—*and up*.

"Zounds!" he gasped. "How tall *art* thou?"

But his captor made no reply. Gloucester gaped as he watched the floor move still further away, followed by the retreating window-frame, succeeded by the receding balcony.

"O, STOP!" the king screamed, but to no avail. As he ascended into the night-sky, he saw the ground gleaming dimly far below. And then he fainted.

"That's better," the professor remarked. "It's harder to fly while you're struggling."

[*Exeunt* FILLMORE & RICHARD, *above.*

SCENE X. — VIENNA. *A street before the palace.*

Enter FILLMORE, FALSTAFF, ISABELLA, CLAUDIO, LABAN; *also* Citizens & Soldiers.

Lab. The villain's safely stashed away, ne'er fear;
And safe he's hid until the Duke returns.

Fil. That's good. Vincentio but waits our word,
And he'll return. Until that time, I vouch
For Claudio. Will you be ruled by him?

All. We will!

Clau. [*To* Soldiers.] Then call those cut-throat sheriffs home;
I'll deal with them in manner kinder than
Those swine deserve. Then I'll return all lands
They stole to Rome. But thou, Fillmore, and thou,
Good knight, wouldst care to serve my steward-court?

Fil. No, thanks.

Fal.   The Duke awaits.

Fil.   Let's cut this short.

                        [*Exeunt* FILLMORE & FALSTAFF.

The professor and the knight returned to Venice. By what appeared to be a remarkable stroke of luck, they found a ship ready to sail to England, nonstop. The Captain was unavailable, so they arranged passage through the First Mate, and soon were under way.

They suffered a slight delay when the *Pembroke* made an unscheduled detour north around the boot and into the Ligurian Sea. Fillmore thought it odd that they put into Genoa at midnight and only stayed an hour, but at least since then, the ship made good time.

"We've passed the Straits," the professor said one afternoon, lounging in a deck-chair, feet resting on the starboard rail. "I figure any time now we'll tack about to northward and head along the Portuguese coast."

"Mff," Sir John Falstaff nodded, mouth full of hardtack. He squatted comfortably on deck, stuffing himself and washing down the dry crackerfood with draughts from his omnipresent wineskin.

"Y'know," said Fillmore, "it's odd, but ever since we stopped at Genoa, I've been hearing funny noises below deck."

"Such as?"

"Subdued sobbing, soon hushed. Like a whimpering child."

"I doubt not 'tis but an animal or bird."

"Maybe," he said dubiously, "but another strange thing, Sir John: how come we've never met the Captain? He keeps to his cabin."

"O, he may be shy."

"Hmph. If I was in another world, I'd guess we were on a ship of Ahab's."

"A-*who?*"

"Never mind."

"Well," said the knight, munching and sipping, "whate'er be his reasons, he's welcome to'm. But what of thee, lad? Hast plans? Seek ye still a mate?"

"Still?" Fillmore repeated with irony. "I never even began. But to tell the truth, I've lost heart for that quest. Maybe I've grown some. The more I think about my amatory adventures, the more convinced I've become that attempting to corner an ideal is sheer illusion. They always seem to turn out smaller than expected. And even if I could find 'das ewig-weibliche,' what hubris has led me to think that I, being flawed, have any right to aspire toward perfection?"

"Ah, well," Falstaff shrugged, "Venus wed Vulcan. But then what *will* you do, friend Fillmore? Quit this world?"

"Not quite yet."

"O, dost'a fear that thing you spake to me about t'other day?"

"'Subsumption'? No; I've given it some thought, and I believe I may have been conceiving things falsely. A man I know once tried to tell me subsumption is a myth, that the umbrella obeys my subconscious desires, that's all. Still, I keep getting this weird feeling, which makes me think I may be stuck in some particular planetary milieu."

"Weird feeling? Canst describe't?"

"Like I was fixed, condensed, notated on a two-dimensional plane . . . as if some artist on my native world was dreaming about me and fashioning a fiction from my experiences."

"That's not occurred to thee here, though."

"Oh, yes, it has, off and on. But for the first time, I realized there may well be an alternative reason why it sometimes appears as if I've become permanently immured in a world, why the umbrella refuses to open up and fly me through the cosmic planes."

"Aye?"

"Perhaps the umbrella only works for dimensional flight when I know, subconsciously, that the sequence is totally resolved—and in a manner appropriate to the derived literature with which I'm familiar."

"Hmmm." Falstaff wiped crumbs of hardtack from his lips and the fringes of his white beard. "If this be true," he meditated, "then thinkst thou it but remains for you to bring the good news to the Duke, collect Boris, and resolution shall've been achieved?"

Uh-oh. Fillmore's face paled. *Too anticlimactic for Shakespeare.* He screwed up his face in fierce concentration and held up one finger at a time.

"What *art* thou doing, James?"

"Trying to see if my exploits here follow the developing-and-falling shape of an Elizabethan drama. I usually think of Shakespeare's plays in five acts, though that was a later scholarly imposition. Still . . . exposition, complication, crisis, resolution, let's see: Scotland's certainly Act I; London, II; Italy must've been III; Austria—*oh, damn!*"

"Dost not work out?" Falstaff asked.

"Worse than that," said the professor, jumping to his feet. "Take a look out there. What do you see?"

The knight squinted over the rail and saw, quite some distance to starboard and behind the stern of the ship, a huge curvature of beach and greenery that formed the eastern extremity of the European mainland.

"Why, James, is't not Portugal?"

"You're damn right it is. Why aren't we steering north and following its coastline? We're still headed west, straight into the Atlantic."

"What ill portendeth?"

"I don't know, Jack, but I'm about to find out." The professor rose and stripped the brown paper from his umbrella. "We'd better be ready for a fast getaway."

Falstaff trembled. "O, no! Not that!"

"Might be necessary. Come along," Fillmore commanded, stumping towards the hatchway, "let's find out what the hell's going on!"

Falstaff waited on the last rung of the companionway and watched the professor pound on the closed door of the Captain's cabin.

"*Yo*, open up! What's happening here?"

With a click, the door swung wide. On the threshold stood a powerfully-built youth with a close-trimmed black mustache and beard. He grinned malevolently at the gaping professor.

"Holy cripes!" Fillmore exclaimed. "*You're* the captain?"

"Aye," said Petruchio. "And now you and I hath a score t'even up. . . ."

He swung a fist at Fillmore, who ducked.

"Back on deck, Jack!" the professor yelled over his shoulder. "*Fast!*"

Petruchio lunged; Fillmore swiftly interposed the umbrella and shoved hard, knocking the other off-balance. Before he could regain his footing, the sailor sustained another blow on the head from the same instrument that felled him in Padua. Again he collapsed.

Fillmore spun around and dashed up the ladder, shoving the laboring Falstaff ahead of him. Bursting onto the deck, they ran sternward, where there was more room to take off from.

"Where d'ye think he was going t' take us?" Falstaff panted.

"My guess would be Bermuda," the professor replied, lofting the umbrella. "Okay, Sir John, hold tight! We're going to fly straight to England."

The knight moaned, but though thoroughly miserable, he bravely put both hands around the umbrella-handle.

"To London!" Fillmore yelled, thumbing the catch. "Boar's Head Tavern, Eastcheap!"

The hood opened. The umbrella began to rise, straining to lift both at once.

Neither saw the seaman who stole up behind Fillmore with a belaying-pin in his hand. With a powerful leap, he cracked the hardwood instrument against the professor's skull. Uttering a muffled groan, Fillmore fell heavily to the deck.

Relieved of some of its burden, the umbrella ascended a few feet higher and floated beyond the ship's rail and out to sea. Falstaff stared in horror at the receding vessel, where his companion still was.

"O, how to control this demon device?" the knight wailed to no avail.

The seaman who felled the professor shouted down the companionway, "O, Captain, my Captain, the prisoners hath tried t'escape."

Petruchio, clutching his forehead, emerged from below, squinting to make his eyes come back in focus.

"O Captain, my Captain," the sailor mourned, "Fatguts hath 'scaped!"

"No matter, Bosun, thou'st done a good piece o' work," Petruchio reassured him, slapping the crewman appreciatively on the shoulder. "The tub o' lard may drown, for all I care. You saved us th'important one."

Fillmore sat up groggily. The skipper stamped over to him, glowering. He growled, "As for you, count thyself lucky, swine, for if'twere not for my commission to deliver thee intact to those more powerful than me, I swear tha'd be dead this instant!"

ACT V.

SCENE. — *The Sea, with a Ship: afterwards an uninhabited Island.*

SCENE I. — *On a Ship at Sea.—A Storm with Thunder and Lightning.*

Enter PETRUCHIO *and a* Boatswain.

Pet. Boatswain,—

Boats. O Captain! my Captain! our fearful trip is done.
This ship can't weather ev'ry rack—

Pet. Pace, pace: thou dost assist the storm!
Speak to the mariners: fall to't yarely, or we run ourselves aground;
bestir, bestir!

[*Exit* PETRUCHIO.

Enter Mariners.

Boats. Heigh, my hearts; cheerly, cheerly, my hearts; yare, yare: take
in the top-sail; 'Tend to the master's whistle. —Blow till thou burst thy
wind, if room enough!

Enter PROSPERO, *the rightful Duke of Milan.*

Pros. Good Boatswain, have care. Where's thy master? He promised
me safe passage when we did's ship at Genoa!

Boats. I pray now, keep below.

Pros. Where is thy master, Boatswain?

Boats. Do ye not hear me? You mar our labour; keep your cabin;
why, you assist the storm!

Pros. Nay, good, be patient.

Boats. When the sea is. Hence! What care these roarers for the
name of Duke? To cabin: silence: trouble us not.

Pros. Yet remember who thou hast aboard. My little girl, whom I
doth love—

Boats. None that I more love than myself. You are a Duke that's dispossessed: if you can dispossess these elements, if you have pow'r to still the still-vex'd Bermoothes, why do't, we'll not handle ropes; use your authority. If you cannot, give thanks you have lived so long, make yourself ready in your cabin for the mischance of the hour, if't so hap. —Out of our way, I say!

[Exit PROSPERO.

An mighty Wave crasheth on the Deck, sweeping half the Mariners *into the Sea.*

Boats. Down with the top-mast; yare; lower, lower; bring her to try with main-course!

Re-enter PETRUCHIO.

Pet. A plague upon this sorcery! no natural storm's this; a witchly concoction, rather: the three weird dames intend t' murther the prisoner and cheat me o' reward, but fie! they'll not play wi' me! Thy worst! I—

A bolt of Lightning striketh the top-mast, which splits and falls on PETRUCHIO.

Boats. Woe! ah, woe! The *Pembroke*'s broke!
My Master! Is't some dream that on the deck
You've fallen cold and dead?
Pet. O yet assist me, friend; I am but hurt!
Boats. What's to be done?
Pet. Go below; release the prisoner. Give him his fair chance t'escape.
Boats. It shall be done.

[Exit Boatswain, below.

Another Wave, which maketh the rest of the Mariners, *save only* PETRUCHIO, *to fall in the Sea.*

Re-enter PROSPERO with MIRANDA, his six-year-old daughter.

Mir. O, what's this noise? O, Father, hast put these waters in this pitch, and made the very waves to howl?
Pros. Nay, child, they drown, wailing as the waters take 'em all. O, what a sorry sight is here: the Master o' th' ship's felled and pinned by a fragment o' the mast! Must be dead; there's blood. Nay, Miranda, look not on't, but hasten thy steps. There's two lifeboats, and I already

stowed the one, some days ago, with waterproofed packets: food, my cape, my books. To't, then.

PROSPERO *and* MIRANDA *climb into the lifeboat. He works the lines and lowers it into the sea.*

[*Exeunt.*

Re-enter Boatswain *with* FILLMORE.

Fil. Thanks again. Where's Petruchio?
Boats. There!
Fil. Petruchio! Are you still alive?
Pet. But little life's left. Yet I would give a thousand furlongs of sea for an acre of barren ground; long heath, brown furze, any thing: a handful o' sod, a few leaves o' grass!
Fil. Let's get this wooden shrapnel off his chest, at least.

FILLMORE *and the* Boatswain *remove the splintered mast from* PETRUCHIO.

Boats. The ship splits! To the boat!
Fil. Help me carry the skipper.

They load PETRUCHIO *into the second lifeboat and* FILLMORE *follows. The* Boatswain *makes to enter, but the ship pitches, and he falls into the Sea, screaming.*

Boats. I'm lost! O, I beseech—
Pet. [*Weakly.*] He's dead, but I would fain die a dry death upon a beach. . . .

[*Exeunt,* FILLMORE *rowing.*

SCENE II. — *The Island: a beach.*

Enter FILLMORE, *dragging* PETRUCHIO.

Beaching the dory, the professor gently lifted the dying seaman and carried him to the shore. Fillmore was not as tired as he thought he'd be; the hardest part of the row was getting away from the pull of the sinking ship and the tempest.

"Funny how calm the weather became all of a sudden," he mused aloud. "The storm only seemed to rage a little distance around the *Pembroke.*"

"No accident, that," Petruchio gasped, "it was an ill wind, blowing no good."

"Shh," the professor cautioned; "save your strength."

"O, do not hope for me, I know I have but little breath left. Sit you down, here upon the sand, and let me give you warning while I've still a moiety o' life."

Fillmore obeyed. "Is there anything you want? A drink of water?"

"Nay, too much o' that element." Petruchio coughed, then spoke again, so soft the professor had to put his ear close to hear. "A trio of witch-hags hired me to haul thee hence; I repent me o't, and bitterly I've paid for my crimes. Revenge, if thou canst, but have an eye o' them, they're somewhere on th'isle."

"What place *is* this, Petruchio? Bermuda?"

"It hath no name. 'Tis uncharted. O, I die; forgive me; but should thou 'scape, wouldst seek my wife? Kate, daughter o' Padua's Baptista; tell her I repent me that I dealt her harsh; say for all my faults, I—"

But he died without finishing the message.

Well, that's probably another loose end for me to tie up if I ever want to leave this world, the professor sighed, digging a shallow grave with one of the lifeboat's paddles. *And that's not the only if:*

If the witches don't catch me.

If I ever get off the island alive.

If Falstaff ever finds me.

That's the toughest IF of all! The time sequence was so mixed up on Fillmore's Avonian world, he couldn't be sure the fat knight had any idea where or what Bermuda might be. Though the island actually was discovered in 1503 by the Spaniards, its existence did not become common knowledge until sometime after 1609, when a nautical expedition led by Sir George Somers landed there to avoid destruction in an Atlantic storm, the very tempest that inspired Shakespeare's next-to-final play. *He killed off Falstaff years before writing* The Tempest *in 1611 or '12, but on the other hand, Falstaff was supposed to be alive during the War of the Roses, which took place when? Oh, hell, there's no way of figuring it out!*

Burying Petruchio, the professor hauled the lifeboat over the pink sands and into a concealing clump of semitropical vegetation. Though he didn't expect to brave the Atlantic again in it, the fact that it might be his sole mode of transportation made the professor exercise extra caution.

He began to push inland. Some fifty yards from the beach he found a brook. As he slaked his thirst, he again pondered whether or not Falstaff was likely to bring help.

Petruchio didn't know the island, but maybe Jack does. If so, I just have to hole out someplace and hope the hags don't find me. The professor shivered. *But if he's never heard of Bermuda—well . . .*

[*Exit* FILLMORE, *worried.*

SCENE III. — *At Sea.*

Enter FALSTAFF, *above.*

Scudding dangerously close to the surface of the water, Sir John Falstaff regarded the churning ocean crests beneath his feet and groaned, utterly wretched.

"O James, good James," he lamented, clutching the umbrella-handle, "shall I survive this fearsome flight? And if I do, how may I rescue thee? Why, what's Bermuda? where is't? What Never-land o' thy fey imagining?"

[*Exit* FALSTAFF, *above.*

SCENE IV. — *Another part of the Island.*

Enter three Witches.

1 Witch. The ship, the ship hath broke!

2 Witch. O, sister, sure, you do not joke?

3 Witch. Didst not thou feel't? I saw it sink.

1 Witch. I smelt a storm, and it did stink.
No earthly tempest toss'd that bark;
I smell a power passing dark.

2 Witch. But did he drown, that Fillmore vile?

1 Witch. O, no!

3 Witch.   He's somewhere on this isle.

2 Witch. Let's catch 'im then, since he's our prey.

3 Witch. O, no! our wrath for him must stay
Until we learn who else is here!
What magic brew'd that storm? I fear
Some evil thing doth rule this strand,
And we may find a war's on hand.

All. We'll give 'em double, double trouble;
And when we're through, they'll be but rubble.

[*Exeunt.*

SCENE V. — *Another part of the Island: a cave nearby.*

Enter FILLMORE.

Uh-oh, thought the professor, *that looks like a footstep in the mud, I'd better go the other way.*

He turned off before reaching the cave-clearing, afraid he'd run into one of the weird sisters. *Who else's footprint could it be?*

Enter MIRANDA, *from cave.*

Mir. O, Father, didst not hear a noise? Methinks
Some creature scuff'leth not too far from here.

Enter PROSPERO, *from cave.*

Pros. Most like. That tempest was a Hell-born storm.
Now do I need those books still in the boat;
The food is stored, I wear my magic cloak,
But if we are to thrive upon this plot,
We must rely upon my sorc'rous art.
Rest thee, love, I'll fetch my lore-packed books.
　Mir. Oh, I'm afraid! Don't leave me, dad!
　Pros. [*Gesturing.*]　　　　　　　　　　Now sleep;
Enchanted rest hang on thy lids, and whilst
In slumber wrapt, no harm shall come to thee.

PROSPERO *draweth a circle in the air with his finger, and* MIRANDA *falleth asleep within it.*

In all ill luck's a grain o' good; had we
Not got away the night we did, we'd been
Bestowed in rotten ship by my false kin,
And sure had sunk or ere we spied this isle.
O, here the sky is clear, the air is fair;
Polluted Milan's stench cannot compare. . . .

[*Exit* PROSPERO.

SCENE VI. — *The Island: a wild place near a Mountain.*

Enter three Witches *and* SYCORAX.

Sycorax was a malevolent crone so ancient and bent with malice and envy that her fingers touched the tips of her toes and her back curved so extremely that, from a distance, she resembled a living hoop. But though she far surpassed the three weird sisters in spite, yet their mastery of the forces of evil much outstripped hers.

Thus it was, then, that the sibling trio dragged Sycorax into a gloomy glade just beneath a bear-haunted peak at the center of the midmost stretch of the elongated isle.

Two of the hags clutched her twitching fingers, preventing her from working further necromantic mischief.

"Tell's now why thou loos'd that superfluous storm!" the Third Witch demanded, gnarled hands on bony hips. "Didst not know that we were here? Might you not ha' guessed to sink that ship might thwart our plans?"

Sycorax first cackled toothlessly, then curled her lip in derision. "From Argier I came, condemnèd for working spells. I had been burned, except I carried child, contrived while I waited i' th' cell. For that reason, those scurvy innocents cast me here, instead, marooning me. Here I've held sway for lo! these twenty decades. None other witch here reigns; you scabs invade my land; *begone!* no wetbacks need apply!"

The Third Witch's saffron pupils shone with an unholy light as she glared balefully. "Then thou refuseth cousin-witches courtesy befitting a sov'reign t' extend to visitors?"

Sycorax scornfully spat. "Kin thou'rt not; I've kin enow. 'Tis my desire, drab, that nevermore shall I set eyes on thee or thine!"

The sisters exchanged a meaningful glance.

"As you wish," shrugged the Third Witch, taking Sycorax literally.

[*Exeunt.*

SCENE VII. — *The Island: a grove.*

Enter PROSPERO, *carrying books.*

A Voice. [*Groans.*]
Pros. This isle is full o' noise; I thought I heard
A mournful sigh, and as I fetched from out
Our beachèd craft, methinks I also heard
A doleful song. Where should this music be
That sweetly, sadly crept by me upon
And o'er the waters; where, O where this plaint?
A Voice. O, hark! I shall not leave thee in the dark:

The Voice *sings.*

Come unto this broken tree.
　　And then help me:
Syc'rax lock'd me in its wood.
　　(And it ain't good).
Foot it featly over here;
And please lift this burden drear.
　　Hark, hark!
　　Blech, *god-dam,*
I hate this pine:
The one that's split—
　　Hark, hark!—
　　Is mine!

　　Pros. I see thy plight. But what's thy name?
　　Ariel. [*Within the cloven pine-tree.*]　　　　Ariel.
The foul witch, Sycorax, imprisoned me
A long, long time ago; I am a sprite
O' upper air, and if thou hast the spell
To free me from this place, I'll serve thee well!
　　Pros. I'll help; must get my cloak; please wait a while.

[*Exit* PROSPERO.

　　Ariel. "Please wait"? A genius he ain't, that *shmoe!*
Just where the hell's he think I'm gonna go?

[*Manet* ARIEL.

SCENE VIII. — *The Island: a wild place near a mountain.*

Enter FILLMORE.

"Well, it *is* a big enough place to hide in, anyway," the professor observed, stepping along stealthily, peering every which way. "There ought to be someplace I can conceal myself for the night, maybe at the foot of that mountain; it's wild enough."

It was not a very lofty peak, more of a super-sized hill, rounded with age. An animal snuffled somewhere from above. *Could there be bears on Bermuda?* Fillmore craned his neck to see what shape seemed to be moving in the brush halfway up the rise, but it was too shadowy in the midst of the thicket to see clearly. *Maybe if I climb a tree?*

Physical labor was not one of his strong points, but adventuring via umbrella inevitably firmed up some muscles, especially those employed in running. He found one reasonably tall tree with enough rifts and branches to make scaling it fairly simple. Taking hold of its lowest branches, he swung himself up and climbed to the top.

Just in the nick of time.

He'd barely time to ascertain the actual existence of a few brown bears upon the nearby peak when he heard some large creature crashing through the forest below. The sound stopped, only to be replaced by the most ferocious howl the professor had ever been unfortunate enough to hear. So terrible it was, he nearly lost his hold on the supporting branch, and had to throw both arms around it and hug tight, lest he fall out of the tree. Fillmore prayed the noise he made passed unnoticed below. When he was sure there was no alteration in the tone or direction of the infernal caterwauling, he ventured a peek downward.

A little ways off in the thicket, he saw two things, neither of which reassured him one bit.

A great twisted monstrosity hunkered on its haunches and wailed over the strangest skeleton Fillmore ever saw: a set of bones curved so unnaturally that he almost doubted it once belonged to a human being —except the skull, surmounted by a long tangle of white hair, was unmistakably that of some long-dead individual.

"Mother, O mother," the misshapen giant raged, gnashing snaggly teeth, "who did this foul deed? Who'd strength to cast down thy colossal wickedness? O, reveal't!"

The jaws of the death's-head opened. The professor thought he'd faint when it spoke.

"*Revenge, son,* REVENGE!" the dead witch shrieked.

Leaping to its fish-webbed feet, the thing below swore a vile oath, then asked the ghost where to find the culprit.

"On the isle, not far from here . . ." it replied, but its voice faded swiftly, and the sentence was never completed.

After the monster set aside the skull and lumbered off into the jungle, Fillmore let himself down from the tree with considerable difficulty, his legs and hands shaking.

So that's Caliban, he shivered. *Spawn of Sycorax and the Devil. Half-man, half-beast.* Caliban was the rebellious servant of Prospero in *The Tempest,* trusted by the magician until the deformed entity at-

tempted to rape his daughter, Miranda. *But how come he's so big? I always thought of Caliban as a runt, something like Lon Chaney playing
Quasimodo.*

Fillmore's first impulse, naturally, was to put as much distance as
possible between himself and the savage. Yet the notion that the monster and he might later accidentally meet was remarkably unappealing.
He might accuse me of murdering his mother!

Deciding it was better to keep track of Caliban's whereabouts, Fillmore reluctantly decided to follow at a discreet distance.

[*Exit* FILLMORE.

SCENE IX. — *The Island:* PROSPERO's *cave.*

MIRANDA *still sleepeth; enter* PROSPERO *with books.*

Pros. My precious child still slumbereth. O, if
A witch doth dwell yet on this isle, as poor
Ariel saith, 'twere best to strength the spell
That keeps Miranda safe while in this round.

Setting down the books in the cave, PROSPERO *maketh a large circle
with his finger about* MIRANDA.

Peace, the charm is firm and good. My cape;
'Tis meet I put it on.

He donneth his magic cloak.

Enter CALIBAN, *rampaging.*

Cal.   Thou filth! O, piece
O' dung! I'll rip thy entrails out!
Pros.   Why, what
A bestial knave art thou? To burst on me
And mine, who've hurt not thee, and threat to kill?
Who'rt thou, clay? Thy proper name pronounce,
I conjure thee—
   Cal.   By all that's vile!
Pros. [*Gesturing.*]   Thy name!
Cal. 'Ban, 'Ban, Ca—Caliban!
Pros.   Too long;
I'll call thee Caliban: why rail on me?
   Cal. I saw thee making magic whirlings in
The air; 'tis thou that killed my dam!

Pros.   You lie!

Cal. Have at you, then!

Mir. [*Wakes.*]   O, father, ha! what is't?

CALIBAN *sees her and stops, fascinated.* PROSPERO *takes advantage of the distraction to gesture toward* CALIBAN. *The creature screameth and becomes twisted, bent and small.*

Cal. By cock, give back my shape, thou stoup o' stale!

PROSPERO *gestureth again at* CALIBAN.

Pros. Thou'lt keep thy shape, slime-tongue. Be dumb! Begone!

CALIBAN *discovereth he can no longer speak.*

[*Exit* CALIBAN, *mewling and gibbering.*

MIRANDA *flieth, frightened, to her father's side.*

Pros. O, be not fear'd, my child; the beast is gone.

Mir. O, grave new world that hath such creatures in't!

Pros. New neighborhoods are always strange.

Mir. [*Still fearful.*]   But who's
That lurking yet within the woods?

Pros. [*Peers suspiciously.*] Hm, who,
Indeed? Thou skulker, show thyself or taste
My wrath.

Enter FILLMORE, *sheepishly.*

Fil.   Excuse me, Duke, I wasn't sure
If it was safe to show my face.

Pros.   If thou
Be true and good, there's naught to fear from me.
But what's thy name?

Fil. [*Smiles.*]   To conjure with? Fillmore.

Pros. A name to conjure with, indeed! Then you
Survived?

Fil. The shipwreck? Yes, I did. But how—

Pros. Thy name's well-known in Italy: the man
Who freed us from the tyrant Austria!
And even I, though foolishly enwrapt
In books o' grammarye, could not escape
The talk of how one man, Fillmore, deposed

Vienna's deputy; but where's that thing
You stole him with?
    Fil.   My friend, Falstaff, took off
To summon aid. We sailed, you know, upon—
    Pros. The very vessel where I was. I heard,
Yet saw thee not.
    Fil.   I was a prisoner.
    Pros. Then evil work's afoot!
    Fil.   You're telling me?
    Pros. That beastly Caliban—
    Fil.   He's not the worst.
I think there's witches, two or three, somewhere
Upon the isle.
    Pros.   'Tis like *they* kill'd his dam.
    Fil. Uh-huh. What should we do?
    Pros.   Stay here. I'll go
Enlist some supernatural aid. But guard my child.
    Fil. Of course I will.
    Pros.   I'll be right back.

                            [*Exit* PROSPERO.

                FILLMORE *sighs.*

    Fil. So you're Miranda, huh?
    Mir.   That's me. I like
Your smile.
    Fil. [*Nonplussed.*] Uh . . . thanks.
    Mir.   And yet it seems you frown
Much more than you do smile. How come?
    Fil. [*Shrugs.*]   I guess
I don't have much to smile about.
    Mir.   O, sad!
Yet if I kiss thee, sir, perhaps thy life
Will grow more glad, for all the fairy tales
That I have heard doth stipulate that lips
O' one who rues thy fate, saluting, sets
Thee free; then, may I make thee ever glad?

    MIRANDA *kisseth* FILLMORE's *cheek. He stares at her, speechless for a second, then, laughing, gives her a big hug.*

    Fil. You are a doll! Your father's fortunate

To have a daughter nice as you. [*Aside.*] It's just
My luck: the sweetest female character
That Shakespeare ever wrote, I have to go
And meet when she is much too young for me.
   Mir. Ah, did th'enchantment work?
   Fil. [*Smiling for her benefit.*]   You bet it did!
Now how 'bout you? I'd like to do something
To make you happy, too.
   Mir.   Wouldst play a game?
   Fil. Why, sure.
   Mir. [*Claps hands in glee.*] O, goody-good! But do you know
A game called Hide-and-Seek?
   Fil. [*Laughs; Aside.*]   I'm glad to find
Some things don't change from world to world. — Do *I*
Know Hide-and-Seek? Why, that's my favorite game.
Miranda, hon, I'll bet that I'm the best
Darned Hide-and-Seeker that you'll ever meet!
   Mir. Why, if that's true, thou must be fair with me,
And in that case, thou must be firstly It.
   Fil. You've got it, kid.
   Mir.   So you must hide your eyes
And count to ten times ten, nor never peak.
   Fil. [*Hides eyes.*] Here goes: *a*-ONE, *a*-TWO, *a*-THREE,
a-FOUR—

MIRANDA *silently runs about, looking for some place to hide while*
FILLMORE *continueth to count.*

Fil. A-FOURTEEN, FIFTEEN, SIXTEEN, SEVENTEEN—

After a time, MIRANDA *chooseth a Tree a little way within the For-*
est. She hideth behind it, but peeketh out at the still-counting Professor.

Fil. A-THIRTY-NINE, *a*-FORTY, FORTY-ONE—

Out of the Woods creepeth CALIBAN, *an evil leer on his ugly face.*
He sneaketh up behind MIRANDA *and clappeth one distorted claw over*
her mouth. She struggleth.

Fil. A-SIXTY-SIX, *a*-SIXTY-SEVEN, 'EIGHT—

CALIBAN *lifteth the kicking child and stealeth off silently into the*
Forest.

Fil. —TY-NINE, *a*-HUNDRED! There! Ready or not, Miranda, here I come!

FILLMORE *puts down his hands, looks about, amused.*

       [*Calls.*] I'll bet I know
Just where you are: you're either over here . . .
Or over there . . . right by the cave, or near—

                             [*A scream, off.*

MIRANDA, *hey!* What happened, hon?
  Mir. [*Off.*]   O, help!

FILLMORE *runs in the direction of her voice and peereth.*

Fil. Oh, cripes, it's Caliban! He's kidnapped her!

He begins to follow them, but stops abruptly.

Aww, hell, I'd better leave a note to let
Her father know what's wrong—
  Mir. [*Further away.*]   O, help me, friend!
  Fil. No time; can't wait, must chase—he'll run too far
Away, and I won't know just where they are!

                      [*Exit* FILLMORE, *running.*

SCENE X. — *The Island: on* CALIBAN's *mountain.*

Enter eight Bears, *frolicking.*

Halfway up the mountainside, Caliban stopped and set Miranda down upon a narrow ledge. Behind them, some of the hillside was scooped out, forming a recess too small to classify as a cave, but ample enough for the web-footed mooncalf to keep a stock of noxious food and a few trinkets his mother, Sycorax, once gave him as souvenirs of her native Argier.

"Please let me go," Miranda pleaded, shrinking back from both Caliban and the bruins cavorting near her, "I ne'er harmed thee."

The monster gestured to his mouth and, growling, shook a fist at her. His guttural grunts frightened the bears; yelping in terror, they scampered off hastily.

"O," Miranda lamented, "I forgot my father rendered thee dumb!"

Nodding angrily, he hopped from foot to foot, gesticulating wildly. Though Prospero's spell both robbed him of stature and speech, it had no effect on the creature's strength, and as his fury mounted, Caliban pounded the rearward slope with his fists, knocking off great chunks of stone that tumble-crashed down the side of the mountain to the forest-floor.

His rage terrified Miranda so much that she began to cry. But as soon as she did, the sound and spectacle of tears checked his choler. Cocking his head, perplexed, Caliban squatted beside the cringing girl and, with a gentleness foreign to his nature, tentatively touched her on the shoulder with the tips of his fingers.

Fillmore watched them from below. When he saw Caliban calm down and try to comfort Miranda, the professor felt great relief. *Shakespeare hinted at a rudimentary capacity for higher feelings in Caliban. Now if I can just think of some way to appeal to his better nature . . .*

But when he pictured the way Caliban treated the rocky mountainside, Fillmore hesitated; he decided to mull over more carefully the wisdom of stepping boldly forth to parlay with the brute.

Some hours later, when darkness fell, he was still busy mulling.

[*Tableau.*

SCENE XI. — *The Island:* PROSPERO's *cave.*

Enter PROSPERO *and* ARIEL.

Pros. Why, what is wrong? Why, where's my child? Did I
Do wrong to trust that stranger so?
   Ariel.   O, no,
O master mine: here's work that I do sense
Doth stem from nothing mortal; no; the tang
O' witchcraft warreth here.
   Pros.   But not the hag
Who locked thee in that tree; she's dead.
   Ariel.   She had
A son, a thing called Caliban.
   Pros.   I know
That beast! I shrank him down, and made him dumb.
   Ariel. He's ta'en revenge! Best follow me!
   Pros.   I come!

[*Exeunt.*

SCENE XII. — *The Island: by* CALIBAN's *mountain.*

FILLMORE, CALIBAN, MIRANDA, *as before.*

The professor hardly was able to keep his eyes open. Miranda had stopped crying long before, and Caliban did not bother her, but neither moved from the spot they'd been hours ago. Once, the beast withdrew some food from the recess and offered a little to the child, but she turned up her nose at the rank stuff, so Caliban dined alone.

The moon came out early. No one budged.

Shades of King Kong, Delia and Prince Albert, thought Fillmore. *If only he'd fall asleep so I could make a run for it with Miranda. Wonder if she's smart enough to know I'm here?* He smiled. *I'm sure she is.*

For the first time in his life the professor pondered the putative pleasures of parenthood.

Which is why he missed the first evidence of help arriving from an unexpected source.

Caliban caught it before the professor. His squat nose suddenly twitched. He growled deep in his throat and cast suspicious glances everywhere, but mostly towards the top of the mountain.

Fillmore rubbed his eyes in disbelief when he looked up where Caliban's head was turned.

It's not possible . . . is it? So soon?

Almost afraid to hope, the professor intently watched the stupendous shadow float down past the peak towards the forest-floor.

It must *be him!* the professor reasoned. *Who else in all the worlds could be so fat?*

Perhaps ten feet above the ground-line, the elephantine silhouette came to rest upon the slope, startling another group of growling grizzlies.

Fillmore was positive it was Falstaff. *But I never expected to see the knight on Bear Mountain!*

He hurried in his direction.

[*Exit* FILLMORE.

SCENE XIII. — *The Island: on* CALIBAN's *mountain.*

CALIBAN *discovered;* MIRANDA *sleeping.*

Dumb show: CALIBAN *peers at* MIRANDA, *satisfies himself she really is asleep, then steps silently away to investigate the strange shadow he*

*just saw go past. But when he reaches the extreme edge of the ledge,
he freezes in horror, looking outward and upward.* CALIBAN *faints.
Enter, from above,* BORIS *and* BAPTISTA, *clinging to the professor's
umbrella. They stop on the ledge; the hood folds up.* BORIS *regards*
CALIBAN *for a moment before speaking.*

Bor. O curses! Scorned again!
Bap.   Ah, see: a child,
And she is beautiful beyond compare;
What doth she here in this forbidding, cold
And lonely spot?
Bor.   I cannot tell. Wait here.
I'll go and seek the knight and good Fillmore.
Bap. And leave us here alone? What if that weird
Thing wakeneth?
Bor.   You know that looks deceive:
Despite his form, he may be mild.
Bap. [*Agitated.*]   Or wild!
Protect me, please! protect this helpless child!
Bor. [*Sighs.*] I will; calm down; relax and don't get riled!

[*Exit* BORIS, *carrying* CALIBAN.

SCENE XIV. — *The Island: at the foot of the mountain.*

Enter FALSTAFF *with new umbrella.*

"I am accursed to fly in that pair's company," the enormous knight
groused, stumping along and thrashing with his new, extra-strength
umbrella to prevent himself from bumping into trees. "Why the devil
could they not stay close, as I requested? Bah! I doubt not but to die a
fair death for all this—"

"*Pssst!* Sir John! Over *here!*"

"Ha! Who's't?"

"*Me!* Don't make so much noise! Walk *this way!*"

"O, *any* way is equal torture," Falstaff lamented, "eight yards of
uneven ground is threescore and ten miles afoot with me!"

But, despite his discomfort, the fat man stumbled in the direction of
the whispering, and soon he and the professor were reunited.

"I was afraid you might not be familiar with Bermuda," Fillmore
said.

"I wasn't, Jim, but Boris claimeth to have knowledge o' this Shakespeare, too, and he flew swift to some other place, came back with this

sturdier umbrella (purchased, saith he, of a merchant named Wells) and led us here."

"Us?"

"The lad Baptista clung to Boris' bumbershoot."

"And Vincentio?"

"Returned to Vienna. His crown called him back, as well as a desire to meet that dame, Isabella."

"Yes, they'll probably marry. They do in—"

"Shakespeare, I know, I *know*." The knight waved it aside. "Th' Duke o' Vienna's rewarded thee well. I have a bag o' gold that—"

"Never mind that now, Jack. Where's Boris?"

"Here, O Puissant Professor!"

The voice at his elbow was so unexpected, the professor jumped a good inch into the air. It would have been higher if he'd seen who the Frankenstein monster had slung over his back like a potato-sack. But it was too dark to discern anything but the dim silhouette of the giant's great bulk.

"Boris! How long have you been here?"

"I just arrived a moment ago. But why do we whisper?"

Fillmore swiftly outlined events for his two friends, but partway through, Boris interrupted, chuckling.

"O, fear that fish-thing no further, Friend, I hath him o'er mine back."

"What?" the professor exclaimed. "Let me see!"

Frankenstein obligingly moved a few paces to the left, where a pale patch of moonlight showed him and his burden more clearly. He let Caliban down, but kept a restraining hand on his shoulder. The creature was awake now, eyes bulging with fright.

"Caliban," said Fillmore, "did you hear everything I just told them?"

Still unable to speak, Caliban nodded his head jerkily.

"Then you understand it was not Prospero who killed your mother, but probably the witches who've been making it hot for me?"

Another nod.

"All right," the professor continued, putting into practice his theory that the beast had a better nature, "since you realize we're all faultless, how about releasing Miranda?"

"No need," Boris began, but Fillmore shushed him.

"It's important for him to answer, anyway."

The mooncalf growled. Boris gave him a warning shake.

"Well?" the professor insisted. "Will you promise not to harm her, but willingly give her back to her father?"

Caliban struggled with the problem for a long time, but at last, grimacing horribly, gave one more curt nod to Fillmore.

"That's a *good* Caliban," the teacher reassured him. "Now I know Miranda will be safe from all—" He stopped in mid-sentence.

Two terrified shrieks sounded a second time from above.

They all spun round to see what was the matter—but just then, the moon passed behind a cloud. The mountainside went dark.

"It's *Miranda!*" Fillmore exclaimed. "Come *on!*"

He sprinted toward the slope, ignoring the lash of twigs and nettle-stings. Boris and Caliban hurried after the professor.

"O, 'twill catch our deaths bumblefutzing around i' th' darkness," Falstaff complained, lagging pitifully behind, yet making a valiant effort to catch up.

[*Exeunt.*

SCENE XV. — *The Island:* CALIBAN's *ledge, now empty.*

Enter FILLMORE, *then* BORIS & CALIBAN.

Fil. Miranda! Hey! Baptista! Hey!
Bor. [*Lamenting.*]   O, gone!
'Tis all my fault! I never should have left
Them all alone!
Fil.   You didn't know. You're not
To blame.
Bor.   But that's not all: they bore away
With them th'umbrella that belongs to you.
Fil. Oh, damn! It's all *your* fault! You never should
Have left them all alone!

CALIBAN *gesticulates to catch their attention.*
             Oh, what do you
Want now?
Bor.   See where he points? A note!
Fil.   A note?
Bor. Aye; note it not? O, note the note!

Turning, FILLMORE *sees and picks up a scrap of paper.*

Fil. [*Reads.*] *High-and-mighty,—Come alone at once to the peak's peak, or thy two friends perish.*
Bor. O, Fillmore, do not go!
Fil.   I have no choice.

Bor. A trap! You seek your death.
Fil.   Maybe. Stay here.

[*Exit* FILLMORE, *upward.*

Bor. O, what am I to do? They need my help!
[*Lamenting.*] I'll never see my friend again! O, woe!

CALIBAN *impatiently plucks him by the sleeve.* BORIS *looks at him, begins to speak, but* CALIBAN, *putting a finger to his lips, gestures for* BORIS *to follow him. The mooncalf disappears behind a crevice in the stone.* BORIS *peers within.*

Bor. A secret way? And it ascends? I'll try
It then, for what more, then, is there to lose?

[*Exeunt.*

Enter FALSTAFF, *wheezing and puffing.*

Fal. 'Sblood, I'll not bear mine own flesh so far afoot again for all the coin Vincentio gave th' professor.

He lieth on his back, his belly resembling a beachèd whale.

Fal. Unless someone hath levers hereabout,
'Tis here I'll lie and die, I do not doubt.

[FALSTAFF *manet.*

SCENE XVI. — *The Island: at the top of the mountain.*

Enter FILLMORE.

Just before he reached the top, he saw the flicker of some unwholesome green fire. He climbed over the last rise and stared at the five figures motionless by the central cauldron.

The moon shone; no further clouds interposed themselves. By firelight and moonlight, the professor examined the terrible tableau.

Two of the weird sisters clutched Miranda and Baptista, crooked-bladed knives at the throat of each. The third crone stood nearer to the place he occupied; in her hand was his umbrella.

"At last we meet again," the Third Witch said triumphantly.

"It's a pleasure I could easily have relinquished," Fillmore replied dourly. "Now what?"

"Come closer."

He did not move.

"I said, *come closer!*"

"Not until you release my friends."

Though the night was clear, an ominous rumble of thunder sounded far-off. Yet the sky held few clouds, and the moon was still as bright.

"Let my people go," the professor repeated.

The Third Witch's eyes glared with an evil yellow glow. "Thou'rt in no position, Fillmore, to dictate terms. Approach, or else my sisters shear their throats in twain."

Miranda whimpered, but, remembering that she was the daughter of a Duke, forced herself to stop.

Reluctantly, Fillmore walked slowly toward the witch.

"All right," he snapped, "I'm close enough. What do you want?"

Overhead, summer sheet-lightning suddenly flickered. Thunder rolled again, somewhat closer.

"Damn you all," the professor swore, "I asked you what you want!"

The sisters snickered.

"O, patience," cautioned the Third Witch, "we've waited long and long to face you once more—this time without your ghastly friend."

"I suppose you plan revenge because I helped save Vincentio. All right. You've got me now. But let *them* go, they've had no hand in it."

The crone smiled toothily. "O, that's true, we know, dearie, we know. But small bus'ness did th' Duke's lackey discharge, the child no thing at all."

"Then you *won't* harm them? *Please.*"

"Ah, tha' crav'st a favor of us, whom thou crossed repeatedly? And what's it worth?"

"My life," Fillmore murmured.

The witch spat. "Why, what good's that to us?"

A strong wind sprang up out of nowhere, whipping the white whiskers of the witch wildly.

Storm coming up—and fast, the professor thought, irrelevantly.

And then he saw something that made his heart flipflop. He didn't know whether to be angry or glad. *Depends on how it turns out. . . .*

Fillmore looked the Third Witch squarely in the eye. "Okay, lady," he grumbled, "if it's not my life you're after, then what in hell *do* you want from me?"

Keep her talking . . . keep her talking. . . .

"O, we *had* entertained mortal thoughts on your behalf," she replied, "but chance hath changed our minds." She held up the umbrella. "Instruct us in the usage of this thing, show us how to fashion others like it, and we'll put aside revenge."

Yeah, sure you will.

She jerked her thumb at the prisoners. "Refuse, and they die first, and won't be swift despatched."

Lightning struck, close by.

"And how do I know you'll keep your promise? *Keep her talking . . . just a few more seconds. . . .*

"Well, thou must trust us," she leered wickedly.

Uh-huh. As far as I'd trust a constipated cobra.

"No more delay!" she shrilled. "Reply: wilt tell?"

Judging the time was right, the professor shouted an answer so staggeringly unprintable it actually shocked the witches. For one vital second, they glared, open-mouthed, at him, simultaneously chagrined and respectful. . . .

And then all hell cut loose.

Happily, the storm picked that precise instant to break forth in towering force. Deafening thunder. A wall of water sloshed down and drowned the witch-fire. Skeletal talons of lightning ripped and cracked, totally confusing the sisters. . . .

And Boris and Caliban leaped upon the First and Second Witches, grasping their knife-hands in bone-crushing grips. The Third Witch spun around, astonished at the instant alteration of Fortune. Cascades of water slashed at her, but she shot out a bony hand and started to cast a spell.

Fillmore threw a flying tackle at her legs. He brought her down, twisted the umbrella from her grip and bopped her smartly on the forehead. She dropped back heavily on the turf, wrinkled mouth wide open.

Good, thought the professor, *maybe she'll drown.* He ran to Miranda's side, hugged and comforted her. Baptista joined the pair and huddled over the child to shield her a little from the rain and also prevent her from witnessing the ferocious fight raging on either side.

Boris wrestled with the surprisingly-strong Second Witch. They tottered close to the edge of the mountain. Fillmore shouted to warn Frankenstein, but could not be heard above the violence of the elements.

Caliban, exhilarated to have one of his mother's murderers in his grasp, was more than a match for the First Witch. Slowly, he forced the twisted blade still clutched in her hand towards her own stringy throat.

A scream. Boris staggered back from the Second Witch, blood streaming down his face. Laughing demoniacally, she rushed upon him, knife poised for a mortal blow.

Roaring, Fillmore dashed to his friend's aid, all too well aware he'd never make it in time.

But suddenly, a thing like some enormous toad sprang up and leaped upon the Second Witch, smashing her to the ground. Caliban, finished with his other opponent, grasped the hag's head and, with a savage yank, actually tore it off—a gratuitous gesture, since she'd already landed on her own rune-cursed knife.

Dripping wet and sneezing, the professor continued toward Boris, who still teetered dangerously close to the brink of the precipice. But before he was able to reach him, Fillmore was horrified to see Boris suddenly lurch, pitch, and, with a frightened scream, plunge backward over the side and into the abyss below.

Fillmore froze, rooted to the spot, listening to Boris' fading cry of terror. It did not go on for long, nor could his ears discern any sound of impact, but the groan of agony that ensued was unmistakable.

"O, no!" someone wailed behind him. "O, Boris!"

And then the professor heard another sound, a profoundly chilling one. The Third Witch was laughing.

The storm stopped as abruptly as it started. The clouds cleared, the moon shone again—and Fillmore saw the Third Witch rise up out of the grass close to the place where Boris fell.

"You pushed him!" Fillmore screamed, brandishing his umbrella like a club. But the witch pointed a finger at him and his muscles stiffened and joints locked. He could not take a step.

Behind her, Caliban crouched, fingers flexed in anticipation. . . .

Without even turning, the hag etched a glowing sign in the air, said a few words . . . and Caliban's brain broke down. He forgot his name, his past, all memory of language. She watched him scurry off through the grass like some timid animal. Then, stepping up to Fillmore, she took away his umbrella a second time.

"I've punished your friends," she said, snapping her fingers and dissipating the rigidity in his limbs. "Now let's get back to business. My offer still holds."

He told her what she could do with it.

"Very well. Perhaps you'll change your mind in time to save your *other* companion."

With that, the witch beckoned toward Miranda, and the child, as if in a trance, pulled out of Baptista's arms and started toward the crone.

"Miranda, *no!*" Fillmore shouted, running to stop her. But he bumped into an invisible barrier which the sorceress casually waved into existence.

The girl took one faltering step after another, bringing herself closer and closer to the malevolent hag who awaited her with claws outstretched to encircle Miranda's pale throat.

"Help!" the professor screamed. "Someone, some*thing*—HELP!"

An answering growl sounded. Out of the forest lumbered a great brown bear. Miranda stopped walking.

The witch cackled. "Hast pow'r, Fillmore, o'er all dumb beasts? He'll harm thee ere he'll touch a hair o' me. No mortal thing may pass the magic shield."

The bear did.

Her white eyebrows shot up. "What airy phantom is this? Thou hast no hold on me, we serve the selfsame master!"

The bear bared his teeth and stalked toward the old woman.

"Desist!" she warned. "I' th' name o' Beelzebub, I charge thee, leave this place!"

The bear came closer, rearing up on its hind legs.

"*Go away!*" the witch screeched, pointing her knife at the animal.

The bear began to grow. As he did, he waved a paw in her direction and a bolt of blue flame shot out and crackled along the blade of her dagger. She howled in pain and dropped it; it was nothing more than a hilt by the time it hit the ground.

And now the shape of the bear shimmered, and the entity turned into a colossal Harpy with hair of flame. Swooping down upon the screaming witch, the fell thing clutched her tight and, rising on leathery wings, flew away with her to sea.

"*Daddy!*"

Sobbing with fright, relief and happiness, Miranda ran to her father's arms.

Fillmore walked across the mountaintop to Prospero. "Good work, sir. I imagine the Harpy was really Ariel?"

"Indeed, 'twas," said the Duke of Milan, Miranda's father. "I freed him from arboreal imprisonment and he, in gratitude, hath pledged to serve me true so long as I shall desire't."

"He sure saved our necks. Wish he could've made it here a little sooner, though," Fillmore said sorrowfully. "I lost my good friend, Boris."

"O, that's not true," Prospero smiled. "I cast a spell and slowed his fall. He may be bent a bit—I'd little time to spend in his behalf—and yet I think you'll find—"

Fillmore didn't listen to the end of it. He and Baptista rushed over to the edge. They stared down as the first streaks of dawn painted the sky pink.

Some distance below, they saw Boris standing on Caliban's ledge waving up at them.

"Are you all right?" the professor called.

"Aye! I landed on a soft pillow!" Boris answered.

And then Fillmore heard the voice of Falstaff rumbling furiously.

"Pillow, lout? I'll give thee pillow! How dast thou bellyflop like that? O, what a beastly stomach-ache I've got!"

Laughing in relief, the professor followed Prospero, Miranda and Baptista down the descending path.

[*Exeunt.*

SCENE XVII. — *The Island: a beach.*

Enter FILLMORE & PROSPERO.

Fil. I can't persuade you, then, to leave the isle?
Pros. [*Smiling.*] I can't persuade you, then, to stay?
Fil.   No way.
Pros. I like this clime; the air is clean and pure;
And we are nowhere near a high-rent zone.
If what you say is true, for twelve sweet years,
I'll see my daughter grow, and then a ship
Shall bring a mate to her, and sweet revenge
To me.
Fil.   That's right. But don't forget to keep
An eye on Caliban.
Pros.   I will. He's pleased

To serve me true. I've lifted off the spell
That binds his tongue, but can't restore his brain.
Miranda says she wants to teach him speech.
   Fil. She will. But don't forget to watch him close.
   Pros. I swear I shall.
   Fil. [*Sighs.*]   A shame she's started out
With such bad memories. She might have lots
Of nightmares for a while.
   Pros.   O, no. I've sent
Miranda deep into enchanted sleep.
She'll wake refreshed, but won't recall a thing.
   Fil. I guess it's for the best. But does that mean
She won't remember me?
   Pros.   The spell will blot
Out all that happed until we both took ship.
   Fil. Well, kiss her for me every night, and tell
Her all about me some fine day. [*Smiles.*] At least,
She won't remember what I told the witch!

Enter FALSTAFF, *with umbrella.*

   Fal. Art ready to depart?
   Fil.   I am. Where shall
We drop you off?
   Fal.   If it's all right with you,
Why, lad, I'd like to fly along with thee.
   Fil. [*Surprised.*] Across the void? But why?
   Fal.   O, Boris told
Me much about that fairy glade where he
Hath ruled a veritable Paradise
O' fairy dames! Sounds very good to me!
   Fil. Free eats, and all the wine that you can drink?
I guess that you might like it fine. Let's see:
There's two umbrellas, so we'll have to make
Two trips.
   Pros.   No need; my ever-potent spells shall send
The extra traveler where'er you wish.
   Fil. That's great. Okay, that's that. Where's Boris now?
   Pros. He's on his way, and hath a great surprise
For you.
   Fil. [*Aside.*] Uh-oh . . . surprises still? I thought

This sequence almost over, but what new
Shakespearean reversal's now in store?

    Enter BORIS *and* KATHARINA, *richly dressed.*

 Fil. Now who the hell is *that*?
 Kate.   You knew me in
Disguise; Baptista was I called.
 Fil.   Good Gad!
 Kate. A husband horrid have I had; so bad
Was he I stole away and played a boy.
 Bor. Wouldst ever guess they once proclaimed her shrew?
 Fil. (The last loose-end!) Oh, Kate, I've searched for you
Both near and far! Your husband's dead and you
Are free; he died upon this beach, and begged
For me to find you out to tell, at last,
He did repent the way he treated you.
I think he also meant to say, for all
His faults, he loved you still.
 Kate.   Then I am free
To wed again?
 Fil. [*Startled.*] Well, yes, but don't let's rush!
I'd like to get to know—
 Kate.   Ah, Boris, mine!
 Bor. O, Kate, canst love me true? I'm scratched anew.
 Kate. And if thy face yet bore an hundred-score
O' witchly scars, I could not love thee more!

     BORIS *and* KATHARINA *embrace passionately.*

 Fil. [*Aside.*] Oh, curses! Spurned again!
 Pros.   All's fair, my friend,
In matters of the heart. And now, good speed,
For we must part. I'll send thee off in style,
And if we ever meet again, we'll smile.

                [*Exeunt.*

Epithalamium

Wedding-day in Arcady. Boris and Kate clasped hands and prepared to join in nuptial bands. Falstaff took the arm of the Fairy Queen, a lithe damsel in his eyes. Rimski grinned, flickering in and out of view in his happiness, for, despite mortal law, there was no fairy statute to prevent him from marrying *all* the other sprightly sisters. Which was precisely what he intended to do.

As for J. Adrian Fillmore . . .

"Oh, well," he sighed, "at least I solved the Best Man wrangle by being *every*body's Best Man."

If the professor learned anything from his amatory pursuits, he refused to talk about it with his friends, but at least he responded to one direct question of Rimski's.

"Do you intend," asked the ex-cat, "to make any other cosmic hops in search of *la belle dame avec merci?*"

"No way. I have higher things in mind."

"Like?"

Fillmore shook his head, refusing to elaborate on the cryptic statement.

The wedding march struck up. All began to sing.

Bor.	After much debate delightful,
	I on Katy dear decide,
	Falstaff now may take the Sov'reign,
	Omnes be our Rimski's brides!
Fil.	In that case unprecedented,
	Single I must live and die—
	I shall have to be contented
	With a quest that's rather high.

All.   Or he'll have to be contented
        With our heartfelt sympa*thy!*

Greatly pleased with one another,
    To get married we decide,
Each of us will wed the other,
    Nobody be Fillmore's Bride.

DANCE

CURTAIN